THE SERPENT
WOMAN

THE SERPENT SERIES

SZ ESTAVILLO

OLIVERHEBERBOOKS

Cover design by Kim Killion

Published by Oliver-Heber Books

0 9 8 7 6 5 4 3 2 1

DEDICATION

To the survivors of sexual assault, human trafficking, and child abuse—this book is for you. As a survivor myself, writing *The Serpent Woman* was a deeply personal journey, one rooted in pain but also in resilience and hope.

According to the World Health Organization, 1 in 3 women worldwide experience physical or sexual violence in their lifetime. These stories often remain untold, hidden in the shadows of stigma and silence. The #MeToo movement has illuminated the pervasive nature of these crimes, giving voice to those who have been silenced for too long.

This book is a tribute to the strength, courage, and unbreakable spirit of survivors everywhere. You are not alone.

PART ONE

ONE
THE FUNERAL
EVERGREEN CEMETERY, PORTLAND, ME

VON SCHLANGE HAD NEVER KILLED anyone before. It was not because of moral conviction or societal laws. She'd simply never had a good reason, or at least one strong enough to give her the courage to take the risk. Margaret Ashby—a person Von had taken a great interest in—had nothing left in her life and every reason in the world to want someone dead.

Margaret had only one child: Harper. And she was dead. Anguish for the mother punched Von in the gut. All the poor woman could will herself to do was to look around in a daze, scowling at a group of young attendees, Harper's friends from college. One made a flippant comment about the color of the flower arrangements, as if they were in Ikea, excited about the funeral decor aesthetics instead of grieving for the girl. They pointed at the beautiful, rich amethyst casket. Fresh powder kissed the top of the rectangular box, creating a striking contrast against the purple-tinted lacquer in the most vibrant way.

The trees in the oldest and largest boneyard in the city, which typically boasted autumn copper, apricot, and gold leaves, were now unembellished branches. A musical tune, coming from a yellow-rumped warbler perched nearby, broke the quietude. The colorful passerine birds native to Maine ordinarily migrated seasonally. Von wondered if Harper's spirit was lingering in their midst to say her final goodbye. Once the casket was lowered into the wintry ground, the active warbler with its honeysuckle feathers would be the only trace of vibrance among the white-grey terrain dotted by naked tree limbs and ancient headstones above the decomposed phantoms of yesterday.

According to Von's research, Harper had been the controversial party girl. Girl X, as the media had nicknamed her. In spite of the false name, she had a hard time concealing her identity. Despite the media blurring Harper's face, it was easy even for Von, who'd never met the girl, to recognize that same sparkly silver cocktail dress worn on that fateful birthday. After all, it had been posted all over her social media channels.

What Von gathered was that everyone claimed Girl X was a "survivor," brave enough to come forward with her harrowing report of the assault perpetrated on her as a minor. Still, after her twenty-third birthday bash was over, Harper had jumped from a high-rise Marriott suite. It was her mother who found her, according to the media. Glittering yet broken in her metallic sequined cocktail dress eighteen stories below, like a piece of polished sterling silver awash in cherry glaze.

But the reports had it all wrong. Von made sure of it. She squeezed her eyes shut, recalling the sound of people laughing as they strolled outside of the Marriott in Torrance, where Von made her home. She'd been walking Zeus, her German Shepherd, then suddenly, something caught her eye, something on the top floor. There was a young woman standing there at the edge of her suite, her sparkly silver dress blowing in the wind. Dark hair whipping past her face. She spread her arms out, like a bird ready to take flight. Von's mind raced as she screamed out.

Gravity would not keep Girl X suspended in the air, and neither would faulty wings.

CPR couldn't do anything. Humans weren't meant to survive eighteen-story drops. That horrible evening left Von tossing and turning. Visions burned in her mind. She'd wake up drenched in sweat, screaming out. Sometimes, she'd see Harper suspended in the air, moving in slow motion. On lucky days, she'd awaken before Harper hit the concrete. The scene played over and over in her mind. She kept asking herself, why her? Why Harper Ashby? She needed to push through the anger with grueling gym sessions, punishing her body with weight-training.

It wasn't her duty to save anyone, to fix anything. However, the more she dug, the more she learned. The deeper the obsessive thoughts, the more easily they pulled her into sleeplessness. Von couldn't unsee it. It crawled inside of her brain and ate away rationalities. Every tiny detail about the girl's life—how she'd lived it and the choices she made, both good or bad—gnawed at Von's insides until she was convinced she had an ulcer.

Could it be because Von had walked away from her own loving family?

Completely cutting contact from them, convincing herself that it was what she needed? Hadn't Harper done the same to her mother? Kept pushing Mama away? Judging by the psychiatric hospital bills Margaret Ashby had accumulated, it was clear she had sought help for her daughter, a fact later confirmed by Von's findings.

Zeus, who had been sitting quietly next to her in the graveyard, nudged himself closer to her, bringing her back to the present. Von tried to watch and listen to the goings on at a distance, but that perpetual ache inside was as hollow as the Grand Canyon. For a moment, Mother Nature's embrace around the eerie cemetery enhanced this unnamed feeling, this growing *Thing* building and turning, burning, and twisting.

Disruptive whispers surfaced from the inky crowd of antsy funeral-goers. It was a small and lonely gathering. Like a murky veil, ten of Harper's peers clad in black stood around the burial plot. Other than her mother, Harper had no other family present, which compounded the sadness Von felt a thousand-fold.

Margaret Ashby looked like someone had ripped out her soul and left a walking corpse. Her sunken face and sallow skin, the shade of alabaster stone, screamed out against her black dress. Von could always see Harper standing on the ledge. Now, as Von stood before Margaret, her heart shattered all over again. She knew this moment would haunt her as well.

Shocked that someone their age had died, the curious youth leaned into each other unable to stop the chatter, reeling from the disaster they were fortunate not to experience themselves other than knowing the hapless soul.

"...never found proof," one of the college students said.

"...maybe she was lying," another responded, trying to whisper.

If they could somehow blame Harper it could never happen to them.

"What in the Sam's hell's wrong witchu?" Margaret Ashby sneered, her head snapping up to confront her daughter's imma-ture friends. "Respect the dead, damn you. If ya can't, then get the hell outta here. All of ya!"

The pastor, so quiet Von hardly knew he was even there, tried to reintroduce peace with a Bible verse on love and respect. The whispers stopped, but the force inside Von was boiling again. Her stomach soured, and her teeth clenched until the muscles in her jaw ached. Her fingers went numb. It took her a minute to realize she'd balled them into tight fists that drained all feeling.

Von's chest tightened, mouth cottony and dry. She hated not

being able to act. She hated standing there helplessly, having to wait it out, let the college kids whisper, and watch Harper's mother cry. Margaret's emotionless, bloodshot eyes, tracked the rectangular amethyst box poised to be lowered into the hole cut out of the snowy earth—a gaping, insatiable maw of an abominable beast ready to devour her only child. Once the funeral concluded, gossip spread among Harper's friends like a viral contagion. From her extensive research, Von knew that Harper volunteered her time at the soup kitchen before Thanksgiving dinner every year.

She'd donated her time to women's shelters and abuse hotlines. Every year, she also gave away bags of clothes to Goodwill. While Harper never attended church, she'd been more spiritual than some of her supposed religious friends who gossiped at her funeral.

The disrespect for Harper made Von nearly lose her composure.

Breathing deeply, she told herself that she must remain in control. Von forced her heart to return to normal rhythm. The attendees were nothing more than cockroaches scurrying away. They sped off in their cars, ready for their funeral after-party dinner arrangements, catching happy hour at some downtown bar, moving on with their lives. They all must've wondered what Von had wondered herself, the questions that sucked her in. How did such a good girl become ensnared in a world that had bartered her body, bankrupted her spirit, and taken her soul?

When everyone was gone, Von drew closer and stood beside Margaret, who remained stuck in place, a stoic shell of flesh on bones and a heart too shattered for human language.

The winter sky was a lusterless slate, stripped of sunshine. An ashy mist hung thick in the trees as the warblers resumed their musical soundtrack. On this day, instead of the sun's fingertips reaching to warm them, white flakes descended, sprinkling fresh powder like frozen tears onto the lavender box, the open grave. It hadn't yet been fully covered in snow. The grave diggers waited on the side, giving them extra time. But no amount of lagging could make the eternal parting any easier.

And then suddenly, a lime green warbler with a buttery chest and a black strip on its head, like a tiny bird toupee, perched on the rim of the grave. It pivoted its head in their direction and trilled softly like it was trying to offer condolences. Or was it somehow Girl X? Harper Ashby? Margaret's eyes deviated from the headstone, darted from left to right, then rested on Von, glancing at her from the corners of her eyes. They clung to the moment together, trying to interpret the little creature standing on a dead girl's purple box in the freezing Maine winter snow.

Time stretched a long beat.

The two watched and listened.

Stranger next to stranger.

As the songbird sang.

Then, the warbler fluttered away, taking the magic of the moment and Girl X's spirit on its wings. Snapping out of that frozen moment, Margaret Ashby moved like a robot with damaged parts, rooting around in her purse. Before she could pull out what she was searching for, Von retrieved a brand-new box of Virginia Slims and a lighter from her backpack.

Mrs. Ashby looked up at her with alarm, still rummaging for her own Slims.

Von kept the woman's favorite cigarettes in her palm, waiting for Margaret to discover that the box in her possession was empty. Von had watched her smoke the last one in front of her house just an hour before the funeral.

Von nodded at the smokes still in her extended hand. *Take it.*

Margaret glanced at her with suspicion but accepted. She eyed Zeus, who'd been a good boy sitting at Von's feet. Von pulled a treat from her black satchel, handed it to him, then snagged a Marlboro Red and lit up. She took a long drag, inhaling the smoke deep into her lungs. Holding it in, Von savored her preferred tobacco blend, nicotine, and more than seven thousand chemicals.

"I don't know ya or that mangy dog. Hate all of 'em—dogs, cats, them stupid chinchillas." Margaret Ashby interrupted the silence, gazing at the naked trees accented with virgin snow. "Ya weren't at her birthday party."

The grieving mother exhaled another long drag. The pewter smoke bloomed, blending with her wintery breath. Von noticed details—the same details that pulled her to Harper, to her mother, and to this funeral. She noticed tiny things, like how the insides of Margaret's index and middle finger were a nicotine-yellow, matching her jaundiced-looking skin, wan and prematurely aged, with folds of worry lines on her forehead like ocean waves of despair.

Von shook her head, exhaling frosty vaporous plumes.

Without moving her head, the woman's eyes shifted down to her new pack of cigarettes.

"Whaddya want then? You one 'em reporters?" Cigarette ash burned long on the tip. She flicked it before taking another puff. "Been following me, haven'tcha?" Margaret jabbed her cigarette like a dagger in her direction. *"Haven'tcha?"*

Von didn't answer, but Zeus growled.

"Answer my damn question. Who the hell are ya, and whatcha doin' here at my daughter's funeral and with that mutt no less? Have 'im shit on my daughter's grave like everybody else? Tell me she was ashamed? That she lied? Guilt made her jump? Never did agree to that damn interview she did. Told her not to do it."

Conscientious about littering, Von took her last drag, extinguished the cigarette, and placed the butt in a Ziplock bag containing three others. Then she tucked the bag back into her backpack. "Want one?" she asked, offering an empty baggie. "I've got a whole box."

"Appreciate the smokes, but if you're here to mollycoddle me like I told the rest 'em media-folk, go exploit someone else's pain." Margaret dropped her Slim on the ground and extinguished the cigarette with a defiant stomp of her foot. She kicked snow over it before turning to leave.

"Why didn't you go with that black and silver casket you knew Harper would like, Mrs. Ashby? She despised all shades of purple. You hated that she always wore black, so she chose that silver sequenced dress on her birthday to please you."

Mrs. Ashby turned around.

"Childless folk won't eva understand," she said, the words wobbling out defensively. "And how in the hell did ya know my daughter? You're like the rest of 'em, going on Instagram, seeing them pictures she always posted of that goth-crap she'd wear."

"I'm no reporter. I'm a..." She tried to collect the right words.

How could she explain what she knew, or worse, how she managed to stalk the despondent grieving mother, hire her hacker buddy to gather intel—all to do what with it? Von hadn't decided what to do yet with this growing obsession, this...blistering rage.

"Must've been hard having her eight weeks early," Von finally said. "Must've been torture sitting next to her bedside while she spent six weeks in the NICU due to complications. And the bad postpartum depression didn't help. Even today, you can't shake the guilt. You look back on those early days when she was first born and wonder: if you had done something different, maybe your relationship with her would've been better? Maybe she would be alive right now? Maybe she wouldn't have jumped?"

Margaret shielded a hand over her eyes to unsee the memory. Von continued.

"She wore braces she hated until she was fifteen. But everything changed after that, didn't it? By sixteen, she blossomed. The boys took notice, and you worried like any mother. Then, your worst fears came to pass. She said she thought someone was following her, and you begged her to go to the cops, but she brushed it off. Harper never knew you reported it anyway. But Portland PD wouldn't do anything. They even accused you of overreacting. Claimed you had no proof."

She paused as Margaret gazed out at the unwelcoming frigid landscape.

"That's when it happened," Von started up again. "On one warm May evening during her senior year of high school. There was never a conviction. Because she was too scared to report it after he threatened her. And as much as you butted heads with your daughter—you were certain of one thing—she always told the truth."

Von pointed at the casket, now covered like a slice of amethyst cake with frosting.

"Harper never lied," added Von, "not even when it was for her own good."

Hands unclenching at her sides, Margaret numbly lit another cigarette.

"Don't know who ya're with or how ya dug up all my private info. But I don't talk to no detectives, no FBI, or any other law," she barked.

"Neither do I," Von said, taking two long strides, cropping the distance that separated them. Zeus followed behind her and sat dutifully at her side. "The law failed you, failed your daughter. You begged for help. But they turned their backs on you. I'm not with the PPD or any other police department. Not even here to give you my deepest condolences with generic words, Mrs. Ashby."

She stood close enough to the grieving mother to invade the woman's personal space, her discomfort featured in the way she subtly recoiled. Von handed her a nondescript black envelope. Margaret Ashby opened it, and her mouth dropped.

Bewildered, Margaret stammered, "This is...this is a check for two-hundred thous—"

"You're behind on your mortgage, your car payments. Credit cards are maxed. Creditors are calling you daily. It was all the hospital bills for Harper when she was in and out of the mental ward during her previous...*attempts*. Let's not forget about the lawsuit against the Portland police department that went nowhere. Call your lawyer and cancel that bankruptcy filing."

Mrs. Ashby's eyes had a cold, tired stare. Von didn't blame her apathy. The poor woman had tried repeatedly to save her daughter from killing herself. Until, at last, she failed.

"It was ya, wudn't it?" Equal parts of surprise and realization spread across Margaret's face. "Playing secret Santa? The anonymous financial donor for the funeral? All 'em flowers? The reimbursement for the casket? Every bit of it." Her eyes narrowed. "Ya were the anonymous caller, I bet. Ya lied to the cops. Ya told 'em I found Harper the day she jumped. Why'd ya lie?" Fresh tears fell down her cheeks, and she wiped them furiously away. "Make them believe I was a good mom, like I was there for her, like I tried...like I was the one t-trying to save her?"

"You can't blame yourself—"

"Don't need no saving! Don'tchu be tellin' me which way the wind blows. Ain't answering jack shit until ya tell me who ya are."

She swallowed a breath and, after a five count, responded. "Schlange."

Face twisted. "What in the world kinda name is that?" Margaret blurted.

"German...it means serpent."

"I want ya first *and* last name. Come up here with all my info. Better gimme something, or this conversation's over."

"Von."

"Well, Yvonne—"

Her voice rose with an uncalculated force of its own. *"Just. Von."*

Zeus stood to his feet, ready to protect but with a wave of Von's hand, sat back down.

"Okay, *just Von*." Margaret took a drag of another cigarette. "Whaddaya angling at?"

"I'm not here to blow smoke up your ass with false sympathy." Von took off her sunglasses and gave Margaret her eyes— steel grey, unshielded, and intense. "I am, however, the only person that knows who assaulted your daughter, Mrs. Ashby, and most importantly, how to locate him."

"It don't matter now that my little girl is six feet underground," she said, pained,

"It doesn't matter, huh?" Von answered. "I find that hard to believe."

"Whaddaya want me to say?" Margaret snarled, exposing smoker's unkempt teeth.

Von got in her face. "The truth, Mrs. Ashby."

"Money or no money." Margaret wagged the check in her face. "Don't know ya. Don't owe ya nothin'. My baby's gone. Ain't no one care."

Von's tone softened as she put a firm hand on Margaret's shoulder.

"Odd as this may sound, sometimes talking to a complete

stranger is the only way to get it off your chest," Von coaxed gently. "Now, what is it that you really want?"

"Ya wanna know what I want?" A crimson flush rose to paint her cheeks. "Ya *really* wanna know?"

"Yes, ma'am, I do."

Margaret's lips curled into a snarl, teeth clenched, and body trembled.

"I want 'im to feel the pain that she felt. I want...I want 'im done the way he done to her. Shackled to his bed. Hope he burns alive in the lake of fire. Who eva the hell ya are—go on and call me when it happens. I'll come sit by the cozy flames and roast s'mores over his burning ass."

Von greedily ingested the mother's anger. It fed the already hungry beast inside, that *Thing* that had been maturing. A fresh wave of righteous rage churned in her gut and surged through her veins.

Von leaned in and whispered in Margaret Ashby's ear, "Apt request, Mrs. Ashby. I'll be sure to pass that message along."

No, she'd never killed anybody before. But that was about to change.

TWO

THE HUNT FOR VICTIM ONE

GRINDING HER MOLARS, Von cranked out her second set of fifty pushups. Sweat saturated her sports top, making it stick to her abdomen. With every agonizing dip, she clenched her core muscles, and the all-consuming surge of heat resurfaced.

The toxic combination of adrenaline tainted with anxiety nearly made her crumble, but she grunted through her exercise.

She paused between pushups and stopped herself from wiping the sweat dripping down the bridge of her nose with the bottom of her shirt. She hated showing parts of her body. Flesh out in the open for predatorial eyes. Parts of her on display like a mannequin. Stripped naked by invading eyes. She pinched at the wet fabric for airflow instead.

The underground gym was a muggy locker room of clanking weights and grunting gym rats. Body odor and a mildewed stench hung in the air. Fluorescent lights forced the windowless brick walls to squeeze closer, feeding Von's smothering uneasiness. The claustrophobic feeling, however uncomfortable, drove her.

A couple of floor fans did nothing but circulate sweaty stagnation. Von dipped low to the floor, her figure a rigid, parallel expression of perfect form and practiced grace. Arms bent at the elbows, slow and controlled. Her plank descended until her nose kissed the cement. Blue veins bulged from her upper body, engorged with the rush of blood. Pectoral muscles clenched in time with her stomach and thighs.

She gave one final shove off the ground, righting herself to her feet. Her arms satisfyingly burned and pulsed from the strenuous push-ups that kept them well-defined and lean. With her hands laced behind her head, she paced the length of the gym, taking in much-needed oxygen, guzzling air into her lungs and all the while keeping her eyes on *him*.

Von had been working out near the genial Bob Bixby, a short and rotund guard at the Maine Correctional Center, whom she often caught meticulously wiping down the equipment. She'd been arriving right on Bixby's schedule: 4:55 every morning for the past two weeks. At first, he didn't notice her, but she'd graduated to a head nod and even a cute smile that showed off his missing lower bicuspid.

A week ago, they even exchanged first names and places of employment. She'd been "Von the Uber driver" ever since, helping Bob Bixby drive parolees getting out. She'd proudly driven seven in the span of a week.

Today, the MCC guard was distracted by the local news. Von moved in closer and planted herself right next to Bixby as he listened to the broadcast playing on the gym's TV.

"A young woman, referred to by authorities as Girl X, claimed she was afraid for her life, alleging she was handcuffed and sexually assaulted several years ago by the one man whose release from MCC has locals in Portland scared," narrated a journalist.

The interviewee sat shrouded in darkness. Though, Von could still see that silvery sequined dress glinting where the shadows didn't cover her fully, hitting the light just at the right angle to shine off her thighs. Harper must've done the interview on her birthday before her party.

"I couldn't say anything," began the late Harper Ashby, her actual voice distorted to retain her anonymity. "They swore... they said...they said they'd kill me. So they got away with it. They all did. Now he's being released, and I'm terrified. Everyone should be."

The screen cut back to the journalist, who somberly announced, "Unfortunately, right after she provided this interview, Girl X was found deceased outside of her apartment building. Portland police have ruled out homicide, determining that the death was by suicide."

"They done got him all wrong," Bixby sighed as a female staff member at the gym quickly changed the channel.

Von double-checked her brunette wig, pulled in a ponytail under her baseball cap and dark contacts, in the gym's mirror. Nothing looked out of place. She looked convincing.

"Hey Bob, you know something about all this?" Von asked dumbly.

"Well, hi there, young lady," said Bixby, pointing to the TV. "Sure do. More than I'd care to. How's business other than the drop-offs you've done for me? Heard Uber gets craziest around the holidays with driving the drunks around and all."

"Been real slow. I've appreciated those referrals more than you know," she said, wiping sweat from her brow. "You got someone *special* leaving today?"

"That'd be correct." He absently rubbed his balding scalp. "Got a nice long rap sheet."

"Couldn't help but overhear you, but you say they got it wrong, huh?" Von furrowed her brows, snapping her fingers. "About what's his name? David Fers—"

"Darren Fischer," Bob corrected with a toothy grin. "Reporters only know what they hear. He was a scary dude when he first transferred, but I tell you what, he's a changed man. Lord works in mysterious ways at MCC."

"That's right...Darren Fischer," Von said. "I'm bad with names. Can you do me a huge favor and spot me at the bench press?"

She didn't need his help, but flattery went a long way.

Bob beamed. "Absolutely."

After she racked one hundred and fifty pounds, Von positioned herself underneath the bar. Standing at five feet even, it took her time and training, but she'd been able to bench fifty pounds over her weight for a couple of years now. Impressed, Bob whistled, readying himself in position to help her lift the weight. While he hovered, awaiting her cue, Von pumped out a set of ten, then took a thirty-second break followed by another set. Then another.

When she was done, she let Bob take the bar even though she could handle it herself.

Bob chuckled, then said, "Shoot—I think I need you to be spotting *me*."

It was true Von could hold her own among a weight room brimming with muscle heads.

"Does this Darren Fischer fella need a ride?" she casually inquired.

"Well, I normally wouldn't arrange transport for violent offenders coming out, let alone one with a sexual assault record—"

Von threw a light jab at Bob's arm, then said, "C'mon, Bixby, you're telling me I can only handle the white-collar types?"

Bob laughed until his cheeks flushed a rosacea red.

"You're such a petite woman..." Bixby caught himself with a shake of the head. "Sorry, that didn't come out right. I didn't mean to sound sexist. I know you're strong and all that. But these men are, well, they're *dangerous*. I mean, I think he's a changed man. Lord works in people, even folks with...his kind of record and all. Please understand I've gotta practice caution. That's how Mama raised me."

Von was so close; she could taste victory. "With the holidays and all...could really use the work right now." She turned up the reverse psychology. "But...if you think it's unsafe. Totally get it."

Bob's shoulders slumped. He gave her a look of pity.

Got him.

"Oh...alright. I guess for a born-again like Darren, I'll make an exception. Can you come by at, say, noon?"

"I'll do one better," Von said with a grin. "Be there half an hour early."

————

At precisely 11:27 a.m., Von waited in her car, anticipating her new customer. With the window rolled down, she could hear Darren Fischer and Bob Bixby yucking it up.

"How do it feel, son?" Bob asked the freed convict as they bumped fists.

"Yes, Darren, how does it feel?" Von said to herself.

Zeus, her German Shepherd, sat in the back seat. He was not only the smartest canine she'd ever had but one with a gut instinct. Which was likely the reason the damn dog had been growling for the past twenty minutes. But Zeus would need to mind his manners, hence the muzzle on his snout, and the harness restraining him.

"*Sei ruhig*," she ordered for him to be still. "Shhh."

Zeus obeyed, and she returned her focus to the conversation.

"You tasting free air right now, that's what this is," Bob said. "We sure gonna miss a model inmate."

"I can't say I'd like to return, sir," Darren said politely. "Feels good to have done my time and to finally be free."

"We better not see you back," Bob said, then asked. "What're you fixin' to do? Your Grandpa lives out here, don't he?"

"Grandpa's with the Lord in heaven. He left me the house, lobster boat, and his truck."

Bob whistled, then said, "Son, you got lucky. Most leave prison without so much as a pot to piss in."

"Real blessed. I'm the only grandson, sir. As far as what I'm gonna do, well, fixing to seek God's will, sir. Head to church as often as I can. Like I been doing up in here. Take long walks in the open air." Darren presented a choirboy smile. "Visit Mama, of course. Live it straight. No more bad influences or bad choices. Hell, no more bars, even."

"God bless you, Darren. You did real, *real* good." Bob turned and waved. "Von, you're right on time."

"Early as promised." Von waved back.

Darren crossed the street, and she gave him a disarming smile.

Von popped her trunk, hopped out of her Jeep Wrangler, and stood to meet him.

"Mr. Fischer," Von greeted, "allow me."

After the guard disappeared behind the gates, the freed convict's face contorted. There was a noticeable change in the pitch of his voice—disposition tensing and shifting. When no one was around to watch his back, the former "model inmate" scowled as he shoved the gym bag at her.

"Don't got much in it, just an old bloody shirt," he said, tone clipped, eyes narrowing at Zeus in the backseat. "Didn't know you had a...dog. Ain't no fun keeping him bound up."

Von watched Darren near the passenger door. He seemed perturbed by the sight of Zeus. She quickly unzipped the bag, removed the old shirt with blood on it, and shoved it under the spare tire. She replaced the shirt with an old towel she used at the self-serve car wash.

"He can have a mind of his own," Von said coolly, closing the trunk, "but you're fine to get in. He's not getting free. I've got him tethered down pretty good."

He unfroze and reached for the passenger door handle.

They drove in silence with Zeus on his best behavior, although the dog had been given little choice. Von took no chances. The last thing she wanted was Zeus going rogue and attacking.

Pulling up to Darren's house, she finally asked, "Whose blood's on that old shirt?"

Darren laughed. "It's my little...*keep-sake*."

Von nodded. "They let you keep it in that gym bag upon check-in? Weren't curious?"

"You don't know just how stupid those pigs are, do you?" Darren said.

In an instant, he altered his tone, and that good-natured Christian returned.

"Officer, please...I'm begging you." Believable tears sprouted from Darren's eyes. "That was Daddy's shirt. It's all I got left of him. All I ask is you keep it safe in the locker until after I done served my time."

And then, at will, he exploded into a chortle that rocked his head back. It grew until he was holding his stomach. Darren wiped his eyes.

"Next time," he began, laughter now gone, "you shouldn't drive people like me home."

"And why's that?" Von's eyes remained fixed on his.

Darren's attention darted to Zeus and then back. His gaze dropped to her neck, breasts, and then crotch. Her pulse quickened. With her throat parched, she took a deep breath through her nose as the muscles in her jaws clenched. Her abdomen tightened. Sweat dampened her cleavage, along her neck, and across her brow.

Zeus let out a snarl—a deadly warning.

Darren crept to her right ear, lips grazed her lobe, and his hot breath assaulted her skin. She could almost taste the disgusting last meal he had in prison.

"Why do you think?" he asked in monotone.

Von inhaled through her nose until the air ballooned in her chest.

The words lingered. He was so close a sour stench emanated from his pores. Darren's nose brushed up against the pulse on her neck. His disgusting index finger slid up her biceps, dripping with perspiration instigated by hot flashes that came in waves during anxious duress, despite cold weather.

That confined feeling took hold of her, squeezing her lungs.

"You're the type that would...put up a good and strong fight," he said.

Her arms broke out into gooseflesh as his lingering finger slipped away.

"Damn right I would," she returned in a low and steady tenor.

Amused, Darren cackled, and the hairs on the back of her neck stood on end.

Adrenaline flooded her body, solidifying terror and determination. The moment stretched out as Zeus's deadly growl grew stronger. Then, just when she least expected it, Darren withdrew and backed out of her car.

When the door slammed, Von let out a long exhale. Her hands, despite her pounding heart, were steady. She was glad she wore the wig and dark contacts again to conceal her grey eyes and golden hair. When he was gone, she took out a folder she'd stored in the trunk of her car marked with the filthy bastard's name and sifted through a pile of victims: men, women, animals, minors. Von had to admit, Darren cut a wide swath when it came to who he enjoyed victimizing.

His first had been Harper Ashby.

Von swallowed a breath as she paused at the picture of Harper, a younger, more beautiful image of Margaret without the wrinkles of despair, yellowing smoker's teeth, and the stress lining her face from having to bury her child.

"Several Sex Trafficking Victims Shut Down On The Stand," read a newspaper clipping in the folder she'd created. Von had the article memorized but read it again: *"Daren Fischer gets a light sentence of 5 years for dog fighting and animal cruelty. All other charges against him were dropped, despite previous charges of attempted murder and rape against minors..."*

Von shut the folder and gripped it, nails digging in, wishing she could shred each sin with her bare hands.

"You're not getting away with it anymore, Mr. Fischer," she said aloud, glaring down at the folder, disregarding the dangers lurking in the research she held in her palm and the unnerving first encounter with the serial rapist, serial predator.

She loitered outside his house daily, memorizing his every little movement and schedule, even chomped on some vegan popcorn while she eavesdropped on conversations. Von recalled the exchange she had with her tattooist a year ago when she discovered the ingenious spy app.

"I don't know who the person is, don't know if it's some fifty-year-old woman in Idaho or some college dude in Irvine," said Tommy, "goes by Ace. Met Ace in an underground online chat, the kind that helps you find anything you need. Group rules: no sharing real names, age, or gender. If there's spy shit or hacking you need, Ace'll hook you up."

"If you've never met this Ace-person and it's all anonymous, how am I supposed to make contact with them?" Von had said.

She could still remember that uncomfortable feeling like she was walking into the unknown.

"Don't worry, serious," Tommy assured. "Trust Ace. I just texted you the contact."

After she contacted the hacker, Ace sent an email she'd committed to memory.

The link will prompt you to download the software to your phone. You can dial in and listen to anyone's conversation. The phone won't ring on their end, so they'll never know their mic on the phone's hot. Yep...stuff like this does exist. Scary, right? Easy peasy lemon squeezy.
~Ace

She had tested the spy app on random numbers, and so far, it had worked beautifully. Von called Darren's number and heard him going at it for the umpteenth time with his neighbor Kang Lee, a petite Korean man with a very possessive attitude concerning his property. Since Darren moved into the home he inherited from his deceased grandfather, his irate neighbor had complained about more arbitrary shit—admittedly nitpicky—than Von could count.

So, at 2:15 in the pre-dawn, the neighborly "born-again" reformed criminal spent several dedicated hours shoveling snow into the back of his GMC Sierra and, once the bed was full, backed up into Kang's driveway and dumped fresh powder all over the man's front lawn. Von chuckled to herself, recalling the event. It was the first time she'd done so in a very long time. However, it was short-lived, knowing that the parolee was up to something.

Aside from Darren Fischer having fun pissing off his new neighbor, Von noticed something else. Darren had grown his hair out to shoulder length during his prison stay. That, combined with his thick beard, made him look nothing like his mug shots that were circulating all over the news. Through a camera she'd planted, Von watched him dye his fair hair and beard a Neil Diamond jet black.

She knew that Darren had been running an impressive seven miles each morning. That he'd drink approximately four gallons of water a day for the past week doing a water fast and had lost so much weight, the man now looked like a sprinting Forrest Gump with his long dark hair, beard, and gangly limbs.

She knew what the inside of his home looked like, that his fridge was completely empty save for more gallons of water, some type of green juice, and bone broth for his liquid diet. It was easy to sneak into his home after one of Fischer's long runs had him snoring like a freight train on his sofa. It was the only day he forgot to lock the door behind him. Not only did she make a copy of his house keys, but she remembered in his dresser was some type of leather S&M whip and a set of hand-cuffs on his four-post bed.

Yet another thing she was aware of was that, while she was following Darren, he had been following Kang Lee to Black-stone—a well-known gay bar. She could sense that the predator had something up his sleeve beyond just a big effort to make himself unrecognizable, but she hadn't the faintest clue what his scheme entailed. Parked across from Darren's home, Von extracted her binoculars from her backpack and watched the two men.

"I brought out the property inspector, and I have my property marked. You crossed over my property line," said Kang, pointing a finger in Darren's face. Kang was no taller than Von. At five-feet-even and likely no more than a hundred pounds, he squared himself before Darren, who appeared to be a giant of a man in comparison, towering well over six-feet-two.

"Did no such thing," Darren denied with a smile that was almost genuine.

Something in Darren's calm tone and in the way he looked at Kang unnerved her.

And something in Kang's hostility said he had no idea who his neighbor was.

"Those are your tire tracks." He pointed at his front yard.

"Could've been anyone's."

"They're your tire tracks. I know that lousy pickup. You dumped snow all over my front yard—*on purpose*."

"Was out on my boat all day, Mr. Lee," Darren lied. "Had no time to be hauling snow in my truck and dumping it in your yard."

"That's one big pile of stinky bullshit!" Kang jabbed a finger at Darren's chest. "We need to discuss building that fence, as I suggested."

"Hey, c'mon now, there ain't no bulls shittin' anywhere, but if there were, I'm a Jesus man now. I'd do the neighborly deed and shovel up that bull's shit just for you."

"Jesus-man, huh? I'd trust you types about as much as I'd trust an alcoholic to guard my liquor cabinet."

Von snorted out a laugh and watched their antics, thoroughly entertained.

"Think we might've gotten off on the wrong foot," Darren continued, playing contrite. He stuck out a hand for a formal introduction. "Know your name, but I believe you don't know mine. You can call me Buddy or Bud for short. Why don't we talk it over some drinks at Blackstone, on me?"

"Buddy, huh?" Von pulled out her binoculars and took a closer look at Kang's expression. "Don't do it, Kang. C'mon, you're smarter than that."

Kang Lee sized Darren up and down. "You at Blackstone? You do realize it's a—"

"I do believe we live in the twenty-first century, Mr. Lee. I know what it is," Darren said with an easy smile, "and know your preferences, but I believe...you don't know mine."

His words alarmed her.

"What's that? An asshole who takes the time dumping snow all over his neighbor's lawn?"

"Just a reasonable man," Darren replied, "willing to personally build that fence with these two hands. Now, what about them drinks, eh?"

Kang stared at Darren's hand like he was about to make a deal with the devil.

"Fine." Kang shook Darren's hand. "As long as you don't kill me."

Darren laughed. He laughed a little too hard.

THREE

THE FIRST VICTIM

THE ROOM SEEMED to shrink as stragglers overtook every inch of the bar. She watched the bartender move at superhuman speed. With the grace of a ballerina, Queen floated with ease. She grabbed four different hard liquors, and by memory, poured two different drinks.

Cocktails vanished into boozing patrons before the talented bartender turned to Von.

"Another Deadly Diet? Or something stronger?" The bartender leaned in. "You know Diet Coke'll kill you faster than liver cancer. I'll tell you this—a Yvonne would be drunk right now—not a Von. Not you. How do I know this, honey? Who needs a head shrinker when you can talk to your bartender? When we dish out the truth elixir, watch out. So, what's a straight teetotaler doing in Blackstone so close to the baby Jesus' b-day and the new year, huh?"

"Teetotaler?" Von arched a brow at the formal word that referred to a non-drinker. "First time I've ever heard someone use that term."

"I get paid to get people drunk, honey—I know that hideous

word by heart. Teetotalers are my enemy." Queen made the sign of a cross with her long index fingers. "You're not here for a family vacation, are you?"

Von gave her a lopsided grin. "Astute observation. Call me Scrooge, but I don't celebrate the holidays. I was just in the neighborhood. Heard you got mad skills."

"Reading an article and experiencing this place—two very different things, honey. Allow me to make that boring Diet Coke into something better? A little Bacardi, Carta *Oro*?" Queen rolled her r's. She was a tall, transgender Cuban and one of the best bartenders in town, according to numerous newspaper reviews. Voices chattered noisily in Von's earpiece, and she refocused on her target.

Von checked her spy app and kept her eyes affixed on Darren and Kang.

"I'll take another," Kang demanded, seemingly milking each free round he could get.

"One more Long Island and that IPA, please," Darren called out.

Queen nodded and then turned to Von.

"That one's *definitely* not from here. Duck-Dynasty, four chairs down." Queen nodded in Darren's direction. Von eyed the back of Darren's long, scraggly hair and shrugged indifferently.

Queen slid the drinks in front of Darren.

"Put it on my tab," Darren told her.

"Sure thing, honey," Queen said, but once her back was turned, she made a face.

"You're not feeling the beard?" Von smirked.

"Not a caveman beard. And that hair. ¡Dios mío! Forget about a makeover. What he needs is a lawnmower." Queen wrinkled her nose, making Von laugh. "C'mon, that was a weak laugh. Your face is too serious. I make you that cocktail. Live a little dangerous. ¿*Si o no?*"

She preferred staying in control and had never been a boozer, but one wouldn't kill her.

"Why not?" Von brushed her fingers through her dark brown wig and adjusted her baseball cap in the bar's mirror. "Bacardi."

Queen swiftly dispensed a fresh Diet Coke with a double shot of Bacardi.

"That'll be ten. Starting a tab?"

Von took out a twenty and handed it over, telling Queen to keep the change.

She was not so stupid she'd use traceable credit cards.

"And you don't want anything to eat? We've got killer beef sliders. They're to die for, I'm serious. You take one bite, and you fall over stone dead," Queen gushed, her body dramatically swaying as though she was fainting.

And after all that effort, Von disappointed the colorful bartender. "Vegan."

"Oh no," Queen tsked, clutching at her chest. "You're one of those."

Von smiled and then winced as she took a sip of her strong-ass beverage.

"*¡Dios mío!*" Queen burst out laughing. "And a lightweight, too!"

Suddenly, the TV mounted above the bar made people shift. Yet more news on Fischer's release. Darren turned his head at the television. Several men at the bar, including Queen, paused to tune in. The bartender cranked up the volume.

"...Maine locals are on their third week of protest outside of the Portland Superior Court against repeat offender Darren Fischer's second early release for good behavior. His first early release was five years ago, having served three years for dogfighting, despite being connected with an illegal sex ring operation and serial rapes. The alleged Aryan Nation member—who transferred from Wyoming Medium Correctional Institute to MCC—was never found guilty of those sexual assault crimes. This time, Fischer merely served five years for the near-fatal attacks on Wyoming veterinarians Dr. Robert Chua and his then-fiancée, Dr. Wilder Friedrich, including a concurrent three-years sentence for animal cruelty after killing the couple's dogs. Authorities never found two other men involved in the attack. In other news..."

Von turned away from the monitor and cranked up the volume on her spy app.

"Talk about a get-out-of-jail-free card or what? Just three weeks ago, too. Can you believe it? Heard he's attacked both women *and* men. And he's here wandering the streets of Portland, Maine," Kang said in her ear.

"Pretty crazy, huh?" Darren pointed his beer at the TV. "You never really know who might be living in your neighborhood."

"So, you really think you can put up this fence by yourself?" Kang asked.

Sitting at the bar a couple of chairs down, Von casually glanced over. Darren appeared to be studying Kang in the same way he had studied her. Took her in. Inhaled her like some dish he was dying to eat.

She turned up the volume on her Bluetooth.

Their conversation was coming in nice and clear.

Darren took a swig from his IPA and noisily swallowed. "I can build just about anything. I've got the design drawn out, in fact, back at my house if you'd care to see it?"

On his fourth Long Island, Kang was slurring his words. "Is that so?"

Darren tilted his head. "Yes, sir. Come on by, and I'll show you?"

"Sir, huh? You're flirting with me, aren't you?" Kang said, inebriated.

"Just trying to be neighborly." Darren polished off his beer. He plunked it down on the bar hard enough to generate feedback. Von adjusted the volume on the app again and listened.

"Sure, you are. I think you're flirting. If you wanted to ask me out, you could've just done so rather than make it hell for me to get out of my driveway." Kang snatched a lock of Darren's hair between his fingers and frowned. "And if we're to go out a second time, you'll need to do something with your...grizzly look."

She gulped her diet and rum in two swallows, feeling the Bacardi warm her throat and belly. Her cheeks flushed and sweat dampened her skin. Body heat started to smother her. She tilted the cup until she got a mouthful of ice, hoping to cool down. Having paid the bar tab, she'd heard enough to know that they'd be returning to Darren's home.

She turned off her Bluetooth for now, cutting her connection with Darren to focus on the next step. She didn't need to be at the bar to listen and could've killed him the other night. But she wanted to take her time. Sit and have a drink next to him. Experience what it was like to be inside his head.

Outside, the December Portland night was a frigid thirty-seven degrees, though the cold rejuvenated her. Black ice slicked the roads, but she drove carefully, returning to her warm motel room where Zeus had been waiting. Von took her dog for a quick potty walk around the building before driving to Darren's house. She parked a couple of blocks down the street in an empty lot ensconced amongst trees. It wasn't visible from the street and was hard to find, even for locals. She'd been scouting the neighborhood for three weeks and had every inch memorized.

Von lost the itchy wig and tossed it in the trunk. She retrieved her contact lens case from her backpack and took out the colored contacts that had been irritating her eyes. She covered her face with a ski mask and pulled a pair of disposable latex gloves—of which she had several spares in her pocket—over her hands. Von only took what she needed: an aluminum baseball bat, a one-gallon gasoline can, a book of matches, and the manila folder. She paused, studying the white shirt covered in dried blood. Von picked it up, gripped it in her fists for a beat before returning it under the spare tire and then shutting the trunk.

––––––

Von and Zeus walked a couple of blocks to Darren's. She checked the video surveillance app on her phone connected to a device she'd rigged to the front of the house. It was small enough and strategically placed behind the mailbox where it wouldn't be noticed if he should check the mail.

There'd been no activity since she checked while driving back from the bar. But she knew from her audio spy app that Kang had accepted the invitation to return to Darren's home and go over plans for the fence. She and Zeus arrived before Darren and his neighbor. Sparing no time, Von unlocked the back door that Darren never used. She double-checked the keys on the keyring, noting that they were all there, and secured them in her pocket.

Von used Ace's trick to call Darren's phone and heard him whistling to country music.

The truck stopped, and he turned off the radio. They were here.

When the door opened, she snapped her finger at Zeus, and he followed her to the walk-in closet, large enough to fit both of them without being seen. They were positioned to the left of the bed. The shutters to the closet door were open just enough for ample visibility.

"Where's the holiday spirit? No lights? No tree?" Kang teased. "A bit...macho-macho and a tad...*no*...a lot hetero, but nothing that an interior decorator can't fix. You know that's what I do, right?"

"You don't say?"

"Yes, I'm self-employed. I work on a referral basis. Word gets around, you know? I've *never once* had to advertise. So where are these plans for this gorgeous fence?"

"They're in the bedroom."

"Of course they are," Kang said. "I don't feel too good. I think them Islands are hitting me hard. Can I lay on your couch?"

"Since the plans are in the bedroom, you can have the bed," Darren said.

They shuffled in, and the juxtaposition between Darren and Kang was astonishing. Next to one another, Kang's petite frame was dwarfed by a towering giant.

"Is this a California King?" Kang crawled onto the bed, the handcuffs clanking against the headboard. "I really had too much to drink. Are these real handcuffs?"

Kang played with one of the metal rings.

"Nah, they're trick cuffs for sex games, you know. Release with just a tug. Fun party trick. Try 'em out?"

Kang took the right cuff and locked it around his wrist. He pulled once and then again.

"Uh...Buddy," Kang said, panicking now. "How does this trick cuff come off? Is there a button or something?"

"You've made this so easy," Darren mused. "What if I said Buddy's not my name?"

"Is it your middle name?" Kang slurred—eyelids were now half-open. He drowsily tugged at his cuffed arm. "This sure feels like police cuffs to me...not that I'd know."

"What if I told you my name is Darren?"

"Is that your first name?" He fiddled with his trapped right arm. "I dated a Darren once."

Von's nerves tightened because she knew she couldn't act too quickly. It had to be the right time. Everything hinged on perfect timing.

Darren's tall frame stood on the side of the bed, his back to her. Fuck, she couldn't see shit.

"What if I was the one that mowed down your mailbox? What if I was the one that took three hours shoveling snow in the back of my truck, so that I could leave a nice Christmas present for you. And that cat of yours, kept getting in my yard, meowing all night long. What if I was the one that killed it? Made it look like it had been hit by a car?"

"You...you sick bastard. I knew you killed Venus. I'm calling my lawyer." Kang struggled in the bed to free himself.

"I hadn't considered you for my first bit of fun. But you made it so hard for me to ignore you. Every single day. The nonstop bitching and moaning. I told you to leave me be, but you just wouldn't shut the fuck up." Darren's tone was as flat as a lake on a windless day. He reached for something in his drawer. With his arms tucked in front of him, she didn't have a clear view of what was in his hands. But Von was thorough. The only thing in the nightstand drawer she could recall was a thick leather horse's whip that looked painful if used on horses, let alone humans.

"Get me out of this thing. Uncuff me, Buddy. Darren.

Whoever you are! I swear I've got the best lawyer in town and you're gonna pay."

"What if my last name's Fischer?"

"Oh my God. *Oh, my fucking God.* I d-didn't even r-recognize you. You're...you're that guy on the news. You're that ra-ra-rap—"

"R-r-right," Darren mimicked with a snicker.

Kang's blood-curdling scream sent Von's heart fluttering in a panic.

For a moment, she froze. Everything happened so fast. Darren swung an arm several times, and by the third, she realized it was no whip but a large, curved knife. He must've placed it in the drawer after she'd sifted through it.

Von tapped Zeus. Her alert dog watched her as she made a circle in the air with her finger, indicating to get Darren to chase him. Von tucked herself back in the closet while Zeus launched his front paws into Darren's back, pinning him to the bed. The knife clattered to the floor. Zeus grabbed the handle in his mouth and ran out the bedroom door.

"How'd you get in here?" Darren said, running after Zeus.

She heard Zeus run out the back door she'd left cracked. The door squealed open as Darren gave chase. Von rushed to the bloodied Kang, who was weepy and shaking. He tried asking what was going on, stuttering through shock. But she had no time to explain or answer questions as to who she was.

Remembering the keys to the cuffs she'd seen on the nightstand, Von yanked the drawer open, snatched them out, unlocked Kang from the restraint, and checked his abdomen.

"Hold still...the lacerations appear superficial. Get to a hospital, just in case. You've had a lot to drink. You think you can drive?"

Kang nodded, then cried out, "What about you? He's gonna kill you!"

"Don't worry about me," Von ordered. *"RUN."*

Snatching his car keys, Kang stumbled out the bedroom door. Von returned to the walk-in closet, grabbed the gas can, baseball bat, and secured the manila folder under an arm. Working quickly, she began dousing the bedroom, bathrooms, spare rooms, and finally, the living room.

She dropped the folder on the ground to free her hands. Zeus rushed in from the back door, the curved Karambit knife still in his teeth. Once he reached her, he dropped the blade on the ground next to what contained a thorough record keeping of Fischer's trespasses. She dug into her pocket and gave him a treat.

"Guter junge." She praised him for being a good boy and patted his head.

In the living room, Von quickly glanced out the window as Kang jumped into his BMW and peeled down the street. She tossed the empty gas can on the floor.

Darren came running through the front door, flushed from the cold. "Who the fuck..."

Von ripped off the black ski mask. "You shouldn't let people like me drive you home."

"Ready to play?" Darren snarled and cackled at once. "Bring it, bitch."

The muscles in his body flexed, veins protruded from his neck and forehead. Blood rushed to his face, turning it scarlet as both hands became fists. A growling sound reached her ears, and she realized with amusement that it was coming from Darren and not from her dog.

Her smile widened.

"Hol dir dieses Arschloch!" Von guided Zeus. *"Get this asshole!"*

Zeus rushed forward. Using his hind legs, he leapt with all his might and sank his teeth into Darren's arm. He howled in pain, trying to kick Zeus loose, but it didn't do jack shit. While German Shepherds didn't hold the record for the strongest bite, Zeus would sooner have his jaws broken than ever let go.

Being a big man, Darren managed to pick up a nearby chair with his free arm and threw it at Von. She stumbled back, and he rushed forward. Despite Zeus's teeth embedded in his forearm, Darren seized her ankle, and she fell on her back. Zeus released his arm and went for Darren's hand, where he sank his teeth. Darren yelped and lost his hold on her leg, sprawling on the ground, giving Von time to wrench free and kick him in the face. Blood gushed from his nose, but it hardly seemed to faze him as he stumbled to his feet and lunged for the curved knife on the floor.

She regained control of the baseball bat and called out to Zeus, *"Lass los!"*

Zeus obeyed and released the man's hand. She and Zeus ran into the bedroom with Darren stumbling closely behind, just as she had planned.

Darren bounded in, swinging wildly with the curved knife in hand like a mad butcher.

Zeus sprung at him, chomping into his calf, causing Darren to scream and lose his footing. He dropped the knife on the floor and clutched the bed for support. Desperate to rid himself of her dog's clutches, he punched at Zeus's rib cage with his free hand, but Von's muscular canine didn't so much as wince, let alone unlock his jaw. Darren's large frame hunched over the bed; his head bobbed forward in her direction. It was a perfect shot.

"Oh," Von said, adjusting the bat in ready position, "and Mrs. Ashby sends her regards."

The years of training seven days a week paid off, every muscle burning from constriction. But it was the kind of ache she'd learned to love. Now, she craved the scorch of a sweltering fire. She'd eventually strike that match, which would cause the flames to spread quickly through the gasoline-soaked house, but the last thing she wanted to do was save Darren from an easy death of smoke inhalation. No, she wanted him alive and well through it all.

She stepped into the imaginary pitch and pivoted her hips. Her arms followed through. The bat made a hollow thump as it connected with Darren Fisher's head. Oh, that sweet spot.

FOUR
THE DETECTIVE

DETECTIVE ANAYA NAZARIO was sweating like a dirty politician at a truth-telling contest. The air was muggy and stifling, but not only from the broken-down air conditioning. Why they picked the only conference room in the Federal Bureau of Investigation's downtown office that didn't have a properly working air conditioner was beyond her. Some last-minute "emergency" meeting.

It was a rare occurrence for FBI Associate Deputy Director Everest Frost. In his late sixties, Frost sported salt-and-pepper hair that was a striking contrast to his rich terracotta skin. His face, marked by lines and creases, carried a worn yet wise expression, each fold telling a story of the decades spent in the demanding world of law enforcement.

After a drug dealer crushed her knee in a fight several months ago, Nazario finally healed from both an ACL repair and a torn meniscus that required emergency knee surgery. Living with a full leg brace for three awful months was annoying as fuck. The recovery took much longer than antici-pated, as she couldn't afford to sit back; she was working double shifts in Homicide, as usual. Nevertheless, the determined detective pushed herself to run five miles every morning despite her healing knee and the added challenge of being pregnant.

Her baby bump popped, her ankles were a tad swollen, and the cheap, rickety office chair squealed under the burden of extra weight. Out of habit, her fingers absently toyed with her late father's wedding ring dangling on a braided gold necklace that she never took off. It'd been a very long four months confined to her desk. Nazario didn't "take it easy" well. While great at her job, lack of commitment on Nazario's end made her quite shitty at relationships, and still trying to wrap her head around being five months pregnant while on co-parent status with a quite peeved FBI Agent sitting right next to her.

Huxley's knee bobbed up and down with animated fury. Someone wasn't in a good mood. His exhalations were so loud, Deputy Frost's forehead furrowed. Nazario was forced to be seated next to a very frustrated supervising federal agent—Blake Huxley. She tried sitting a chair apart, but that wasn't even remotely far enough.

Frost eyed the gold band between Nazario's fingers that had once belonged to the famous Detective Lucas Nazario. As if she was caught in the act of chewing her nails, Nazario quickly tucked the necklace inside her shirt.

Huxley blew out another gust of air.

Enough is enough. To hell with this so-called "emergency" meeting.

"Christ, Huxley, it was one doctor's appointment," Nazario blurted, like no one was in the room. "There'll be more."

"That's part me in there," Huxley said, his pale skin turning the color of a bad sunburn. "It wasn't immaculate conception, Detective. Running five miles a day, I hear? Gotta use my sources since I can't get you to pick up the phone. Keep tabs on my unborn child somehow. What're you training to run, a 5k?"

"Maybe I am." Nazario pulled a thin smile across her lips.

"Pregnant women can run. They can also go to the gyno—alone —if they wanna."

"I am the father, and I want to be there. You squeeze me out again, and I'll force my way into the next appointment."

"And I'll omit you from the consent list," she said, folding her arms across her chest.

"I'd like to see you try," he said, his blue eyes glaring daggers. He threw his arms up in the air. "Maybe I should thank you for the emergency meeting. Otherwise, I wouldn't have gotten face time with my baby mama."

Nazario laughed, shaking her head. "Why in the hell are we even here? It better be good."

The deputy gave them a weary look like a parent of feuding children.

"This have anything to do with Informant F's little tip?" Huxley queried.

Informant F had become a valuable asset to the force and to the FBI. Homicide never relied on informants that promised them intel especially when that someone made the FBI look bad. But the anonymous informant proved to be quite valuable, calling with knowledge of alleged criminal activity that had gone down as they said it would. Then, two days ago, they called again to warn them about some house fire. They claimed a woman might be involved but would not give the FBI any further details on their source. That was the deal Informant F had with the Feds. They'd give the FBI leads but not how they knew and certainly not give up their identity.

"As a matter of fact, all of F's tips have been dead on." Deputy Frost folded his hands on the long conference table and leaned forward. "House burned down. Fried the man alive. You'll both be flying out to Maine on the bureau's private jet in an hour. We'll have a team here handling research and intel."

"Hell no," Huxley barked. "The detective's not supposed to

be flying anywhere. Not to mention working around toxic fumes and chemicals."

"The doctor cleared me. It's fine."

"Cleared you to go back to work, maybe. Did he clear you to work a house fire? It isn't fine, Anaya." Huxley raked his hands through the waves of his thick chestnut hair, leaving it disheveled. "It's all kinds of fucked up."

Nazario rubbed her temples.

"Why are we being teamed up? Do we sound like the dream team to you? Why am I being onboarded with him if this homicide is in Maine? FBI's within jurisdiction to jump on anything out-of-state and anywhere in the world. Look, I'm not worried about the flight or the damn smoke fumes. I. Am. Not. FBI. Maine's got their homicide division. Why do they need LAPD?"

Deputy Frost sipped his coffee, swiveling back and forth in his chair before casually setting his mug on the desk.

"What's going on?" Huxley asked, eyeing Frost with suspicion.

"Man fried to a crisp? Darren Fischer." Frost rested his chin on an ebony hand. Dark, shiny eyes darted between the two of them.

"Shit." Nazario slumped in her chair and put a hand on her belly as the baby kicked.

"Goddamn it." Huxley slammed back against his chair and punched the armrest as though he wished he could extract himself from the meeting. The muscles in his upper body tightening.

The baby kicked again.

"Was worried as all hell that the moment he got out, he'd go after Samantha Friedrich," Nazario rubbed her temple. "At least she's safer out here in L.A., since Fischer was transported to Maine to serve his time 3000 miles away."

"Well, it appears someone else got to him before he had a chance to go back in the slammer as a repeat offender," Frost said.

"Just three weeks out of prison is hardly much time at all," Frost mused, sipping his coffee, "With them protests going on and everyone pissed off at his early release...shit, anyone could've killed the man. Heck, it could've been one of them nutcase PETA fanatics—People for the Ethical Treatment of Animals—I think that's the full name? Those folks have gone a little crazy over that dogfighting alone. Not to mention all the other *caca* on his rap sheet."

"Good riddance," Huxley said.

"Karma's one mean bitch with a lighter." Nazario itched her belly. "Unfortunately, scum like Fischer has to be protected, too."

"The downside of our job," Huxley added.

It was the one thing they could agree on.

"Nazario, you led the Fischer conviction, and Huxley, you had a big hand in it as well. We need both of you on this, and we need you working together," Frost said.

Nazario exhaled a long breath. "Was pulling eighteen, twenty-four hours during the Darren Fischer case. Would go two, three days without a wink of sleep. Don't think I was even eating."

Huxley groaned. "Every damn federal agent was working around the clock." He raised a brow at her, giving her a sideways glance. "You can't be doing that no more. That's a human that you're incubating. It's not some dog you decide you can put out on the porch. Can't be doing that self-punishment thing you love to do."

"Save your toxic masculinity lecture. I'm the one blowing up like a balloon. I just love it when a man tries to tell a woman —who's pregnant—what to do and not to do with their own body. Appreciate that you solved my father's murder. Since, apparently his cold case made you quite famous. But that's as far as my thank you goes, Blake."

"Toxic masculinity?" Huxley rolled his eyes. "It's called concern for your wellbeing, and I'll have you know I told you in grad school—nearly thirteen years ago—I'd solve it. And it wasn't for the limelight."

She couldn't believe it'd been fifteen years already since she'd known Blake Huxley. If she had to be honest, Anaya Nazario was the one doing all the running from any commitment with the supervising special agent.

Deputy Frost stepped in. "How about we stick with Darren Fischer? Both of you had been involved in the Aryan Brotherhood case associated with him."

"How can I forget?" Nazario pivoted to Huxley. "I switched my hours around several times when we were working the Brotherhood case, including working graveyard. Yet, there you were," she accused. "Kept on running into you, and I can't help but wonder now."

Huxley rolled his eyes. "Oh please, if you think I was stalking you—you're just a little too full of yourself."

"Okay, now, kids. Here's the bottom line: the two of you are the best we got and Maine's aware that you'll be leading this, Nazario. Don't know if this means anything, but they requested you and Huxley." Frost dropped his pen on his desk. "He did deliver by solving Detective Lucas Nazario's cold case and that was no easy task."

Nazario reached for her father's ring, dangling from her necklace, and clutched it.

Huxley caught her eyes. "Solving it was a heartfelt promise. Not for me. Not for my career, Detective. It was for you, and you know why."

Because he loved her, and to this day, she hadn't even so much as whispered the word.

The deputy leaned in and steepled his fingers. "Law enforcement personnel all across the country know who you are. I, too, knew your father well. I've followed your career: fourth-degree black belt in taekwondo by eighteen—" Frost read from her file.

Nazario couldn't help but feel singled out. She hated the special attention.

"For all the good it'll do me now when I'm as big as an elephant," Nazario huffed.

"All-star track athlete in both high school and college. You've solved dozens of murders, more than anyone on the force. You took down that drug dealer." Frost annoyingly returned to reading her resume without a glance in her direction.

"And he crushed my knee, severing my ACL and meniscus. I was in a full brace from ankle to hip, having to shower with a plastic bag over my leg. You know what it's like going to the bathroom spread eagle on the toilet 'cause you can't bend your leg? So yeah, Deputy, it looks like I lost that fight," Nazario said.

Frost inhaled through his nose, folded his hands, and made eye contact for the first time.

"And you fought like hell. We're talking a three-time UFC champion; not to mention the bastard ran so fast, they didn't call him 'Speed' for nothing. No one's been able to catch up. *Ever.* That's how he eluded authorities for so long. You did. You caught him." Frost pointed a finger at her.

"Whoop-di-do." Her hands shot up. "Don't get brownie points for doing my job."

Frost powered on as if determined to break through her stubbornness.

"You're the first detective—*let alone woman*—to break our

record of solving homicides," he paused for a reflective beat, then continued. "If there's some woman running around out there burning a man alive, and God knows if there'll be more—"

"What do you mean more?" Nazario interjected. "Wait— does the FBI think there could be a hit on the Aryans? Like the whole group?"

"We're bracing ourselves for that possibility, yes, and we need the two of you. Especially you, Nazario. You help us with this, Detective Nazario and we guarantee you, you'll be next in line for chief of detectives."

Nazario slapped both palms lightly on her pregnant belly. "You forget my condition?"

"The doctor's cleared you, correct? I see no reason for any hesitation," Frost said, taking off his glasses. "Doctor's note or no doctor's note, we don't hesitate when it comes to our best homicide detective."

Nazario considered Frost's words and suddenly thought of Mama.

"Your father would be so proud of you right now, following in his footsteps. I used to hate it so much, wanted you to be a Southern Bell like me, do a proper woman's job, but you are doing a woman's job. Bet you're a better detective than ninety percent of the men on the force," Mama had told her the only time she'd spoken about Daddy since his death.

Mama turned to her with that same teacher tone that had made her one of the best. *Promise me that you won't give up. Your father was the highest-ranking Puerto Rican detective. That record can't be replaced. But it's about being a woman of color, Anaya. It's about excelling beyond society's expectations. It's about the pride of ethnic heritage and shattering the glass ceiling for minorities everywhere.*

She refocused her attention on the meeting with more determination. She had an obligation, a duty to fight against racist assholes like the brotherhood. Nazario had to take them down, five months pregnant or not.

"Pardon me, sir," Huxley huffed, "but I'm just a little concerned over her well-being and our child's safety and not whether this case will *boost* her career."

"I can handle it, Huxley," Nazario warned.

"And we would never put Detective Nazario in a position that would jeopardize her life or the baby's life," Frost answered. "The fact remains, Huxley, your *baby mama* is still the best we've got. Pregnant or not. You know it. We all know it."

"Nazario, Huxley, both of you worked on ethnically charged cases like The Bridge Killer targeting undocumented immigrants and did a damn good job. I can't stress this enough— we need both of you," Deputy Frost finished with a candid expression.

Huxley's face turned hot cherry. Blood rushed up his neck and spread across his cheeks. He stared at her belly. His jaw muscles twitched.

Nazario swallowed the lump in her throat, willing back tears of frustration. The pregnancy made her more emotional, despite her uncanny ability to never show it.

Deputy Frost reminded, "We trust the two of you will work together and not against one another. This is a team effort. What's going on between you—none of our business— *seriously.*"

Huxley stirred next to her.

Nazario gave Huxley a sideways look. *Well?* He nodded a silent truce.

"Alright," Nazario said.

"You've got our full cooperation," Huxley offered in defeat.

Huxley and Nazario waited for Deputy Frost to leave his office before leaving.

"You running home?" Nazario finally asked, "cause it looks like we'll be staying the night in Maine."

"Always got my travel bag ready to go in my car." He gave her a tired smile.

"Great minds think alike. I do, too," she said.

Huxley stared out the window for a beat while Nazario gazed at her feet.

The two held onto the silence with equal stubbornness as the baby did a flip, already trying to get Mom and Dad to work together. Nazario opted to keep the gender a surprise and hasn't given Huxley a chance to give his opinion. Which wasn't fair. She was no good at figuring out a way to navigate this whole new mom role with success. Nazario didn't know how to be a mom and equally sucked at accepting Huxley's help.

How *could* he help? Sit there and watch her body get as big as a house?

The baby was in her body for nine months, not his, yet she couldn't avoid the fact that the baby was part Huxley, too. She had a great relationship with her father. Would she rob their child of that same experience because she was terrible at expressing her emotions? He or she had been keeping her up all night dancing in the womb. It didn't help that she battled with ongoing insomnia that not even pregnancy could cure.

The baby stirred again. Nazario grabbed Huxley's hand and put it on her lower belly.

"You feel that?"

"I do," he said, eyes wide. "The...baby's kicking already?"

Huxley put both hands on her swollen abdomen and stayed that way for a long beat.

"I think the baby wants us to get along," Nazario finally said. "Look...Huxley, I have no idea what I'm doing. This whole parent thing...I'm freaked out, okay? You're the father, and I'd never prevent you from having a relationship with your child. I didn't mean what I said back there. I'll fill you in on the doctor appointments from here on out. I'm sorry—"

"No, no, no...I'm sorry. Okay? *I am.* I didn't mean to be such an asshole. I just...I'm here for you...for the both of you and in any capacity you need me to be."

She nodded and whispered, "I've been...a little overwhelmed. Haven't been sleeping."

"I haven't been sleeping much either," he admitted.

She swallowed a shaky breath and nodded. "Can we not allow whatever is happening with the baby to affect our work? Whatever we decide to do—co-parent—who knows? I don't have a crystal ball. How about we do our job and bitch at each other when we're off the clock?"

Huxley nodded. He slipped his hands off her belly and met her eyes.

"We on the same team?" Nazario asked.

"On the same team, Detective," he assured her.

FIVE
THE TRIAL
EIGHT YEARS EARLIER

COLD FEAR RAN through Dr. Wilder Agatha Friedrich, fear that speaking the truth might kill—if not today, then someday. The protective big sister wished she could run to Sammy, hug her close, and save her from having to deal with the stress of testifying. Wilder squeezed her eyes shut and laid her throbbing head in her hands. The courtroom shuffled back in from recess. She imagined her sister sequestered somewhere in a back room for her safety.

Waiting to be called upon like a death row inmate anticipating her execution.

She could picture Sammy's hands fidgeting in her lap, the way they always did when she was nervous. She could imagine her shallow breath and sense her heart accelerating to a frantic speed, causing her stomach to twist. Sammy must've had to run to the bathroom multiple times by now. Wilder's seventeen-year-old baby sister always got sick when her anxiety was exceptionally high. How would Sammy handle being a key witness in a controversial trial, the one voice speaking for countless young women too scared to come forward, and who could blame them?

What would happen if Sammy spoke the truth?

Who might come after her little sister or their family seeking revenge, and when?

If Wilder could crawl into her sister's skin, get into her mind, and erase what had happened, maybe it would release the guilt that had kept Wilder awake every night. If only she hadn't been busy at the clinic. If only she had been with her sister, then Sammy would never have been...

Oh, dear God...She couldn't even say the words. With her head buried in her hands, Wilder shut out the world, wishing the five-minute sidebar would stretch forever. Two people she loved would have to testify soon. Where they were seated, the press circled like predators around a wounded animal. If they weren't chasing her mother, they were hounding Wilder's father.

A reporter whispered to her mother, "Dr. Friedrich, as a famous psychologist specializing in trauma—"

"Oh please," Wilder heard her mother whisper back in an effort to avoid her temperamental husband overhearing. "Do call me Dr. Katrine. There are three Dr. Friedrichs present."

"My bad, Dr. Katrine. How're you handling the trauma, given your daughter's unfortunate association with the sex ring?"

Not this, Wilder pled silently.

"Fascinating question—" the psychologist began, level-headed as usual, but the hushed conversation couldn't escape her husband's excellent hearing.

"Verpiss dich!" Wilder's father snapped at the reporter. "Can't understand German? Allow for me to translate—*I said fuck off!*"

Wilder pressed her temples. The court she had tried to shut out was returning to session.

"Bobby's on the stand, dear," her mother said in her ear, putting a hand on her shoulder.

Nervous for her fiancée, Bobby was surprisingly calm about testifying as an expert witness.

Wilder opened her tired eyes and looked over at the defense table. A group of Caucasian men sat next to Pilar "The Pit Bull" Velázquez. The female Hispanic defense attorney was as expensive as they came, and she lived up to every bit of the ruthless reputation she'd earned in the courtroom. Once again, she seemed to have succeeded in casting reasonable doubt.

Prosecutor Roger Hale's questioning was straightforward. Bobby recounted treating a dog that had been badly injured in a dogfight and speaking to an eyewitness about the elaborate ring. Once Hale sat, Velázquez stood with an ironclad posture and steely glare. The Pit Bull planned to sink her teeth into Dr. Robert Chua. Wilder was sure of this.

Velázquez launched right in, "Dr. Chua—you and your fiancé Dr. Wilder Friedrich co-own the veterinarian clinic in Casper, Wyoming?"

"Yes, we're co-owners, co-partners in life. Wilder also runs advanced dog training classes. We work in shifts like any other clinic," Bobby said, looking at Wilder. She smiled supportively.

"According to your statement, Santiago Torres had come by the clinic to drop off a dog suffering from multiple lacerations—is that correct?" Velázquez asked.

"Correct," Bobby said.

"Could the dog have been injured in a fight with some neighborhood dog?"

"Well, no. It was quite clear to me that Mr. Torres' account of a dogfighting ring was true based on the type of gashes Princess received. Ordinarily, a street fight gets broken up quickly, so the injuries are different. The injuries Princess sustained were severe. The type that would be evident after an animal being forced to fight for a lengthy period until one dog is incapacitated or dies," Bobby said.

"Did you yourself see who was responsible?"

"Mr. Torres said they were associated with the Aryan—"

"Answer only the question asked of you, Dr. Chua," the judge rebuked.

The Pit Bull repeated her question. "Did you, yourself, see who was responsible?"

"Well—no—of course not. I didn't directly witness the dogfighting ring. I can only attest to the condition that the dog was in and, frankly, Mr. Torres' condition. He had received a terrible beating."

"So, you have no way of really knowing if my clients beat Mr. Torres or had anything to do with the dogfighting ring?"

"Well, as I said, I wasn't there. I was treating the wounds on Mr. Torres' face and waiting for the ambulance to arrive. Mr. Torres relayed that the men who attacked him were white. He also claimed they were associated with the Aryan Brotherhood," Bobby said.

"White men?" Velázquez grilled, "Dr. Chua, you're Filipino, correct?"

Bobby took off his glasses and then said, "Excuse me, but I don't see how that's—"

"Objection, your honor," Hale threw his arms in the air. "What does Dr. Chua's ethnicity have to do with anything? He simply imparting information provided to him by Mr. Torres while Princess was being treated for fight wounds at his clinic. He's not the one on trial here."

"Your honor, I'm making the point that Dr. Chua's state-ment here in court and what he told the police is hearsay. Since he brought up my client's ethnicity, my question is a valid one," Velázquez said.

"I'll allow it." Judge Estevan glared at Hale. "Continue, Ms. Velázquez."

Of course, Judge Estevan would overrule, thought Wilder.

"Yes, I'm of Filipino descent," Bobby blurted out with an exasperated huff.

The palms of Wilder's hands began to sweat as her body sank into the wooden chair. The courtroom melted and swirled into a giant black hole, sucking them in.

"You said this eyewitness identified white men. My clients are white," Velázquez pointed at them. "Gang affiliations can be any ethnicity. Isn't it true that your older brother Alvin Chua is currently serving time for criminal activity associated with the Satanas? You know, the very well-known Filipino gang here in Southern California?"

Wilder's mouth fell open. Bobby had told her that Alvin died in a car accident.

Her mother's hand was on her knee. Wilder could feel analytical eyes studying her.

Bobby took off his glasses and looked right at her, his face dark with an apology she didn't want to hear. The Pit Bull had no further questions. Bobby stepped off the stand and stormed out of the courtroom, not staying for Sammy's testimony.

The courtroom broke into a murmur. So did her parents, who often spoke about her in the third person as though she wasn't sitting right next to them and she wasn't twenty-nine, soon to be thirty. As if she was still a child. Guilt filled Wilder again. It was no wonder Sammy hated living with them and begged to move in with her big sister. Had she said yes...if only she had said yes, this wouldn't have happened.

"Roger Hale is an *idiot* like Bobby. I told Wilder she could do better," her father said under his breath. "Told her she shouldn't have moved to Casper, Wyoming, in the middle of nowhere with that *idiot*."

Had she not moved, she could've gotten a place with Sammy in California.

In a hushed tone, her mother replied, "Wilder didn't expect Bobby's testimony, dear."

Oh, shut up. Just shut the hell up—the both of you, she wanted to order them. But she sat there and said nothing, instead. Behind her, a hurried dialogue between two reporters rattled away before the judge could yell again, distracting her attention from her infuriating parents. Yet another conversation that only made her panicky in a way she'd never experienced before.

"Velázquez with Judge Estevan presiding—lethal combo, eh? Estevan's a damn tyrant. I'm writing that in my column 'cause it's the fucking truth. You think he'll bully the star witness like the others?" Wilder heard the reporter say.

"Judges chastise witnesses all the time...but yeah, Estevan's a particular asshole. He's as nasty as they come. My money: These dirtbags get a guilty on dogfighting. Go scot-free on the sex ring and rape. It's a real shame. It's disgusting," the second reporter replied.

Judge Estevan slammed the gavel. "Order."

Wilder's nerves cinched tighter.

When the courtroom eventually settled, the prosecutor called his key witness, and Sammy walked up onto the witness stand. Freckles dotted her face, her golden hair highlighted from the sun. The amber dress she wore matched her eyes. She might be seventeen, but it looked like she could be twelve.

She sat with a touch of grace. This was their Sammy— sweet, child-like innocence.

Sammy tucked a wisp of hair behind an ear and kept her gaze cast down. Never once did she raise her eyes, glancing away from her family. Wilder couldn't comfort her, and that hurt her heart. Roger Hale made his way forward in a moderate stride as if trying not to frighten a kitten.

"Samantha, would you like some water before we begin?" Hale said.

Sammy, with eyes still cast down, shook her head.

"You said in your statement: 'I've never been academic, and I'm never going to medical school.' Given that your father's a world-renowned neurosurgeon, mother's a famous psychologist best-selling author, and your sister's a veterinarian—any pressure from the fam to excel?" Hale asked.

Sammy stared at her hands for the longest minute of Wilder's life. "Definitely."

"Objection." Velázquez stood. "Relevance other than flaunting the family resume?"

"Sustained," Judge Estevan said, "get to your point, Hale."

Hale did so. "Is this why you got a fake ID and entered a bar alone at fifteen?"

Her sister hugged her arms against her chest and avoided eye contact.

"Everyone knows my family. It's been really hard to...to live up to." Sammy paused, and Wilder held her breath. "So, yeah, I got me a fake ID and went to a bar solo. I suddenly felt less sheltered...like I was all grown up or something. That's when I met a couple of guys at the bar. It was...they were cute. I was stupid and lonely. It was a huge mistake. A mistake that took me away from my family for two years. The biggest...the biggest mistake of my life."

For the first time, Sammy met Wilder's gaze. Her sister's mouth went slack as if trying to find the words, but nothing except a sharp exhale came out. Eyes welled up with moisture, but the tears never fell. Sammy stared at Wilder from the dock with a distant look of loss and shock.

Instantly, Wilder was a teenager again, eating a stick of beef jerky on the deck, her baby sister a toddler. She could see their neighbor's intimidating Doberman Pincher, Dallas, escape the yard. Sammy freezing, her pouty lips agape, large doe eyes looking right at Wilder. Eyes that asked Wilder to save her, to protect her from harm. Wilder could feel her own panic, see the Doberman's bared teeth as Dallas charged toward Sammy. Wilder shouted his name, catching his attention. She threw the jerky toward Dallas, the powerful dog veering away from her terrified little sister.

Wilder hastened toward Sammy, arms outstretched, and scooped her up.

On the witness stand, Sammy was two years old all over again. Her plump rosy cheeks smudged with dried peanut butter. The pull-ups she'd been wearing for potty training sagged at her thighs as she gripped her favorite Winnie The Pooh stuffy. Her hair was still tangled after waking up from her nap. Frightened eyes called out to Wilder.

Save me, big sissy.

"Samantha," Hale hesitated, "need to take a break?"

Wilder's eyes never left Sammy's.

Sammy gulped and shook her head no.

"Sammy, did you overhear Jerry Bell call from San Quentin?"

"Yes." Sammy's gaze withdrew downward again. She chewed at her bottom lip.

"Did you hear the men in this courtroom take orders from Bell? Including his right-hand man, Darren Fischer?"

Another minute dragged, each second tightening the nausea in her gut.

"Orders? Not so sure if they were orders," Sammy said in a small voice.

As Estevan glared at Sammy's uncertainty, Velázquez sported a satisfied grin.

Wilder's stomach turned ulcerous and sour. The courtroom stirred once again.

"Why'd that bloody psychologist give Hale the okay to put Sammy on the stand?" her father grumbled to her mother, loud enough for Wilder to hear him.

"Because Samantha passed the psych-eval and therefore deemed her fit to testify."

"Clearly, she was wrong. Clearly. I'll have her license revoked. Mark my word."

Wilder didn't always agree with her hot-headed father, but she did about this.

"I *will* have order in my courtroom," the judge demanded, slamming the gavel again.

"How about we back up," Hale said gently.

"By all means," Estevan snarled.

The prosecutor glanced at the judge, who was ten degrees above vexed. As if Roger Hale was fresh out of law school instead of a prosecutor with twenty years of experience. Hale cleared his throat, continuing. "You said you met two men at the bar. Did you willingly leave the bar with them?"

Sammy, still not looking up, nodded.

"You must answer in words," the judge admonished.

"Um," she swallowed, eyes shifted nervously, "yes."

"After you met these men at the bar," Hale continued, "when did you know something was wrong?"

Sammy hugged her arms to her chest and took in a deep breath.

"There wasn't a specific moment." She bit her lower lip. "They said we were going to a party. So, I left with them, and then...then I knew something wasn't right. I knew I couldn't leave."

Hale said, "Can you explain what you mean specifically?"

Sammy began curling a lock of hair around her finger, a habitual dance of nerves. Finally, she lifted her gaze to meet their parents. Her father was a volcano, red-faced and agitated, on the brink of eruption, as if he wanted to shake his youngest child, scream at her to answer the questions directly. There was nothing more Dr. Anton Jörg Friedrich hated than indirectness. On the other hand, their mother maintained the same clinically inquisitive expression as when the other young girls were on the stand.

"Uh-huh." Dr. Katrine Adele Friedrich was aware of something no one else was.

Sammy's eyes darted away from them.

"Young lady, you're under oath for a serious matter—a federal crime," the judge barked. "Answer the questions concisely"

Sammy jumped and began trembling.

"Were you free to leave?" Hale asked with more directness.

"Um...I don't think so? I mean...there weren't fences or barbed wire or anything like that. It's so...so very hard to explain."

Estevan rolled his eyes and shook his head with incredulity.

"Ms. Friedrich, 'I don't think so' is not good enough. It's certainly not what the court would consider an understandable, direct answer. Need I remind you that this isn't just a trial about illegal dogfighting accusations. Identifying men who have been accused of sex trafficking of minors and other sexual crimes requires certainty," Estevan said, throwing his pen across the bench. "*I don't think so* is not satisfactory."

Wilder covered her mouth with a clammy hand. The courtroom sunk further into the abyss of despair. Her father dug his nails into the seat in front of him with such force that she was sure they'd break. Meanwhile, her mother wrote in a small notepad that fit in her purse. It was the same one she'd seen the psychologist use with her clients hundreds of times.

She wrote one word down and numbered it as though she'd have more to add.

1.Intimidation

Mr. Hale's ordinarily blanched face flushed with a sudden rush of red-hot humiliation. The prosecutor fumbled with his legal pad, flipping pages with an unsteady hand. Wilder glanced over at The Pit Bull. Velázquez bit the end of her pen cap with a toothy grin.

Wilder felt like she'd been gut-punched. She wanted to stand up and scream at the judge.

Leave my sister alone, you asshole!

She wanted to snatch her sister away from the witness stand and testify for her. She wanted to smack her father's disappointment right off his high and mighty face. Rip to shreds her mother's stupid notebook full of psychoanalysis, as though hired as an expert witness, as she had been for numerous other high-profile trials. Instead, she glanced warily at Dr. Katrine's notes.

More one-word observations in a neat little numbered row on a single horizontal line.

1.Intimidation 2.) Vagueness 3.) Shut down 4.) Not-guilty

Just like that, her mother had the entire case figured out in four words. Wilder clenched her molars with such force that her jaws ached, worsening the ever-threatening migraine that sought to incapacitate her. Her misery, however, was nothing compared to what her sister had to endure. Wilder followed Hale with her eyes as he walked right up to the stand. He was inches away from Sammy now.

"Were you forced to have sexual intercourse with men?"

The air left Wilder's lungs. "Yes," Sammy's voice trembled, and their eyes met again.

"Can you identify the men you were forced to have sex with? Do you see the men who raped you in this courtroom?" There was an air of confidence in Hale's tone, as though his witness would elaborate in his favor. Hale waited until his face turned a darker shade of degradation. The courtroom rustled.

The jury began to shift uncomfortably, glancing around. Her father murmured a German swear word under his breath.

"We're all waiting," Judge Estevan demanded of Sammy.

When the star witness couldn't answer despite aggressive prodding and reminders of being under oath from the judge, plus having the question repeated, the prosecutor changed tactics.

Hale cleared his throat. "More specifically, did you witness this sex trafficking of other minors similar to your age at the time?"

Sammy sat very still and looked past Wilder, beyond her parents and the courtroom.

Judge Estevan raised his voice, demanding an answer. But Sammy remained frozen, staring at the wall. She never responded with hysterics. Instead, tears trickled from the corners of her eyes. She neither wiped them away nor looked at anyone in the courtroom. An all-consuming paralysis took over her baby sister's body as Sammy blinked blankly.

Having no further questions, Hale heaved into the chair, sunk by his own witness.

When it was Pilar "The Pit Bull" Velázquez's turn, the defense confidently rested.

In that very moment, Wilder knew what the entire courtroom and—more importantly—her mother predicted. It was all over. Wilder glanced at the defense table. Darren Fischer captured her gaze with his steel-blue eyes and with the slightest tilt of the head. No one else seemed to notice. Time paused, and it was just the two of them. Wilder's heart slammed against her rib cage.

These men...these men would be set free.

Eyes locked on hers, Darren ran his tongue along his upper lip and gave her a wink.

SIX
THE DETECTIVE

FIRE HAD TURNED the December snow in Portland, Maine, into a sludge-fest that dulled any holiday cheer. Thick, blackened muck was everywhere, making it difficult to walk without getting most of their pant legs wet.

It wasn't even mud season yet, but she sure was glad she'd brought her all-weather shoe protector. As she sloshed through the mire, Nazario felt lucky she'd spent some time in the Laurel Mountains just west of Salem, Oregon, where the average rainfall was one hundred and twenty-two inches. Her feet stayed dry and mud-free thanks to the anti-slip, bright yellow shoe protectors that shielded her calves just below the knee. Huxley wasn't so lucky.

Each step emitted a crunching sound as his dress shoes became more buried in ebonized slush from fire and ash.

"Shit," Huxley cursed.

"Sure looks like it," Nazario teased, "don't it?"

Huxley scowled at her, not finding it funny.

"Sorry, Huxley, I only brought enough for me. I'm surprised you didn't change out of those Italian leathers."

"My snow boots," Huxley grumbled, "are conveniently

home in my closet. It's not like we had a whole lot of time to pack. I brought what I had in the trunk of my car."

Nazario almost lectured him for his lack of preparation just to get under his skin but figured it best to shut up.

The smell of the campfire was forceful. The stench of black soot was everywhere. Charred wood particles scratched Nazario's lungs, triggering a round of coughing fits. Onyx and silver ash varnished the landscape in a circular pattern surrounding the home, now a crumpled heap.

"You alright?" Huxley leaned in, face pink with concern.

Nazario nodded but continued to hack as the ash went down her esophagus. She pulled out an N95 facemask and handed one to Huxley. She at least had extra masks. He took the mask, thanking her. Even with the mask, it was hard to breathe without getting lungs full of cinder and soot.

Two men in plainclothes and similar all-weather foot protectors approach them.

"Maine Homicide division. Detective Grover Riggs," the bald, thin man said. Despite the bald crown, a thin strip of graying hair clung to the lower part of his head from ear to ear, like a determined survivor. He'd aged gracefully, in a rugged, Ed Harris sort of way. In fact, he was a dead ringer for the actor, prompting Huxley to ask the obvious.

"Anyone ever tell you—"

"All the time," he laughed, then nodded to a stout black man with a laid-back way about him. "This is my partner, Detective Keaton Mack."

Detective Mack shook Nazario's hand. A crime scene photographer exited the front door, and Huxley handed him his card.

"Emailing you the password," he said, "photos will be uploaded to the database."

Maine Homicide didn't give two shits about letting them

know what side of the law they were on. Nazario eyed two medical examiners sipping coffee and listening to talk radio while they waited in their van. Their hazmat suits were on except for their headgear and masks. Neither of the Maine detectives appeared to care if the case dragged on.

She returned her attention to the two detectives and divided a look between them.

"If it were my case, I'd give the perp...a little head start." The laid-back Detective Mack smiled, his bright teeth gleaming against his dark brown skin.

"We'd be out of a job," Nazario said.

"You *are* aware that I'm a federal agent?" Huxley warned. "This is a homicide scene. We're not supposed to have a prejudicial sway one way or the other."

"Oh, really? What color am I, Supervising Agent?" Detective Mack said, tone measured. He let out a short-lived laugh. "Badge or none. You better believe I hold prejudicial sway against this skinhead who got away with raping both men and women. All he really served time for was dogfightin'. We should be congratulating the perp for taking him out. Had this Darren Fischer been a black man such as myself, he'd have gotten the death penalty."

"Scene's around four hours or so old," Detective Riggs said, dispelling the heated exchange with his partner. "Of course, the fire investigator confirmed arson, as we suspected. Kept the scene unmolested for y'all, a gift from us Mainers to you LA city folk."

The truth—Darren Fischer had been murdered *after* serving his time.

His killer still needed to be found.

The law wasn't written to allow people to kill those who deserved it. No, an eye for an eye was *not* how the criminal justice system was supposed to operate, and it certainly wasn't how Nazario operated. Of course, Deputy Frost had foreseen that it was the one thing she and Huxley had in common. Feelings came second to solving homicide cases.

Huxley nodded towards the house. Her belly led the way.

Burnt cinders tickled her nostrils as the musky campfire odor intensified. Nazario adjusted the facemask to cover her nose. She waded through charcoal debris, the carpet beneath invisible. Pulling on latex gloves, she retrieved a plastic bag she always carried to a homicide scene. Huxley entered the bedroom first, but Nazario scanned the living room, hoping to find the smallest piece of evidence. She quickly crunched numbers. The middle of the floor was approximately two feet in front of where she was squatting.

Nazario moved to the center of the room, where two people might meet. She crouched low, guided by her gut instincts. Nazario glanced up at the door and then back to the accumulated debris covering the floor. If someone came in through the front and there was an altercation, it might have taken place in the living room.

Precisely where she was kneeling now.

Nazario skimmed the ground and then caught a glimpse of something ivory. She palmed through the black soot and fished it out.

"Looks like Scooby-Doo lost a tooth," Nazario said, loud enough for Huxley to hear as she bagged it. She'd gotten damn lucky spotting the dog's tooth amid the ruins. It was unlikely there would be anything else to find. Huxley helped her to her feet. She waddled through another mound of ash, scanning one last time to be sure. Finding nothing, they shuffled through the rubble towards the bedroom.

Nazario handed the bag over to Huxley, who inspected the incisor.

"Good find, Detective." He inspected it at various angles. "I haven't had a good barbeque in a long while."

Huxley's stomach grumbled aloud, making her wonder how he could be hungry at a time like this. He leaned closer, taking an inventory of Darren Fischer's charred remains. His ankles and wrists were bound. A strap around his mouth was melted against his crispy flesh—black rubber from what used to be a ball gag—liquified down his throat.

What a painful way to die.

"Say we jet over to Salvage Barbeque afterward, heard they some mean baby back ribs in Portland." Huxley rubbed his stomach, which complained aloud for a second time.

"You got some timing," Nazario tossed over her shoulder, studying the body.

As if a cooked Darren Fischer instigated Huxley's appetite, he said, "A man's gotta eat."

The victim's eyes were wide. Lacerations and dried blood encircled the circumference of the wrists and ankles.

He'd fought against the restraints.

Nazario scanned the charred arms, and sure enough, teeth marks. They were so small they could be missed amid the distracting smell of fried human flesh. There was an anguished look on Fischer's blistered face. The bulging eyes appeared to be looking right through her.

"Perp has a dog." Nazario pointed at the tiny puncture wounds on the right bicep.

"Didn't even see that," Huxley said.

"Bet the dog lost the tooth locking onto Fischer's arm," Nazario said.

She looked closer at Fischer's head. The smell of singed hair wafted up to her. Oddly, she didn't feel like throwing up, which she'd been bracing for. However, an Egg McMuffin was the quickest way to lurch the contents from her stomach.

A body burned alive? Nope. Especially not Darren Fischer's.

She inspected his hair, mostly burned off, matted with ash, and crusted with blood.

"B.F.T., depressed fracture of the superior orbital rim," she said, pointing to the blunt force trauma to Fischer's left eye socket and skull. "Been hit upside the head with something hard. They fight out in the living room, but it ends up in the bedroom. If the perp is indeed a woman, Darren's a big dude. It'd be too hard to drag him. Perp swung at him, some type of club, knocks him down, gets him off-balanced. Nothing too heavy like a brick, otherwise his head would've been caved in, and we'd have seen brain matter."

"Fischer must've fallen to the bed after the blow across his head, then tied up with his own restraints and cooked alive," Huxley finished. "Now, let's talk victimology. Why not shoot him or stab him? Poison the guy? Why bind him with the ball gag and restraints?"

"A simple death would be undeserved. This is about humiliation and punishment. Humble him with his own...tools." Nazario stretched her throbbing lower back. "Female killers don't kill for the same reasons men do. This is...personal."

"Remember that Girl X? Shame it ended in a ten-fifty-six," reminded Huxley, "said she was handcuffed and assaulted by him."

"Terrible what happened to that girl," Nazario agreed, "I'll never forget my first ten-fifty-six. A real mess. Blew his brains out all over the place after he lost his money—forget how. Some guy from the South Bay."

"Yeah, I remember. Lost it in stocks," Huxley sighed, "that rich dude in Manhattan Beach."

"Wonder if we'll find S & M gear?" Nazario said. "From

Fischer's history, bet he's a sadist. Bondage, torture, likes to control his victims—all that good stuff."

"You should take a look at what was left outside."

Nazario and Huxley about-faced. Two men from the medical examiner's office in hazmat suits who were sitting in their van earlier stood at the doorway now donning their head-gear. She already knew that the men were assistant medical examiners because the actual ME very rarely made an appearance on a homicide scene.

A middle-aged man with square glasses and an impressive beard smashed against his mask ogled Nazario. The assistant ME lectured, "You should've worn something more protective, in your condition and all."

"Eyes up here," Huxley directed. The man flushed, fogging up his mask.

"Sorry, my wife just had a baby and—"

Huxley broke in, "My partner's just fine. She wouldn't be here if the doctor and the head of FBI and chief of homicide hadn't okayed it."

"Assuming SID came out for a sweep," Nazario broke the tension, "anything that could be collected that wasn't already burned?"

The assistant ME offered a friendly smile and nodded. His associate, who looked like an apprentice fresh out of college, was already beside the bed with a navy leather body bag.

"It's CSI up in these parts. And yes, they have. We're up next," the ME assistant responded. "Anything else you might need, revisit the body, and all that good stuff, stop on by."

Weaving around the scorched home, they hopped over crumbled concrete, and navigated around the stretcher on the front lawn, its grim presence as eager as a grave waiting for its occupant. Then, they walked past the Portland Detectives. Both were chewing on donuts. They must've gone for a quick munchie-run.

One of the detectives saluted them with a half-eaten, oozing jelly-filled. "We gotta box if y'all want one?"

"No thanks." Nazario waved off with a tight smile.

"See," Huxley pointed out, "I'm not the only one that's hungry."

"That's called 'I don't give a fuck,'" Nazario clarified.

Huxley laughed. "I think you're correct, Detective."

"We saved the best part for last," said the Portland detective. "Fifteen feet over that hill."

Huxley and Nazario headed in the direction, south of the crumbled ash heap of a home. At a distance, she spotted a small white plastic bag on top of a snowy mound. They crouched next to it. Using a gloved hand, she felt around the exterior for what might be inside.

"Feels like a folder," she said, "that our perp made sure to keep from getting ruined."

"Why would she leave a folder behind?" Huxley said. "Got a theory?"

"Given your criminal psychology background, shouldn't I be asking you?"

"Ladies first." He winked.

Nazario studied the folder—nothing on the front. She flipped it around and frowned.

"Got no idea what the hell this says. Need your linguistic aptitude," Nazari told Huxley, who looked over her shoulder. "What's it say?"

"*Die Schlangenfrau,*" he reads. "German—The Serpent Woman. Think it's her signature."

"Personal meaning. Has to be. All of this...it's real personal, especially for female killers."

Nazario opened the folder. The first item was a collage made of a young woman from her baby pictures through adulthood. Early twenties. Warm brown eyes. Straight chestnut hair to her shoulders. In all of her adult photos, she was in black clothes. The following images were labeled by the Portland police department's sexual crime unit. Her face was beaten so badly that both of her eyes were swollen shut. There were wounds along her wrists and ankles. A copy of the medical report was on file that confirmed rape, along with a detailed statement from the young woman.

"Harper Ashby," Nazario said, "she's our Girl X. Perp's sending a clear message. One of justice or the lack thereof."

"Could it be Harper's friend out for revenge?"

"No way." Nazario flipped through the folder's contents. "Check this out. It's a printout of everything Fischer has ever done. From parking tickets to assault with a deadly weapon charge and battery on a police officer. Shit, animal cruelty charges, dogfighting, attempted rape, and rape. Some of the sexual assault reports were from men. Which doesn't happen very often."

"I hate to think of the number of victims out there that never came forward to report it, out of shame or embarrassment," Huxley said. "These reports and documents are classified. You need access to the PPD and the bureau."

"Which is why I can't picture some twenty-something college student at a library printing out this stuff. This is a highly sophisticated individual. Someone who painstakingly planned this all out. This took a heck of a lot of time, research, and thought."

"Take a good look," Huxley said, picking out a photo of a lanky man with a gaunt face and unwashed, stringy, long black hair that gave his skin a jaundiced hue, made worse by his beard that looked more like a scruffy tumbleweed.

Nazario needed a full minute to study it before it came to her.

"Holy shit." She cupped her mouth. "It's Darren Fischer."

"Think about it. Your face is plastered all over the news. You just got out of prison. People want you dead. Belonged to one of the most well-known racist organizations. Would you mosey around town where people would recognize your face?" Huxley said.

"Guess I'd be finding a way to hide, too," Nazario said.

Huxley frowned at the photo. "He lost a lot of weight. The body's too fried to see much, but I'm impressed by his dedication to change his appearance."

"What gave it away for you?"

"It's all in the eyes, they never change," Huxley explained. "Lost weight by fasting. I'm a gym rat, I recognize people no matter what diet they go on. I noticed a singed book in there on liquid dieting. Same one I read a while back. Fridge got nothing but water and other such liquids. Running shoes in his closet were worn something good. He's been hitting the trails."

Detective Riggs, the Ed Harris doppelganger, stood on the hill, sun to his back. They looked up at him, still chewing on his bear claw. "We got us a witness y'all should chat with."

"Witness?" Nazario blocked light from her eyes with a hand.

"Said he might've been killed if she didn't help free him," Riggs said.

"Interesting," Huxley said under his breath. "Perp saves a man and kills one."

Nazario chewed on Huxley's words, words that had been plucked out of her own head.

The baby kicked, and she realized they hadn't really eaten anything. It was going to be a long day. This serpent woman became more intriguing as time passed. Nazario spotted movement at a distance and watched the MEs hoist the navy body bag onto the stretcher.

Nazario glanced at the folder, then back up. "I normally don't eat after a homicide scene. But the baby and I can be down for barbecue. Say we grab lunch before hitting the station?"

"Great idea," Huxley sported a victorious smile.

Nazario thought about Fischer. At one point, he was alive and well, disguising himself so that he could do what exactly? Sexually assault someone? Again? He ended up getting busted for dogfighting. But all the innocent victims were marred for life.

Where was justice for Girl X, Harper Ashby, and Sammy?

Justice failed, and the killer took matters into her own hands.

This was a man who preyed on victims until he became one.

Yeah—Nazario thought—*those barbecue ribs sound like a tasty idea.*

SEVEN

THE SECOND VICTIM

THE ROADS IN MANCHESTER, New Hampshire, wouldn't be drivable if not for snowplows. Lucky for Von, she was smart enough to rent a Jeep armed with snow chains on its tires for the occasion. It had been three days since driving in from Portland, Maine, which took longer than the normal two hours due to inclement weather.

The entire time, she'd been monitoring the Airstream trailer nestled in a thicket of trees on a large lot of land, where everything was enveloped in a rich, compact layer of frosty white. Festive Christmas lights bordered the front frame. Every morning, Sean Martin got up at 6 a.m. and headed to the gym, where he lifted weights for forty minutes and ran on the treadmill for twenty. Day one, she oriented herself to her surroundings. On the second day, Von left Zeus in the hotel to protect him from the frigid temperatures, as she would never leave him for an hour in the car when it was twenty below zero.

Going to the gym felt incredible, making Von grateful she'd packed for every occasion.

Von immediately hit the chin lifts and busted out five sets of twenty. Several men paused their workout to watch her, complimenting her "Bruce Lee" physique. She'd been compared to the martial arts icon a few times thanks to her small but shredded stature and incredible strength.

"Dang girl, you ripped *and* strong," said a stout muscular personal trainer wearing a tight T-shirt with the gym's logo across the chest. "You on a day pass? You ain't from around here."

Von hit the floor, watching Sean do arm curls.

"Not from here, no," she breathed as she cranked out fifty pushups. Sweat slipped off her forehead and down her chin. It soaked her chest and abs that burned with each rep.

"I like your HIIT routine. You ever compete? If not, shit girl, you should," he said after she was done.

"Nah, not my thing." Despite her personal rule against showing skin, Von grabbed her shirt and wiped her face with it, temporarily exposing her six-pack and something else.

"Killer abs and one mean scar," he noticed, then grimaced. "I'm sorry, they call me big-mouth up in here."

"Don't worry about it." She dropped her shirt. Her eyes followed Sean to the treadmill. She timed his routine and knew his keys were in a top middle wall cubby on the other side.

"Alright, Bruce Lee, better see you here tomorrow." The personal trainer handed her a seven-day pass and a gym towel. "On the house."

On her way to the ellipticals, she moseyed by Sean's cubby to double-check his keys with her own. The Airstream master key ordered two weeks through a third-party company was an exact match. She returned Sean's keys and considered her cardio options.

Despite many treadmills being free, Von chose the one right next to Sean Martin.

———

On day three, Von and Zeus entered the trailer for the second time. However, on this occasion, she was prepared with a tiny off-market video camera that wasn't sold to the public. It was funny how people were willing to sell you what you needed for the right amount of money.

She placed the tiny device on the backboard of a built-in desk that looked to have been customized. Behind a torn paper with a Bible verse scribbled on it was a perfect spot. She checked her phone app connected to the spy camera. The position was perfect. Zeus sniffed around before sitting to patiently study his master's movements. She'd be able to see his password log-in. She looked around the Airstream. It was roomier than anticipated. Various Bible verses were scattered about the walls. She'd skipped reading them during her first recon. A worn King James Bible sat on the built-in couch. It hadn't moved since the last time she was there.

She picked it up and scanned through various highlighted passages.

Highlighted was Leviticus 18:22, which frowned upon homosexuality.

General theme: Temptation. Perversion. Abominable sexual sins.

There was a cute miniature Christmas tree next to the bed and a cross made of unfinished cedarwood on the wall. The place was spare and exceptionally organized. Martin lived with just enough and without excess, perhaps an admirable quality. Von opened the door to his full-sized fridge and looked inside. She'd have to get an Airstream for herself, she thought. The trailer kept impressing her.

There was a gallon of milk, bottled water, salad, and lunch meat. Von reached for the lunch meat. Just because she was a vegan didn't mean she must let Zeus suffer. Dogs, by nature, preferred flesh to foliage. It would be cruel to refuse him his favorite treat.

"Hungrig?" Von asked Zeus in German if he was hungry, and he barked once. He'd been such a good boy; he deserved to be fed well. She offered him a few slices of turkey and ham, then put the container back in the fridge's deli drawer.

She opened the freezer and peered inside. It contained frozen chicken breasts, a couple of steaks, and a bag of fish that might have been freshly caught. A couple of fishing poles and a tackle box leaned against the wall.

Von had tried to access his laptop the last few times she was there. Today, she decided she'd work smarter and not harder. She looked at her watch. It was time for Bible study. Von eyed his Bible on the couch.

"He forgot something," Von said and then told Zeus it was time to leave.

Von ensured everything was exactly how she found it and locked up. Zeus followed her into the woods, where they were covered enough to not be seen but in a perfect position to monitor the man, as they had for the last few days. She took out the binoculars, and sure enough, Sean's blue metallic Chevy Silverado with customized oversized tires slowly made its way up the open field toward the trailer. He left the truck running, ran in, and returned with the Bible in hand.

Von watched him leave and returned back to her hotel room, figuring she could use her spy app to listen remotely. She dialed in as usual and turned on her Bluetooth wireless buds. Most of the Bible study was lackluster, from the introductory singing to reading the day's verses. But the topic of temptation was synchronistic to the inner demons Sean had been warring against.

A man droned on about restraining oneself from worldly evil.

The room was mostly silent until there were murmurs, and then someone apologized.

"Sean," the man said, "where're you going?"

"I...I'm not feelin' so good," Sean said.

"Are you struggling? Son, this is the place for the struggling. Ain't nothing wrong with admitting to it. It ain't weakness."

"Said I'm fine," Sean said in a clipped tone. "My lunch didn't agree with me."

"Alright, y'all, how about we pray for Sean?"

"I said I can't stay," Sean's voice boomed so loud feedback announced itself in her earbuds, making her wince. "Don't want no prayer. Don't want no more talkin'. Leave me be!" She adjusted the volume on her Bluetooth device through the app on her phone.

There were audible gasps.

Von rubbed her chin. He was right on the edge.

"What's wrong, Sean, hitting too close to home?" she mused to herself.

Sean's breathing was so heavy and rigid, she could hear him through his cell phone. His footsteps thundered. Von followed him in her mind's eye from the church through the crunching snow. A door slammed, and next came the revving of an engine. A traditional Christian song blared through.

"Fuck you," he said, and then a punk song replaced the hymn.

Von glanced at her watch. He'd be home in ten minutes.

She got up and snagged the vegan salad she picked up from Whole Foods in Bedford, just twelve minutes from Manchester. While up, she took out a packet of organic lunch meat she bought for Zeus and gave him a few slices. He greedily ate his snack. She balanced meat with grain-free dog food because she wasn't one of those vegans terrified of getting near meat. She and Zeus had that sort of relationship, opposites that respected one another.

An angry scream squealed more feedback in her earbuds, forcing her to remove them.

She could hear Sean even with the earbuds on the bed. Von raised her brows, ate a forkful of salad, and turned on her laptop. She heard a *thud, thud, thud,* and turned on the video spy app that was not only on her phone but on her laptop as well.

He stood with his back against the discreet video recorder mounted behind the piece of paper above his laptop. It captured him banging his head against the wall. After at least a handful of punishing blows to his forehead, he stopped and began to pace.

"No," he said, hitting his forehead with a fist. "No, no, no."

Sean turned around, face pink. His hands clenched and unclenched at his sides. He took in large, exaggerated breaths that caused his chest to rise and fall in rapid succession. Von watched his body language. The bastard was nearly hyperventilating.

Sean unpinned himself from the wall and powered toward the laptop driven by need. Von recorded the entirety of his actions, so that she could slow it down when needed. Sean typed in his password. The camera was wide-angled and captured every single key stroke.

She pressed a couple of buttons to zoom in and watched closely.

"Got it, you son of a bitch." Von scribbled in her notebook.

She watched him click through his computer.

He gritted his teeth, a hand pulled down his pants, and the other started yanking at himself viciously. It was more than masturbating. It was a raw, punishing assault of both pleasure and pain.

Von turned off the video and then helped herself to another

forkful of vegan salad. Despite not wanting to know the images that inspired his relapse, she had an idea based on her thorough recordkeeping of Sean's criminal history.

And she'd be coming to collect further proof.

———

She waited only hours until he was asleep. He went to bed at exactly 11 p.m. Twenty-five minutes later, she called his mobile via the audio spy app and heard him snoring. By 11:48 p.m., she and Zeus quietly entered the mobile home.

Zeus plopped down on the ground next to the laptop and let out a huff.

She walked toward Sean's bedroom and checked on him. Zeus lifted his head and followed her movements with sharp, watchful eyes and without leaving his comfortable spot on the ground. Sean was still asleep and snoring.

She walked back to the laptop and opened it with gloved hands.

After doublechecking the note she'd been carrying, Von typed the password slowly.

Bingo.

Several pictures of a boy popped up on the screen: playing in the playground, walking out of his school, and leaving his house with his dad. He'd been following the child. They were likely captured by Sean's cell phone. She closed the pictures and returned to a single folder. Other than the collage of photos, Sean's desktop, like his living space, was clean.

The folder on his desktop where the pictures were saved was titled "Psalms."

Von took a deep breath and clicked on the folder.

There were more pictures of this boy along with the subfolder "Leviticus 18."

She right-clicked: 850 GB. Videos. There had to be videos in the folder.

Her jaws clenched as she squeezed her eyes. She pinched the bridge of her nose.

I can do this. I can do this. I can do this.

In the Leviticus folder, Von found dozens of sick videos. She quickly clicked on each and confirmed her suspicions—child pornography. Von looked at her watch. It was already 12:21 a.m. Unconcerned whether Sean would notice, she unplugged his laptop and took it with her, including the power cord. Before leaving, she moved Sean's Bible, which had been sitting on the couch, and placed it in the empty space where the laptop used to be.

———

Von slouched in her idling car the following day and opened a manila folder, the contents of which she'd memorized. She looked down at Sean Martin's mug shot as he smiled brightly, like he was proud that he finally got caught. This was the same man that was singing church songs a day ago. The mug shot was from the only case the serial pedophile had served time for.

She gritted her teeth and white-knuckled the steering wheel.

And then, she spotted them. The little boy in all of Sean's pictures on his laptop was now holding Sean Martin's hand and getting into the bastard's Silverado. Von opened a school roster and thumbed through pages until she found the boy's photo.

Joey Adrian Worsham, Caucasian, eight years old, third grade.

She closed the folder while Sean's truck pulled out onto the road. Von followed the pickup at a distance, her nostrils flaring with each deep inhale, her chest rose and fell in quick succession to the rhythm of sweltering fury souring her stomach.

Joey, the child Sean had been stalking, needed her.

Who else would help him? The cops? They wouldn't look twice at this truck—*just another hardworking white guy with his son.* And what about the judges who let him off with a slap on the wrist? Where the hell were they right now? And the lawmakers who'd allowed this registered sex offender to live within a mile of an elementary school? Would they stop what was about to happen?

The entire system had failed this boy. Von's system would not.

Less than five miles away from the elementary school, Sean Martin pulled into the barren field encircled by trees, where his lone silver Airstream was hidden in the woods. Von parked her car at a distance, thankful that there were enough trees around to conceal her vehicle.

Zeus observed her with steady eyes to see if it was safe for him to prop his head up.

Von reached for the aluminum baseball bat in the backseat. She hated guns and refused to carry one, although having one would make her mission a hell of a lot easier. Time wasn't on her side. Every second Joey was in Sean Martin's trailer was too long. Von couldn't bear to imagine what might happen. She gripped the baseball bat and Zeus hopped out of the car, keeping close beside her, and waited for her cue.

She closed the car door without making a sound, then looked at Zeus and made a swirl with her index finger.

Get in. Attack. Get out.

Zeus perked his ears, ready to bark, but she put a finger to her lips, and his mouth closed.

"*Rette den Jungen,*" she whispered in German for Zeus to save the boy.

Zeus moved ahead in silence—the gravel muted beneath his paws.

The morning air was crisp. It danced across Von's face, brushing her cheeks and giving her a frosty kiss. A waft of scent from the surrounding pine trees soothed her soul, as Von harkened back to the days when she lived ensconced in woods and isolated from city life. Fresh nostalgia that soured as she drew closer to the Airstream.

She unlocked the door with her master key.

Zeus rushed in; Joey was kicking and yanking at his arm, trying to wrench free.

"Let me go," Joey cried. "I want my daddy."

"Joey," Von called out.

Sean turned around. "What the hell?"

Zeus lunged forward, clamping hard against Sean's upper arm. He screamed out in pain. Joey followed Zeus's example, biting Sean's hand, causing the man's fingers to lose their grip. Joey wiggled his wrist free and ran into Von's arms.

"Bleib bei ihm," Von told Zeus. *"Keep on him."*

She picked Joey up. He wrapped his legs around her waist, and she jogged out of the small trailer. When they got to the car, she put him in the back seat. Von knelt in front of the boy who was crying out for his dad.

"It'll be alright. Listen to me, Joey. Need you to lay on the back seat here, okay, sweetheart? I'm gonna lock the door. Stay down, and don't you move." Von gripped Joey's hand. "Can you be a brave boy and do that for me?"

Lower lip trembling, Joey nodded. He laid down, and she covered him with a blanket.

Von took out a gas can and matches from the trunk and ran back, pressed for time. Rushing back in the trailer, she found Zeus stubbornly on Sean's arm, but not for long. Sean punched Zeus in the ribs, but the dog didn't budge. He stumbled back and managed to reach for his rifle, which Von hadn't had the time to grab. She had been too focused on subduing him. Zeus unclamped his jaws and dodged. But Sean, one-handed, maneuvered the long barrel and fired a shot, nearly hitting Zeus. Von grabbed a knife in the kitchen just as another shot went off, pushing her body forward causing her to drop the knife.

Von gripped the sink, feeling the bite of the bullet lodged somewhere in her left bicep.

"Don't care who you are or what the hell you want, but I'm fixin' to kill you," Sean snarled, trying to shoot at her a second time.

Zeus lunged for Sean's gun arm, biting him so hard, Von spotted blood pooling in her dog's mouth. Sean howled in pain and dropped the rifle. Before she could command him, Zeus took the rifle in his mouth like he was playing fetch and ran toward Von.

"I hate guns," she seethed, pointing the rifle with her left arm, ignoring the fact that she'd been shot in the left bicep. Sean thrust his quaky hands in the air. She grabbed the baseball bat with her right, glad that it was her dominant arm, and slammed it brutally into his head, cracking his temple. He fell hard, body quaking and convulsing, blood coughing out, gushing from his nose.

She dropped the rifle and stumbled back, leaning against the kitchen counter for support.

Above the kitchen sink, a newspaper clipping taped on the wall caught her eye.

"New Hampshire Bill Would Soften Distance Restrictions on Sex Offenders," read the headline. She scanned the old 2014 article, where the state attempted to pass a bill that would've allowed pedophiles to live within 2,500 feet from a preschool, elementary school, playground, or childcare facilities.

Von snatched the article from the wall.

Suddenly, her heart started to sprint. Blood rushed to her face, blotting out the pain in her arm. She retrieved the knife she dropped in the sink and then returned to the body: head hit with enough force to leave the pervert semi-conscious. Despite her livid emotional state, she managed to remain collected and in control—every part of her body calm, especially her hands.

"Draußen," she ordered Zeus outside. He did as he was told and jogged out of the trailer, finally leaving her alone with *him*. Sean moaned. His body shifted in slug-like motion, trying to back away from her. She pulled a fresh pair of latex gloves from her pocket and put them on. Her left bicep continued to ache as blood left her body, drenching her shirt.

Von yanked off his pants and boxers until he was lying there naked from the waist down and then knelt on his thighs to prevent him from squirming.

She lifted the knife, and Sean stirred, coming to.

"Oh, God!" Sean begged. "Please..."

"He's not coming to save someone like you," Von said.

Sean's eyes widened, and then he let out a terrified scream.

EIGHT

THE DETECTIVE

NAZARIO NOTICED Kang's cherry-glossed fingertips; they looked to be professionally done gel nails, along with his waxed, arched brows. The petite Asian man sat hugging himself in Interview Room A at the Portland police station. He sniffled and wiped his face with the back of his hand, pausing his recount of the Darren Fischer encounter.

"Venus," Huxley said dumbly, "was?"

Kang bit his lower lip. "My cat. She was ten years old. I miss her so much."

"He admitted later to killing her, correct?" Nazario asked, and Kang nodded his head.

"I kept finding his tire tracks on my property. He was doing it on purpose to drive me crazy. He even snowed out my lawn, so I couldn't drive out. I was trapped."

"How'd you manage to go out for drinks prior to the time of the attack, given there was so much hostility between you and Darren?" Nazario asked.

"I got in his face about that pile of snow he dumped on my yard," Kang explained. "He claimed he wanted to make peace and said he'd build a fence that would divide our property like

I've been asking. Denied any involvement at first to the snow deposit and the rest."

"So, you meet up for drinks," Huxley said, moving the story along, "at a local gay bar you frequent. His idea. And you weren't suspicious?"

"At first, but figured he was making amends. Talked about the fence, then I had too much to drink, and let my guard down." Kang's nostrils flared. "He seemed, I dunno, nice. Flirty even."

"We know this is hard, but can you tell us what happened next?" Nazario queried gently.

Kang took a breath and then explained how he managed to cuff himself to the bed.

"He said they were trick cuffs, and you believed him?" Huxley made a face.

"I was drunk, okay." Kang slammed a fist on the table and Huxley apologized.

Nazario leaned in and put a hand over his in reassurance.

"I-I didn't recognize his face. I swear he looked like a totally different person. Super tall and very skinny. Long black stringy hair and a beard. Who wouldn't recognize his face the way it used to be, unless you live in some bubble? It was all over them TVs mounted above the bars. But he looked *nothing* like that mug shot. No one in the bar even knew. Here we all were watching a broadcast about this Darren Fischer guy, and the fucker was sitting right there watching along with us. Like we were a bunch of idiots."

"Don't blame yourself for not knowing who he was," Nazario affirmed. "The man was a master manipulator."

"He used a knife on you, correct?" Huxley redirected. "Any deep wounds?"

Kang shook his head and then explained how their perp and her dog worked together.

"To hell with jail. They saved my life. *Reward them.* She and her German Shepherd."

Nazario leaned back in her chair to stretch her lower back; it pulsed and throbbed.

"So, the dog understood commands? Was helping the perp?" She adjusted uncomfortably on the plastic chair that felt more like sitting on cement slabs.

"It was like a tag-team effort," Kang said, allowing himself a light laugh, despite his eyes growing wet. "I went out for a drink to talk about a stupid fence with a man I thought was named Buddy. Didn't expect to find out that Buddy, my annoying neighbor, was Darren Fischer, the serial rapist. An added bonus —he happens to be a skinhead. I sure as hell didn't expect to be a knife slash away from death and then saved by a dog and a little woman! Little like my size. *Then he gets burned alive?* I can't believe I was there."

"Did you see what this woman looked like?" Nazario handed Kang a tissue, and he thanked her, dabbing his eyes. "You left the scene before you could witness the actual murder, correct?"

"I wasn't fixing to stick around. As soon as she uncuffed me, I got the hell up out of there. I drove straight to the hospital. And, no, I didn't see her face—ski mask. Lovely grey eyes, though. As I said, she was real petite. Can't be more than my height. Size zero." He paused to admire his cherry nails. "When I heard he was burned alive, I got my nails done a festive red, opened up a bottle of wine, and I CELEBRATED!"

Nazario's phone buzzed. She looked down—*Deputy Frost.*

"Need to take this," she excused herself and stepped out of the interrogation room.

"Whatever y'all are doing—wrap it up," Frost said with a serious tone.

"Interviewing Fischer's neighbor. Was very close to being a DB if not for *her*, sir."

"Manchester, New Hampshire, victim two, pedophile, scene's still hot," Frost said.

There was only one pedophile on the FBI's list connected to Fischer.

If this was the serpent woman's second target, Nazario was looking at her second female serial killer case: first Madison Vanwell targeting vulnerable undocumented immigrants that didn't deserve it. Now, this *"Die Schlangenfrau"* had moved on to her next hit.

Her voice lowered to a hush, "Wouldn't happen to be *Sean fucking Martin,* would it?"

"It would." Frost exhaled static into the receiver. "Was ready to call you. Hoping you'd get to him before *she* did. Makes sense, given Sean Martin's been a long-time Aryan Brotherhood member."

"And who did she...*save?*"

A long silence settled on the other end of the line.

"Sir, you still there?"

"A boy. Joey Worsham." The words labored out of the deputy's mouth. Bile started to rise in Nazario's throat, as she sighed. "I texted the address. Manchester's homicide—they're cued up for y'all."

Her phone chimed, and Nazario looked down. "I got it, sir. Heading there now."

———

They wrapped up the interrogation, thanked Kang, and then headed south. The drive from Portland, Maine, to Manchester, New Hampshire, took around an hour and a half. As they drew closer, the route wound into aimless, unmarked roads.

"I'm following the robot lady, but I'm beginning to feel like we're lost." Huxley glanced to his right and left, then followed the navigation's directions.

"Rural roads out here," Nazario said, "so, I'm sure we're fine...I hope. You know there's no state-level restriction where a sex offender can live in New Hampshire, right?"

"Yes, ma'am, I know all about it," said Huxley, "I believe it goes by city municipalities—usually 2,500 feet from a school or only a half mile. It can be hard to find a place to live. I wouldn't be surprised if Sean Martin lives in some mobile home out in the sticks," Huxley said just as they stumbled upon two unmarked cars parked beside a lone silver Airstream, situated on a barren lot nestled among a thicket of pine trees.

A couple of fire trucks slushed past, leaving the cold, snowy lot.

A Spanish woman and an Italian-looking man were talking to what seemed to be the crime scene photographer. They were likely New Hampshire's homicide. The couple nodded at Nazario but didn't approach, likely giving them room to investigate the scene without interruption. Nazario thanked them, studying the burnt cinders and ash soot surrounding the mobile home—similarities between victims one and two apparent, like some trademark.

First thing in their path was a body part they did *not* expect to stumble upon.

"Well, I'll be," the Italian New Hampshire detective mused, looking down at the snowy ground. He plucked latex gloves from his back pocket, put them on, and heaved in a generous gulp of air. "Looks to me like a lonely lost penis in the woods. Poor thing, shriveled up and scared—"

"For Christ sakes, stop talking to it," Huxley barked.

Nazario shoved the New Hampshire detective aside.

"Oh, get the hell back," she groused, massaging her bulging belly, "the both of you."

Both men took several steps with Huxley leading the way like an experienced line dancer. The New Hampshire detective followed the supervising agent's body language, taking large steps back to mirror Huxley.

She put a pair of latex gloves on and inspected the frozen, dismembered genitalia.

"The coroner's office'll be taking care of it," Nazario said. She gently squeezed it—still soft. "Judging by the purplish color and pliability, it's been freshly severed. Had it been longer, there'd be no lax consistency whatsoever. It would've been frozen solid."

Huxley avoided looking altogether and instead picked up a large clear plastic bag left on the ground. It was similar to the one left fifteen feet from Fischer's scorched home. Inside the bag, there was a manila folder and a Dell laptop. Most likely Sean's PC, and once again, the perp took care to protect both from getting damaged by snow.

"*Die Schlangenfrau,*" He read aloud and then opened the folder, whistling as he thumbed through its contents. "Our serpent woman autographed this one, too. Damn, she did some research. Don't know whether to arrest or hire her on the bureau. Who the hell knows how she got a hold of this stuff? I wonder what could be on the laptop? Sean's, I'm assuming."

"Lemme guess...a record of his trespasses in the folder?" Nazario said. "Most likely child porn on the Dell."

"Another folder with stuff not available to the public, not even to the police. Only the FBI was privy to it. Everything we were trying to pin Martin for, she already had it printed out here in this folder. A civilian couldn't have had access to it."

Huxley leaned in to take a closer look at the gloves and the knife lying on the ground.

"She left the evidence, the weapon of choice, even the gloves behind," he said, puzzled.

"Eh, not getting the hacker vibe. She's smart and resourceful. My guess—she knows who to tap for help," Nazario said as they stepped into the trailer.

Inside, the trailer felt claustrophobic, but at least she hadn't thrown up yet.

The Airstream's frame was blackened and singed. The center portion of the main body was aluminum alloy, and since it was riveted over a steel frame, most of the trailer remained in decent condition. This told Nazario that lighter fluid or gasoline was poured over Sean Martin and not the rest of the home. But had it been a traditional trailer made of wood, there'd be nothing left.

The kitchen, upon first examination, looked clean. But when she went over it a third time, near the knives were small drops of blood. Nazario leaned in closer, looked around on the ground, and found a shell casing hidden between floor cracks. She retrieved an evidence marker from a separate Ziplock bag she packed and placed one next to the blood splatter and another next to the shell casing. CSI had its own evidence markers, but she didn't want it overlooked.

Could Sean's killer have been injured? If this was their perp's blood, it was likely not a lethal wound, Nazario reasoned, because this serpent woman managed to kill Sean Martin, save a boy, escape, and only leave a small amount of blood behind. Nazario walked over to the body.

Sean Martin had his pants down, dick chopped off, body charred like Darren Fischer.

"It's a rather clean cut," Nazario rubbed her chin as she examined the amputated member between his crispy legs. "I think she's skilled with knives."

"Looks like it," Huxley said, as he hung back with the New

Hampshire detective, the only other male present. Couple of yellow bellies, keeping their legs pressed closed as if someone would come along and chop theirs off, too.

Nazario drew a little closer; the skin looked to be fried. Like Darren, Sean Martin's flesh was bubbled and blistered, eyes bulged and extended out of their sockets like squeezed goldfish. The body and surrounding circumference were more burnt than anywhere else in the home.

The wide-opened mouth caught her attention. She leaned in, placed two fingers inside, and retrieved what looked like a piece of newspaper stuffed in Sean's esophagus, blocking his airway near his tonsils. She handed it to Huxley, and he read the headline aloud. The article validated his earlier suspicion: the state nearly passed a law permitting sex offenders to live closer to children.

"She must've cleared the boy out of the way first," Nazario began.

"While the dog stays on Sean," said Huxley.

Nazario continued, "There's a confrontation. He gets his rifle, shoots, she's hit—"

"But not dead," Huxley said, "thanks to Cujo."

Nazario squatted lower for closer inspection. There were bloody dog prints around Sean's body and familiar bite marks on the man's bicep. She studied the bite closer and noticed a missing tooth. Same dog. Inspecting Sean's head, there was a nice fracture and indentation.

Blunt force trauma. Same deadly swing.

"B.F.T. to the left frontal bone. Hit him nice and good," Nazario pointed out, "then sliced off his...member, lit him up, and didn't bother with the rest."

After she was satisfied with the inspection, Huxley helped her to her feet.

The Hispanic woman who had acknowledged them earlier walked up.

"Manchester Homicide?" Nazario said.

"That'd be us. I'm lead detective, and we've got a first-timer." She pointed to a stocky, twenty-something Italian man—Manchester's homicide trainee. "Nice to finally meet the famous Detective Nazario. Saw you got to inspect what's left of his—"

"I did," Nazario confirmed, then pointed to the kitchen, "and the shell casing and blood."

The lead detective nodded toward the evidence marker, admitting, "Totally missed that."

"Saw the blood my third pass. Easy to miss. Counters were burgundy. Casing was tucked away between a floor crack." Nazario nodded to the rifle next to the door as they exited the trailer. "Shot by that Remington, 7 mm bolt action. Never used one. Have you?"

"I indeed have. It's a range hunting rifle, pretty standard," Huxley added. "Perp dressed in layers to soak up the blood. Must've gotten shot where it wasn't lethal."

Outside, they congregated together and waited, not knowing if the medical examiner's or the coroner's office would show. Finally, a coroner's van pulled up. Similar to Maine, two young assistants fresh out of college shuffled to greet her. Huxley allowed her the honor of briefing them on the semi-frozen piece of male anatomy lying in the snow.

They quickly retrieved it and ran it back to their van.

When they returned from the errand, they were flushed and shiny with sweat. One of the two men muttered something about having contained the dismembered penis. Neither coroner apprentice made direct eye contact.

When CSI came on the scene, she briefed them on what they'd found.

Huxley added, "I'll need to go through the contents in this folder."

"As you know, sir, we require everything in the folder be recorded and labeled for evidence, so we'll make photocopies and provide you with them," one of the CSI men said.

Huxley handed them the folder. "Can I get it today?"

"Sure can, just as soon as we're wrapped up here," the crime investigator said, following his partner into the torched Airstream.

"I'll be hanging on to the laptop, as it's in the bureau's custody now," Huxley said.

"There's not a whole lot in the trailer that's not all burned up, save for blood on the kitchen counter—a tiny amount too—and a single shell casing between the floor cracks," Nazario called to their backs, then at the lead Manchester detective. "Where's the boy?"

"Returned safely to the police station," she said. "He showed up with a note. Martin didn't have a chance to do anything to him from what we gathered."

"Thank the Gods," Huxley said.

"She came on scene just in time," Nazario redirected the conversation. "We'll need to talk to him. Joey might not be in the mood, but maybe I can go in and talk to him. Might warm up to a pregnant woman."

The lead detective handed Nazario the handwritten note Joey had brought with him.

"Paul Worsham, single dad, widower. Wife died of cancer. Construction worker. Pissed as all hell. Big dude, maybe not as big as you, though—" she nodded to Huxley's muscular six-foot-four frame.

"Don't inflate his ego," Nazario warned. Huxley shot her an amused look.

The young homicide trainee, who'd been quiet, piped up,

of sleep beckoned, and for the first time in months, she slept. She slept soundly and without the haunting nightmares that now seemed a world away.

Gone for now.

Gone in the warmth of his embrace.

———

In the morning, she found herself lying on Huxley's chest, their legs tangled, his hand brushing against her cheek, nuzzling her awake. She wanted to stay like this for hours longer, lingering in bed. A deep, carnal desire inside her yearned to ravish him. But she rose, pulling herself from the comfort of his warm body, and got dressed in the bathroom.

Nazario felt rejuvenated after the best night's sleep since her pregnancy, but she couldn't shake the sense of vulnerability she hated. Focusing on the case was the best distraction. She found Worsham's number and made the call.

The phone rang twice before Paul answered. "Hello, Paul? Is this Paul Worsham?"

"Speaking." Irritation heavy in his tone. "You wouldn't be the detective they told me would call? And if my suspicion is correct, I'm not ready to put my son through some Q and A with a bunch of cops. He's still shaken up."

"I'm Detective Nazario, and while I understand your concern, it won't be a bunch of cops, okay. It'll be Special Agent Huxley and me—"

"Oh, it gets better, an FBI agent? Don't think so."

"Mr. Worsham, we just need to ask Joey a couple of questions. If it makes you feel more comfortable, it'll just be me. Special Agent Huxley doesn't have to be there. We're looking for a killer, and we're on a nationwide hunt for her."

Paul breathed hard into the receiver.

She was close, close enough to get a yes out of him.

"Look, I'm six months pregnant. Think I'm harmless. I'll go gentle. You can be right there in the room. Maybe your son will feel comfortable talking to me?"

"Fine," he groused. "Ten minutes. Questions about that fucking pervert—off the table. Questions about that woman, fine. Frankly, I'd like to find her myself, thank her personally. Heard what she did. I'd give her a million bucks if I had it for chopping off his filthy—"

"Got it," she said, Paul's words echoing what so many had already said.

They'd arranged to meet within the hour. Huxley and Nazario grabbed a quick continental breakfast, free of charge in the hotel lobby. They spoke strictly about the questions they'd be asking Joey Worsham, avoiding any mention of the snuggling, cozy night where a broken heater and fully booked rooms had drawn them a little closer together. Although words weren't spoken, there was a stir in him, the same stir inside her, and it made her wonder how long she could be around Huxley before their "professional relationship" became something else once more. Nazario didn't want to hurt him, yet already felt like they'd crossed a line. The line they both agreed couldn't be, shouldn't be.

Because she knew neither of them would be able to control what happened next.

NINE

THE DOCTOR

WHITE FLAKES FELL INTO THICK, billowy cushions of lush, fresh powder. Under the torrent of wind, the windows froze into sheets of ice. Casper, Wyoming, received fifteen inches overnight.

In the morning, the sun crested beneath the mountains, its light peeking through the frosted ponderosa pine branches. During the springtime, the sun would expose a riot of dead foliage and sometimes dead animals hidden beneath the melted snow. Wilder had buried dozens of animals in her yard. Preserving their spirits was the right thing to do, giving the poor frozen creatures a proper burial.

On this morning, a dense veil of nimbostratus clouds hovered low enough to kiss the Earth, their opaque arms enfolding the cozy two-story, three-bedroom cabin-style home on the outskirts of Casper. It was one of a handful of customized homes built in the urban forest and spread out far enough from one another. She loved that there wasn't a neighbor around for miles and miles. The twelve-hundred-square-foot cabin was pleasantly sequestered from the world by nature's branches. Large custom glass windows, channeling light from the inside looked onto ominous terrain marked with nothing but mounds of white flurry.

The rich aroma of coffee wafted into the air, mingling with the low hum of the television downstairs, gently reminding Dr. Wilder Agatha Friedrich of the simple, comforting rhythms of life. She retrieved her stethoscope from her black medical bag and went into the spare bedroom. The small sound of whimpers escaped from the room. She smiled down at Lucy, her Kuvasz dog, and her seven adorable five-day-old puppies. Lolo, the father, stood up and stretched. He ambled toward her, wagging his tail.

"Hey, Daddy." Wilder stroked Lolo's head, running her hand down his back. Lucy lifted her head, panting as the puppies crawled and fought over nipples. One whimpered, losing its way. She picked up the pup gently and redirected it back to the food source.

"How you doing, girl?" she asked Lucy, stroking her face. Lucy licked her hand and then lowered her head. She looked tired. Wilder inserted the ear tips in and brought the stethoscope to Lucy's heart as it thudded nice and loud. Lucy had a stage four heart murmur, and Wilder worried the pregnancy would make her weaker. There wasn't much she could do but let Lucy nurse her puppies. The congenital heart defect occurred because of age, and it was why Wilder had her on a strict diet and vitamin supplement regimen.

Lucy and Lolo were both AKC-registered Kuvasz breeders who'd come from a proud, long line of show dogs. She sold the puppies and decided that this would be the last litter for Lucy and Lolo. Wilder had planned to have both of them spayed and neutered in a few months, wanting to ensure their well-deserved retirement.

Wilder checked each puppy, and they all seemed to be doing well.

She stopped to gaze at her diplomas on her wall and the local "Best Veterinarian" award she'd received three years in a row. She could hear her father's displeasure regarding what his eldest daughter chose to do with her life.

Samantha was the "troubled one" and the only Friedrich not to have gone to medical school. Regardless, it was Wilder and her father who never saw eye to eye. Dr. Anton Jörg Friedrich didn't even like animals. In fact, her father hated them and considered becoming a veterinarian to be a "waste of a medical degree." That was precisely why Anton insisted on eating meat in front of his veterinarian, animal-loving daughter. Wilder was disappointingly—*vegan*.

Wilder sat in the chair next to Lucy and the puppies and pulled out her phone.

Her finger paused over her sister's number, hesitating before calling.

The phone rang four times before Sammy picked up.

"What?" Sammy spat.

"God, it's so good to hear your voice," Wilder gulped, gripping the phone against her ear as if trying to hug her sister through the device. "I just wanted to see how you're doing? That's all, is that so wrong? I miss you so much."

"Mom's been calling and driving me crazy, using that psychologist tone of hers. She quoted passages from her own book—again!"

Wilder sighed, closing her eyes. She hoped Sammy would not hang up like she had a dozen other times. Their mother did her very best to keep the family unit in "open communication." The accomplished psychologist wrote the bestselling nonfiction psychology book *The Psychology of Trauma* and spoke worldwide. Her client list was so long that she hadn't taken a new patient in years.

Wilder opened her eyes and pinched the bridge of her nose.

"Oh Sammy...I'm so sorry. You know Mom loves you. I love you. We're worried about you—"

"They blame me, don't they? For freezing on the witness stand. You know what? I wish the LAPD never found me. I'm not so sure what's worse anymore, having my body sold or never being able to go a day without one of you blowing up my phone or giving me that look. Like it's my fault they're free. You're the good daughter. The one that went to veterinary school, and I'll always be the one without a fancy degree. Kidnapped and sold to a bunch of disgusting men who..." Sammy paused to weep. "I'll never stop feeling dirty or stupid for not being able to speak up for myself when I had the chance."

"No one blames you for the trial, sweetheart," Wilder's voice broke with the lie. Her eyes scanned one of several news clippings framed on her wall, *Judge José Estevan Eludes Witness Intimidation Accusation In Aryan Sex Ring Case.*

"The hell they don't."

"Sammy, if you need space—"

"Yes, I do, actually," Sammy said and then screamed. *"Stop smothering me!"*

The phone disconnected. Wilder picked up one of the puppies and held it close to her chest. She scanned another news article mounted on the wall. It'd become a daily reminder.

Suspects Remain Free Despite Aryan Sex Ring Bust.

She'd never forget receiving the call from her mother. Wilder had been euthanizing an old Border Collie with a terminal tumor when her mother called.

"Wilder, honey," her mother said over the phone, her psychologist's tone undone. "They found her. Narcotics and Gang unit found Sammy."

Her little sister had been a victim of kidnapping, sexual assault, and sexual slavery. Sammy and a few other young girls around the ages of fourteen through seventeen had experienced trauma from captivity and were forced to endure horrific, sadistic torture.

Her mother got a personal taste of what she longed studied. The trial had gone terribly, and it never left Wilder's mind, causing her to live in fear. Every time she closed her eyes, Darren Fischer was glaring at her with that sadistic look, licking his lips, giving her a wink. A shiver ran through Wilder as she brought herself back to the present.

She returned the puppy nuzzling against her chest to Lucy's engorged breast.

"Take care of Lucy, Lolo," Wilder told the new father, rubbing his face. As she descended the stairs, Bobby had her morning coffee on the dining table. Wilder thanked her fiancée, and he glanced up from reading the paper, returning her kiss. But then froze as the news hit her ears.

"Darren Fischer was released from prison three days ago," the news anchor said.

Wilder muted the television, and her gut twisted, remembering the trial all over again.

Did Sammy just see this on the news? Was that why she was so on edge? So upset? Is that why her mother's been calling? Wilder had been so busy with the clinic that she put off returning her mother's call.

"Bobby, did you hear this? Why didn't you say anything? Why didn't you tell me?"

"I thought you heard. It's been all over the news within the last couple of days." He sipped his coffee and took off his rimless glasses.

"My God...he's out. Darren Fischer is really out?" Wilder hugged her arms to her chest.

"Well, you've been at the clinic," he continued in his usual analytical manner. "If you'd answered your mother's call or checked your voicemail—"

"This detachment thing you do, this...compartmentalizing...I can't deal with it. Fischer's part of a racist organization that's been known to kill. I'm worried, Bobby. This is real fear." She paced, raking her fingers through her fine hair. "We should leave. Let's get out of here, fly to Los Angeles, or drive. We can take the SUV."

"Now you sound like your mother. I'm not detached. I hate that word. It's psycho-babble. I hate it when you say it."

"Because you are!"

"So, your brilliant idea: We hop into the SUV with two large dogs and seven puppies, not even a week old and drive along roads covered in black ice? Honey, are you even thinking this through? Even if we were to catch a last-minute flight, you know it's not safe for the puppies to fly so early. It's not safe for Lucy's heart, either. She'll stress out. All because that Darren guy got out of prison? He's got more important things on his mind than us. I think your mother's gotten you paranoid."

"Stop bringing my mother into this," Wilder hissed. "You realize what those men did to my sister? Do you realize how dangerous they are?"

"It's been three years since Sammy testified. Since I testified. Like, if Darren's ring wanted to do something, don't you think they would've done it by now? There're more of them out there that weren't locked up. So, one got out a few days ago. So what?"

Her phone pinged, alerting her to a text message. It was Lisa, the vet tech.

Injured German Shepherd. Gunshot. Emergency.

"Is it bad?" Bobby asked knowingly.

"Yeah," Wilder sighed. "Gunshot wound."

Be right there, Wilder texted back.

Bobby got up and put his arms around her. He kissed her and grabbed her hands.

"It'll be fine. It's my day off. If you need me, I can jump in. Otherwise, you better tend to that emergency. Lolo and I will watch Lucy and the puppies. We'll be fine."

Wilder gripped his hands in hers. "I'm worried, and I'm scared. I'm tired of living this way. We had plans to start a family...have our wedding. As long as they're still out there—"

"Wilder, no one has threatened our lives. Where're you getting this idea from? We can start having a family now. We don't need a wedding for that," Bobby stroked her cheek. "Look, if we need to move, we'll move. Okay? We'll have to sell the practice and start fresh somewhere else. Maybe somewhere warm and sunny like Florida."

Wilder nodded and hugged him tightly. She whimpered against his shoulders, gripping him against her. He shushed her, rubbing her back, whispering that everything was going to be okay. But why did her gut tell her that everything was about to change?

———

When Wilder arrived at the clinic, the first person she recognized was the contrite soldier sitting in the passenger truck, face swollen from tears. With the windows rolled down, the reek of booze assaulted her nostrils.

"It was...an accident. I tried to kill myself, but he wouldn't let me," the soldier said numbly, lifting his eyes to hers. "He wouldn't let me," he repeated, ghostlike, as if his spirit fled. Wilder had to pull her gaze away from the face that looked too young to be a soldier, too young for such heavy sorrow.

The veterinarian hurried into the clinic. There was only one dog she'd taught gun-to-head that understood the command. How could she forget? She'd trained him specifically for war.

He'd been and still remained the brightest canine to ever attend her dog training classes.

In the examining room, Zeus lay panting on the metal table. Blood matted his left shoulder. Wilder put on gloves and felt around with her fingers.

"Shattered scapula," she said to Lisa and then noticed a tall soldier looming near the chairs at the far back wall.

"He gonna be alright?" the soldier asked. "I'm Sergeant Berg. My Lance Corporal, well, he hasn't been right since we got back. I think it's for the best, Zeus...well..." Berg raked a hand down his face, "he deserves to be with someone more stable, someone better with their German. Someone without PTSD. Preferably a civilian. We don't need him with another head-scrambled jarhead who's got a personal death wish."

"Prep the room for surgery," Dr. Wilder instructed.

Lisa handed her fresh gauze. The doctor thanked her assistant before replacing the bloody dressing at the entrance wound with a new set.

"Pearce, he tried to..."

Dr. Wilder nodded.

"Yes, he...informed me." She pressed on the wound. *"Du machst das großartig."*

She reassured the dog in German that he was doing great.

"I was coming in to do a wellness check and heard a gunshot," the Sergeant said, stepping back to give her room.

Berg babbled while she began unlocking the wheels to the metal table so she could move Zeus to the operating room.

"Pearce hadn't expected Zeus to stop him from killing himself. How'd Zeus even know what was going on?"

"I taught him." She brushed the gloved hand that hadn't been bloodied by the wound across Zeus's nose. Lisa came back in, propping the door open.

"Well, you saved my soldier's life, Doc," Sgt. Berg exhaled. "And I think it's time that we retire this soldier."

Sgt. Berg nodded to Zeus.

"Zeus, he isn't an ordinary dog. No other canine could recall the command and execute it. I taught him when he was eight months old. I'm as surprised as anyone," Wilder said and briefly glanced at Berg. "I'll take him. Zeus is smart but he's dangerous in the wrong hands."

Two other vet techs came to wheel Zeus out. Wilder thought Berg whispered what sounded like *thank you*, but she'd already been out the door, rushing to save the dog's life.

TEN

THE THIRD VICTIM

VON RIPPED a piece of her t-shirt and tied it around her upper arm as a tourniquet to prevent further blood loss. Zeus watched her with worried eyes. His head lifted and flinched as if ready to help somehow.

"*Beruhige dich,*" she directed. "*Settle.*"

They pulled into the motel. Von purposely chose run-down and cheap.

"Need a single for the night for me and my service dog." The words came out clean, any sort of pain pulsing at her biceps hidden.

Von hoped she didn't sound injured.

The young receptionist texting on her cell hardly looked up to notice.

"Yup, got several. How about a view of the pool?" She smacked her gum and dangled the keys. "That'll be seventy-five a night."

Von paid with cash.

"Up the stairs to the—" The receptionist looked up. "Sick-ass tat! I love the snake and the roses. It's so detailed. Did it hurt? I heard it hurts when you get inked on your head."

Von rubbed her shaved scalp. "The artist was very good. It hurt at first, but then you sort of become used to the pain," she said, unable to shake the double meaning. Her body had grown accustomed to certain pains, while others lingered, impossible to ignore.

Von wanted to wear the baseball cap but got it a little bloody, trying to wrap her arm. She'd need a new one. A shopping list was in order, maybe a wig and definitely a new hat.

"Thanks, I'll find the room."

Von was relieved that her luggage bag was small and came with wheels and a handle, so it was easy to maneuver up the elevator to the second floor. The cheap motel room had a lingering odor of old, stale linen and mildew. The drapes embraced the window, blocking light and casting darkness throughout the small room. She turned on the lights. There was a television, a queen-sized bed, a nightstand, a cheap coffee maker next to the TV, and a mirror on the wall. It'd have to do. Working quickly, she opened her luggage and retrieved a black faux leather bag.

She took off her shirt in the bathroom. The faulty lights twitched and flickered.

A shadow across her abdomen accentuated the hideous scar, an inch wide and six inches long. The keloid scar was massive, beginning at her sternum and stretching below her pubic line. Thickly roped, it rose about a half-inch above her skin and coiled in an S-shape like a discolored venomous snake screaming against her ivory flesh. The marquee of the pale blue-green bathroom lights made it appear alive and moving. Every time she saw it, she was reminded of her purpose. It gave her strength and fuel.

Zeus followed and laid on the floor with his head down, not wanting to see.

The pain from her first gunshot wound wasn't as bad as she

thought it would be, though, the burn and dull ache wasn't what concerned her. If she didn't work fast, the bullet wound could get infected, and the blood loss would weaken her, cause her to lose focus of her objective. But it was not just her arm that had prompted her to stop by the grocery store and stock up on a dozen sugar-free Monster drinks.

A young girl was in the clutches of the third man on Von's hit list.

Blood dripped down her arm as she opened Walter Yang's folder. There were too many underage victims in the Chinese business mogul's folder to know for sure who his prisoner was. All Von knew was that she was pleading for her life.

She turned up the volume on her phone and tuned in via spy app to Walter's activities.

"I can't...," the young girl begged, "never done that before. They'll hurt me."

"Stop your sniveling," Walter ordered. "It's a done deal, Mia. They come to pick you up tomorrow night. You will enjoy it, and if you make them force you out of lack of cooperation or refusal, two things will happen. Number one, all of our fun little videos will be all over the Internet. The first people that will be emailed will be your parents. The videos don't show me, just your pretty little face and naked body. I made sure of that."

Von quickly shuffled through a stack of young girls. More blood oozed from her wound. Each sheet contained a detailed workup of everything from their names, ages, education, background, ethnicities, where they lived, and how long they'd been missing.

Mia Lee Hong, a sixteen-year-old Korean, has been missing for a year. She was last seen in August walking to her high school in Syracuse, New York, but never arrived. Her teachers and friends alerted her parents, who had not stopped looking. Finally, six months ago, a one-hundred-thousand-dollar reward for information about Mia Hong's whereabouts was made public.

"No, don't...please don't," Mia begged. "It'll tear my parent's heart out. Please. I'll...I'll cooperate. I promise. Please don't post those videos. Please. I'd rather...I'd rather die."

Von's watch read 7:13 p.m. She needed to excise the bullet and make the drive to Boston now instead of tomorrow morning as she had planned. If she didn't get there on time, she'd lose Mia, who'd now been promised to more men. She dug into her black bag, took out a scalpel, needle, thread, and narrow-nosed forceps with serrated jaws.

Luckily, the bullet was located on the outer bicep, a reachable location.

The first step required disinfecting the area with rubbing alcohol.

Von continued listening to Walter and Mia's conversation. Gritting her teeth and without stalling a second longer, she poured a generous portion of rubbing alcohol over the wound. It burned, but this was not the hard part. It was locating the bullet and extracting it or leaving it in and suturing the area closed that was the challenge. If she got it wrong, trying to dig out the bullet could cause sepsis. She'd attempt the extraction first, and if it was lodged too deeply, she'd have to leave it alone and stitch up without the removal.

"Good girl," Walter said. "Because option two will grant you your wish. I can make you disappear for good."

Mia sobbed uncontrollably, and a loud slap made Von wince.

She was running out of time. Von inspected the bullet wound. It had pitted the skin, causing the blood to coagulate. It collected at the bottom of the depression, appearing almost black, a deep burgundy where the entry wound occurred. It clouded any evidence of the bullet and how deep it was. She inspected her left triceps—no exit wound. Well, there was only one thing to do. The area had to be opened up to allow her room enough to collect the culprit.

Von took three large puffs—one, two, three—causing her cheeks to balloon.

"C'mon, you got this," she coached herself.

She gently gripped the scalpel between her thumb and index finger, hand steady. Without so much as a flinch, she made a clean vertical incision, focusing on the operation, dismissing the razor-like pain pulsing through her arm. She made a second horizontal incision until the marks formed a cross. She knew that natural endorphins were flooding her body, working to help numb the pain that would otherwise make her scream in agony. Von inhaled deeply as her cells reacted to the incision.

She swayed, lightheaded. The spasm in her arm escalated, forcing her to grip the sink.

She meditated on the burn spreading through her arm in the same way Darren Fischer and Sean Martin were consumed by fire. She thought of them, of all the victims they tormented, all the disgusting things they got away with. The pain spurred her rage, and Walter's laughter made it that much greater.

"Mia, I'm a very powerful businessman with contacts," Walter said, as Von operated. She repeated the scalpel slices, only cutting deeper to ensure she had enough space for the removal.

Von, defying her body, ingested the moment like a spectator.

As the entire area throbbed, the quick scalpel slice blended with the constant dull ache that remained present since being shot. It could be worse. It could always be worse. She could've been shot in the heart, in the head, in the gut—somewhere fatal.

Her mind was like a laser, aiming to remove the foreign object and do it quickly.

No time to cry out. No time to let the pain win. It would not succeed.

Mia would not be a lost life, another missing girl without a body for her parents to bury.

She took the forceps, grabbed gauze on the counter, and dabbed the open wound. The white sheet of cotton turned crimson, soaking up the blood. It did its job to improve visibility and help locate the bullet lodged somewhere in her bicep, but only temporarily. She dug the narrow-nose forceps deeper into her arm to widen the perimeter. A scalding feeling blazed through her body like a razor blade skinning her alive.

She cursed in German, growling through the pain.

Zeus let out a whimper of concern as he tilted his head at her.

Sweat drenched her forehead and ran down her face, completely soaking her shirt that was now plastered against her chest. Finally, the silver bullet peeked out from the bottom of the pool that continued to pump, threatening to bury it again. She dabbed more gauze to mop up the blood.

Zeus whined once more. She saw him in the mirror on the floor, burrowing his nose under his paws until his eyes were covered. *"Es wird schnell vorbei sein,"* she assured Zeus that it would be over soon. Von dipped the pointy nose of the forceps, luckily not too far down, about a quarter inch.

There. It's right there.

She felt it. Saw it even clearer now. Clamped down.

"Gotcha, bitch."

Walter continued in her earpiece, reminding her once again to move speedily.

"You won't be the first that I've had killed and disposed of without a trace," he threatened, heckling as Mia cried. "No one will ever find you, and that I promise you. Try to escape again. I dare you."

"We'll see about that, Mr. Yang," Von snarled as she retrieved the bullet at last.

Hearing enough, she disconnected, just as the forceps and bullet clanked in the basin.

She soaked the wound with rubbing alcohol and squeezed her eyes shut for a beat, nostrils flaring with each rapid intake of breath as she clutched the sink. Von retrieved sutures she'd taken out of a sterilized pouch and left it on the bathroom counter, ready to grab.

Without a second's delay, she pierced her flesh with the needle. Each puncture brought on fresh perspiration and agony, but she powered onward with intensified focus. She sutured herself, moving with precision until the entry wound was expertly sealed. Von took another fresh square of gauze, soaked it with hydrogen peroxide from her bag, and dabbed the suture.

Once the wound healed properly, she'd cover it with more ink.

Zeus turned his head to the right and left, glaring at her, whining again with canine concern. She was certain her dog sensed his owner was doing something crazy, like performing surgery on herself without numbing the pain. Von had lidocaine injections in her black bag, amongst stronger anesthesia she could've used but didn't feel the need.

She survived thus far by *feeling* it all.

It was 7:45 p.m. The stitches only took thirty minutes. She redialed Yang via the spy app.

"Put that red lipstick on and those sunglasses to hide your eyes," Yang ordered. "You'll wear that black dress and those red high heels. You hear what I said? *Stop your crying...*"

"P-put the gun away," Mia begged. "I heard what you said. Black dress. Red shoes. Red lipstick. Sunglasses. Please...the gun isn't necessary. Haven't I done everything you asked?"

"Good girl," Walter said. "I need you to look nice. We've a late dinner reservation at Ruka. 9 p.m. sharp."

Von checked her watch—shit. It only took fifty minutes to get to Boston from Manchester, New Hampshire. However, with traffic and the snowy roads, it could take her at least an hour and a half.

Von had heard enough, but Walter called out once more.

"Maria?" Walter's voice hollered in her ear. Von turned down the volume.

Maria? Von wondered who this could be and if she could be of help.

"Yes, Mr. Yang?"

"I need you to stay late tonight. We need fresh bedsheets. There's a little...blood on them. Throw them out and replace them, please."

"Blood, sir?" Maria's voice shook.

"Ten years and that gives you the right to question me? I have no loyalty to you. Question me again, and you're done. Am I understood?"

"Y-yes...Mr. Yang, I'm sorry. But I've got to run home first. I have to put my kids to bed and read them a story. I do this every night. My husband comes home at 9 p.m. I can be here by 9:15."

"That's fine as long as you return before we do," Walter said sharply. "We'll be at dinner for at least an hour and a half. You have plenty of time to straighten up in the bedroom."

"Of course, sir," Maria said.

Von turned off the spy app and quickly jotted a note to herself on her iPhone.

Maria – Yang's house cleaner. 9:15 p.m. deadline.

She removed bleach wipes and gloves from her bag and disinfected the bathroom sink and all areas with her blood, including the forceps. The disposable needle was placed in a

Ziplock bag and taken with her so she could later dispose of it safely. She ran the forceps under hot water and washed them well before returning them to her black bag.

Von looked down at her watch. It was now 7:52 pm. Time to get to Boston.

————

She didn't have the gate code to Walter's mansion. Not yet. She waited beyond the mansion's gate, which was made of thick cement walls. It was a fortress-like compound no one could escape. There was a video camera pointed downward toward the entrance where Walter could monitor who came and went.

Her watch now read 9:10 p.m.

The camera must be disabled. She put on her ski mask, grabbed her bat and checkbook.

Zeus sat up, ready to follow.

"Bleibe," Von said, ordering him to stay and he sat back down. She shoved her checkbook into her jacket pocket.

A car approached from a close enough distance. Von stood to the side of the video camera, avoiding being directly in front, and swung the bat a couple of times until the camera body hung on by a thin wire. She ripped it off just as a car pulled up.

It was 9:15 p.m. A tall Italian woman got out of the car.

"Maria?"

Fright in her eyes, Maria gasped, "Who...who are you? Please, I don't want any trouble. I just work for Mr.—"

"What's he paying you?" Von asked. The maid hesitated. "C'mon, I'm short on time."

"He's cheap. Thirty thousand a year. It's not the best pay, but I do need the money. I can't afford to quit. I've wanted to many, many times...but I can't. I have a family. I don't understand what's going on. Whatever it is, I really can't get involved. I got kids."

Von took out her checkbook from her jacket. She wrote a check for one hundred thousand dollars from an account reserved for emergency situations under the business name *Z Dog Walking Services*. She handed it to Maria. The maid scanned the check and placed her hand over her mouth.

She looked down at her watch: 9:25 p.m. It'd take ten minutes to get to the restaurant.

"Find another job. Save the money for your family and get rid of this." Von handed her the destroyed head of the video camera. "I'll need your help with a few more things."

Maria looked up, hands still shaking. "W-what do you need me to do?"

———

It was now 9:36 p.m. They'd arrived in time for dinner. She and Zeus sat in her car, parked across the street from Ruka. According to Maria, it was a nice, expensive restaurant known for its fusion of Peruvian, Japanese, and Chinese food.

Even at a distance, she recognized the Asian man having dinner with a much younger girl. Von took out her binoculars for confirmation. It was him, for sure. Mia's red lipstick didn't cover up her busted bottom lip. The Gucci sunglasses Walter had her wear indoors was probably hiding a black eye. Perhaps Mia tried to escape, and he found out.

The FBI hadn't been able to bust Yang in connection with the Aryan Nation Brotherhood sex ring. While the racist group despised anyone other than "their own kind," they had an affinity for the color of money. Chinese or not, the racist group couldn't turn away Walter Yang's type of cash. According to Von's meticulous research that sat in a folder on the seat next to her, Mr. Yang had been the brotherhood's best paying client. Yang paid off FBI agents and other law enforcement officials, buying himself immunity not only from being charged with the rape of a minor but also from allegations of violence against ex-wives and the "disappearance" of mistresses.

It was as though none of his criminal sexual indiscretions ever occurred.

Yes, Walter Yang's threats to Mia Hong were real and terri-fying. If the Chinese business mogul promised he could kill the girl and no one would find her, not the FBI, CIA, or any other law enforcement agency, Von didn't doubt him for a second.

A biting chill filled the car, freezing the seats and making her breath frosty in the dim light. She turned on the heater and waited patiently through dinner, deciding to watch instead of listen this time. Every once in a while, Von looked to see how their meal was progressing. Their actions said everything. Each time the waiter came by Mia didn't say a word. A half bottle of red wine sat between them. Walter said something to the waiter, and he poured Mia another glass. After the waiter left, Walter put a palm down on the table. Mia jumped.

Von pressed the app button and finally listened in.

"I can't drink anymore. I'm not feeling so good," she whispered.

"Finish your glass," he ordered sternly and then leaned in again. "Or I swear to God…"

Von looked down at her watch: 9:50 p.m., time to prep. She revved the engine and headed back to Walter's lush estate. She parked the car down the street where Yang shouldn't notice, took the folder, steel baseball bat, and then decided to bring along the white t-shirt covered in old, dried blood she'd stolen from Darren Fischer's gym bag.

Zeus walked alongside her. Hurried, she glanced into her folder and punched a number code into the keypad—courtesy of

Maria. The gates opened wide, and she and Zeus rushed in. When she got to the front door, it was already open. The alarm system was deactivated.

Thanks again, Maria.

Courtesy of Yang's former maid, she opened the folder with the mansion's layout, so finding the master bedroom upstairs was effortless. Within ten minutes, Walter Yang and Mia Hong made their way in through the front doors.

"Maria," Walter called out. "You left the door unlocked and didn't put on the alarm again! This is the fifth time you've done this. Maria…Maria? Stupid ingrate isn't here. Come on, Mia, in the bathtub like last night."

Von and Zeus hid in the bedroom closet. Her heart pumped with adrenaline.

Yang's walk-in closet was enormous. She hid in the back behind a rack of business suits, and Zeus stayed low to the ground. She tensed, worried the closet doors would open any minute. When they didn't, and the sound of running water echoed instead, relief flooded her.

"You disobey me like last night, and there'll be consequences. Understand me?" Yang said. When Mia didn't respond, the sound of a slap forced Von to shut her eyes, waiting for the precise timing to act.

"Yes," Mia whimpered finally. "Please…please put the g-gun away."

"I don't trust you. Get undressed and in the bathtub."

"Please…please put the g-gun away," the girl whimpered.

The sound of another slap echoed through the room.

"Get naked right now. In the bathtub, you little whore."

Mia began to sob.

"Jetzt," Von ordered Zeus. *"Now."*

They stormed out of the closet, Zeus leading the way. He launched himself so high that his teeth connected with Walter's neck. Not having time to react to his intruders, Yang toppled to the ground with Zeus's teeth locked around his throat.

Mia screamed.

"Keep your clothes on," Von said to her. "Wait for me downstairs. I'm here to bring you home. Can you wait downstairs for me?"

Both of her eyes were blackened, blood seeped out of Mia's nose and her cracked, swollen lip. Shaking, she nodded and stumbled down the stairs.

Walter's gun had fallen several feet away. It was a close call; neither Zeus nor she was shot again. It'd be a real inconvenience having to perform another impromptu surgery on herself. She snatched up the gun in her left hand and gripped the steel baseball bat in her right. Walter thrashed, desperate to rid himself of Zeus's grip, but it did him no good. Von told Zeus to get off, and he obeyed. Walter's neck was bloody and punctured.

Von didn't give him time to say much. She dropped the old bloody shirt and folder on the bed to be found by authorities, then took the baseball bat and whacked his stomach as hard as she could. He doubled over and curled on his side, gasping for breath.

She pointed the gun at his head. "In the bathroom." He tried crawling on his knees. *"I said, GET THE FUCK UP! NOW!"*

Grimacing, he stumbled to his feet, raising his hands in a gesture of surrender. "If it's that reward money you're after," he muttered between gritted teeth, "I can pay you much more than what Mia's parents are offering. Name your price. I'll have it wired tonight."

"In the bathroom," she ordered. He shuffled into the bathroom with his own gun pointed at his back. The large Jacuzzi-like tub was nearly full.

"Please," he begged. "I'm not exaggerating. I can literally pay you *anything*."

"I don't want your money. Were you the first to have had Samantha?" Von asked.

"I don't...I don't know who that is, I swear—"

Von shoved the barrel of Walter's gun against his cheek. "Wrong answer."

"Okay, okay...I was her first bidder. I had her first," Walter admitted shakily. "Please, I'm worth a lot of money. Let's sit down and talk. Whatever you want, just ask!"

Von placed the gun that was in her left hand on the sink. He relaxed, expecting freedom.

"Ich will dein Leben," she said, low and lethal. *"I want your life."*

Gripping the steel baseball bat in her right hand, she swung for the fences.

ELEVEN

THE DOCTOR

THE WORLD WINKED awake in an unfocused, hazy veil. Every part of her body hurt. Though it was her torso, the entire abdominal region felt torched. It burned with a terrible fire-like quality that pulled an involuntary moan from her gut. Her throat, dry and raw, was most likely caused by an endotracheal tube they had inserted into her esophagus. They had to have placed her under general anesthesia, Wilder reasoned.

"Wilder, honey?" her mother sniffled, coming now into focus. Dr. Katrine Friedrich wore a grey business dress suit, her pale hair tied into a slick ponytail, her lipstick the perfect shade of rose. She looked like she was ready to command an executive board meeting. As always. Wilder's eyelids felt sticky and heavy. When she tried to open her mouth, her cheeks felt fuller, swollen.

She wanted to speak, but the words wouldn't come out.

"Your dog's safe, dear. He's in a kennel. Treated for—well— he's fine now. We can get permission to have him here. I'm certain that would bring some comfort to you," Katrine said, unable to separate the psychologist's role from that of a mother.

Wilder paused for a long moment before nodding.

Her mother began to weep.

Wilder looked away, incapable of tears or pity.

"Robert is fine, too," Katrine said when her daughter didn't respond. "He survived, and it looks like he'll recover nicely. Your father is...having a *discussion* with your doctor."

She could hear him in the hallway, his booming voice penetrating the walls.

It was no surprise Dr. Anton Jörg Friedrich was going off on the doctor's incompetence.

"It serves no one keeping such information from my daughter," he bellowed. "She'd never willingly wait around to find out later. Her mental health will not suffer any less, pretending everything is fine, only to spring it on her later. Just ask my wife —she's a leading expert in trauma, for Christ's sake."

"Dr. Friedrich, please lower your voice—"

"No one tells me to lower my voice. And do *not* interrupt me. I'm not finished." Every word deepened Anton's anger. "I'll have you know that I looked at her stitches. It looks like a job a blind man performed."

"Dr. Friedrich," said the doctor tried calming matters. "I'm fully aware of your resume, and Dr. Katrine—"

"Well, then drop the doctor prefix, the bloody formality. We're all doctors here, including the victim in there—my daughter—who would have died if not for that mangy dog. To hell with hospital policy. He is trained. Wilder trained him. Frankly, I detest dogs. They're filthy. They're more needy than babies. But you *will* allow that German Shepherd to stand guard at my daughter's hospital bedside immediately."

"Doc—*Anton*, I already spoke to hospital management earlier this morning, and we'll make an exception for the canine...for Zeus, rather. Now, regarding Wilder's condition, this wasn't brain surgery. It was abdominal, and therefore, it came with severe complications along with its own set of difficulties. We did our very best considering the condition your daughter was in when she was brought to us. I will inform *my patient* about the details of such complications resulting from her wounds when it's appropriate to do so."

Complications? What complications?

Katrine's eyes met hers: steady, unyielding, and no longer crying.

"I'm sorry you have to hear this, honey." Her mother's lower lip quivered, but she took in a deep breath, straightening her spine. Then, putting her psychologist's experience to work, calmly explained, "You know your father. His outburst shouldn't shock you. It's a natural response to a crisis. People respond in different ways; paternal reactions are quite strong."

Wilder wasn't surprised. But she was touched that her father would argue on Zeus' behalf and that he would acknowledge that she was a doctor, however much he'd considered veterinary medicine to be below the Friedrich lineage—even though veterinary school was much harder to get into than medical school. Regardless, Wilder knew that her father had hoped she would follow in his neurosurgery footsteps.

If she was a disappointment then, how much more was she now?

Still unable to form words, to get them out of her bruised body, Wilder placed a hand upon her abdomen. She'd never been the trembling type. Not even as the patient. The victim. Like her father, that was what made her great at her job. *Steady does it,* she thought, as she breathed in the sanitized hospital room. Calm fingers grazed light against the thin hospital gown.

Wilder gulped. My God...how many stitches were there? Seventy? Eighty?

She felt a light breeze against her right scalp and could see with her fingers, feel the woven pointy threads holding her scalp together. More stitches? Twenty? Maybe twenty-five?

"Your best was hardly good enough," her father hollered at the surgeon.

Her father swung the door open and stormed into the room with her doctor following.

Eyes met hers in widened surprise that she was conscious.

"I see you're awake," her father said, then yanked his gaze away. He was loud enough for the entire hospital to hear. He shifted in place, swallowed, and then took two long strides toward the window where he gripped the sill, looking out of the hospital, jaws clenching and unclenching.

She deciphered remorse in her father's eyes, and something else.

Was he detesting that he had to see her in her present condition? Imperfect now. Botched. Wilder never met his standards before the attack, and she certainly wouldn't now. The doctor with whom her father had been fighting lingered a few feet behind. His steps were quiet and careful as he made his way toward her bedside.

"Dr. Damião Sequeira," he said with a faint accent, then clarified, "Brazilian—I get asked *a lot*."

The attractive Brazilian doctor was young, perhaps in his early thirties. He had a goatee, midnight hair, and thick ebony eyelashes, with brows most women would envy. His large, deep brown eyes seemed to penetrate and search her soul.

"Dr. Friedrich, may I address you by your first name? Since, as your father put it, there are three Dr. Friedrichs present?"

She nodded once.

"Wilder, before I get into the...details about your surgery. Look, you don't have to worry about my asking you the generic 'how are you feeling' question because I can't begin to imagine. I'm certain you are in pain, and I can prescribe you medication to get you through it." Sequeira paused before softly asking, "You called 911, and the police arrived at your home. Do you recall what happened between the time you called and when they arrived? Do you recall the—"

He caught himself as tears sprung in her eyes. She bolted that door of emotion and pushed the memory down. The doctor strode next to her bed and pulled up a chair. He extracted a couple of tissues from the box sitting on the nightstand and put them in her hands, cupping them with his. He looked down at her with those soft, endearing eyes that made everything in her body mellow, even the fright that caused her voice to shut off from the world. His touch was warm and electric. A tiny wave rippled through her, reminding her that she was human, and the nightmare that nearly killed her hadn't destroyed her.

Wilder stared at the handsome doctor, lost and unable to perform even a nod. Time stalled, sequestering her temporarily from her painful reality. He wasn't wearing a wedding ring and for the first time since meeting Bobby, a flutter stirred beneath the dozens upon dozens of stitches that sewed her up.

Dr. Sequeira slipped his hands from hers.

"A couple of detectives would like to know if you're able to answer any questions. You've been through serious trauma. We almost lost you, and if you're not ready to answer—"

Wilder stared at him, focusing on his words. But whatever force that kept her voice from activating was soothing. She couldn't bring herself to leave the shelter of the quiet place inside her mind, the sacred space that protected her from the pain.

"Had Samantha spoken up instead of letting that bastard judge intimidate her on the witness stand—" Her father finally said the words Wilder had known he'd been harboring in his heart.

"Not now, dear, Wilder's in shock," her mother shushed her husband, then turned to Dr. Sequeira. "I don't expect she'll speak to anyone anytime soon. I can't speculate how long she'll remain mute. Sometimes, it can last for a few hours, a few days, months, even years."

Sequeira sighed. He turned to her parents as though reading Wilder's mind.

"Can I speak with my patient alone, please?"

Relief swept over her; she loved her parents but couldn't bear their presence for a second longer. She couldn't take her mother's psychoanalysis and her father's temper. This had happened to her and not to them. She was the one who'd been attacked. Yet, she couldn't help but feel as though they'd made it about them again.

"I understand your concern for your daughter, but she's my patient, and her privacy right now is paramount. Not to mention the need to limit stress," the doctor said.

"How are we adding to her stress?" her father reeled, insulted. "We're her parents. We've every right to be informed as to what will be the next protocol for her medical treatment. Such as how long she will be here in the hospital and whether or not we've got to move her elsewhere to get the best treatment from *competent* doctors."

The doctor stood up and faced her father. They were inches apart.

"Please leave, Dr. Friedrich, or I'm calling security to escort you out," Dr. Sequeira said, leveling his eyes at Anton. "You've been nothing but hostile. This isn't helping your daughter."

Dr. Anton Friedrich scoffed, then leaned in to confront the young doctor.

"*Verpiss dich!*" her father spat angrily. "*Fuck off!*"

Sequeira returned in Anton's native tongue, "*Sie hat ein Recht auf Privatsphäre und wird Sie auf Wunsch über ihre medizinische Behandlung informieren.*"

"*She has a right to privacy and will inform you of her medical treatment if she wishes.*"

Sequeira's German wasn't just good, but his pronunciation was impressively native. Wilder hadn't expected the Brazilian to know German, and her parents were surprised too.

"I lived in Germany for a little over five years," the doctor explained, then told her parents goodbye, essentially kicking them out. *"Auf Wiedersehen."*

Wilder wanted to applaud the doctor's cultured attitude and his courage to use it as armor.

No one had spoken to the famed Dr. Anton Jörg Friedrich in this way *ever*. In fact, as well-known as her father was in the neurosurgery world, he was equally known for his temper and being extraordinarily difficult to work with. He'd gone through numerous surgical technicians, and they all couldn't handle working with her father's challenging personality. He'd been sued dozens of times, accused of humiliating and screaming at them during surgery, abusing them verbally with his harsh criticisms and demands for perfection.

Her father had settled most of the cases out of court in cash payments and non-disclosure agreements. But everyone knew, non-disclosure agreement or no, that Anton was as brilliant of a surgeon as he was a giant asshole. How their mother had put up with him all these years without even a single thought to file for divorce was beyond her. Wilder and Sammy had always believed that their mother should've separated from him long ago. But Mom had control over her emotions in that annoying psychologist way.

Anton straightened his back. "You're a linguist. Good for you," he snarled.

Her father turned to her and paused—opened his mouth, shook his head, and stormed out.

"I know he meant to say that he loves you, and you know I love you. We will be here if you need anything, honey. If you can't talk, that's okay," Katrine assured her.

In a flash, Wilder was her mother's patient. Uncomfortable knots twisted her insides. Now she understood why Sammy had a hard time with their mother after she'd been captured and forced into sexual slavery. Wilder had been the strong one for Sammy. Wilder was the daughter that, at the very least, had her life together. Where did this attack leave her now?

Her mother continued, shaking Wilder's mind back into the moment.

"If you need to say something, write it down. Don't push yourself. Give yourself time to heal. Experience what you need to experience. Don't try and fight it. It's best to feel it, remember it, and walk through it. It's the only way to exorcise the trauma. If you push it down, you will delay the healing process. I can refer you to a psychologist when you're ready, honey."

When they finally left, Wilder pulled the longest breath into her lungs and closed her eyes. She could hear the doctor apologize and felt his body draw close, the chair scooting next to her bed, the beep of the machines monitoring her heart, and the taut tape keeping the IV in her vein.

"As your mother said, it's okay if you can't talk. But I must ask you a couple of questions, so I know what you're comfortable doing. Nod yes or shake your head no, okay?" He put a pensive hand on a pen and paper. "The detectives asked me if I would...if you feel comfortable writing down what happened? They'll be stopping by for your statement."

Her skin froze all over again at the memories wanting to return. In her mind, she could see herself pulling up to the house. She could see Zeus going mad in the car, barking and scratching eagerly at the passenger door. Wilder shuddered, closing off that memory and locking it away in a vault. A hammering began at her memory's door, the doorknob rattling, the memories fighting to be set free.

No, no, no. She shook her head again and again, squeezing her eyes shut.

"Okay, okay...hey..." He gripped her hand, and she squeezed back. "No one can force you to talk or do anything against your will. Understand? You have my word. I'll do everything in my power to hold them off. You don't have to write it down right now. Alright? Would you like for me to go over the surgery and the details surrounding it?"

She didn't always agree with her father, but she did side with him in the case of bad news. It was much better knowing sooner than later.

She nodded yes.

"Are you sure? Wilder, it will...not be easy to hear."

She nodded yes again.

None of this is easy. Let me hear it. Just tell me.

"You received ninety stitches on your abdominal region alone and twenty-three to your right scalp. The lacerations were quite severe..." Sequeira hesitated for a beat.

With her eyes still shut, Wilder braced herself.

The doctor continued.

"You received extensive uterine wounds. We had to perform an emergency hysterectomy. There were...severe tubal lacerations as well, and your ovaries were equally damaged. We had no choice but to perform a bilateral salpingo-oophorectomy, the removal of your tubes and ovaries." Dr. Sequeira gulped air and removed his glasses. "You are in surgical menopause. If we hadn't performed it, you would've bled to death. This is the hardest part of my job..."

Menopause? I'm thirty.

Wilder opened her eyes and turned to face the doctor.

"When we ran an emergency blood panel, you were...you were pregnant, Wilder. Judging by the HCG levels, you weren't that far along in the first trimester. But the damage...the pregnancy could not have survived. *You* wouldn't have survived. I'm so *deeply* sorry."

Pregnant? I was...pregnant?

Wilder shuddered, grazing lightly over her belly with her fingers.

She'd been stitched back together like a disemboweled pig.

"At the very least, we did try to save your uterus. We tried to prevent the hysterectomy," Sequeira paused, looking down at his hands as regret weighed on each word. "It was a complicated surgery. The hardest I've performed and the longest. It lasted for six and a half hours. You lost so much blood. For a moment, we thought we'd lost you. There was nothing we could do to prevent the miscarriage or avoid the hysterectomy."

Suddenly, she felt detached as an all-consuming numbness dominated every cell.

Wilder turned her head and stared up at the ceiling, feeling a slow storm whirl deep within her. It dried her tears and filled her with a growing venom, unlike anything she'd ever experienced. She then opened the door in her mind and allowed the clawing memory to burst free.

Perhaps her mother was right. She would use her memories as fuel.

And then she gave herself permission to be human.

Wilder allowed herself to feel the pain and to at last remember—*everything*.

TWELVE
THE DETECTIVE

OUT OF HABIT, Nazario found herself comparing any dude labeled "a big man" to Huxley's stature. While Paul Worsham came close, he was more on the lumbering side. He was meaty and not nearly as defined or tall as the Supervising Agent. Nonetheless, his steely edge was intimidating.

Composed, she met his angry eyes and nodded. "Paul, thank you for agreeing to meet," she said, then looked down at Joey, who was staring at her belly.

"Is that a baby in there?" he asked. "Can I touch it? If my mommy was here, I bet I'd have a baby brother or a sister, but she's in heaven now."

"Joey—" Paul put a meaty hand on his son's little shoulder.

"It's alright," she assured Paul, then smiled at the boy. "Yes, a baby. You can feel."

Joey's eyes went wide, and he giggled. "I felt it, Daddy, the baby kicked!"

Paul ran a large hand through his son's chestnut hair. Joey looked a lot like his dad, making Nazario wonder who the baby would resemble more—her or Huxley? She pushed the thought aside and refocused on getting the interview started. Glad that

Joey had started to feel comfortable, she also knew full well from prior experience how children could clamp shut, especially after suffering trauma.

"Joey, I'm glad you're here. Thank you for coming. This won't take long. Okay?"

Joey nodded, and she continued.

"Can you tell me about what happened?" she asked. Paul narrowed his eyes at Nazario and shook his head no. So, Nazario switched tactics. "Joey, let me rephrase that. Can you tell me about the woman who helped you get away from the bad man?"

"I was leaving school, and he pulled up, and he said that he worked with my dad and..."

"Joey," Paul warned, "answer the lady's question."

"Dad, would you just let me finish?" Joey said. Paul sighed and leaned back into his chair, raking his hands over his face.

He continued. "I thought he worked with my dad. He was bald like my dad. He said we were getting ice cream, but we kept driving, and then that's when I got scared. I told him I wanted to go home, but he wouldn't let me. We were in this metal trailer in the woods. Never seen a metal trailer before. I was scared. I tried to kick him, and then the door opened, and there was this small woman, she wasn't tall like my mommy in heaven. She was real short, but her dog was *huge*."

Joey's eyes grew wide as he gestured with his hands.

"The biggest German Shepherd I've ever seen, and we got three at home! But this one, I really mean it, this one was super big. He was smart, too. He attacked the guy."

The boy's eyes opened even wider now, words tumbling out without a breath in between.

"And the lady told me to come with her. She carried me back to her car. It was a black Jeep Wrangler. I remember that since my dad keeps saying our next car'll be a red Jeep Wrangler. We've gone to the Jeep dealership to look several times already, but he needs to save more money first."

Paul let out a loud grumble and rolled his eyes.

"A black Jeep Wrangler," Nazario tapped into her iPhone notes app. "And when you got to her Jeep?"

"She told me to lay down. She promised to take care of the bad man so that he couldn't hurt anyone else."

Nazario was thankful she also had the digital recorder because Joey was talking fast. Despite what he went through, he couldn't hide his boyish excitement.

"Can you tell me what she looked like?"

"Yellow hair like Mommy's, but part shaved off, and there was this tattoo on her head like a snake or something. It looked really cool. I laid down in the car, and I waited. Then I could smell fire. I almost lifted my head. But she told me to stay down, so I did, but I could smell smoke. She came back, and there was, like, real blood all over her arm. Think she was shot or something. But her arms had muscles, but not like a she-man."

"She-man?"

"Yeah, like Aunt Shirley. Dad said steroids are drugs that make your muscles grow really big," rambled Joey, then whispered, "Aunt Shirley, she takes lots and lots of steroids, and her voice sounds like Daddy's, too."

"Joey, for the love of God—" Paul's face was now fire hydrant red.

"But that's what you said when Aunt Shirley knocked you out that one time, that she's a she-man and—"

"Aunt Shirley has nothing to do with this interview. What have I told you? Stop repeating everything that adults say," Paul said, his face still flushed a dark cherry and the picture of parental mortification.

Flushed, he turned to Nazario with an awkward explanation.

"To help with...context. My little sister's a...professional bodybuilder."

"Stop saying stuff in front of me you don't want me repeating," the eight-year-old pointed out, scolding his dad.

Paul lifted his face to the ceiling, tightly folded his arms across his chest, and shook his head, mumbling incoherently to himself.

Nazario coughed unnecessarily and then attempted to steer the conversation back to Joey's mysterious rescuer. "So, the woman who saved you...she wasn't as muscular as your Aunt Shirley. More like...real fit?" Nazario explained in language he'd understand. "Am I close, Joey?"

"Yeah, what you said. She was bleeding in the car, but she was tough and didn't cry at all or show any pain on her face. Like a superhero," Joey said, punching the air with a fist. "We drove to the police station, and she parked her car down the street. Zeus, the dog, walked me to the police station. Dad lets me walk our dogs. Never been walked by a dog before. Oh...and she gave me a note to hand to the police, so I did, and then the cops asked me some questions about the guy. But I think he's dead. Is he really dead now?"

Nazario met Paul's worn eyes. He pinched the bridge of his nose and let out a loud gust of air from his lungs, swearing under his breath. He waved at Nazario to proceed how she wished.

"That's not important, Joey." Nazario smiled. "What's important is that you're safe now."

"He's dead. He has to be. I wished I could've seen his body. He was burned alive, wasn't he? Daddy was talking about it with someone on the phone. I've never seen a dead body before, not in real life...only on TV."

"Joey! For Christ's sake. That's it. You're not watching any more of those scary movies. No more sneaking onto Netflix. You don't think I know?"

"Aww, come on, Dad, that's not fair!"

"No more scary movies for you, and I mean it." Paul pointed at Nazario's belly. "Pray it's a girl you've got in there. I tell you, boys—"

Paul shook his head and didn't finish.

Nazario flashed a weary smile. "I think we're all set here, Joey. Thanks for answering my questions. In the future, don't go off with strangers. No matter what they say. Okay, buddy? It's very dangerous."

"Okay," Joey said, shoulders slumped in defeat. "Really thought he worked with Dad."

"I know you did, sweetheart," Nazario reached for his hand and squeezed it. "It's okay you made a mistake. Best thing to do is learn from your mistakes, okay? Listen to your dad."

Joey nodded. Nazario stopped the recorder and shook Paul's hand. She thanked them and walked them out of the interrogation room.

In the hallway, she met Huxley, who was armed with a folder and an intense look. He had some news. She was afraid of what that news entailed.

"What is it?"

"Am I that easy to read?" Huxley laughed. "We've got another cold one."

"Jesus, another victim? Where?"

"Boston."

"Just how many DBs are we fixing to have?" Nazario scratched an itch on her belly. "This is a serial killer we got on our hands, Huxley. Second female I've ever handled. But this one's a whole lot more hands-on. Need to dig. FBI dragged me into this, but I don't have access to some of your top-secret records. There must be some list, some connection. Need to find it and get to them before she does."

"I realize that," Huxley said, pacing the hallway. The soles of his Italian leather dress shoes squeaked against the waxed linoleum floor. "Already on it. Our guys are doing some research. Let's brainstorm tonight; I got the file and my laptop. We're scheduled for a video sesh tomorrow with Deputy Frost. Guess he has a sketch of our girl, thanks to Informant F."

Huxley paused and swiped a hand across his face.

"But—first things first—let's get our asses to Boston."

———

The black ice on the I-93 between Manchester and Boston was a Slip 'n Slide. They swerved and spun, turning a complete 360, nearly hitting the honking car behind them that maneuvered around.

Huxley skidded to a stop on the side of the road, breath stuttering in fragmented bursts, his chest heaving. He was still gripping the steering wheel at ten and two.

"You alright?" He searched Nazario's face and body for injury.

"I'm fine," she reassured, even though she felt like she was going to hurl.

"I'm glad you weren't behind the wheel."

"If I was, we wouldn't have been driving so fast on black ice."

"I deserved that," Huxley admitted, returning the car on the road.

Huxley learned his lesson and drove slow the rest of the way, taking them twice as long to arrive in Boston, where the temperature was barely twenty degrees. Six inches of pristine powder framed the freshly plowed street as they drove through a wealthy neighborhood, just five miles from downtown. They reached Woodland Road, where a one-hundred-million-dollar, twenty-seven thousand square-foot mansion sat on fourteen acres of land. A fifteen-foot-high newly built cement wall surrounded the compound.

"All that's missing is barbed wire and a security tower with a damn guard armed with a high-powered rifle," Huxley said. "Looks freshly erected."

"It certainly does look a tad prison-like, either trying to keep people out or—"

"—trying to keep someone in," Huxley finished.

They parked the SUV next to several vehicles, one being the CSI van, another belonging to the medical examiner, the rest were likely Boston's homicide division.

"Well, at least she didn't burn this one down," Nazario said, inhaling the air. It smelled clean, not a trace of smoke. Conceivably a fire could've started in one of the rooms but was put out before it spread. But absent was the campfire smell or the presence of the fire department.

"Curious to see how our girl did this one. A gun?" Huxley wagered.

"Nah," Nazario rubbed her belly. "Gut's telling me that she's not the gun type. Darren and Sean had similar head wounds from being struck hard with something. Maybe our girl used to play a little softball."

"If your theory is correct, Detective, she's got one hell of a swing and is ballsy as hell for not carrying anything more than a bat."

He opened the door for her and walked in behind her.

"Don't forget the dog." Nazario breathed a little heavier. She hadn't been running, and the lack of regular exercise made walking around feel more of a chore. "Zeus—he's her weapon."

"I'd like to learn more about that dog," Huxley admitted.

"Same here."

The mansion's interior was both vast and strikingly minimalistic, blending modern décor with open yet airy spaces. Nazario's eyes were drawn to the grand staircase spiraling upwards, its sleek lines and polished finish adding a touch of elegance to the contemporary design. Voices bled from the second floor.

"Well, fuck me." She put her hand on her lower back and stretched.

"Think that's how we got into this situation to begin with, Detective," Huxley gave her a sassy smile. "I bet there's an elevator. If not, I'll carry you."

Nazario grinned. "Carry your own ass up the stairs."

"Just thought I'd offer." He winked as she made her way up ahead of him. She held onto the rail, feeling her hamstrings burn with each step. She paused for a breath.

The staircase was endless, but they eventually found the main suite. It was as large as her one-bedroom apartment in Los Angeles. The burst of camera flashes illuminated the scene. A rotund crime scene photographer filled up a good portion of the bathroom, where all the action appeared to be taking place.

The photographer snapped away as two CSI personnel dusted for fingerprints and gathered any evidence. He took a couple more pictures before wrapping up.

"Wicked pad and all, but I'm all set. I'm hungry. I need suppah," he said in his Boston accent. "Will upload and password protect."

Boston accents were never easy for her to follow.

Huxley gave the crime photographer his card. "Send us the link and the password to all the photos, please."

The man's wide frame labored to rise from kneeling, his weight a burden on angry, popping knees. Huxley lent his hand, helping the photographer to his feet while the CSI team made their formal introduction, exchanging names and titles.

"Any luck on lifting prints?" Nazario asked one of the crime scene investigators, scanning the bedroom that appeared to be immaculate. She leaned in and sniffed the bedsheets. They were freshly clean.

"We got nada. Dog hairs and small drops of blood in the bedroom," the investigator said, moving to the bathroom with his fellow CSI partner.

"Most likely from our victim being attacked by the dog," Nazario said, eyeing the blood spatter on the floor next to the only evidence marker. "It's real clean up in here. I wouldn't expect prints or much evidence unless she leaves it for us. Our perp isn't sloppy or stupid."

Huxley squatted down for closer inspection, then added, "Didn't bleed a whole lot. Started in the bedroom and finished him off in the bathroom."

In the luxurious lavatory, one of two senior detectives in blazers stuck his hand out for a formal greeting. "Detective Carducci and my partner Detective Tripi," he said in a thick Boston accent.

They exchanged a round of handshakes.

"Yous go on and getta look," Detective Tripi said, "it's pretty cut and dry. Floater in that big ass custom-made behind yous."

Nazario rose a brow and exchanged a look with Huxley. They made an about-face.

"Water instead of fire this time," Huxley said loud enough for Nazario's ears.

The bathroom was as expansive as the rest of the house. The large tub indeed appeared to be customized and much bigger than a standard Jacuzzi. Nazario took gloves from a box sitting on the bathroom counter, and Huxley did, too. They pulled them on and squatted to inspect the body that was faced down. Huxley turned the corpse for a better look.

An Asian man she didn't recognize, but she bet Huxley knew who it was.

"Recognize him?"

"Sure do," he answered, cursing under his breath. "Walter Yang, business mogul."

"As in the Yang liquor stores and restaurants? Isn't the chain nationwide?"

"Correct," Huxley said. "Our sex trafficking division had him on their radar."

"And he wasn't busted?" Nazario frowned.

The man hadn't bloated yet the way floaters did when submerged underwater for three to four days. A combo of bacteria in the gut comingled with carbon monoxide, methane, and hydrogen sulfide resulted in an ugly concoction that caused the body to swell in a disgusting way. It'd been a day, maybe two, since the drowning.

Like Darren Fischer and Sean Martin, a bloody contusion dented the right temple denoting where the killer struck.

"Blunt force trauma to the head, like the others," Huxley said. "It's rumored that Walter Yang had paid off a couple of cops and the Feds. Wasn't my department, but I know there were a few agents fired and charged. That was about five years ago."

"Anything else on his rap sheet? Usually, there's more," Nazario said. "Domestic violence, I'm assuming? Sexual assault tends to go hand in hand with DV."

"Yep, DV and got off scot-free," he said.

"Apparently not." Nazario scanned the body. Puncture wounds on the neck from a bite appeared deep. "That dog sure got this one real good."

Huxley stood and helped Nazario to her feet. He raised a brow at a folder on the bathroom sink. On top was an old shirt with dried blood. Nazario grabbed the shirt and inspected it.

"Looks like this blood is old...my guess...years old," she said. "If it's with the folder, our suspect wants us to run DNA."

Huxley called CSI over, and Nazario handed them the evidence to process.

"We need DNA on this bloody shirt and an approximate timeframe of when the incident might've occurred," Huxley said. "We need this stat."

"We're backlogged," one of the crime scene investigators said, "but we'll do our best."

"I think I already know what that contains," he said, nodding at the folder. "What I don't understand is how our girl was able to gather classified intel on each of her vics."

"She had help," Nazario reasoned. "Wonder who she saved this time around. I'm thinking someone who was a part of the sex ring. It must be connected to the brotherhood in some way."

Huxley removed his gloves, put another pair on, and grabbed the folder.

He thumbed through it and whistled.

"Damn, she's good," he said, as Nazario peeked at the open folder. "Even has intel on all the women he's assaulted. *Allegedly.*"

There was a picture of Mia, a young Korean high schooler, along with her demographic background: ethnicity, birthday, age, part-time after-school job, and the date she was kidnapped. Huxley flipped to the next image, and Nazario's mouth dropped.

"Wait. That's Sammy." Nazario put a hand over her mouth. "One of my students."

"That self-defense class you and Gus used to teach every Saturday afternoon?"

"Still do, up until I was pulled onto this assignment by your boss."

"Swear I had no hand in the FBI signing you on. Had I been asked, you know what my answer would've been," Huxley said. "I was given no information about our little meeting."

"I knew Sammy was rescued," Nazario began, raking her hand through her hair. "I didn't know too many of the details."

"It's like she was passed around." Huxley pointed at a star next to Sammy's name. "Look, only select profiles have this star-like symbol. Sammy, Mia, and a couple of others in the folder. They had 'favorites' men could pick from. These rings run like an auction until the highest bidder wins. Usually wealthy men."

Nazario was sick to her stomach, and it had nothing to do with being pregnant. She couldn't look at any more pictures in the folder. Nazario strode over to the Boston homicide detectives. Huxley followed with folder in hand.

"That's a copy, so it's all yours," Detective Carducci said. "We had it made for you."

"Thanks. Appreciate it," Huxley said. "Did the original have German writing on it?"

"Is that what that was?" Detective Carducci said. "Die Sh—something. I dunno."

"*Die Schlangenfrau?*" Huxley rose a brow, glancing at Nazario.

"Yeah—whatever you just said." Carducci laughed, but Huxley and Nazario didn't.

"The girl?" Nazario said, "Where's Mia? We'd like to talk with her."

"Conducted an interview with her already—recorded it for yous. We needed to act quickly; she was shaken up pretty bad, came in with a busted lip, swollen eyes. He beat her good," Detective Tripi said. "Video interview is on this thumb drive."

"Got the rundown on the other two vics. Burned alive, huh?" Detective Carducci said.

"Daddy not worried about you being on this nationwide manhunt for a serial killer?" Tripi asked. He handed the thumb drive to Nazario and smiled down at her belly.

"Daddy's always worried," Huxley interjected, giving Detective Tripi a stiff smile.

Tripi's eyes darted between the two of them. "My bad." His hands shot in the air.

Nazario cut in. "Thanks for the video and for interviewing Ms. Hong, not delaying things. If we need to ask follow-up questions, we'll be in contact with her." She handed them her card. "Please let us know what CSI finds."

When they got to the hotel, they checked in and made it upstairs to their room. Once inside, Huxley fired up his laptop and popped in the thumb drive. After a couple of clicks, Mia's interview filled the screen. The sixteen-year-old endured being repeatedly raped, beaten, her life threatened at gunpoint on several occasions.

It was excruciating to watch, making Nazario relieved they didn't have to question her. When asked, Mia avoided answering questions about the woman who had saved her. Instead, she explained events in clipped sentences: She was instructed to wait downstairs. There was a dog. She heard Walter Yang cry out in pain. The next moment "was like a fuzzy drunken blackout," she said, and the next thing she knew, the killer was dropping her off down the street from a police station. Mia couldn't recall the time between leaving the mansion and walking to the car.

"I didn't think I'd ever leave," Mia said. "I thought Walter would kill me like he promised, dozens of times. I thought I'd never see my parents again."

"We know this is tough. But we need to confirm, so we're asking you again," Detective Carducci began off-screen, the camera tracked closer. "Can you describe this woman that came in? Can you describe the dog?"

"No," she said. "I was in so much shock my mind went blank."

Mia's eyes darted to the left.

She was lying, lying to protect whoever saved her, lying to protect Walter Yang's killer.

"Okay, Miss Hong," Tripi interjected, "if you start to remember more, anything that can help, give us a call."

Mia looked down and nodded once.

"The FBI's trying to locate this woman," Carducci said. "So, if you can remember anything else, anything that would help, please call. Day or night. We'll pass it along to the feds."

Off-camera, Carducci and Tripi rose to their feet. Chairs scraped against the floor. A hand was on the camera. It shook as one of them got ready to turn it off. Mia remained sitting.

"I do have one last thing to say," Mia whispered, "may I please?"

Still recording, the bouncy camera movements stopped.

"Sure," Tripi said, behind the camera. The lens zoomed in closer.

Mia looked into the camera; it was a tighter close-up of her beautiful face. Beautiful despite the bruised eyes and swollen lip.

"I...I have a message from her." She swallowed. Eyes stared directly into the camera with grim seriousness. "You should've done your job."

Mia's last words were like a punch to the gut.

THIRTEEN

THE DOCTOR

WHEN SHE'D STOPPED EATING, they had moved her from the after-care surgery rooms to their mental health wing at her mother's insistence and professional recommendation. The department not only monitored those in need of psychiatric care, but those with eating disorders.

Wilder was relieved when the hospital honored her request to allow Dr. Damião Sequeira to remain her primary doctor. While she'd been nonverbal for months, she'd managed to write down what she needed.

Not a lot went through her mind in the months since she crawled inside her shell.

While she lost track of time altogether, she forced herself to recount every single second with vivid recollection. The way Zeus began to growl with animal instincts as they pulled up to the driveway, knowing that they were walking right into danger.

Bobby had been on the floor in the kitchen, sputtering out blood but breathing.

Shocked tears wet her face, as Wilder briskly inspected his wounds. He received a defense wound stabbing on his right arm and a puncture wound to the abdomen. She grabbed the kitchen towel and pressed it against his stomach, took out her phone, and dialed 9-1-1.

"9-1-1 what's your emerg—"

Screaming out, she wasn't aware her frantic words had tumbled out unintelligibly.

"Ma'am, try to calm down. I can't understand what you're saying. Take a breath, ma'am and please, start slowly."

"Someone's...oh my God...someone b-broken into my home. I-I knew they would. I told him...*I told him*. I had a feeling they'd come. They...they stabbed my fiancée. He's alive, but he may not be for long. You need to come here now; I think they're still here—"

"Slow down, ma'am..."

"I don't have time to slow down. They're here somewhere, I know it. I knew they'd come. I knew it. Send someone now!" Wilder hollered.

"Who, ma'am? Who's they?"

"Send someone now!"

She rattled off her address and hung up the phone. Knowing she was likely not alone. She ran up the stairs taking the steps two at a time, following the sound of Zeus whimpering. And when she reached the top of the stairs...

The pain was intense. The agony that ripped at her soul was worse than the physical pain she would later endure. They were all dead. She checked them one at a time: Lucy, Lolo, and their puppies. In a panic, she rushed to see if there was life still, one that she could save. The sound of footsteps and voices alerted Zeus, causing him to power down the stairs despite having just come out of surgery from a bullet wound.

The dog was insane.

Everything happened so fast. She needed to go back to Bobby; she needed time to absorb the devastation but had none. It was survival. Escape or die. Only, she hadn't escaped. Wilder ran down the stairs and out the door after Zeus. Suddenly, there were three masked men grabbing at her. She remembered screaming, trying to fight them off. She couldn't. There wasn't a thing she could do. They tore off her clothes. She could still feel their hands squeezing her breasts, groping between her legs.

There were three of them, and they were all masked. But she focused on the little things she could remember, like the fact that they all had one thing in common. The same tattoo. On the neck, one of the men had a Confederate flag in the background and in front of the flag were two hammers crossing over one other to form an "X."

Another man had it on his left forearm. Zeus had managed to sink his teeth into the third man's face tearing the man's mask off. That was when Zeus was stabbed and thrown to the ground. There was so much of her blood everywhere that the third man cursed as he took off his jacket, changed out of his bloody shirt, and placed them in a duffle bag along with his torn ski mask.

With his face unmasked, the third man looked her in the eyes. It was a disturbingly intimate moment she'd never forget. He thrust a knife into her belly again and again. His breath was hot against her ear as he muttered, "No one gets away. *No one*. When we find Sammy—and we will—she'll be dead just like you."

She could hear sirens at a distance. The other two men reminded the third that they were out of time and had to leave.

She coughed up blood, feeling her face wet with tears. She couldn't move her cold body, nor could she discern what part of her was hurt. Pain burned in every cell, tormenting her with an inescapable agony. What she resolved to control was what she would force herself to remember. The tattoo the three men shared. The last man, whose mask was torn away, the only one that she was able to identify from the scene.

She traced the keloid snake scar winding down her

abdomen, a constant reminder of what she lost. Wilder watched the nurses and doctors bustle down the hall, tending to the madness and wild rantings of varying patients with mental illness—many paranoid schizophrenics, though others appeared more normal than even she did. Her mind traveled to how it all began.

Beyond the slaughter of her dogs, Bobby nearly dying, being left for dead herself, naked in the snow—the death of the life that had been growing inside her cut the deepest. She thought about the baby she would never have and the babies that would never come thereafter. She thought about motherhood and the fetus inside her womb that she'd never feel kick. She thought about the newborn she'd never get to hold in her arms, how she'd never know the bond between mother and child. The miracle of carrying a human in her body would never be. She'd never get to breastfeed, co-sleep, watch her baby smile for the first time, take his or her first steps.

Sure, she could adopt. She could try IVF, donor eggs, and have a surrogate carry for her. There were options for women— women like her. Women who would never be able to have a biological child. Forced into surgical menopause at thirty. More than the attack itself, what started as sadness morphed into something else like an out-of-body experience. She repeated every micro-second that went by in vivid detail and, each time, kept in mind the child that had been in her body. The fetus that once grew there. She imagined the heart beating, beating until her baby was murdered inside her. Robbed of the chance at life.

She didn't want a surrogate or adopt.

What she wanted, what she really wanted more than anything, was taken from her—ripped from her body. Wilder didn't know how long she lay there, but every time she looked out the window, she forced herself to remember. She made herself replay it until all the tears died.

It took her a while to finally let herself feel anything but rage.

It took her a long time to let herself turn away from the window, to acknowledge the brave canine who lay on the floor beside her. Zeus had single-handedly saved her life. She knew he was smart because she'd trained him. But she underestimated his instincts. How he knew there was danger before they even entered their home. How he knew to keep her body warm by lying his body on hers.

Zeus lay there on the ground across the room, watched her with steady eyes, but never pushed her for attention. Knew just what to do and for five months lay in kinship with her silence. Held the sadness, the hurt, and the anger for her, with her. As if it was his duty to bear sorrow, a type of comprehension, and emotional intelligence, no one, not one human she'd ever known, could exhibit. Wilder quickly grew to realize she trusted Zeus more than she did a single human in her life, and that included Bobby. That included her mother and father and even her little sister.

Sammy had finally come to visit her after she'd spent months in the hospital. Unlike their parents, she sat quietly at Wilder's bedside. Like Zeus, Sammy didn't ask Wilder questions and didn't talk about her as if she wasn't in the room. Wordless, her sister sat like a meek child next to her. Wilder thought about the two horrendous years Sammy was kidnapped and forced into sex trafficking. She remembered all the times she called Sammy when she came back after her ordeal and how their parents worried about every tiny thing. She remembered how they all loomed and filled Sammy's personal space until she had none. Sammy stopped answering their calls. They'd smothered her. Bought her groceries, tried to coddle and care for her.

Wilder didn't understand back then what she understood now.

Wilder moved her arm for the first time and put her hand out. Zeus lifted his head to the snap of her fingers. He arose and slowly approached her, put his head under her palm until she finally touched him. Zeus let out a whine-like cry, and she was briefly seized with a pang of guilt for emotionally neglecting him. Her little sister took off her jean jacket and her baseball cap. That was when Wilder noticed Sammy's shaved right scalp mirroring hers, and her arms weren't like Wilder's bony frame. Her little sister looked like she spent the last two years not only hiding from her and their parents but lifting weights.

Wilder took her sister in, raking her eyes over Sammy. From head to toe, Sammy exuded the kind of strength Wilder had never seen before. There was a determination in her eyes that told Wilder that Sammy had grown into a woman who was no longer a victim, but a survivor. The sun painted her skin a warm bronze, accentuating the sculpted lines of her biceps, triceps, shoulders, and chest, while her hair shimmered like spun platinum in the sunlight.

"Shaved my head in solidarity with you," Sammy finally said. "And...I'm vegan, too. Dad had a fit. He blamed you, of course, and Mom played family psychologist again—but what's new?"

Sammy put her hand on Wilder's, placing a photo in her hand.

Wilder regarded the picture and smiled. It was of her, Sammy, and Zeus as a puppy jumping off Havasu Falls. In their younger years, they used to vacation during the summers at Tar Creek, when it had been open to the public. Though in 2009, the famous cliff-jumping creek, well known to attract adrenaline junkies, closed for good. A five-thousand-dollar fine plus jail time was posted for anyone who plunged off the seventy-foot cliff. Tar Creek was within proximity to the 53,000-acre wildlife Sespe Condor Sanctuary and had remained a refuge for the endangered California condors. These young condors, still learning to explore their vast terrain, were particularly vulnerable. So, when a young condor, just barely old enough to fend for itself, was found strangled by climbing ropes, the creek became off-limits.

Wilder and her sister had frequented other cliffs as well. It was what they did together. They sky dove eight times, but when that became dull, they made it a mission to cliff jump as many cliffs as they could travel to. Tar Creek, her favorite spot in California, was followed by a whopping eighty-foot drop in Red Rocks Park in Vermont. But the best in the U.S., bar none, was Havasu Falls in Arizona, which touted a one hundred-and twenty-five-foot plunge.

They had jumped from Havasu dozens of times. Zeus, in fact, had been jumping since he was a pup. She trained dogs to be fearless—but Zeus stood out as exceptionally so. Being trained as a military dog had always fit his personality. By six months old, as a part of his training, Wilder and Zeus were leaping out of planes with soldiers—no hesitation, no fear. His first jump, however, was Havasu Falls. The picture brought back all sorts of old feelings of an innocent, blissful life before brutal reality would tear her family apart.

"That picture...you know I feel like we were the happiest in our lives?" Sammy said. "It was the first time I met Zeus. I didn't expect to see him again. You remember me, huh boy? I knew you before you went off to war with that soldier." She leaned in and stroked Zeus's head. "It was a month before I was kidnapped and before this happened to you. This is my fault, and it is up to me to make it right."

Sammy clenched her teeth, rage flashing in her eyes. The anger Wilder felt churning inside moments ago, she could see in Sammy's eyes. And for the first time, the dormant words inside, words that had been silent, escaped her mouth.

"None of this was your fault."

It was the first words she'd spoken to anyone in months.

"They were the same men, weren't they?" Sammy bit out, rage in her eyes.

"You're a vegan now?" Wilder dodged, trying to change the subject.

"They were in the Brotherhood? *Weren't they?* I choked during that trial. I'll never live that down. For a while, I thought maybe it was a good thing. No conviction meant that they'd leave us alone? But then Darren gets out, and—"

"It was a blur. I...I didn't see their faces." Wilder lied. She knew they'd come. Known it in her gut, despite Bobby dismissing her concerns. "You really need to stop blaming yourself for all of it."

She had recalled one face, the only one that Zeus managed to unmask. Darren Fischer. But Wilder could not bring herself to share this piece of memory with her little sister. Nor would she speak of the small but defining tattoos the three shared. Sammy would find out soon enough after Wilder spoke with detectives and would likely be subpoenaed to testify in follow-up future court proceedings.

"But I *know* it was them," Samantha insisted. "They came for you. They told me if I ever escaped, they'd go after my family, and they'd—"

Sammy let out a sob and threw her arms around Wilder.

"They didn't kill me, Sammy," Wilder spoke with strength. Having survived, she wasn't going to let this experience kill her soul.

Sammy sobbed in the crook of her neck, and they held each other tight. Wilder found that, after a long contemplative time, after experiencing the event that would change her life forever, and after reliving it repeatedly—tears didn't come because they were no longer necessary.

Washed away were her tears, and in that moment, she was steady.

Steady for her sister, whom she let cry.

"You...look different," Wilder finally said, brushing Sammy's hair back.

Sammy sat up and wiped her face. She flexed her lean biceps proudly. "I've been training at the gym with a personal trainer in Los Angeles four days a week and also with this martial arts expert twice a week. Detective Anaya Nazario, fourth-degree black belt in taekwondo. She's a real badass."

"The change is—well—it's quite remarkable," Wilder said. "I'm very proud of you. As you can see, I've lost quite a bit of weight. Partly why I'm here still."

Wilder's petite frame was now skeletal. Every time she looked at herself in the mirror, the emaciated woman staring back was someone she hardly recognized.

Sammy kept her hands firmly in hers. Gripping Wilder's fingers as if afraid to let her go.

"They can't get away with this," Sammy said. "I have to do something about it."

"Like what, Sammy? Get yourself killed? Stay away from them," Wilder warned.

"Then let me do something for you," Sammy began. "You might think I'm crazy, but...I can give you my eggs—"

"Sammy—"

"No, please, *please* listen. I'm sorry it took me so long to come and visit. I knew...knew you needed time." She looked down at their hands laced together. "I've...been there."

Wilder's voice cracked. "I didn't know what you'd gone through. Not like I do now."

Sammy took her free hand and ran it through Wilder's hair. A tender touch Wilder hadn't experienced from her little sister since she'd been found by the LAPD Gang and Narcotics unit.

"Let me finish, please," she begged, and Wilder nodded for her to go on.

"There's IVF, I've already checked. They told me I'm young enough and in perfect health. I'd be willing to do egg retrieval, and you can fertilize them with Bobby's sperm. I'd carry for you. I would," she said.

Oh, Bobby. He had appeared a handful of times, but Wilder wasn't ready to see him.

Wilder gripped her hand and looked her in the eyes, trying to reassure her. "I appreciate the offer. I really do. But it won't be the same."

"That's the misconception. That's what you think now. I've done so much research on this. I've joined all these IVF Face-book groups. The baby, it'll be part me. And when you hold the baby in your arms, I promise you...you will bond. You'll still be Mommy. Please, please let me do this one thing for you."

Despite her new gym shape, Sammy had this innocent look, this sweet baby face that she never outgrew. Wilder could see how this might attract filthy men who wanted to taste and tarnish her. Sammy, despite what she'd gone through, wasn't tarnished. Big, hazel doe-eyes turned amber with flecks of fairy dust in the sun. Her pouty, full lips and simple beauty made her look like a sunflower—an angel. Sammy had always been the sister Wilder begged her parents for.

Wilder loved Sammy and would do anything in the world for her.

What happened to Wilder was evil, but what happened to her little sister demanded justice.

"It's the single kindest thing you have ever offered me...that anyone has ever offered me. But...Sammy, I can't," Wilder shook her head. "I haven't wanted to see Bobby since...well, I haven't been myself. You're the first person I've spoken to since waking up in here."

"Mom told me you were...mute," she swallowed. "There's nothing at all I can do?"

"Take Zeus for me. He understands German. You're fluent, and he knows you. At least until I'm out of the mental unit with a sound mind and back at home." Wilder said, allowing herself a laugh causing pain to shoot through her bruised abdomen.

"Of course." Sammy stroked Zeus's head. "What...what was it like? Not talking for five months?" Sammy broke into her thoughts, squeezing her hand until Wilder turned to face her.

Wilder looked out the window, the same window that she'd stared out of for months.

"It felt like surrender," Wilder said.

"Surrender?" Sammy snapped. Wilder was surprised by the sudden outburst. She stood up abruptly and took Zeus's leash. "They're not getting away with this."

"Sammy—I said stay away from them," Wilder pled. "What're you planning?"

"Ich werde mich nicht ergeben," Sammy said. *"I will not surrender."*

Wilder called out Sammy's name, but she and Zeus were gone.

FOURTEEN
THE DETECTIVE

NAZARIO AND HUXLEY spent most of the night scouring through the detailed case folders left at each crime scene. All the victims had one single thing in common: They had several criminal charges expunged from their records. No one would know such intimate, sensitive information unless they had access to FBI classified intel. The charges brought against the perps ended in lenient sentences or were dismissed altogether.

"This is infuriating," sighed Nazario, scattering the files across the bed in disgust. "How did our perp get this information? There's got to be a leak somewhere. We need to seal it up."

Huxley picked up the folders, piled them up on the desk, and powered up his laptop.

"Pisses me off, too," Huxley admitted.

Emotionally and physically drained, Nazario plunked herself next to the hotel window and watched the snow. The string of unsolved homicide cases had started to feel like an anchor around her neck. Drowning her during the most joyful part of the year—Christmas and New Year's. Now, she doubted if she'd ever enjoy the holidays in the same way. Something about corpses of murdered men and bright Christmas lights, along with the incessant cheery seasonal tunes playing everywhere she went, clashed in a disturbing way.

She clutched the gold necklace that once held her father's ring in her fist.

It was the one thing that made her feel safe, like an invisible protective force field. In all her years as a police officer and as a detective, she'd never taken it off. This was something most on the force knew, especially everyone on homicide. Then last night, out of nowhere, the necklace broke in the shower, and her cherished father's ring came clattering down like a bad omen warning of impending disaster. She sipped cold decaf coffee and fiddled with the ring between her fingers, unable to shake a somber feeling.

When Huxley asked what was wrong, she told him about the broken necklace.

"I can't just put it in my suitcase," her voice cracked, eyes still squeezed shut, "it's like I'm...like I'm boxing him up and burying him all over again."

"Know the best place for it," he said. Her eyes slowly opened along with her fingers. He took her father's ring, met her eyes, and then asked, "May I?"

She hesitated for a ten count, protective over the heirloom that ceased being a mere piece of jewelry long ago. It was her father's heart that had beaten against hers since she was eighteen. It was the first time it'd been off her body. She felt naked without it but swallowed an apprehensive gulp of air before finally nodding her approval.

"I think it's..." Huxley inspected it carefully, "...just the right size."

Her breath caught in her throat as he slipped it onto his left ring finger.

It was a perfect fit. Nazario bit her lower lip, blinking back a whirl of unsaid emotions.

"Let me keep it safe for you," he said gently, "at least until you can get another necklace. It won't be buried at the bottom of some suitcase. It'll be right next to you. Right here with you."

Unsure of how to respond, she stared at his strong hands that were so much like Daddy's.

She pushed aside the symbolic connotations and tried on her best professional tone.

"Don't be mistaken, Supervising Agent, this ain't no proposal or anything," she finally said, allowing the levity in her words to coax a chuckle out of him.

"I learned long ago not to read between the lines, not with you, Detective," Huxley said. "You're much too direct to be the subtle innuendo type."

"If you can...keep it from slipping off, I'd... I'd greatly appreciate it," she said, clearing her throat.

Huxley tugged on it, demonstrating that it was indeed secure, and she sighed with relief.

With his left hand, he brushed the backs of his fingers against her cheek. Her father's ring was cool against her face. It was the closest to her father's kiss she'd felt in twenty-six years.

"Hey...I promised you I'd find who killed your father, and I delivered, didn't I?" he said softly, tucking a strand of hair behind her ear. "Anaya, I promise you it'll be right here when you need it. I'm honored to wear it—*temporarily*. Your father was a true-blue legend."

"We should..." she paused, aware of how close he'd been standing, "probably get to our meeting."

"Okay, boss." He took a couple of steps back until there was ample space between them.

Admittedly, her father's gold band looked good on his hand, as if always meant to have been worn by him.

"Temporary," he reminded her, watching her eyes, reading

her thoughts. "I'm just keeping it safe until we wrap this case up, and then it can be snug at home with you."

He did an about-face and sat in front of his laptop at the motel desk. Nazario pulled up a chair next to him and changed the subject.

"Let's see what's so important. I hate to guess what it could be," Nazario sighed.

"Ditto." He launched a video conferencing software unfamiliar to her. "Looks like we've kept them waiting."

The video screen popped up. Deputy Frost sat in his office at the bureau, sweat sheened across his forehead. It looked like the FBI hadn't fixed the air conditioner in the stuffy room.

"Glad to see the two of you haven't killed each other." Frost laughed, though it wound down quickly as he returned to their agenda. "How's the investigation? Progress? In terms of victimology—thinking revenge?"

"Not to oversimplify—female serial killers are wired differently than men, sir," Nazario said, "we've reason to believe the motive is much more complex. Beyond chopping off Martin's... you know...we're still trying to unpack it."

"We heard you had the honor of...inspecting it?" Deputy Frost cleared his throat, returning the conversation back to Sean Martin's...separated male member.

"Sure did," Nazario said, matter-of-factly, "it was still nice and squishy. Wasn't totally frozen, sir."

"Yeah, anyways...went over the three folders left behind by our girl," Huxley redirected. "Some of it was news clippings and stuff anyone can get access to. I mean, hot damn, it's honestly the best fucking intel I've ever seen, sir. The classified kind."

Huxley gestured to her, and Nazario briefed them on all the victims, explaining how each was connected to the sex ring. She explained that while the unsub took lives, she also saved them.

"Anything that jumped out at you in these folders?" Frost asked.

"We did have a surprise in Yang's folder. Which brings us to Samantha Friedrich. I haven't seen her in a couple of years now. She seemed angry the last time I saw her, kept saying she wanted the men to pay for what they did. At the time, I brushed it off, figured she just wanted to learn how to defend herself."

"She's your student in that self-defense class you teach, correct?"

"Yes, sir," Nazario answered.

"And you're thinking Samantha's connected to these murders?" Frost frowned.

"Don't know yet, but we got her DNA on file. We'll soon be able to compare blood samples found inside Sean Martin's Airstream." Nazario raked a hand over her face. "But, judging by the positioning of the photos of the women..."

"We believe Sammy was one of their *prized* women they auctioned off," Huxley said.

"Well, doggonit, how many were there?" Deputy Frost asked, leaning into the camera.

"Seventeen under-aged, give or take." Huxley provoked a curse under his boss's breath.

"The way the pictures were stacked, first one, of course, was Yang's victim—Mia. The second was Sammy's pic. There's something there, something about the order," Nazario said.

"Hopefully, what we're here to discuss will help." Deputy Frost emitted a long sigh. "To get back to the reason why I called this meeting, we've got two significant discoveries. We've got a sketch of the perp, and we know who the hacker is."

Huxley looked at her. "Well, Detective? Behind door number one or two?"

"Let's see our girl first."

"Sharing my screen," Frost said, and the sketch populated. "Von Schlange. That's what she goes by, there may be other names."

"Schlange...isn't that German, sir?" Nazario asked. "Sounds familiar."

"Yeah, it means serpent. Makes sense. Remember, her signature? *Die Schlangeenfrau.* The Serpent Woman. She picked the name: Von Schlange. The reason remains to be known. Informant F referred to her as *The Serpent Woman*," Huxley explained. "Makes a lot of sense now."

The name was a mystery, but the detective knew there was something deeper behind it.

Huxley and Nazario leaned in to study the artist's rendering.

The face was serious. The head was shaved on the right side, and on the scalp was a serpent tattoo. A separate sketch revealed forearms with similar Viking-style tattoos. Her face was sullen, eyes deep and penetrating, body petite. The serpent inked on her scalp, coiling through roses, was undeniably unforgettable. Her muscular arms harmonized perfectly with her distinctive look and powerful build.

"She's real strong, lifts weights regularly. Maybe where she gets her good swing?" Nazario remembered the first time Sammy joined the self-defense class. The first thing Nazario had noticed was Sammy's arms.

A chill ran up the detective's spine.

She inspected the image and then added, "Sammy, she's built like that. Had enough anger and motive, too. The jaw's different, but those eyes...she didn't have tats back then."

Huxley inspected the image of their unsub. "But she could've gotten them recently. There's a resemblance, for sure, but close isn't good enough. A DNA match will clear this all up for us."

"The arm tattoos mean something—" Nazario rubbed her chin.

"Tree of life and the other, the connecting triangles—Valknut. It's the symbol for life and death," Huxley clarified.

"That serpent on her head," added Nazario, as she stared at it, "superb artistry."

"*Jörmungandr*. It means huge monster. It's the world's serpent. Norse mythology—Thor's arch-nemesis. The serpent that represents war," Huxley deciphered, then pivoted the conversation. "Let's see what's behind door number two."

Deputy Frost took off his glasses, and the atmosphere suddenly changed.

"What's going on? Who's the hacker?" Huxley demanded.

"We've reason to believe it's our informant."

"Informant F?" Nazario's mouth dropped. "That means it can be—"

"Right, it can be anyone," Frost finished. "We're surprised ourselves. We trusted them, whoever the hell they are, and now the bureau's got egg all over its face. But we have to keep them talking, keep the lines between us open."

Nazario leaned in, concerned. "Did we get their identity yet?"

Deputy Frost rubbed the bridge of his nose, folded his hands, and studied them for a five-count before putting his glasses back on, then continued.

"Not yet, but we're trying to strike a deal. Immunity in trade for their—*skills*—if you will." Deputy Frost leaned back in his chair. "They claim they can't recall certain details."

"And you believe them?" Huxley rose a brow.

"We honestly don't know what to believe," the deputy admitted, then said, "but they did mention something about a judge. The thing is, there were several shady judges in connection with the sex ring and dozens more like Darren and

Sean. Not all the men were skinheads—case in point, Walter Yang."

"Aside from the shaved head and some tattoos, our unsub looks like she could be any gym rat. We need to identify her, that dog, her motive. We also need a list of everyone associated with the brotherhood and the sex ring who's on the FBI's radar," Nazario said.

"We'll certainly provide that list. But fair warning, it's extensive," the deputy said. "Now, about that dog. Think we got something. A Lance Corporal Jefferson Pearce. Talk to him. Sending you his contact along with that FBI list connected with the sex trafficking ring."

"Let's try and find out who this Von Schlange really is and quick. When y'all do, don't be putting it on blast. You feel me?" Frost made a zipping motion across his lips.

"Sir?" Nazario frowned. "We're not—"

"No, we're not," Deputy Frost chopped the air with a horizontal hand swipe. "Everything about the killer remains one hundred percent confidential. That's a strict order. Some woman going around executing men on the FBI's list? Scum that we didn't clean up first, and more importantly, didn't prosecute in a timely fashion? It don't look too good."

"So, we're covering our asses, is that it?" Huxley raked a hand through his hair. "What're we telling the damn press?"

"So, we're going generic," Frost began neutrally, "we've reason to believe the killer may be a—'former member of the brotherhood.' Get what I'm saying?"

"That's our cover story?" Huxley let out an incredulous laugh. "Why not just take the media spanking we deserve and tell the doggone truth?"

"Huxley," Deputy Frost gave him a paternal smile, "that's why I like you so much; you're so...*honest.* Honesty, son, isn't an FBI prerequisite. It is secondary to the bigger picture. If it's any consolation, we're real sorry y'all will be spending the holidays doing a nationwide chase of this serpent woman."

"Yeah, well, operation normal." Nazario exhaled and considered that this new year would be at least memorable. "We'll be talking to you next year, sir."

Directly after their conference, Nazario and Huxley started digging through the files. The FBI's list of the men associated with the trafficking ring was indeed daunting. It would take them months that they didn't have to track down each name unless they could identify the killer and her motive, which could immensely shorten the process. Out of one hundred and twenty or so men, any of them could be Von Schlange's next target.

"How do you feel about this informant being used by the Bureau?" Nazario broke the long silence that had settled in the stuffy hotel room.

"I don't like it," Huxley admitted, "and we better pray it don't make things worse. Shall we call this Lance Corporal Jefferson Pearce?"

Nazario agreed, figuring the dog might provide more clues.

Huxley fished his phone from his pocket, and Nazario retrieved her own. She showed him the text message Deputy Frost sent with Pearce's number. He dialed, and the conversation lasted all of five minutes before the soldier agreed to a video conference—stat.

"That didn't take a lot of persuading." Nazario mused.

"The Lance Corporal sounds sauced." Huxley tapped his temple. "He ain't all there."

"Multiple deployments, likely during the Iraq and Afghanistan years. Lucky he's drunk, he may open up to us a little more," Nazario reasoned.

"Let's cross our fingers and toes," Huxley said, swiftly

sending the drunk soldier a link to the encrypted video conference.

In three minutes or less, Pearce had joined the conference call.

"He must be eager to talk." Huxley clicked a button that expanded their screen.

A young, red-faced Hispanic-Anglo soldier appeared, reminding Nazario of her own mixed heritage of Puerto Rican and Irish. Sweat glistened on his cheeks, and fresh beads trickled down his sideburns. Pearce's beard was scraggly and not military smooth. That, coupled with the fact that his disheveled hair hadn't been cut in a while, made Nazario doubt he was still enlisted. He was shirtless, numerous tattoos wrapped around both arms and shoulders.

"This about Zeus, isn't it?" he slurred with a country accent. Glassy-eyed, he took a swig of brown liquid, that Nazario reasoned was some kind of whiskey. "Served three tours in Iraq, two in Afghanistan, found hundreds of bombs, saved countless lives."

"Zeus?" Huxley looked perplexed. "This a cute nickname for some badass soldier?"

"Talking 'bout a badass dog, sir," Pearce responded, "and Zeus is a soldier trained for war. But...he was a whole lot more. Dog's a weapon, smarter than shit. Smartest dog all of us had ever seen, and we've worked with dozens of them. Not a dog like him."

"You still enlisted?" Nazario asked gently.

"No ma'am, medically discharged from the Marine Corps after..." The words caught in his throat, and his eyes grew moist. He stared numbly and unblinking as if transported away in an instant. Pearce's voice cracked.

"We were in Kabul. It was mid-afternoon. We were in this run-down building. Set up there on a special mission. All of us were there. Fifty total. We didn't hear it coming—the rocket—but Zeus did. He barreled into me like a damn semi-truck, all muscle and instinct. When he gets going, boy, it's like a truck comin' atcha. Next thing I know, I'm out the door on my ass, disoriented. Thought he'd gone crazy, and then it happened so fast. The entire building crumbled." He gestured an explosion with both hands. "Most of my men...they didn't make it. Handful of us survived. We redeployed, medivacked back home, and...and I wasn't right after that."

Pearce reached off-screen, returned with a bottle of Jack Daniels, and took a swig.

"I'm sorry. It was a traumatic situation," Nazario said, tone tender. "Thank you for sharing. I'm no soldier, but my job as a homicide detective is dangerous and stressful. I'm very familiar with PTSD, as well as drinking."

Huxley put a hand on her knee.

Pearce stared down at the Tennessee whiskey, didn't look up, but nodded.

Nazario continued, tone soft and low. "Where is Zeus now? Do you know what happened to him? When was the last time you saw him?"

"Been five years now. When we got redeployed and was home...I wasn't right to him. I never used to hurt him, but the nightmares were so bad. Horrible. I wasn't sleeping. Had me on a shit-ton of meds, a whole cocktail, and ain't none of 'em work. I started...I started..." he choked out a sob, "...kicking him. I resented the fact that he saved my ass and most of my men, all my friends, my brothers, they...died."

Pearce coughed out an anguished cry. "So, one day, I just...I just couldn't fucking take it no more. I c-couldn't keep on living. That's when...that's when it happened. I tried to end my life. I took my gun, and the moment Zeus saw it, it was like he... *knew*."

Pearce took another swill and wiped his face. He looked up to meet their eyes.

"Take your time, Jefferson," Huxley whispered.

"Tried pulling the trigger, even got the gun all the way up to my head, but...Zeus, he done stopped me. He went after the gun. That stupid dog tried to save me—*again*. So, I screamed at him: '*hör auf mich zu retten.*' It means..."

"Stop saving me," Huxley translated. "He understands German then, the dog?"

"Yeah, he only understands German commands. Was trained that way. And anyway, the gun went off, and I shot 'im in the shoulder. It was an accident. I swear this on my mama. Sergeant Berg, he rushed in when he heard live fire. We drove to the vet clinic, went to the same doctor that trained him. Recognized her. Berg said she performed emergency surgery. Last time I saw 'im. Zeus ain't safe in the wrong hands. Especially... mine."

Nazario and Huxley exchanged a look. "You recall the doctor's name?" Nazario asked.

Jefferson shook his head. "I can't remember her name. Blonde, small, and pretty in a simple sorta way. It was some clinic in Casper, Wyoming. She also trained service dogs, that type of thing. What does Zeus have to do with this case you say you're on?"

"Might be involved somehow," Nazario said. "That's all we can disclose."

The soldier nodded. "Like I said, Zeus's capabilities are shocking. And I ain't exaggerating. He's very loyal to his handler. That's the way he was with me. He'd die...die trying to protect me and nearly did multiple times. He's trained to save lives," Pearce paused, took a long swig from his JD, looked up with bloodshot, watery eyes, "but he's also trained to kill."

Nazario had never felt a connection with anyone like the

one she had with her father. But as she looked at Huxley's left hand, adorned with her father's wedding ring, and felt their small, growing child in her belly, she began to ponder the nature of bonds.

Bonds between humans were strong, but those between humans and dogs could be stronger.

Whoever the perp, she wouldn't be Von Schlange without her beloved dog, without Zeus.

FIFTEEN

THE DOCTOR

BABY BIRDS SQUALLED outside on the newly thawed trees that were boasting freshly sprouted leaves. The spring sun's brilliant rays sliced through the oceanic sky. On a clear night, the stars freckled the darkness, tiny firelights of hot gas in the atmosphere.

So far away and yet closer than ever before.

Wilder stared for so long. She felt more connected to the cosmos, to nature. She needed to find the strength to leave the hospital but knew they wouldn't release her in her current condition. So, she requested a personal trainer, and that was when she met Briar Carson Rogers, former up-and-coming minor league baseball player. A rotator cuff injury ended his sports career and was the beginning of his new profession.

With Briar's daily visits to the hospital for moral support and a little motivational coaching, Wilder began eating solid foods. It wasn't long before her request for Briar to train her was granted, and five days a week, for at least two hours, she was able to leave the hospital. In the first two months, she had already packed on twenty-five pounds.

While she missed Zeus, she knew that he was in good

hands, and Wilder needed the time to become the person she always knew she could be. Briar started her off with unconventional Cross Fit training methods to not only rebuild her torn abdominal muscles but her entire body.

"Come again?" Wilder scowled. "I've never swung a bat in my life. I haven't an athletic bone in my body."

"This'll help to strengthen your core." He placed the tips of his fingers on her abdomen.

He handed her a baseball bat.

"Feet apart...there ya go. Now swing as hard as you can at the punching bag. Step into the swing. Remember you draw power from your legs. Step with your left foot, rotate at the hips, keep your back leg planted, and give it your all."

She botched her first swing. The bat slipped from her fingers, clattering to the floor.

"Keep your grip at the bottom of the bat," Briar explained. "Open your hips, step forward, and rotate." He demonstrated proper footing and hip rotation in cadence with his swing.

It took a few attempts until she perfected it, and once she did, it was addicting hearing the bat strike the punching bag with a loud THWAT! She broke several wooden bats until Briar bought her an aluminum one. The first thing she noticed was that her appetite increased as she amped up her weight training regimen. As she filled in, the second thing she noticed was that her gaunt frame was transforming.

"You've got great genetics," Briar had said. "It doesn't take very long for muscle to show up on you. You're real lean, and so you build up pretty fast. I can already see great definition. Your strength has also improved immensely. Remember, you couldn't do one chin-up, and now you just busted out three sets of ten. I'm very impressed, Dr. Wilder." Briar had encouraged after another successful strength training exercise.

"I'd like to get to five sets of twenty," Wilder said, stretching her arms. "That's my goal."

"Oh, we'll get there. I don't doubt you for a second." Briar put a hand on her shoulder and looked in her eyes. "When you put your mind to something, you are capable of just about anything. And I'm not just blowing smoke. You're more determined than anyone I've ever trained."

"I can't believe it's already been four months," Wilder said, wiping sweat from her brow with a towel. "I really couldn't have done it without you."

"To think you were eighty pounds of bones when we first met, and now a buck-twenty and nothing but muscle," Briar announced proudly, and then his face turned serious. "You... uh...doing alright otherwise? Have you heard back from your sister?"

"Not yet. Sammy...she does this sometimes." Wilder paused, then admitted, "I miss Zeus."

"He's your dog. If he's as smart as you say he is, he'll be wanting to come back home to you. Try calling Sammy again. I bet she'll show up soon."

"No need to call me," Sammy's voice announced from the back of the gym.

Zeus barked. Sammy unhooked him, and he came running.

He tackled Wilder with one-hundred pounds of muscle. She laughed, and for the first time in a while, her stomach no longer hurt. Zeus gave her wet kisses all over her face.

"See? What'd I say?" Briar said with a smile. "See you tomorrow?"

"Bright and early," Wilder promised, then turned to Sammy. "Can I catch a ride?"

Sammy drove Wilder in total silence. Back at the hospital, Sammy waited next to her bed while she showered and changed clothes. Once dressed, Dr. Damião Sequeira came in, surprised to see Sammy.

"Nice to see you back, Sammy." Dr. Sequeira turned to Zeus. "And you too, Zeus."

"So, you're Dr. S?" Sammy smiled, raising a brow. "Hello, Doc."

Dr. Sequeira flushed, briefly meeting her eyes. "Wanted to see how training went, Wilder."

"Went well, getting stronger." Wilder smiled. The nervous flutter in her belly returned.

"That's wonderful. What remarkable progress," he said with a glint in his eyes. Something she couldn't quite label. Dr. Sequeira cleared his throat. "Anyway...lunch will be in about an hour. You have time for your visit."

The mental health unit had everyone on a very strict schedule, especially those with eating disorders. The structure became something Wilder thought she'd hate but oddly grew to appreciate.

When Dr. Sequeira left, it took a moment for Sammy to finally address her absence.

"I'm...I'm really sorry," she began. "I dunno what I was thinking. I almost...I almost did something stupid, something illegal. But I...I changed my mind, and then I felt stupid."

"You don't have to explain," Wilder said. "No need to feel stupid."

"I needed time to think...but Zeus, he seemed...I dunno... depressed," Sammy said. "He missed you."

Wilder brushed a hand on Zeus's head and down his back.

"Can I...can I ask you something?" Sammy began. She looked nervous. "Never mind."

"What?" Wilder asked. "You can ask or talk to me about anything. You know that."

"Did they...did they...r-r...?"

Sammy stuttered over the words that their parents wanted to say but couldn't, using other words instead. Dr. Sequeira knew she hadn't because they'd performed a rape examination straight away, and it returned negative. Sammy looked to be choking for air—breath hitching, chest heaving in rapid, shallow bursts, palms slick against Wilder's dry, steady hands.

Sammy was on the verge of a panic attack.

Wilder brushed the back of a hand against her wet cheeks.

"No, Sammy, they didn't rape me," Wilder said the word.

The evil word that somehow made what had happened to her feel smaller.

"They just killed the baby growing inside me and made it so I am now in surgical menopause—like some woman in her fifties. Made it so that I can't have children anymore."

She picked up the hand mirror next to her bed and briefly looked at herself. The woman who now stared back wasn't the woman lying in the snow, defenseless and left for dead. Her words were flat, and eyes smooth as grey stones, wiped entirely of emotion.

Wilder put down the mirror and casually finished her thought.

"Maybe if the weather wasn't thirty-below, they might've been in the mood," she explained in an almost clinical, doctor tone. "I do remember hearing the sirens. The cops were already on their way...so I suppose there were time constraints."

"God, Wild..." Her hands flew over her mouth. "I didn't mean to make this about me. I'm sorry I even asked."

"It's okay." Wilder lied because nothing was okay.

Voices rose out in the hall.

"I think it's Bobby," Sammy said, turning her head towards the door. "He sounds livid...is everything okay? Never mind, it's not at all my business."

She recalled all of the times Bobby tried to visit her.

"What do you mean she won't see me?" Bobby had said after Wilder had first awakened in the hospital months ago. *"I was there, too. Need I remind you that I nearly died as well?"*

"I realize that, and words can't begin to describe what both of you experienced. But as her doctor, I have to abide by my patient's wishes. She does not wish to see you. I'm sorry," Dr. Sequeira had said.

She could hear them from behind the hospital walls seemingly made of paper-mâché.

"She blames me, doesn't she? She blames me for the attack?"

"As I said before and will repeat to you as I have to her parents. My patient is non-verbal. I do not know what she thinks. I can't read minds. Nor is it any of my business what is occurring between the two of you. All I know is that my patient has gone through major trauma, and when she's ready to speak with you or to anyone else, for that matter, she will."

Sammy rose, breaking her out of her thoughts. Giving Wilder a fierce hug she whispered, "Now that Bobby's here, will you at least consider my offer of donor eggs and surrogacy?"

Wilder didn't have the heart to reject Sammy's kindness again, so she nodded instead.

Yes, carry a baby for me because I no longer have a uterus. While I experience hot flashes, night sweats, mood swings, and other menopausal symptoms, you can get knocked up with a child I'll never be able to physically experience growing inside of me.

Wilder knew that a baby wouldn't make her whole again and that maybe somewhere deep inside, she might eventually become resentful. Resent her little angel, her perfect little Sammy, for still having the reproductive organs that had been extracted from her body.

Resent her belly that would grow. Resent that her sister got to have the experience.

Or...

Maybe, it would be perfect and even bring them closer. A child, part her little sister, part Bobby. Maybe the child would still resemble her, and maybe no one would ever really know. She could have the family she always wanted, and Sammy could help her. It would be amazing to start a new life somewhere else, to put this all behind her. Maybe she and Bobby could start a clinic elsewhere like they'd discussed, someplace warm like Florida. She could see a chubby adorable toddler running down the beach, giggling infectiously the way Sammy did when she was happy.

Sammy would be there; she might even move into their home.

They'd have a house off the coast, a beach bungalow, and they'd get more dogs.

Maybe a handful of German Shepherds like Zeus.

Then she took the mirror on the nightstand, lifted her shirt, and stared at what was left of her. During an earlier visit, her father came in and said the word "schlange" over and over, accusing Dr. Damião Sequeira of, "Turned my daughter into a schlange."

Schlange, she thought, was her beast. The serpent, slithering up her body. A thick maroon keloid scar twisted up the length of her abdomen, ending at her pubic bone. It was precisely what she was, what she had become. Rather than getting offended by her father's remarks, she inwardly thanked him.

Schlange, yes, the German word for serpent.

The door flew open, Bobby barged in.

"Dr. Chua, please, I told you she's not ready to see you," Dr. Sequeira said.

"Then I'm here to break hospital policy," Bobby said. "She'll see me."

"I'm calling security—"

"Then call them."

"It's okay," Wilder said. Words continued to make her feel naked before the handsome doctor. It still felt strange talking after being mute for one hundred and fifty-two days, nearly half a year. Unfortunately, she'd been avoiding talking to Bobby the most.

Dr. Sequeira adjusted his glasses. "You sure, Wilder?"

"Well, of course, she is," Bobby bit out.

"Dr. Chua, my patient was mute for months, and then she stopped eating altogether until she dropped to eighty pounds."

"I'd have loved to be here for my fiancée, had I been allowed," Bobby spat. "Eight months of being shut out. EIGHT!"

"Her wellbeing has been my chief concern, and to see to it that she isn't under added stress. That means honoring her request as to who she wants to see and who she does *not*," Dr. Sequeira returned tersely, then softened his tone as he turned to her. "Wilder, please press the button if you need someone to come—because if he's hassling you, I'll get security here."

"It's alright. It won't take long." The moment she said the phrase, Bobby looked like he'd been slapped in the face.

"And...as a reminder, you've got fifteen minutes." Dr. Sequeira turned to Bobby. "If you care about your fiancée, Dr. Chua, you must leave in fifteen minutes. She can't afford to miss her lunch. We've worked very hard to stop force-feeding her through an IV."

Bobby waited for Dr. Sequeira to leave before he spoke. His face smoldered in frustration from the long months of being denied visitation rights. What she had with him, any love, died that night, died eight months ago. Wilder lifted a hand to hush him, and Bobby shut his mouth, gritting his teeth, causing the muscles in his jaws to dance. She reached for her engagement ring on the nightstand and extended it toward him.

"I don't understand. Why are you doing this? Is it because you blame me? I didn't know that you were pregnant. My guess is that you didn't know either. I didn't know that they would come. I know you had this 'feeling', but I didn't think—"

She kept her hand extended—the two-carat diamond glinting against the light.

"Can you at least talk to me? Explain? It's over, just like that? Seven years together and no explanation? Nothing? I know that what you lost—"

"No, you don't," she said, words calm and deliberate. "You have no idea what I lost. You have no idea because you've got your cock and balls still dangling between your legs."

His eyes widened. He took off his glasses and paced the length of the room.

"What the hell has gotten into you? So, you hate all men now? I'm now in the category with those men that attacked us?"

"Men? Is that what you're calling them?" She laughed despite rage flooding her body. "I call them animals. They were animals, Bobby. Not men."

"You've never used such language with me, and this tone. It isn't you. You're...different. You've been...lifting weights?" His nose crunched making a face as he adjusted his glasses. Bobby inspected her arms like he didn't recognize her anymore. "This...isn't the Wilder I know. It isn't the promising doctor I love. You're not the only one who lost something that day. The entire event was traumatic for me, too."

"Had a lot of time to think. People change, especially being left for dead with my guts torn to shreds," she said. "There's nothing to explain, Bobby. You want some kind of long-winded song and dance? A discussion? Some big, dramatic drawn-out break up with pleading and tears? Don't think so. Don't have the energy to fight. Don't have the energy to talk about my feelings. Don't have the energy for couples counseling, all that nonsense I grew up hearing about. Psychobabble, horseshit that my mom is so good at spewing. This is what I need right now, and yes, women can lift weights, Bobby. They can learn to defend them- selves, too. I won't apologize for not being the vision of weakness you so loved about me. I am *not* that woman anymore."

"You're twisting my words," Bobby said through clenched teeth. "Wilder, this is simply not rational."

She felt her voice—felt its strength for the first time. After so long staying silent, it felt good to speak her mind.

"You don't get it? Tough," she grated, "All my life, I've done the right thing. I've done good things. I was the good daughter. I was the one that went to veterinary school, became a doctor. I've cared about the environment, global warming, climate change, animal cruelty, and people. Giving my time to soup kitchens, donating money to battered women's shelters—"

"And that's a bad thing? Those are the reasons why I love—"

"I've always put my needs last. That's all changed now. You damn right I'm not the same woman. I'm thinking about me from here on out. I'm thinking about what I want and what I need to do. And my plans, they don't include you. Now, please leave."

"Plans? What plans? What are you planning on doing? And what about our clinic?"

"Keep it. Pay me out. Take over my clients. Find a nice girl, get married, have babies since you've still got all your working parts," Wilder said bitterly.

"Now, that is *not* fair."

Sammy's voice returned to her mind, giving her an out, a chance to make things right again. Though reality had been shattered by the serpent, now a permanent, grotesque scar on her womb—a forever reminder.

"I'll be moving."

"Moving? Where?"

"None of your damn business."

Bobby strode toward her and snatched the two-carat diamond engagement ring.

He exhaled a gust of air, shoved the ring in his pocket, and stormed out, slamming the door behind him. Trauma and tragedy, Mother always said, often did two things to a relationship. It either brought people together, or it tore them apart. In most cases, however, the latter occurred.

As always, her mother, *the* Dr. Katrine Adele Friedrich, was painfully correct.

PART TWO

SIXTEEN
THE KILLER

LEARNING how to shoot a gun meant nothing if you didn't have access to one. Sammy learned this lesson when she was kidnapped, and now Von would have to reconsider whether she should arm herself. It was not like she'd forgotten how to shoot.

"You'll learn to shoot and defend yourself, and that's that. This isn't up for debate," Anton scolded her with firm conviction. "You're a Friedrich, Wilder. You and your sister will go to the range, and you'll learn how to shoot. My daughters will learn to defend themselves."

She only ever fired at the range with her father, but a paper target and the real thing were quite different. It couldn't be too difficult, especially with the steady hands she'd been gifted with. A family trait: aim for the heart and be cautious of the kickback. She never shook during the attack, not even after, when she lay in the hospital for months in total shock, staring at the snake scar on her stomach with a mixture of horror and fascination.

Of course, her hands never quaked through any of the murders, either.

That was what made it easy to perform surgery on herself.

It also helped that she'd performed hundreds of surgeries on animals. More dogs than cats, though she performed a C-section on a pig that had difficulty delivering her piglets. Her progress was poor after straining in labor for two days. The owner knew something was wrong. Despite the odds, Schlange delivered four healthy babies.

She had no idea that the emergency animal surgery would hit CNN, NBC, ABC, Fox, and hundreds of other smaller news outlets and papers across the nation. The media attention of course included mention of her father with pictures of the two of them side by side.

She wasn't sure what he'd say. Would he scoff and express embarrassment that he, the best neurosurgeon in his and everyone else's mind, was pictured side by side with his daughter, a lowly veterinarian? But she'd never forget his response.

"It looks like you delivered a handful of little piglets, didn't you?" her father had casually mentioned over family dinner. "They claim you broke records, how swiftly it was performed."

"Oh...I haven't paid much attention," she said dismissively. "It isn't brain surgery, but I had to act quickly, or the sow and her piglets would've died."

He'd sipped his wine and then said, "Don't underestimate that it takes more than steady hands; it requires a skilled doctor to do what you do."

It was the one moment in her career, her life, where she felt a little parental approval.

It had been years since she last saw her parents and little sister. When she left the hospital, she left a note asking them to take care of Sammy and informing them that she was leaving and would not be traceable. Schlange changed her name, number, and address. Time slipped by at a rapid pace yet provided ample opportunity for her to prepare. It changed her, as did her sister's experience.

Her chest tightened to the ache in her soul as buried emotions threatened to free themselves.

"Not now. Not this right now," she told herself, swallowing a knot in her throat.

Schlange broke out of her thoughts, the drafty motel air chilling her skin.

January was the coldest month in Florida, especially in Niceville. The city apparently lived up to its name as being one of the best places to live and raise a family in the Sunshine State. Schlange opened the drapes an inch or so, allowing the early morning sunlight to break inside and lift the gloom of the hotel room. But she was careful not to open the drapes too wide. It was the one thing she missed about her old lifestyle, though determination to complete her mission—no matter the cost—had erased old sentiments and comforts.

The all-too-familiar dark hotel rooms and closed blinds had become a depressing reality.

She admitted she missed her old life. Family. Friends. Career. The days when she didn't have to always look over her shoulder. But everything had changed for her, hadn't it? Since the attack, she didn't regret for a second leaving Bobby. He paid off her portion of the clinic while she sold the cabin that had been under her name. She'd saved enough money to live off of comfortably for the remainder of her life. Especially after the ten-million-dollar settlement she received once Dr. Anton Jörg Friedrich sued the clinic that performed her surgery.

"A skilled surgeon would've been able to save my daughter's uterus, save her from being infertile, and avoid surgical menopause. Dr. Damião Sequeira butchered my eldest child and took away the one thing she wanted the most: motherhood," her father said with conviction on the stand.

She'd never wanted the settlement money and still didn't.

What she wanted was to feel like a real woman again, instead of a gutted one.

She was grateful she had resources. Grateful that during the attack, the one thing she didn't lose was her sound mind and memory. While Zeus's sharp teeth ripped off Darren Fischer's mask, she paid attention to the smallest details. Wilder couldn't have identified Sean Martin among the dozens of brotherhood members linked to the underground sex ring without their Confederate flag tattoo. Without identifying marks, any one of them could've been the culprit.

But she remembered that exact tattoo was on Sean's neck.

There was a third one out there. The final man, the one that wore it on his right shoulder. She remembered seeing it when he stripped off his shirt during the attack as she'd told the Casper, Wyoming, detectives when she'd finally spoken to them.

"Thank you for your help in identifying Darren Fischer," Detective Tae Mun had said. He had a gentle touch. One that almost made her tell the truth.

"But...are you certain, Dr. Wilder, that you don't remember anything that can identify the other two men that were wearing ski masks?"

"No," she'd lied. "One had neck tattoos, and another one had one on his shoulder."

"That's quite broad. Not trying to give you a hard time, but anyone can have neck or arm tattoos, ma'am. In order to catch the men that did this to you, we need details. Did you see what the tattoos were? I know a lot was going on. But it would help us greatly if you could remember specifics."

"I'm...very sorry," she continued with this untruth and didn't know why. "Like I said, it was all a blur. I'm afraid my mother would call it 'a state of shock.'"

She figured at the time that her hint was enough for them to catch the other two men. The detectives and FBI would notice

Darren Fischer's distinctive tattoos and would also discover that there were only two other members with identical ink. When they didn't, she came to discover her own true intentions. Her mother would've explained that perhaps Von's subconscious didn't trust local law enforcement to deliver justice. Next, the psychologist would have reminded her that Von should be happy she could retire early and never have to work a day in her life again.

No, she never wanted the money. It never once brought her joy.

She did miss the log cabin she'd sold in Casper. She missed its large open windows and the perpetual fragrance from a collection of different tree species, all of which merged and wafted through the air, leaving behind traces of clean, green scent of spice, bark, and pine. In the spring and summer evenings, she would often leave the windows wide open. When the weather turned cold, she and Bobby would stoke a fire in the fireplace, sip red wine, and listen to classical music while they each read books.

Last time she'd checked on Facebook, Bobby had married Lisa, the vet technician. Lisa's banner picture on her profile page was of their adorable baby, with Bobby kissing one cheek and Lisa the other. It was a tiny, newborn girl swaddled in a knitted blanket, the perfect shade of bubble gum pink. Her tiny fingers poked out, and her face looked so peaceful as she slept with pouty lips that could make even the iciest hearts melt.

Seeing the picture several months ago sliced her open again. Once again, she was lying back down in the snow for what felt like an eternity. Frozen. She felt stranded like her spirit was cemented in some tortuous middle world. She stared at the couple, her fingers tracing the screen, lingering on the baby's peach cheeks. She imagined the softness, the sweet baby smell, a tender innocence just out of reach. She didn't cry as she thought she would. Instead, Von inhaled the pain, each breath pulsing with raw, searing intensity, like shards of glass in her lungs.

She had sworn she would fracture from it.

Each passing year the desire never dulled.

The sad longing for motherhood persisted.

The truth was she didn't choose her path.

The truth was her path had selected her.

Rising voices from the television jolted her back. She shook her head, warding away ghosts that still haunted her. The ghosts from her past must be left behind, but the beast inside her stirred. She took off her shirt, staring not at Dr. Wilder Agatha Friedrich but at Von Schlange.

Von's eyes returned to the scar. Studying it. The serpent was her true self now.

She turned up the television and immediately noticed the belly of the tall, lean Detective Nazario, who was speaking into the mic before a press conference. She was even more beautiful with her pregnancy glow than in all of the pictures and taekwondo videos Von had of her. Like the men on her list, Von had a folder on Nazario, too. A muscular and tall Supervising Special Agent, Blake Huxley, stood next to her. The federal agent had an intensity about him that made her pause.

"That's correct," Nazario answered a reporter. "I was asked by the FBI to partner up with Supervising Special Agent Huxley on the case. There have been multiple murders, as you all know. Darren Fischer, Sean Martin, and Walter Yang. We're still looking for the killer. Currently, we are thinking—" Nazario looked directly into the camera. It was as if the detective was looking right at Von. "Likely a male suspect, potentially an ex-Aryan member. We're thinking it's gang-related. Retaliation."

The detective's eyes shifted; she shuffled in place for an awkward beat.

She was lying through her teeth.

Von's mouth dropped. There were three victims she'd saved from the three men that she'd killed. They knew what she looked like and certainly knew the difference between a pussy and a cock. Why ought a man take credit for her work? Fury roiled and warred with another contradictory emotion—relief— perhaps? Ever since the surgery that had brutally gutted her female parts, she'd experienced mood swings, hot flashes, horrible night sweats, and renewed fury. A 'welcome to surgical menopause' that had imprisoned her by a gaggle of emotions. Until she cannibalized them, letting all her 'feeling' digest into a rage that would ultimately scorch the frightened little crybaby she used to be.

Von gripped the aluminum baseball bat and belted the bed.

Zeus lifted and then tilted his head.

She wasn't sure whether she was relieved that someone was covering up for her or worried over the FBI's motives. Von paced the room. Why were they lying? Left without answers or the time to continue watching the press conference, she turned off the television and hurled the remote across the room. It hit the wall, causing the batteries to fall out and clatter to the floor. Zeus padded towards her and licked her hand. Von apologized with a pet on his head.

Her earpiece came to life.

"What are you doing tomorrow? I need to see you," said the voice she recognized. It was him. Three doors down. So close, she could taste him. Adrenaline pumped through her body.

"C'mon, José, what about your wife? Is the divorce still going through? I mean, I don't understand why you came down here with her. First, you say you're leaving her, and then you bring her down here, knowing I live down here. For what? A romantic vacation? You need to make up your mind," said a woman.

When Estevan and his lover went down to the hot tub, she

was able to quietly sneak into the judge's hotel room. Estevan had left his wallet behind, giving her the chance to take pictures of his credit card information and the wallet's contents—anything that would help her access his bank account and free Estevan's wife. Then, she used the spy app on her phone to listen in on the judge's conversations.

His wife, Alisa Marie Estevan, had been admitted to a mental hospital on several occasions, orders issued by the judge himself. In medical documents that the judge gathered against his wife, words like "unstable," "suicidal," and "a harm to herself and others" surfaced. Though something wasn't right. Prior to the marriage, Alisa Marie Holton had a thriving career as an executive of a marketing firm. She'd graduated top of her class and had an MBA from Stanford. She had no prior mental health history, no criminal record, and grew up in a stable, loving Catholic home. Most of Alisa's successful career was easy to track and all over LinkedIn and the web.

However, her new history of mental health issues was just as easy to find.

In fact, they were posted on her Instagram, Facebook, and X accounts. It didn't seem like something a once-ambitious, yet private executive would blast on social media. Some of the posts were downright embarrassing. Sharing things that went a little too far, and it surprised Von that such posts weren't banned or taken down by various sites. Thoughts of hurting herself amid excessive gushing of José and how "amazingly supportive" he'd been.

How he'd helped her through her "fragile mental state."

In Los Angeles, she posed as a private investigator and managed to get a hold of one of Alisa's friends. It was easier than she'd expected to gather intel on the judge and his wife. Piecing the puzzle together wasn't hard. The writing was on the wall, but Von had to be sure. Soon after their wedding, Alisa stopped working, gave up her career entirely. At first, Von thought that maybe Alisa stopped working to raise children, but the couple had none. During the marriage of ten years, Alisa never once held a job. Stella Dwyer, one of her former co-workers and best friends, said Alisa cut out all outside contact with friends.

"It's José, I know it is," Stella said with conviction. "She was so strong-willed and sharp. She'd never think of hurting herself. Her friends were everything to her. She had this huge social circle, made more money than some of the men at the firm...I mean she was the head executive there. It's like he's brainwashing her or something."

"Did she try contacting you, or did you eventually reach her?" Von had asked.

"Once. I called, and she finally picked up the phone. I asked if we could go to dinner. She was whispering her answers. It didn't sound like the Alisa I knew—the Alisa who kicked ass, ran a whole marketing agency. She said something about José giving her a weekly allowance, some bullshit about it helping her learn financial discipline. She turned down dinner, said he had her on a strict diet."

"Classic controlling narcissistic abuser," Von said, reciting the terminology from having a mother who was a well-known psychologist, "keeping her isolated."

"Like her social media accounts, he took over all of the bank accounts, too," Stella said.

"How do you know this, if she's cut off from friends?" Von prodded.

"I visited her at the mental hospital. José made sure he had the medical documentation, psychologist testimony, and evals as evidence that Alisa was mentally unfit to handle her finances. When we spoke during her last stay at the mental hospital, she explained it all: the manipulation, the paper trail, the money. And this is one of the smartest women I've ever known."

"I'm here to help Alisa." Von gripped her hand. "You have my word."

What was most troubling was what the FBI didn't have on their list.

The judge wasn't just an abusive husband. He had partaken in the brotherhood's sex ring, which explained why so many members weren't convicted or received lenient sentences.

Von could still see each girl on the witness stand.

"Can you or can you not help us identify the members of the sex ring?" Grilled Pilar "The Pit Bull" Velázquez, the defense attorney from hell.

Like Sammy, each girl stared down at their hands.

"Are they in this room, or have you been lying—"

"Objection, your honor," Mr. Hale stood up, the prosecutor who looked a little too insecure through the proceedings. "Badgering the witness. There's a difference between being frightened and lying."

"Overruled," Judge Estevan said, turning to one of the girls. Now Von remembered a tiny detail she'd forgotten. The way one of them looked at Estevan, swallowed a breath, tears crawling quietly down her face, hands shaking. It was a look of recognition as if the judge had paid a good price to have sex with her against her will, and she was too afraid of the judge's powers to say a word about it.

Yes, that's why Darren Fischer received light sentences for multiple convictions, such as five years for dogfighting, and wasn't convicted on any sex trafficking charges.

"You'll not scare me into silence, you piece of shit," Von swore. Zeus lifted his head and looked curiously at her. "We're getting a very bad man," she told him.

Von wasted no time and speedily logged online to see if there was a way to access Judge Estevan's bank account, knowing it would be next to impossible without help. She was no hacker but wished she were, desperate to find a way to help Alisa. When she'd begun gathering her *list*, she didn't expect she would discover who the actual victims were.

She had grown attached to each of them, formed a bond that couldn't be broken. And then an urge overtook her, one that saw the bigger picture. Take a life to save a life.

She jumped at the sound of an email alert that shouldn't have come in. At first, she assumed it was spam. The email was addressed to Von. No one had her email address, especially anyone who knew her by her original given name, Dr. Wilder Friedrich. She lowered the volume on the wireless Bluetooth device connected to her computer and Estevan's conversation.

The sender...Black Dragon?

Who was Black Dragon? An undercover federal agent?

Von's heart sped, fingers hovered over the keys, and then she clicked open.

SEVENTEEN

THE HUNT FOR VICTIM FOUR

Sender: blackdragon6@dragon6.com
Subject: Done

*How's Miami? I see you've been quite busy, given I've tracked
your moves. Some road trip you've been on. You thought if you
could take a picture of dickhole's debit card that you could do this
solo? Don't worry, I'm here. Several bank accounts will be
emailed to you. Click the link, and the username/password will
automatically populate. How's this possible? I've embedded
myself onto your computer. LOL! There's no way to find out
how, so don't even bother. What matters, dickface no longer has
access to his own accounts. Wifey does. All she needs is the login
and passwords. Easy peasy lemon squeezy. FYI – the Feds know
about what I did, but the dummies still can't figure out my real
name.*

Stay safe, okay?
Your #1 fan.
~BD

P.S. That detective and that big ass FBI agent did a video inter-
view with me. Not about you. About Zeus and my time with him.
I don't drink no more, but I faked it. They thought I was
hammered. Wasn't hard to get myself to cry about that shit in
Afghanistan. Now those tears were real.

HER PHONE CHIMED A FEW TIMES, signaling that more
emails were coming in, just as Black Dragon said. She tested the
links. Each automatically logged her into several bank accounts
stocked with millions. The name on the account, though, had
been changed. Her heart hammered as she paused, listening via
Bluetooth to the conversation happening a couple of doors
down.

"Your wife, José," a woman's voice hissed in Von's ear. "I
want her gone."

Lips smacked. They were kissing again.

"Don't worry about that crazy bitch. I'm already taking care
of it. What do you think is happening right now?" Estevan
responded. "I'm getting rid of her—for good. Suicide is a nasty
thing when it comes to mental health."

Laughter and more kisses filled her Bluetooth earpieces as
she listened in.

She focused back on her computer screen. Fear that she
might be too late coursed through her. She'd saved the account
info on a separate document, along with a new complex password and then reread the email one last time.

Black Dragon? My number one fan? WTF!

Von turned off her computer. Afghanistan? Answering
questions about Zeus?

"Motherfucker!" Von raked her hands through her hair and
paced the room.

A year ago, Von had turned to an unlikely source for help.

She kept running into a veteran marine honorably discharged who'd spent most of his days at the library. He loved her tattoos, but especially took to Zeus. It was like her dog knew the veteran, and that caught her by surprise.

Von recalled how she got to talking to Jefferson. "I can learn just about anything. Master most things I put my mind to, especially computers," he said matter-of-factly. It wasn't a brag. It came out more like a boring truth he'd accepted about himself.

Von laughed. "I've got a dare for you. I bet you can't hack into the FBI's accounts."

The soldier rolled his eyes.

"Try me," he'd said. "You looking for someone?"

"Several someones. They're all bad news. Evil. When I say evil, in no uncertain terms am I exaggerating. Not so sure one of our country's heroes should be getting involved," Von said, then narrowed her eyes at him. "Don't I know you? Haven't we met before?"

She knew she'd seen him once before but couldn't place him.

Jefferson Pearce shrugged. "I got one of those faces," he said. "All us soldiers look alike."

"You look like someone...a soldier that tried to kill himself," Von stopped herself from giving away more. When she was Dr. Wilder Friedrich, she'd saved Zeus from his former handler. Usually she could remember names, but it was a fog in the void. All she remembered was rushing to save Zeus's life. "He used to be Zeus's handler."

"We've had quite a few bomb-sniffing German Shepherds, trained war dogs that deployed with us," Jefferson admitted. "Honestly, they all look like your dog. Just like in uniform, we all kinda look alike, don't we?"

Jefferson laughed and Von gave him a tight, wary smile.

Von had been skeptical initially, but Jefferson's expertise was far more than some research skill. The former soldier either partly lied to Von about the extent of what he was capable of behind a computer screen or understated his own abilities. Though, as much as he'd helped her, she knew that she couldn't keep relying on Jefferson for his help. Especially given that Jefferson had been discharged from the military due to his mental health. What would happen to him if he was caught? He'd committed a federal crime, one that would even be classified as a terrorist cyber-attack.

When she finally asked Jefferson about Judge Jose Estevan, the twenty-five-year-old baby-faced Mexican-American former Marine and trained sniper, he immediately had dirt on the judge, as if he had been expecting the question.

"You know he lives in Beverly Hills?" Jefferson had said.

Von nodded, and the ex-Marine continued.

"But...he'll be vacationing in Miami for New Year's. With more than just his wife."

"That doesn't surprise me," Von said.

"His wife's trapped, needs a whole lotta help. I'm not too sure what you're up to," Jefferson had claimed back then, but now that Von recollected the conversation something in his face told her he knew more than he'd ever admit to. "I dunno what it is you're planning, but if I can help in any way...haven't had this much excitement since Afghanistan."

But he had known, hadn't he? Von's gut told her that Jefferson Pearce had lied to her face. Somewhere inside, he got off on helping her out like it was a big middle finger to the establishment, to the rules, and to the country he vowed to serve and had once almost cost him his life and sanity.

They initially started talking about the book Jefferson checked out at the library, which an advanced computer programming and coding book. She quickly learned that he was a bit of an undiscovered genius in computers, coding, research, and the underground world of hacking. She'd given him instructions to dig up information on a list of names, and he completed his assignment at a speed that almost scared her off her mission. She didn't think he could actually break into the FBI's top-secret files.

Now, he'd broken through personal and professional barriers.

Jefferson was *Blackdragon6*.

Jefferson Pearce was that baby-faced Lance Corporal who had been in the truck, his eyes swollen and raw like he'd been punched repeatedly by sorrow. Smelling like booze. He might've sobered up now, but he drank back then. She could still smell the whisky. He was the same soldier who'd unsuccessfully tried to end his life, had it not been for Zeus remembering his training. As Dr. Wilder, she'd taught him "gun-to-head." Knowing when a soldier was about to kill themselves and designed to prevent it from occurring. There had been numerous deployments back then. The anti-suicide safety training was uniquely her idea, a program that only her veterinary clinic—and specifically she—had developed. She trained service dogs to be paired with soldiers.

And then, two things hit her from the email: *Ace* and *Easy peasy lemon squeezy*.

She remembered her tattooist giving her the hacker's email and recalled Ace's instructions with those exact words. Jefferson didn't just ask her about her tattoo or her "cool dog" for the hell of it. It was all a part of his plan. He was not only Black Dragon but Ace as well, the hacker who'd helped her install listening spyware on her phone. How many more aliases did the soldier have?

But then, hadn't she been hiding who she was as well—for better reasons, right? She tried to make excuses for her actions, to make herself better, more justified, but at the end of the day, Jefferson Pearce was scarred like Dr. Wilder Friedrich. The difference between her and Jefferson: she sought revenge, while he seemed to want to help out of boredom. He was a thrill-seeker who, upon retiring from the Marines, began dabbling in the dark web, hacking stuff for people for cash while he'd been collecting disability for his PTSD.

Jefferson was dancing on dangerous ground, not realizing what he'd gotten himself into.

She recalled having to meet up covertly at the library, coffee shops, and diners.

Then, she started to notice an SUV that kept showing up.

"Were you careful?" she asked when they met at a Denny's.

"Of course, why you asking like that? You know I take the bus, right? Been taking it since my license was revoked—second DUI," Jefferson had said. "Girl, you're acting kinda strange. What up, Von? Think we're being followed or some shit?"

Von spotted two suspicious men in the same black SUV. She recalled seeing them at the library, twice near her apartment, and almost every time she met up with Jefferson. At first, she thought she was being paranoid, but it couldn't be a coincidence. She knew it then and now. She wondered if the Aryan Brotherhood was still following her. She had managed to evade detection recently. But why hadn't they struck? Were they biding their time, or was it the FBI tracking her movements now?

With each passing day, gnawing uncertainty intensified— was her time running out?

"Hell yeah, I think we're being followed. Look, I can't involve you anymore, man. I just can't. We need to terminate."

"But I'm already involved. Come on, what're they gonna do?" Jefferson rolled his eyes.

"Many, many things, Jefferson," Von hissed. "Bad things. Murder being one."

"I can defend myself." Jefferson laughed. "Kinda was my specialty when I was enlisted, you know. I was a sniper, remember?"

"Been planning this for too long for you to threaten our mission and go rogue. Start playing GI Joe. Shoot-em-up. This isn't Iraq or Afghanistan, Jefferson. These people, hell, there's an entire network of these fuckers—"

"Same with the Taliban."

"It's a whole lot different this time. A military operation that's backed up by your country versus illegal domestic activity that can put us in jail for life—two totally different things, Lance Corporal. Two very, very different situations. They know who you are. Guarantee they know your capabilities. They've seen us together. We must be strategic. I need to cut you loose. You're a liability now. I pulled you into this and I shouldn't have."

"I ain't stoppin' now. No way in hell. I'm almost done with the list. There ain't no way we can stop now," Jefferson said, then pleaded, "I can do this. I know I can. I'll be safe. Look, the Marines cut me out for the same reasons. Liability. Don't do the same. Promised you the list of those dirtbags didn't I? I need to do this. Okay, maybe at first, I kinda thought it was a fun thing to do—I get bored. I hack shit. I drink. Sometimes I like fucking with people for no real reason."

"Which is why we should stop. 'Cause these assholes aren't someone you just fuck with."

"Dude, it's deeper than that. Zeus saved my life, and it was your training, Dr. Wilder, that made it possible. And then you saved his life—"

"It's Von," she interrupted, hating the sound of her former name. "And that...it was a long time ago, alright?"

"For my soul...for my fucking soul, I have to do this. I *need* this. Please, Von," he'd begged, correcting himself and addressing her as the person she'd now become. *"Please."*

Von swore to herself, raking a hand over her face. Why did she cave into those big brown eyes of his? Why couldn't she have found an ordinary, reasonable hacker? Some old, middle-aged bald man with a beer belly and not some twisted genius ex-Marine who was now risking his life for a second time. He'd been trying to live his life straight since being medically discharged. He was trying to get off disability and get a civilian job until she came along and pulled him into her dark world of vengeance.

How long could Jefferson continue to deceive the Feds? Even with the FBI monitoring Jefferson, he might not back off. When it came to money, people were weak. Many would do just about anything for a large lump sum of cold, hard cash—José Estevan's preferred motivation. This wasn't a video game or a fun hacking joke. What Jefferson was now involved in was something that could kill him, and anyone associated with him. Von had felt zero guilt or remorse for her mission. Until now. To have involved a young twenty-something former soldier with his mind all scrambled from war and leading him down the wrong path. It was as bad as that fiery agonizing pain in her gut from being gutted and stitched up like a stuffed animal.

The former Marine was going down a path that could lead to his death. Could she live with herself knowing he'd been a hero and survived the war, only to come home and get killed by a white supremacist group or put in prison because of her?

If something happened to Jefferson Pearce, she'd never be able to forgive herself.

She packed her things and signaled for Zeus.

José would find out quickly that he'd been locked out of his bank accounts. She didn't have much time. Von had to pull this one off quickly and flawlessly. The FBI would figure out soon that one of the prominent judges on the list connected to the other murders was the honorable José Estevan.

Because they'd figure out the connection to the brotherhood's sex ring.

"Yo, listen to this." Jefferson leaned in. "Walter Yang, the Chinese businessman in Boston, millionaire—he got all these domestic violence charges dropped."

"And? How's Yang in Boston connected with Judge Estevan in Los Angeles or associated with the brotherhood?"

"Judge Estevan, he had a friend he went to law school with —a judge in Boston that pulled strings, got all of Yang's charges dropped, and expunged!" Jefferson had said.

Von found pictures of Estevan arm-in-arm with the Boston judge having fun at a bar over a couple of beers. These images, easily found via a Google search, meant nothing to the public but made a lot of pieces connect for her. According to the news, Detective Nazario and Agent Huxley were close. In fact, the press conference was in Boston—a twenty-one-hour drive away or a short three-hour flight.

They were on her trail, and damn it, they were close.

Von pulled her baseball cap tight over her eyes and kept her head down. Zeus followed her out the door. Thank God José and his lover hadn't left their room yet. Once in her car, she gunned it to José Estevan's luxury beach house. It didn't take long to pull up to a gorgeous, modern oceanfront abode. It was listed at 6,612 square feet with six bedrooms and six and a half bathrooms. Von noticed that the square compound had floor-to-ceiling windows. In fact, the entire beach house was made mostly of glass, including the balcony with its black railings. Everything about it screamed uber-chic. She parked a couple of blocks down the street and walked the rest of the way carrying a duffle bag large enough for essential items.

Zeus walked a few feet ahead, sniffing the ground. As she

drove up, Von noticed a Miami police car parked within walking distance of the beach house. Her heart quickened. The knot of tension tightened in her stomach. As she passed the empty police cruiser, her awareness of her surroundings heightened. Concerned, she approached the house with care, every step deliberate and cautious.

Taking her chances, Von tried the front door. It was unlocked, likely left that way by the cop who'd parked his cruiser in the driveway. She stepped into the massive luxury home, finding it just as spectacular inside. The white furniture, highlighted with wood trim, matched the modern aesthetic of the place. This style was further accentuated by glossy wooden ceilings, marble floors, and recessed lighting throughout. The living room overlooked a large rectangular pool, the color of deep cobalt with lights embedded in the walls, creating a watery glow.

No one was downstairs. But she heard two voices coming from upstairs: one belonging to a man, the other to a woman. Adrenaline rushed through her. Von hoped the woman was Alisa. In the kitchen, she noticed that the refrigerator had been chained shut. In the living room, there were handcuffs connected to the sofa's railing. The remote was pinned against the eighty-inch television mounted on the wall, and what was playing shocked her.

The woman looked to be in her late-twenties, early-thirties. Von was good with faces and was certain she didn't recognize her as one of the victims of the sex trafficking ring operation that had been so thoroughly researched. Her voice also matched the woman in the hotel room. Von put on latex disposable gloves and grabbed the remote. She pressed pause and suspected that the judge was a "collector." There must be more videos some-where of underage girls.

A single, half-empty glass of water sat on an end table. Was

Alisa made to sit here watching her husband with his lover, handcuffed and without food? It made her stomach turn to think that Alisa endured this torture for hours.

Zeus sniffed and paused at the staircase. Von pointed to the second floor, and Zeus rushed up the stairs, Von following. Voices began to draw closer with each step.

"Ten minutes away?" a man said. His accent a mix of East Coast and Spanish. "*Bueno*. The note's been written. She'll have killed herself by the time you get here."

The man laughed, and Von could hear Alisa cry.

"Please don't do this. I'll leave. I'll disappear. We can get a divorce. I've signed the prenup. He can keep everything. Why's he doing this?" she sobbed.

"Because you know too much."

"I won't say anything—"

"You're a liability. Now, shut your face or I paint the walls with your brains."

A call announced itself, sounding like it was put on speaker.

"Officer Alberto Montoya here, there has been a suicide," he said. "White female, Alisa Estevan. Judge's wife has shot herself at their beach house off Venetian drive."

"Copy that. Patrol units and ME are both delayed, sir. Thirty minutes out."

"No rush," he said, tone clipped as he ended the call.

Alisa's cries were muffled, as though she was being gagged with the barrel of the gun.

Zeus had three steps to scale before he reached the room.

Von pushed her body, taking the long winding stairway two at a time. In less than five seconds Alisa Estevan would've committed suicide according to the local news and the truth of her murder might never be revealed. Von was almost at the top of the stairs. Hoping she wasn't too late, she counted to herself as if each step brought her closer to Alisa, closer to life over death.

Five

Four

Three

Two

One...

EIGHTEEN

THE FOURTH VICTIM

ZEUS REACHED THE TOP STEP, then launched, and Officer Montoya let out a yelp. The gun went off, and the crash of shattering glass—without a cry from either Zeus or Alisa—meant neither was hit.

Von let out a breath she didn't realize she'd been holding.

She reached the top of the stairs. The large bedroom had a fantastic ocean view with what had been wall-to-wall glass before parts of it fractured. Gusts of the Atlantic air swept through the room. Officer Montoya was on the ground. Shards covered his navy uniform. Zeus stood over him, teeth on his throat.

Dropping her duffle, Von's heart thumped hard with a rush of fear as she glimpsed Alisa's skeletal form. Curled into a tiny ball on the bed, Alisa wound her frail arms around her knees. Her skin was sallow, cheeks sunken. Alisa looked nothing like her former executive profile picture on her LinkedIn page. She was emaciated. Her cheekbones were morbidly visible. Dark, ashen circles framed eyes no longer sparkling emeralds, but dulled to the color of mold. Her protruding collarbones and rib cage—discernible even under her shirt—were evidence of starvation. Not days, but weeks. Maybe months.

"Alisa...can you hear me? You, okay?" Von asked quickly.

Alisa recoiled, as a mixture of shock and fear appeared on her sunken face.

She shook her head.

"I won't let them hurt you, I promise."

Officer Montoya struggled to get up from the ground. He pounded his fists on Zeus's back, trying to get him off. Montoya's gun was just out of reach. He scooted forward, inching closer. Zeus clamped tight around his throat, and blood trickled down the cop's neck. Montoya tried to hit Zeus again, this time nudging him loose enough to reach for the gun. Von dove to the floor and grabbed the gun right in time.

Officer Montoya escaped Zeus's stranglehold and was swiftly back on his feet. He launched for Von, and they grappled over the Glock 22, standard issue service pistol. Montoya managed to strike her jaw in the process, but she threw a right hook hard enough to break his nose, spraying blood. Zeus bit into Montoya's hand as it grabbed at the weapon. Montoya yelped and stumbled back. Von wrangled control, fingers wrapped around the grip. She backed up, giving herself room. Montoya rushed toward her.

Von's heart steadied. To hell with not using a gun. *Thanks for the lessons, Father.*

She aimed for the center of his chest, given he was not wearing a bulletproof vest, and fired three times. He staggered backward against the glass wall. Von recalled her time at the shooting range, aimed slightly higher, and the fourth bullet landed right between the eyes. Brains splattered against the glass window as his body slid down.

Von aimed at the partially shattered glass, and the fifth

bullet collapsed the wall, sending broken glass and Montoya's lifeless body cascading to the ground below.

She hadn't planned on killing anyone other than the judge, let alone a cop. But did she have a choice? Besides, Montoya was dirty. Would the Feds and the Miami police department side with her? Likely not.

"Montoya..." José Estevan's voice boomed from the first floor. The thud of his footsteps drew closer as he ascended the staircase.

Von rose to her feet and grabbed the baseball bat and rope from her duffle bag.

She took the rope and worked quickly; she'd already prepared the noose in advance. At the end of it was a hook, which she preferred instead of a knot that might come undone. She secured the end of the rope around the black metal railing that once held the window in place.

Von hid behind the door. "Stay under the covers," she whispered to Alisa.

"What the hell!" Estevan bellowed as he entered the bedroom, glaring at the shattered glass wall, its shards across the marble floor.

"Hol ihn, Junge!" Von screamed. *"Get him, boy!"*

Zeus ran at the judge, leapt, catching enough air to clamp down on José's upper arm. Von readied herself, swung the aluminum bat, and kneecapped him. He screamed, stumbling backward onto the ground.

Von dropped the bat, picked up the gun, and leveled it at the judge.

Alisa poked out from under the covers.

Estevan moaned in pain, gulped and looked up at her. "Sweetheart..."

Tears inched down Alisa's face, mingling with mucus from her nose.

"Why not let me walk away and get a divorce?" she screamed at him. "Why force me to watch? Why the torture? You had some cop try and kill me, make it look like a suicide? For what reason, José?"

"She's lying. She's mentally unstable," he sputtered. "My wife...is experiencing another delusion. Officer Montoya was here on a wellness checkup and nothing more."

"Get your hands up!" Von yelled, and the judge did as he was told. "Where are the other videos?"

"Who the hell are you?" José snarled. "Maybe you're fine killing a cop, but you wouldn't be stupid enough to kill a well-known judge, would you? Name what you need legally, and I'll pull every string you can imagine. You go away quietly, and we pretend none of this happened."

Von strode towards José and shoved the gun roughly against his head. "Where're the other videos? You having sex with underage girls? I know you got them."

"I have no idea what you're talking about," the judge sneered.

"Walk," Von ordered.

The judge struggled to his feet and shuffled toward the smashed wall of glass as Von kept the gun aimed at his head. She picked up the rope.

"I'm helping..." Alisa said. She got up from the bed and scurried towards them.

"Stay out of this, Alisa. Keep your hands clean," Von responded.

"I need to do this," Alisa cried. "Please."

Von handed her the gun. "Keep it pointed at his head. Don't shoot. A bullet is too easy. He doesn't deserve a quick death."

"I love you, sweetheart," José begged. "Think about what you're doing. You're not well. Don't listen to this crazy woman.

She's totally unhinged. Can't you see that? You can't possibly take direction from a cop killer?"

"No one is ordering me to do anything anymore. All I have to do is pull the trigger and plead insanity." Alisa laughed madly. "And a jury will believe me, thanks to you."

"Please...whoever you are," José turned to Von. "I can help you. Let's sit down and talk this out."

"I don't need your help. I'm not here for me. I'm here for Alisa. I'm here for Sammy and all the other girls you victimized," Von said. A sudden flicker of recognition sparked in Estevan's eyes. For a moment, they were back in the courtroom.

Von would never forget how the judge had glared down at her and her parents from the position of authority as he gave the verdict. There'd be no official charges brought upon Darren Fischer and the other men for their alleged involvement in the sex ring. Sammy, along with the other minors associated, had been too scared to tell the full truth, destroying the prosecutor's case and strengthening the judge's ability to abuse victims using his power of authority.

Alisa wiped her face, but the tears were no longer there. Strength and determination shone on her features. "You love the control. That's all you love. What you did to those girls... what you did to me? The way you paid everyone off to keep quiet. I'm not your victim anymore, José."

Alisa trained the gun on her husband. Von took the noose and looped it over his head and around his neck. She secured it until it was tight, making him gasp and whimper.

"Asking you again. Where are the videos?" Von demanded.

She maneuvered him towards the edge, the rush of the ocean below a reminder of just how high they were. No one would survive the fall.

"Okay...okay, it's in the cabinet, under the television," he choked out, as Von pulled the rope tighter. His face turned burgundy.

"Locked safe. Combination is 80-12-40. Please, let's negotiate..."

"Negotiate?" Alisa looked crazed now. *"Negotiate, José?"*

"Sweetheart...Alisa...I love you...please..."

Alisa's jaws clenched. Her finger tightened on the trigger. Sweat trickled down her brows.

"Give me the gun," Von ordered Alisa. "You're no killer. You've got your future ahead of you. C'mon, Alisa...the gun."

"I have no life. He's made sure of it. He's ruined everything, and I...God, I let him." Alisa walked closer until the barrel of the gun was pressed against José's cheek.

"You'll have a new life, Alisa, I promise you. You need to trust me. Gimme the gun."

After a long beat, Von was awash with relief as Alisa surrendered the weapon and turned her attention to José. Had the judge given Darren Fischer the sentence he deserved, Von would've never been attacked. Maybe she'd have a five-year-old child and perhaps another little one, too. Von had always wanted at least two kids.

"The jury's in, your honor," Von said.

"No...no, please...don't do this! Please!" The judge shrieked in terror.

"Rot in hell," Alisa croaked, her breath dry and harsh.

"Let a monster like you go free," Von sneered, ignoring the judge's cries. "I don't think so."

———

"There are four accounts in total. Checking, savings, and two offshore accounts in the Cayman Islands. They're all yours now

—all under your name," Von explained as she and Alisa hovered over her laptop in Alisa's SUV. They sat in the parking lot in front of her motel room.

Alisa had packed quickly and followed Von's rental car.

"There's at least ten million between all the accounts. I did a little number crunching."

"Oh my God...really? How on Earth did you...They're really under my name? Why...why are you helping me? Who are you?" Alisa gasped.

"Von Schlange."

"Serpent?" Alisa translated.

"*Du sprichst Deutsch?*" Von asked if Alisa spoke German and Alisa nodded.

They began conversing. Zeus lifted his head as if he understood.

"That folder you left behind. Did you leave it for the cops? I took a look inside, and there's so much I didn't know about José. I knew some things, like the sex ring. I overheard him talking about it. He threatened that if I said a word to anyone, he'd have me killed. I had...I had a gut feeling about this vacation," Alisa recounted. "How do you know so much about my hus—José?"

"I got my sources." Von paused and snapped her fingers at Zeus, knowing he didn't care to sit in an idle vehicle for long stretches. He nudged his way forward until her hand scratched that sensitive spot behind his right ear.

"As far as my reasons, well, they're personal." Von drew a breath. "Let's just say Zeus and I both have a good idea of what it's like to have survived trauma. Remember, you're no longer a victim, Alisa. You're a survivor. You've got all the accounts and passwords. I suggest you change the passwords again. Make sure it's complicated and at least sixteen characters or longer. Also, change your phone number the second you have a chance."

Alisa began to cry.

"What if the cops or the FBI find me and start asking questions? What do I do? Say?"

"You've done nothing wrong and nothing illegal. You were psychologically manipulated, emotionally abused, starved, held prisoner. Need I go on? Has he ever hit you?"

"Never physical, no," Alisa's voice quivered as she slouched over her folded hands, biting a fingernail.

"But he did enough damage," Von noted. "If the detectives and the FBI track you down and ask questions, which I'm certain they will, then you tell the truth. Simple as that."

"They'll ask questions about you. What you look like and what happened and all that. What do I say? It'll sound crazy. This tattooed stranger, a small woman with a mean-looking German Shepherd, killed my husband and a dirty cop, and I'd like to thank her? As crazy as it sounds, it's the truth. I know I can't begin to repay you monetarily for what you've done; there simply are no words, and thanking you sounds trite. You have no idea...I owe you my life, and I'd like to transfer a million to you for saving my life."

"You owe me nothing. You don't even have to thank me, and I don't want your money. Don't need it. All I ask is that you get it together. Never ever let a man control you again, manipulate you. Get your life back and live it." Von's voice cracked.

Von's phone chimed. She had an email under her serpent identity and wondered if it was Jefferson playing games again. But when she glanced down, her heart stopped.

Subject: Little Sis in Boston

Sammy? How did she get her email? She was in Boston? Did she think Von was still there? It'd been five years since she'd spoken to her sister and parents. If it were indeed from Sammy, she'd have to wait—Alisa couldn't be there when she read it. Her little sister reminded Von of what was possible—survival. If

Sammy could get through horrific abuse, having been forced into a life of sex trafficking for two years after her kidnapping, Alisa could also live to become stronger after her ordeal.

"Do you need to get that?" Alisa asked timidly.

Von shook her head no and faced her again. "You've got your entire life ahead of you."

Alisa threw her spaghetti arms around Von and hugged her tightly.

Von found herself hesitating to return the embrace, settling for a pat on Alisa's back.

"You better go. There's a lot for you to sort out and enough money for you to disappear."

"Whatever you plan on doing...please be safe." Alisa pressed her face against Von's shoulder, her muffled words blurring into a sob.

"Get this SUV outta here. Fast. Either give it away or dump it—five-o's crawling everywhere," Von said, eyes scanning the street from the passenger seat. "And lose the guilty face. You've got nothing to be guilty about. *I* killed that cop. And your piece-of-shit husband. Not you."

Von gave Alisa a faint smile, opened the passenger door, and watched her disappear into the night before returning to the motel room with Zeus at her heels. It'd been an hour since she'd left José's vacation home. They would need to remain mobile. Staying at the motel was too risky. She sat at the edge of the bed while an exhausted Zeus lay at her feet. In German, she cooed that he did a good job as she ran her fingers down his back.

Zapped of energy, Zeus closed his eyes and was asleep within seconds.

Von took a deep breath and checked her email.

The address was indeed from Sammy's personal account.

Subject: Little Sis in Boston

Wilder,

*I went to your tattoo artist Tommy and not to get a tattoo. I heard
you went there, and I've been trying to find you for a while.
OMG, girl, I can't picture you with a tattoo! Tommy was nice
enough to hook me up with Ace. Please don't be mad, but Ace
helped me find you. Ace gave me your email and said you're in
Boston but gave me nothing else. I've been here for about a week
now and will be here for another three weeks, taking some time
for myself. Took me some time to get up the nerve to write this
email. Please, I want to see you, Wilder. Please. It's been so long,
and so much has happened. I really, REALLY regret ever
pushing you away.*

*Mom and Dad don't know I'm here. They don't know that I
tracked you down. I don't even know your number or where you
are exactly. Please, will you come meet me? My number is still
the same. I'll be waiting anxiously for your call.*

I love you, Wild. I miss my big sister.
Sammy

Von covered her mouth with her hand as her stomach
twisted. She *was* in Boston—past tense— and wasn't about to
make the twenty-hour drive back up north. Now was the worst
time to meet up with Sammy. She had never seen her as Von
Schlange. What would she think of her big sister now? The ex-
doctor. The ex-good-girl.

She lay on the bed and reread the email a few more times to
herself. The time stamp on the email revealed that it was sent
yesterday at 8:30 a.m.

Von's fingers hovered over Sammy's number.

I can't. Not now, Sammy. Not now.

Von squeezed her eyes shut and hit her head with a fist.

There was a time when she would have dropped everything at a second's notice to see her baby sister. Now? Now she couldn't pull herself away from her mission, and it made her angry. That she couldn't stop. Not even her sister's heartfelt pleas could sway Von's stubborn resolve.

Suddenly, her phone rang. It had never rung before—no one had the number. Could it be Jefferson? Could he've given it to Sammy? She pulled the mobile from her pocket and stared at it. It rang several times, stopped, then started again. Von took a deep breath, pressed the call button, and put the receiver to her ear without saying a word.

A strange, machine-like voice answered.

The robotic cadence spoke German.

"Ich nehme ein Leben für ein Leben auch," it said. *"I take a life for a life, too."*

Von's stomach tightened. *"Wer ist das?"* she asked. *"Who is this?"*

The altered voice returned in its eerie baritone. Scrambled, part machine, part human, and now in English, he continued, "The last man on your list."

"Wild? W-Wild..." Sammy's voice broke into a sob.

Von stood, clutching at the device pinned against her ear. "S-Sammy?"

"The Schultz brothers...Butch and Josh!" Sammy screamed.

A sound of a loud smack caused Von to jump.

The robotic voice returned. "This is for my men," it said.

BANG!

"SAMMY!" Von screamed.

"Der Soldat ist der nächste," the voice warned. *"The soldier's next."*

She collapsed at the edge of the bed, her head slumped heavily into her hands. For the first time since the attack that cost her a child and her womb, Von wept. It wasn't a soft or faint cry but a soul-shattering, anguished sob. Her blind fight for justice had now cost her the one person she loved more than anyone.

It felt as if she'd taken another life. Only this time, the victim was her sister.

NINETEEN
THE DETECTIVE

BRIGHT GOLD BLOOMED through the bedroom windows, painting the walls with winter morning colors of saffron, blush, and butter. Nazario should've been exhausted, but a sudden burst of energy sped through her as if she'd mainlined coffee.

She looked at the clock. It was five-thirty in the morning.

Obsessed with the case, Nazario thought about Sammy's photo. It had been bugging her, her mind rewinding to just the night before, scanning each folder in order: Darren Fischer, Sean Martin, and now Walter Yang. But why was Sammy's picture behind Mia's in Yang's dossier? It meant something—other than Sammy being one of the misfortunate young women Walter had purchased through the brotherhood. The picture was stacked at the front for a reason. Why though? Especially given the Chinese businessman had been with dozens of young women after Sammy was rescued, many of them underage.

She knocked onto the adjoining room door. When Huxley didn't respond, she barged in.

"Hey...what's wrong?" Huxley searched her face. He was in nothing but tight briefs that hugged his tree-trunk thighs and rock-hard glutes.

She gulped and suddenly found herself unable to look away. Nazario raked his body with her eyes. Heat rose to her face, through her body.

"You're such an...early riser." She blushed, suddenly aware of the innuendo.

Huxley shot her a sly smile.

"I didn't hear you knock." He put on his jeans, arms and chest flexing with each movement, causing his muscles to ripple.

Dear God. Nazario rubbed her temples, fighting a carnal urge.

"Something is spinning in that brain," Huxley said.

Yes, you and me naked, she thought.

"I was going over the files again," she said instead, businesslike. "Sammy's picture was placed behind Mia's, and it's nagging me. Because we're still missing something, Huxley. All of this must be intimately connected to our girl. We're seeing a dark pattern here: from the men, our perp chose to kill to the details around the victimology, the method she used, plus the individuals she saved at each homicide. What's her trigger? We're missing the trigger other than the fact this Von chick is one pissed-off woman."

A bubble of laughter sprang forth. He walked over to her with his shirt in hand.

"And what's so funny?" Nazario frowned at him, snatching the shirt from his hands.

"You. You don't ever turn it off, do you? Give me back my shirt."

Nazario hid it behind her back, making her belly pop. "Come and get it."

"You're looking at Walter Yang's folder. That's the last vic," he said, brushing strands of her hair back. "What about the beginning? Let's start with Darren, shall we? He was in prison for dogfighting, released, and then...didn't he go back to prison?" he said, stepping closer.

"Attempted murder," she said, breath racing to match her heart, "a veterinarian couple."

"Keep the cheap shirt. I got another," Huxley said, running the pad of his thumb along her lower lip, sending an electric current through her. "A veterinarian couple? So we do a search for veterinarians near the attack."

"That's a good idea," she murmured, both of them drawn to this intoxicating game where they teased the professional line neither wished to cross. Her hand broke through all of her hard-fought discipline and reached out to touch him, like being drawn to a hot stove.

Huxley took a step back, but it was a little too late to pull back from the temptations they'd entertained. Her palms and fingers roamed freely up the planes of his flat abdomen, along the width of his muscular chest and brawny shoulders. She could hear him breathing more ragged, struggling to keep it together, though a low moan escaped.

In their twelve-and-a-half—going on thirteen—year history, she knew his aversion to recycling the past. It ran deep. All their false stops and starts stemmed from her lack of commitment. She put both hands on his face and brought him to her lips. Her mouth opened—yearning, hungry. Their tongues found one another, dancing to a rhythm that was theirs alone. Slow. Gentle. Unhurried. As if relearning something lost. With her kiss, she shared her heart—and everything she'd never been able to say: too scared, too late, too much.

When they finally parted, they each struggled to find air.

"I can't do this whole modern co-parenting bullshit," she finally admitted, "this separate lives. 'Daddy has you every other week.' Custody battles. God, Blake, that's not what I want. Not anymore."

"What do you want, then, Detective?" he asked, searching her eyes.

"Just you," she answered with more honesty than she'd ever given him. She brushed a hand on his, the one that carried her father's ring. "I mean it in my gut. Only you. That's all I want. All I ever wanted."

"Until you decide you don't anymore," Huxley said matter-of-factly.

"Don't you do that."

"Do what, Detective? Tell the truth?"

And just like that, they were back to that familiar place. A romantic moment soured by mistrust.

He looked at her father's wedding band on his ring finger.

"You know how many times I've imagined you as my wife?"

Nazario looked down at her feet and then out at the snow-frosted window.

"I'm sorry that I pushed you away after our miscarriage. But that was more than a dozen years ago. We were young. I was young. I was scared. It was wrong for me to have taken off like that," Nazario said. As the words awkwardly stumbled out, embarrassment washed over her because she knew how pathetic she sounded.

There was simply no excuse for how she treated him, how she left things.

"I was scared too. How many times do I have to say that?" he countered, turning his back to her, pacing now. "She was our baby, Anaya, *ours*. You took off, and I thought I could move on, and I did the whole 'get married' bit. Then she kept begging me to have kids with her. I couldn't stop hurting over the child we lost. *Together*. That night you started to bleed...I felt so help-less," his voice cracked. "All I could do was hold you. There was not a single goddamn thing I could do to stop it."

"I honestly...had no idea how you felt," she said, rocked by his words.

He strode across the room, putting distance between them.

"Because you never bothered to ask. I mean, you full-on ghosted me."

"I *never* wanted to be the cause of your pain." Nazario lifted her eyes to meet his. "I was a bitch, alright? I know that now. I own it. I take responsibility."

"And now with this pregnancy, all you've done is shut me out *again*—from every doctor's appointment, when you're the only woman I've ever loved and the only person in this world I would want to carry my child. What I can't figure out is when you'll change your mind about me. One moment you're cold, and the next you're not, and then you're cold again?"

He stalked over toward her and held her face in his hands.

"I still love you. That's never for a second changed. Not even during my failed marriage. I couldn't let go in all these years," Huxley said and then dropped his hands from her face. "But how many times do you expect me to put up with this? I can't keep getting my heart disassembled, Detective."

"I'm different now. Just...give me time to earn your trust."

"Different how?" Huxley threw his hands in the air. "Different than a few weeks ago when you could barely stand to be in the same room as me during our first meeting at the bureau?"

Nazario's phone rang and she cursed under her breath.

His face flushed with annoyance. "Just my damn luck."

"Shit. I'm sorry," Nazario said. She handed him back his shirt, and he put it on.

Her phone continued to ring. He looked at her with that pissed-off glare. That look that told her he'd been waiting for a very long time for her to open up to him, only for work to get in the way. *Again.*

She leaned in and whispered in his ear. "To be continued, okay?"

"Whatever," he contended, gesturing to the phone. "Better answer it."

She put it on speaker.

"Detective Nazario here," she announced formally, not recognizing the number.

"Hope yous're still in Boston?" a familiar Bostonian accent began. "Detective Tripi here. Yous...uh...yous need to come by. Cold one, scene's real hot. This one...it's the kind that'll keep you awake at night. Know what I mean? Warning yous now. I...I personally can't look anymore."

Detective Tripi's voice wobbled.

"Hey, Detective Tripi, Agent Blake Huxley here. Who's our vic?" Huxley asked. "Unless it's related to the case, I'd imagine Boston homicide's handling it?"

"It's one of the...one of the girls in Yang's folder," he said. "Already texted the address."

They ended the call. Huxley glanced at the text message sent by Tripi on Nazario's phone.

"We're close. The location is ten minutes out. Looks like it'll be a grab-and-go continental breakfast downstairs," Huxley said, returning them to co-worker status.

"Blake—" his first name shivered out of her mouth as she grabbed his hand.

"Next time, don't barge into my room if I don't answer, please," he said snatching his hand from her grasp.

"Meet you downstairs, Detective."

Once Huxley disappeared down the hall, Nazario made a bee-line for the bathroom, where she shut the door and let herself cry.

———

Yellow crime tape marked the perimeter of the Boston Harbor. A thin layer of falling snow already dusted the naked body. Nazario's panic attacks returned. Her chest squeezed as though her heart was in a vice grip. There was a sense of breathlessness, of oxygen being stolen. Her gut told her that she didn't want to know who was lying on the cold concrete.

Detectives Tripi took a quick drag of a cigarette, no doubt one link in a long chain that had kept him alert on-scene. Carducci sipped his coffee instead. Of the two detectives, Tripi was the one who was visibly shaken. He turned his back on Nazario and Huxley.

How bad could it be?

The crime photographer snapped pictures while CSI fished for DNA under the corpse's fingernails. Nazario gripped her chest and tried desperately to take breaths, but the air wouldn't enter her lungs properly.

"Breathe," Huxley coached. "Have they returned? The panic attacks? Do you want me to see who it is? I can—"

Nazario gave a slight shake of her head. Together, they moved toward the body.

Flakes of snow sprinkled the blonde hair that covered the woman's face. Heart hammering, she pulled on latex gloves, then swiped strands from the face, revealing the victim's identity. Her hands jolted up and covered her mouth as a loud gasp escaped.

Sammy. Oh God, no...it can't be her.

She smoothed Sammy's hair back further for closer inspection. There were dark teeth marks on her neck and shoulders. Nazario's hands shook as she breathed through her nose, feeling the squeeze in her chest punishing each attempt. She flipped Sammy on her back. Her face was swollen and bruised.

Huxley asked if she was okay. She didn't respond. Her father's words came back, uninvited.

If you wish to do what I do, no matter how hard and how much it rips at your heart, you keep your emotions separate from the case you're trying to solve. Focus on solving the case. Worry about emotions later.

The bullet hole at the temple looked to be a couple of hours old.

Nazario voiced her observations, "Execution style shooting. Burn mark on the skin. Barrel was pressed to her head."

Huxley reached for the jaw and moved it to the right and left. "Broken."

"Sammy put up a fight—" Nazario started, then paused as her eyes watered. She blinked away her emotions, recalling their time together in the self-defense class. Sammy had worked so hard to get her strikes down so she could throw blows that would knock someone out.

"Again," Nazario encouraged Sammy as she faced the punching bag. *"Now I know there's a stronger strike inside of you. Picture their face on this punching bag."*

"Kihap," Sammy exhaled the taekwondo shout, only it sounded as weak as her punch.

"C'mon Sammy, again," Nazario barked.

"I'm not good at this. The other girls are way better than me."

"I believe in you, Sammy. Again."

"KIHAP!" she screamed, landing a solid blow that rocked the punching bag.

"Atta girl," Nazario hugged her student and then helped her out of her gloves.

She'd never forget how bruised Sammy's knuckles were after the exercise. Nazario scrutinized Sammy's lifeless hands. They were both bloodied and swollen, with blood pooled under her broken fingernails, violently torn from their cuticles.

"She c-clawed the ground trying to get away. The nails on her index and forefingers are ripped off. She fought with...with everything in her," Nazario said, lifting both of Sammy's hands to inspect them. "She threw a bunch of strikes. It's the one thing I taught her."

Nazario turned around and lifted her head to the sky.

"Sit this one out." Huxley put a hand on her shoulder. "I got it from here."

She inhaled through her nose once more and dug her nails into her palms until she was sure she'd cut through soft flesh. Shaking her head no, Nazario turned around. Sammy needed her right now more than ever.

She was not letting anyone else assess Sammy's bruised body.

Her eyes scanned over the girl, starting with the head. "Bite marks on the neck, shoulders, both b-breasts. Deep bruising on the stomach," Nazario took two fingers and pushed lightly down around the rib cage. It was loose. "Broken ribs. She was kicked or kneed a few times."

Nazario analyzed her thighs and pointed at hand marks on either side of her hips.

"They held her down," Huxley said. "Bite marks on her inner thighs. Quads and knees are torn up pretty bad. She was—"

"Dragged along the concrete." Nazario closed her eyes for a five-count.

Breathe through your nose. Breathe through your nose. Breathe through your nose.

She inhaled a shaky breath, opened her eyes, then continued. "The handprints on her hips are quite fresh. Don't think they pinned her down while she was alive."

She scanned below the waist and then froze.

Nazario raked her hand over her face, and all her composure left.

"Goddamn it!" she shouted, unable to contain it.

At a distance, Detective Tripi gave Nazario a solemn look. He retrieved another cigarette and lit it. Detective Carducci tilted his head at her. It was a gesture from one detective to another. It was an understanding that while they were trained to handle any homicide case, they were made of flesh that bleeds and bones that break.

They were human, after all.

Huxley stayed quiet. He put a hand on hers and held it there.

A couple minutes crawled by—no words, just the two of them staring at anything but the defiled body of her former student. A young woman with her whole life ahead of her. Sammy had fought like hell only to be dragged back into it. When Nazario was ready, she gave Huxley a nod, and they returned to the job at hand.

Nazario squatted with Huxley following suit.

A bloody bottle was stuffed approximately three-fourths up Sammy's vaginal canal. There was a note in the bottle. The labia looked to have been torn and punctured. Nazario attempted to steady her hands but was unable to stop them from quaking. She reached for what appeared to be a green Heineken beer bottle and slowly extracted it.

The tip of the bottle was broken enough to cause severe internal damage. Several jagged shards were stuck to the inner vaginal wall. Nazario tugged gently, and it finally came free. Blood dripped down Sammy's pale, bluish legs, which were now covered in a fresh, thin layer of snow.

Breathe through your nose. Breathe through your nose. Breathe through your nose.

"Judging by..." A wave of nausea washed over her.

She gagged, then stopped, and then gagged again. Huxley put a hand on her back to show support but knew better than to interrupt or ask again if she was okay. When the dry-heaves stopped at last, she continued.

"Judging by the gunshot wound to the head...and those all over her body, an altercation most likely occurred first. Other injuries came after death," Nazario reported.

"Necrophilia? Is that what you're thinking?" he asked. "Think you're right—the handprints on the hips and the bite marks all look fresh. But the gunshot residue's been there a lot longer."

"Thinking the same. Vaginal bleeding's likely from the assault with the...broken bottle. But the labia and vaginal tears look consistent with a...with a rape victim. They shot her first. Then they...then they raped her postmortem. The autopsy will confirm it. I'm guessing at least two men were involved."

Nazario turned the broken bottle upside down, retrieved a pen from the inside pocket of her jacket, and used it to fish out what appeared to be a newspaper clipping. She pulled it free and handed the bottle to Huxley.

Two crime scene investigators walked over.

"We left it in," one of them remarked, "'til yous had a chance to—investigate."

Huxley handed the bottle over, and it was placed in an evidence bag for further examination at the lab. "Appreciate it," he murmured.

She waited to open the newspaper excerpt until Huxley stood beside her.

Headline: "Respected Veterinarian Left for Dead After Vicious Attack."

Nazario and Huxley scanned the article. It described how Dr. Wilder Agatha Friedrich, a local veterinarian in Snow Country Casper, Wyoming, was brutally slashed open and left for dead. She was pregnant at the time and lost the baby. Dr. Friedrich had survived, but the senseless attack resulted in an emergency hysterectomy, after which she was left unable to have children. Darren Fischer was charged with a reduced sentence. However, two of her attackers were never identified. At the top of the article, in red ink, was the warning: "Ace is next."

Nazario took a picture of the note with her phone.

She turned to Huxley. "We need to figure out who this Ace is, but first, I think we've found our killer. I'll call Detective Tae Mun. We used to spar together. He transferred from LAPD to Wyoming. Moved to Casper when he and his wife became pregnant."

"You think he can send us digital files, stat?"

"If anyone can, it's Tae. He's hella fast," Nazario said, scrolling through her phone. She stepped away from the body, and in three rings, Tae answered. After a quick volley of questions about his wife Helen and the couple's rambunctious two-year-old girl, Nazario cut to the chase. Just mentioning the Darren Fischer case made Tae rattle off a string of swear words.

"Need the files on that attack. Yeah, Doctors Chua and Friedrich. Digital files would be great. You're sending them now? Hang on—"

Nazario muted the call, impressed that Detective Mun hadn't lost a step. She checked her inbox, and Huxley leaned in. She showed him the email with the attached zip file. His eyebrows rose in surprise. She unmuted the call and let Mun know that she'd received the file.

Nazario hung up and handed the newspaper to CSI to scan for fingerprints.

All of it felt overwhelming, like a thousand pounds were pressing down on her chest. After the call with Tae Mun, the tightening in her lungs returned. Nazario looked back at Sammy

—lying on her back, covered in bruises, blood drying between her legs, and fists still clenched with proof that she'd used every bit of her training to fight back.

So, why did Nazario feel like she failed her?

The ME approached. "Are we good to go? CSI done? You got what you needed?"

"Yes, we're all set," Huxley said when Nazario fell silent. He gave her a concerned look.

When the ME left, she shuffled beside Huxley to meet with Carducci and Tripi.

Tripi took a drag of his latest cigarette. "My daughter, Carlotta, she's in college. Looks exactly like her—same age as the vic. I remember when she was just born. Every time I look at her, I still see that innocent little baby."

Tripi took another drag of his cigarette. He pointed at Sammy as the MEs picked her up and placed her in a body bag. "I couldn't even breathe when I saw the girl lying there. Felt a... a pain in my chest. Thought I was having a heart attack," his voice broke. "God...she looks so much like Carlotta."

Huxley glanced at Nazario, knowing her silence meant that reality was hitting her, too.

He spoke for her. "We knew Sammy well..." Huxley paused, rubbing his chin. "A good friend of ours in LAPD's Gang and Narco saved her from the brotherhood a while back. It looks like we...we got here too late this time."

"Nothing yous could've done," Carducci said in a monotone, Bostonian-Southie accent. His tone was so flat it was as if the veteran detective was discussing geological rock formations with a bunch of bored-to-tears college students. "We'll send you the intel when we get the DNA reports. Vic fought good. Maybe we'll find something under the fingernails. Hopefully, we get a match on someone yous've been tracking."

"Still don't make it easy, Charlie. What if it was your daughter?" Tripi flicked his cigarette. "You wouldn't know what it's like 'cause you ain't got kids. She was someone's child, Charlie. She was someone's baby. And you sit there talking about her like she's some roadkill."

Tripi spat on the ground in his partner's direction and stormed off.

"C'mon, Frank..." Carducci pleaded.

Nazario watched Tripi leave. She gripped the chain running along the Boston Harbor and looked out at a cluster of sailboats floating by at a distance. Despite the frigid thirty-seven-degree snowy weather, the sky was so blue and cloudless you'd think it was a beautiful, perfect day.

Sammy. Oh, Sammy, I'm so sorry I failed you. We failed you.

A frosty breeze blew against her skin, making her feel anesthetized.

She heard Huxley give the Boston detective his contact info for the second time since they'd found a drowned Walter Yang at his Boston mansion. Nazario numbly turned from the harbor and shuffled back to the car on autopilot—no signal to Huxley, no goodbye to Carducci.

———

They sat near Boston Harbor as Nazario opened the zip files on her laptop, not wasting any time. In the first crime scene photo, Dr. Wilder Friedrich lay naked in the snow after a vicious attack. Her clothes were slashed from her tiny frame, and a massive German Shepherd nearly obscured her. They must've taken a picture thinking she was dead.

Another photo was of her bloody abdomen nearly shredded to pieces. Nazario covered her mouth, taken aback. The fact that she'd survived at all was a sheer miracle. Zeus, the dog, had to have saved her life by applying pressure from his body and keeping her warm in the snow until the Casper PD arrived. Huxley pulled up an article on his phone and then paused.

The article detailed how Samantha Friedrich, Dr. Wilder Friedrich's little sister, had been kidnapped three years prior to her big sister's vicious attack by the very men who almost killed the well-known veterinarian. They methodically studied the rest of the photos, including the post-surgery images of a gruesome keloid scar. Dr. Wilder looked like a different person. They studied the two women. Juxtaposing the sketch of Von, now muscular and tatted, next to the emaciated doctor recovering in the hospital five years prior.

"We might as well be looking at two different people," Nazario said.

Just then, another email from CSI in Boston. She quickly scanned it and showed Huxley.

He read it and then said, "DNA on that extra-large men's shirt he took to prison with him after the attack on the veterinarians in their Casper, Wyoming home was from Dr. Wilder Friedrich and not Sammy. From when she was attacked."

"Shirt was probably Darren Fischer's," added Nazario. "Never forget, that was the court date where Sammy had to testify against Fischer. Since she froze along with other witnesses on the stand, they didn't have anything incriminating except for the dog fighting. Surprised the prison allowed him to keep that bloody shirt. That was enough evidence, had they seized it."

"Unless there was a gross mishandling of the case by Casper PD, Darren must've taken that shirt with him instead of leaving it at the crime scene. Otherwise, they would have bagged it as evidence."

Why didn't they see it before?

"They're not men," Nazario seethed, "they're monsters."

A wave of despair washed over her.

It was the kind of dejection that stuck to your rib cage and zapped all the fight in your spirit. She wearily closed her laptop. On the drive back to the hotel, neither said a word. Nazario walked dazedly to her hotel room and laid down in her bed, curling up in a fetal position. She stared blankly out the window, her emotions a mélange of grief, shock, guilt, regret, and something else—a love for Huxley she'd never been able to express.

The bed dipped quietly, and Huxley's warm body curled behind hers. He pulled her into his embrace. Warm breath against her neck, he secured her against him protectively until not a single sliver of space stood between them. He gripped her hands, and she squeezed his. Her phone rang, the special ring tone announcing Deputy Frost. She let it go to voicemail. For the first time, they shared the same decision: whatever his call was about, no matter how dire, it would have to wait for at least the next thirty minutes. As two human beings, they should be allowed time to process everything, even if it meant a slight delay.

And so, for the next half hour, Huxley held her tight while she quietly wept.

TWENTY
THE KILLER

ORDINARILY, HER PARENTS' Palos Verdes estate remained illuminated 24/7. Even the fountains on the front lawn never took a break. *"Our electric bill—it's almost as high as the rent for a New York City apartment,"* her mom once boasted to her earth-loving, vegan daughter.

But now the compound sat shrouded in darkness. The grand fountain, with cherub angels she once cherished as magical when she was a child, remained motionless. Floating insects and dead leaves polluted the filthy water. The massive windows on the house were blackened, curtains drawn, shutting out the world. The lush roses that once surrounded her childhood home were dead thorny vines.

The time since Sammy's death had passed in a haze. The urge to return here grew until Von knew: although she was risking everything, the visit was non-negotiable despite the sense of foreboding that swept over her. How had her parents endured losing Wilder and Samantha as they once were—the two heiresses of the Friedrich fortune, now mere ghosts in the twilight? It was as though the home that once held an aura of antique beauty suddenly ceased to exist, the premises cloaked in raven mourning, bloodless and without a soul, robbed of the two little girls giggling and playing in its gardens and halls.

The sound of Sammy's laughter echoed from a time when the sun shone brightly. Von saw herself chasing her little sister around the fountain and through the garden—their favorite place to escape, a lovely maze of rose bushes boasting red, pink, white, and yellow. Dr. Katrine had always been the type to overdo things. Instead of a few roses accenting the landscape, she insisted on thousands. Every guest who arrived had spoken of the Friedrich compound as though it was more splendid than anything else to be seen. The house's cathedral ceilings, expensive paintings, and the entire décor were the best money could buy.

But it was the garden that had changed her. It was what made Von love nature, what called her to love animals and pursue a career in veterinary medicine. Now, only twisting, thorny branches and vast patches of barren land remained of what had once been her wonderland—as if it reflected, not only her own life, but also Sammy's tragic death.

Though the men she'd killed deserved their fate, Samantha Friedrich did not.

Von approached the dilapidated remains of her childhood sanctuary, her key a relic from another life. The locks, still unchanged, whispered of unspoken hope. Did her parents cling to the fragile dream that their last living child would one day find her way back home?

But after all these years, it was not the idea of seeing Mother but confronting her father that caused anxiety to rise.

Sammy was dead.

She'd repeated this again and again, but was still unable to come to terms with the traumatic reality. What was worse, had it not been for Von's vengeful actions, her little sister would still be alive. Jefferson had survived the war only to come home and get caught up in her vengeful web, which could've already cost him his life. Their last exchange entailed her warning him to go into hiding and getting no reply. It was her fault. There was no one else to blame.

There was enough information left behind to incriminate not just her targets, but herself. The real victims she'd saved knew not only her face, but her canine accomplice. Zeus left enough of himself behind at each scene, from dog hairs to teeth marks. Then, of course, there was Jefferson to identify them both, too.

Maybe her lack of an escape plan had been what she truly intended. Maybe Von wanted to be caught? Perhaps all of this was nothing more than one big suicide mission? She'd told herself many times that she wouldn't change a single action, a single kill. At first, each murder became soporific, inducing the best sleep of her life.

Her conscience was at peace. *Was.*

But since Sammy's death—and Jefferson's likely capture— fresh insomnia stalked her.

When she stepped into the marble-floored foyer of her childhood home, a shiver ran up her spine. The grim, lightless place she once called home filled her with a sadness she didn't expect. Perhaps her parents neglected it, unable to bring it to life with Sammy gone. Although past midnight, a single light gleamed from the second floor.

Her hand touched the smooth metal railing, and, ever so slowly, she ascended the staircase, each step like trudging through quicksand. Zeus moved with more confidence, charging ahead of her, leading the way. Von could remember when she was five, seven years before Sammy would be born. Her earliest memory was staring at her father's office, as the doors were always closed.

It was the one place Anton loved to shut himself in, and no

one was permitted to disturb him. Now, ironically, the oak sliding French doors were open. The light from her father's office offered the only indication of life. Zeus's nails tapped against the bamboo floors. He didn't enter the office. Zeus wouldn't—not without her. Instead, he stood in front of the open door. The swiveling chair squealed as her father turned.

"*Katrine, ich dachte du hast deine Schlafmittel genommen,*" Anton said.

Katrine, I thought you took your sleep medication.

There was a long pause followed by an audible gasp.

"Zeus?" he said, the name scratching out. Zeus barked once. Von, with her back pinned against the wall, closed her eyes and took deep breaths in an effort to steady her heart. The last time her father saw her, she was Dr. Wilder Agatha Friedrich. But that person no longer existed, and if Wilder wasn't good enough for her father back then, what would he think of Von today?

Zeus turned toward her, waiting for her to join him. Unable to delay longer, Von emerged from the shadows and stood beside her dog. The glass of red wine in her father's hand came crashing into tiny shards on the floor. He blinked at her, his eyes a well of emotions—once veiled, now foreign to her. She wasn't used to her father expressing such raw feelings. He scanned her from head to feet, his eyes lingering on the tattoos on her forearms and, at last, the large serpent on her skull that covered the long, jagged scar.

His mouth fell open, but he was unable to form words.

"Hello, Father." Von stepped into his office. "Am I...more the way you've seen me all along? Do I better fit your standards?"

"W-Wilder?" he stuttered, gripping an arm on his oversized leather office chair. His eyes were wide now. A look of shock washed over his weathered face. Hues of burnt orange flickered from the fireplace, illuminating his skin just enough to reveal dark rims under his usually bright green eyes. Eyes that were now mossy and sullen.

Von lifted her shirt to reveal her hideous keloid scar in the shape of a snake.

"Von Schlange!" she bellowed. *"Es ist eine Schlange, erinnerst du dich an Vater?"*

My name is Serpent, remember, Father?

"I...I have always loved you. You're my daughter," he said.

"Bullshit," she replied.

His eyes pooled with unrecognizable emotion. For once in her life, she watched tears crawl down her father's pained face. Even when her grandparents died tragically in a car accident, the talk among everyone at their funerals was how Dr. Anton Jörg Friedrich, their only child, showed no sign of human sentiment. His back had been so straight, it looked like he'd snap in half if he should bend at the waist.

"Where've you been all these years?" He wiped his cheeks. "Your sister...your sister..."

He choked, turning to the fireplace, gaze now distant. The flames crackled again, making his wet cheeks glow with a mellow amber hue that softened his usual stiff features. By firelight, the neurosurgeon looked like an old man who'd lost everything.

"I know," Von said. "She was murdered. I promise you—*I promise Sammy*—I'll find him."

Anton kept his gaze fixed on the fire. Deep worry lines creased his forehead, and the bags under his weary eyes revealed the toll of the five years she'd been gone. Her father had aged, but not gracefully.

"The FBI was here asking us questions. Questions that we couldn't believe they were asking." Anton turned to face his daughter now. "What have you done, Wilder? What do you mean you'll find who killed Samantha? Your mother and I, we know that what had happened to you...it was pure evil." Anton's voice rose and cracked. "But, what in God's name have you become?!"

"Was ich sein sollte," she said with cool regard.

What I was meant to be.

Light footsteps made the wooden floors creak, accompanied by a familiar floral scent—one that could only belong to her mother.

"We've missed you, honey," Katrine said, the words wobbling out.

Von turned around to face her, and they locked eyes.

Mother looked at her as though she hadn't changed.

"They may be watching the home. Listening right now. It could be bugged. Honey, it's not safe for you to be here," Katrine said. "Will you...please let the authorities handle Sammy's killer?"

Von raised her chin and then said, "That's why I can't stay. I just...came to tell you that while I don't regret what I did—but I'm sorry for what it cost. Sammy's dead because of me. I can't bring her back...but I *will* make them pay."

"Make who pay? The authorities wouldn't tell us anything. They were very secretive. We don't even know what's going on. How is our daughter—a veterinarian who can't hurt anything that breathes, has no criminal history whatsoever, and doesn't even like to eat meat, for Christ's sake—suddenly involved in something where the FBI is looking for you? Whatever it is you've done, if you turn yourself in—" her father pleaded.

"She's dissociated," Katrine cut her husband off, donning her psychologist hat. "It's highly unlikely she'll turn herself in." Her mother turned to Von. "I'm sorry, honey. We spoke about you again in the third person, didn't we? It's Von, is it?"

Despite feeling like one of her mother's mentally ill patients, guilt became a relentless tidal wave. She'd let her mother down. She'd let Sammy down. Now, with Sammy gone, she wondered what book her mother would write next. Would she write about surviving the pain of outliving her daughter or daughters? After all, it was highly likely Von would succeed in her mission. Since the start of her vigilante justice, Von factored in the probability of her own death or capture.

She hadn't foreseen that Sammy might be caught in the crosshairs. Victimized because of her rage. Sammy was the worst collateral damage—an unexpected error in Von's years of planning and one she'd never forgive herself for.

Five years ago, she had legally changed her name and moved from Casper, Wyoming, to Los Angeles. Little did her parents or Sammy know that, while no one knew her where-abouts, Von had never even left California. Hiding in Los Angeles among its ten million residents was relatively easy. Her mother prodded her thoughts, repeating her new name, ques-tioning if this was truly what she wished to be called, as if in a psychotherapy session with a delusional client. How long had her mother been standing there, listening to her argue with her father? Long enough to hear her correct Anton—that she was no longer Wilder.

Feeling awkwardly psychoanalyzed, Von nodded at her mother's query.

"Okay—*Von*—whatever you wish to answer to now—" Her mother began in her usual controlled manner.

"Sammy's been murdered, and now this?" Anton bit out, hardly able to contain himself. The asshole in him returned with fury.

"Das ist Wahnsinn!"

This is insanity!

He ripped through her mother's unnerving professionalism, throwing his arms in the air.

Katrine ignored her husband's sudden outburst. "Whatever

it is you've done...we'll always love you. Always. No matter what. You hear me, honey? No matter what."

Katrine strode toward her daughter and pulled her into a fierce embrace. Von hesitated for a moment before wrapping her arms around her mother's waist. She couldn't remember the last time she hugged her mother this way.

"Won't be attending Sammy's funeral, and I'm not coming back," Von said, reluctantly pulling away. "But I promise that Sammy will not have died in vain."

Anton shoved himself forward, wedging himself in front of his wife.

"Anton, sweetheart, this outburst of yours, while under-standable, will do no good," Katrine said, so calm it was unnerving. "It will not change the fact that we bury Sammy this week and that Wilder, well, she's been buried, too. We have Von now; she's all that's left. Denial and anger won't change that reality."

"Oh, for heaven's sake, Katrine. Enough! Can you stop for once? This is our daughter—" he jabbed a hand at Von. "Our children are not your bloody patients. I am not your bloody patient. Samantha is dead, and yes, I am beyond anger—I'm destroyed."

Spittle flew from his mouth.

Her mother put a hand to her chest. "Darling, I—"

"We are *not* a bloody idea in your book. Our trauma is real. *Our* trauma—it happened to us. It happened to our children."

His face went crimson.

Katrine's eyes grew wet, but she nodded, silently acknowl-edging her husband's words.

Anton turned to face Von now. "I've always been proud of you. I've always loved you. I might've been caught up in my work, but you were my firstborn. My little girl and you still...you still are."

Anton let out a cough and then sobbed. His shoulders

bobbed. This was a man she'd never known—the father she'd always wished he could be.

"Daddy..." It was a whisper, delicate as a breeze, and they embraced in a fierce hug. He wept heavily against her neck. "I'm sorry," she said. "But there isn't any other way. I've come too far to turn back now."

Von pulled away from his grip.

"It is *not* your fault. Sammy is *not* your fault," her father said. "You can't blame yourself or make matters worse."

"You're wrong. It is," Von said.

"*Lass uns gehen.*" She stroked Zeus's head. *Let's go.*

"Your father's right, it isn't your fault," her mother said and then let out a light, incredulous chuckle, one that conflicted with the anxious look spreading across her face. "You're no *murderer.*"

She met her parents' eyes. "*Oh, aber ich bin es.*"

Oh, but I am.

Anton took off his glasses. Katrine gasped. Her mouth dropped open.

Von, not able to stomach her parents' expressions, turned and walked out the door, down the driveway, and through the large gates. They called out, and her mother ran after her, sobbing. Zeus paused, glancing back for a final look. Von clicked her tongue, and he obeyed. She knew—without looking—that Anton would hold his wife, and that they'd cry together as they watched their only living child leave for good.

Von wiped her eyes with the back of a hand and didn't look back.

TWENTY-ONE

THE DETECTIVE

IN HER MIND, Nazario could see Sammy, her bright, dimply smile so young, so sweet. She always knew when her pupil spent too much time at the beach because Sammy would come into the dojo smelling like suntan lotion and sand. Her golden hair would turn platinum, and the freckles dotting her nose would darken.

And when she laughed too hard, she'd snort from her nose and give herself the hiccups. Sammy was a hugger. Every single time she left a session, she'd throw her arms around Nazario and give her a sweaty kiss on the cheek.

"Love you, Detective," Sammy said each and every time.

Nazario's stiff reply was always the same.

"Did real good today, kiddo."

"I'm fixin' to make you say the L-word if it's the last thing I do," Sammy promised.

Dozens of little memories like this swirled while Huxley asked her again if she was okay.

But the words lodged themselves somewhere between her heart and throat. Deep inside, where human language went to die when there was a loss far too great for the body to process, especially over a short thirty-minute work break. She thought about Dr. Wilder Friedrich—Von—and she wondered what the serpent woman was experiencing right now. No matter the pain the killer might've endured or what Von had done, Nazario knew there were certain homicides where loved ones should never know the specifics.

She heard Huxley on the phone with Deputy Frost and didn't recall him leaving the bed.

Another DB, this time Miami, Nazario heard from a distance, but her mind was elsewhere.

Nazario rose and gazed out the frosty hotel window at the Boston landscape, where snow dusted the ground like fine sugar. Then suddenly, Sammy was standing in front of the window. A manifestation of grief, one that was very real. It had happened once before, when her father died. He'd appear everywhere, her mind and heart unable to let him go, let him rest in peace. Sammy was...she was so real. Naked before her. Jaw hanging broken to one side. Eyes partly swollen shut. Face puffy and blackish-purple from the blows she received to the head. A portion of her skull was gone from the gun blast to her temple. The bruises and bite marks all over her body were more pronounced now from the rigor mortis. Dried blood stuck to her inner thighs and between her legs.

Please, Detective Nazario, Sammy's ghost began, her voice a haunting echo in Anaya's mind as though they were both in a long dark hallway. *Don't tell them what happened. They don't need to know. Promise me? I don't want them to remember me this way.*

I promise, Sammy...I love you, Nazario returned in her mind.

Too late to hear these long sought-after words, Sammy dissolved into the sunlight.

Nazario buried her face in her hands and began to weep.

The bed dipped, and Huxley returned swiftly to her side.

"Come here..." He turned her shoulders toward him, and she buried her wet face against his chest. "I'm right here, Anaya. I'm right here. If you need to cry, well, you go on and do it. We've got time to be human, Detective."

She heard Sammy's voice yet again in her head. The night Sammy stopped by to do her makeup because Nazario was utterly clueless. It was the first night she and Huxley went out for an official date months ago. The same night, they became pregnant.

Detective, can I ask you something? Sammy's voice, now a phantom from the past.

Am I nervous? Yes, I've never worn a dress, and I don't do makeup, Nazario had recalled confessing to Sammy.

Sammy laughed as she applied her finishing touch, red lipstick, to Nazario's lips.

Why are you so afraid to say the word? I mean—hell—you can't even say it to me, she said. *I can see it in your eyes. The way you look at me. It's just like my sister does with a protective kind of look. Just like I know you love him. You just can't say it, though, can you? You can't live your life afraid. I learned that after they found me.*

Sammy paused to brush a couple of curls back away from Nazario's face and continued.

I lived like a prisoner even after I was released by those men. Afraid. Afraid to leave my house. I pushed my family away. People that loved me. It's no way to live, Detective. Pushing people that love you away like that. There's a lot of evil out there. I get it. You've seen it so long. Maybe you stopped realizing that... there's a lot of good and love out there, too.

You're incredible. You know that, Sammy? Nazario had met Sammy's eyes. *That after all you been through...you still see the good in people. I admire you so very much.*

Don't wait until it's too late, Sammy had warned her; the words seemed loaded. *You don't know when someone will be here today and then tomorrow—poof—they're just gone.*

Just like Daddy, Nazario had thought. One minute alive, and the next, murdered.

Sammy had thrown her arms around Nazario in a bear-hug.

If you love him, Detective, Sammy whispered, *just tell him.*

Huxley stroked her face with his fingers, pulling Nazario from the past.

"Hey...I can go check out this next vic alone. You're pregnant, and that scene was—" Huxley didn't finish. He inhaled a long breath and raked a hand down his face. "I filled Frost in on everything. Sammy's...brutal murder was a message to Dr. Wilder—*Von Schlange.* Get this, they...they think they know who Ace is, but they wouldn't share more, said they'd fill us in after Miami. Frost was concerned after Sammy...he was worried about overwhelming us."

Nazario nodded absently. He gently wiped the tears from her face with his strong fingers.

"While you were asleep...I reread Dr. Wilder's statements to the police after her attack. She mentioned tattoos on her attackers. It was right under our noses. Darren Fischer had one on his forearm, Sean Martin had one on his neck—matching Confederate flag tattoos. There's a third guy with one on his shoulder. He must be on her list. These men were the ones who attacked her. We suppose Walter Yang had been Sammy's first buyer. Frost confirmed it. Guess the feds found some buried records that one of our guys dug up. Guess who went to college with the Boston judge who dismissed Yang's case, helped expunge other charges from his record? Guess who presided over the brotherhood's trials, including Dr. Wilder's?"

Nazario pulled away from Huxley and got up from the bed.

With her back facing him, she gripped the window frame where Sammy had been standing just moments ago.

"Estevan...he's our vic in Miami, isn't he?" Numb, Nazario looked out on the snow falling.

She heard Huxley walk toward her. He placed his hands on her shoulders.

"I'm sorry, Anaya," Huxley said. "I didn't mean to be insensitive and start talking shop like nothing happened. As I said, I can go alone. Maybe you...sit this one out?"

Nazario fell silent for at least five minutes. Huxley nudged her a few times to talk to him, but she stared out at the window watching the snowplows clear up the roads. She rested a palm on the frosty window, a chill running up her arm. As she absorbed the winter through the freezing windowpane, she couldn't help but wonder what the medical examiners would say.

How long was she alive, on the brink of death before she was shot?

And then Sammy's words returned to her again.

If you love him, Detective, just tell him.

"Say something, Anaya, please..." Huxley begged again. "You got me worried."

She took a deep breath, heart pounding in her chest. For so long, she had kept her feelings buried, afraid of what might happen if she let them surface. They had agreed to co-parent, live apart, do their best for the baby. But now, as she looked into Huxley's eyes, she knew she couldn't hold it back any longer.

The weight of her emotions grew heavier with each passing second. Her voice trembled, throat tight with fear and anticipation. Tears welled up in her eyes as she continued, "I can't keep this to myself no more. Trying to live apart, pretend I can do this without you, it's breaking me." She studied Huxley's face, searching for any sign of his reaction. The silence between them was deafening. "Every day, I miss you more," she added, voice barely a whisper. "I want us to be a family, Huxley. Not just for our child, but for us. I...I love you."

Huxley gasped. He rested his head against her back as his arms wrapped around her.

"I love you. I love you. I love you," she repeated with firm conviction. "And I can't keep pretending otherwise."

"I would've waited another fifteen years to hear you say that," Huxley said.

She turned around to face him, meeting his blue, crystalline eyes.

"I can't...I can't do me without you. Not anymore. Sammy once told me that I shouldn't be afraid of love," her voice cracked. "Her death...it just hit me so hard. It made me...it made me prioritize what really matters."

He sighed, as though he was expelling deep relief and drew her tightly against him. The moment felt eternal rather than the ten minutes they barely had, since they must hit the road stat. Huxley ran his fingers through her hair and whispered his love that never faded. She wished they had more time, instead of feeling rushed and having to jump onto their next homicide scene. But she closed her eyes and savored every second she could hear the beat of his heart against her ear.

Huxley finally added a kiss to her forehead. "Does that mean you're not sitting this one out, Detective? Relax, eat a bowl of ice cream at the hotel while you let the man you love do all the work?"

Nazario blurted out laughter and wiped the moisture from her eyes.

"No way in hell am I gonna sit this one out—let you play lone cowboy." Her eyes softened, and her tone turned tender. "Besides, we're a team. Remember?"

"We're a team, Detective." Huxley gave her a quick peck on

the lips. "Let's get our asses to Miami, shall we? We got a judge to see."

―――――

The gorgeous modern estate right off Miami Beach overlooked the ocean. The temperature was 60 degrees, about the coldest Miami got in January.

A black Cadillac Escalade, a couple of Miami police cruisers, and the ME were parked in the driveway. The fifth vehicle was a plain white van that was likely CSI. Yellow crime tape encircled the mansion that appeared to be five to six thousand square feet.

Nazario and Huxley made their introduction to two Hispanic men in jeans and blazers.

"Miami homicide," the first man said, shaking both of their hands. "You arrived quick. CSI wanted to wait until you got here."

The Miami detective pointed three stories up at Estevan's vacation home. A bright yellow tarp was suspended around a shattered window. But Nazario and Huxley could see the body was that of honorable José Estevan still dangling by a rope. His face ashen, eyes bulging out of their sockets from the pressure to his neck.

Nazario instinctively put a hand on her throat. Huxley rubbed her shoulder. He leaned, checking in on her. Taking a long deep breath, she nodded. Her stomach turned, but the wave of nausea thankfully passed.

"There's a note for you inside," the Miami detective said. "Not an actual *note* note, just addressed to the both of you. A folder on Estevan, detailed as hell, and a box of DVDs. I personally don't think I'd have the stomach to watch them."

"If you haven't watched them, how do you know what they contain?" Huxley queried.

"Based on the one that was playing in the living room," the Miami detective filled in. "A homemade sex tape starring the judge and his lover. The DVDs were actually marked, all of them by names of young girls and their ages. They match the folder's contents. Most no older than sixteen. Makes me sick. My daughter just turned sixteen."

"Judge José Estevan's have been on our radar. The more power, the more they think they can get away with," Huxley said.

"That intel—" the Miami detective pointed at the folder.

"Heavily researched and detailed as hell," Nazario finished.

"Impressively so. We've been asked to release the folder and the DVDs to you straight away without logging them in our database since you're the lead on this nationwide hunt," said the Miami detective.

Nazario walked backward, tilted her head, and shielded her eyes with a hand to take in the full expanse of the window that the judge hung before. The wall-to-wall, floor-to-ceiling vista had been blown out. Shattered glass sprinkled the front lawn. She looked down and walked a few feet next to a large outdoor pool. Huxley and the two Miami detectives followed.

Nazario squatted before the body of a Miami police officer who was lying on the marble tiling outside in a pool of his own blood and covered in fragments of glass. She rubbed her chin.

"He was unplanned," she said with certainty.

She noted the familiar canine teeth marks on the officer's forearms.

"What's his story?"

"Officer Alberto Montoya," began the Miami detective, "was dirty. It's no surprise he was here. We got a hunch that the judge called him here to take care of his wife. The fridge was locked. There were handcuffs on the bed and on the couch and that sexually explicit video of him playing on repeat."

"What makes you think Montoya was here to take out the judge's wife?" Huxley asked.

"Like we said, Montoya was as dirty as they come. Seriously. Suspended multiple times. Should've been fired for all sorts of shit. IA still has several open cases on him," he explained.

"Internal affairs, huh?" Nazario frowned.

"Yes, ma'am, and it looks like he had friends in the right places to buy himself immunity, keep his job. Thirty minutes before the EMTs arrived, Montoya called in Alisa Estevan's suicide," said the Miami detective.

Nazario and Huxley exchanged an amused look.

The Miami detective continued, "EMTs specifically stated they'd been called for a gunshot to the head. Had it been called in as a general suicide and not specifically naming the judge's wife, the EMTs might've initially figured it was the judge himself that had hung himself. Though it wouldn't have explained why Montoya was shot or the bruises and contusions to the judge's body. We were notified and arrived shortly after. We let the ambulance go since everyone left on the premises is leaving in a bag."

"Estevan would never kill himself," Huxley said. "Too much of a narcissist."

The Miami detective explained, "CSI found blonde hair on the couch and on the bed along with what they think are Alisa Estevan's fingerprints. It appears she was handcuffed and couldn't access food. Who knows how long she was locked up here? When we got here, she wasn't the one that was dead."

"Looks like our girl got here just in time," Nazario said. "And she used a gun."

"Not a bad aim, if you ask me," Huxley said. "Three taps to

the chest and one between the eyes. He wasn't using a vest because he wasn't expecting our girl."

Nazario struggled to stand, putting a hand on her lower back. Huxley helped her up, and they headed into the house.

"Nazario, I must ask, and please don't take this the wrong way. I mean, I know all about your career—you're quite famous, Detective—but...all those DBs across multiple state lines don't make you a tad queasy?" the man's face was awash with genuine puzzlement. "My wife couldn't hold anything down. It was like morning sickness for the entire pregnancy."

"No offense taken," Nazario waved a hand and smiled wearily. "The dead don't do it for me. Eat an Egg McMuffin in front of me and forget it."

The Miami detective laughed. They entered through the sliding glass door and proceeded into the kitchen. The locked fridge screamed out at the detective, as did the handcuffs on the couch in the adjacent living room. Nazario eyed the position of the sofa, directly in front of the television. "She had to sit here and watch her husband having sex with his lover?" Nazario said. "You say it was on repeat?"

"Disgusting piece of shit. It was playing on a loop," said the Miami detective. "The DVD's in that box with the others. Everything else has been left untouched, except for what CSI gathered on Alisa and in the area, such as dog hairs They've gathered skin under Montoya's nails. We're not sure if the DNA belongs to Alisa or the killer."

They walked up the winding staircase and to the bedroom on the second floor, where there was a breathtaking view of the ocean. There was a second set of bloody handcuffs on the bedpost, as if Alisa had been fighting to get herself free and injured her wrists. The tarp outside did little to thwart a cold breeze blowing through the blasted window. The rope contained a metal hook with a ring at the end to secure it. Nazario got close to the edge and looked down.

Thump. Thump. Thump. Estevan's body thudded against the lower portion of the remaining window that hadn't been shattered. The rope creaked and whined from dead weight as a bluster of wind disturbed the corpse.

Huxley was next to her, a hand on her upper arm.

"Don't get too close to the edge," he warned protectively.

"She had this rope ready to go," Nazario reasoned. She took a step back from the window, glass crunching under her shoes with each step. They walked back downstairs and seized a brown box containing the DVDs and a thick folder.

The note attached was barely legible and taped to the top of the box.

Nazario & Huxley - Alisa is fine.

It was the first time the serpent woman, Dr. Friedrich, had addressed either of them. Huxley leaned in and read the message over her shoulder.

Huxley to the detectives. "And no sign of Alisa Estevan anywhere?"

"Nope," answered the Miami detective. "They've got a home in Beverly Hills. We called LAPD and they put out a BOLO to neighboring jurisdictions."

"Don't think she'd fly back to L.A.," Nazario said.

"I was just thinking the same," Huxley answered.

Her phone rang, but she didn't reach it on time, and it went to voicemail.

"Frost," Nazario alerted Huxley, who rose a brow.

"Shall we?" Huxley carried the box containing DVDs, likely of rape videos of underage girls. Nazario wasn't looking forward to reviewing them. However, the folder containing an incriminating and detailed criminal history of the judge ought to be interesting.

"Give us a ring if there's any other intel that comes up," Nazario said, handing the Miami detective her card. "After CSI runs DNA, and all that."

She knew the DNA was likely from Dr. Wilder Agatha Friedrich. The serpent woman. Their girl. Nazario's mind struggled with the image of the innocent-looking doctor in her white lab coat, smiling as she posed with a group of dogs. This was the same doctor who had hung a judge, shot a corrupt cop, burned two men alive—one of whom she had given a Lorena Bobbitt special. Yet, she still had the conscience to save lives. Alisa Estevan, while missing, most likely was rescued by this vigilante out for justice.

They walked back to the car. Huxley turned on the engine, cranking up the heater. The car shivered as it shook off the cold, and he gave it a little gas to warm it up.

"I'm not sure I got the stomach for those DVDs," Nazario said, buckling her seatbelt.

"I most certainly don't," he said, releasing a weary sigh. Huxley gazed for a long beat out the window, fogging from the discrepancy of body heat and the cold January chill.

Nazario broke the silence. "What're you thinking?"

"You really meant what you said?" Huxley turned on the windshield wipers to dispel the moisture. "Pardon me if I'm a bit in—disbelief."

"Every last word," she assured. "I'll earn your trust. I promise you."

The car idled. Nazario reached for Huxley's hand and squeezed.

"Sounds cliché, but you're looking at the *happiest* federal agent alive." Huxley kissed the back of her hand. "Does...this mean we finally move you into my house? Save you from renter's hell?"

Nazario smiled. "Maybe."

"I'll take that as an eighty-five percent chance I'm getting a yes?" Huxley grinned. "Got an extra room for the baby."

"Ninety-nine," she said, and his face lit up.

Nazario's phone rang again. Deputy Frost. She put him on speaker. "What's the update?"

"We've got reason to believe our perp is heading back to the city of Angels," the deputy said, "think it's her final stop."

"What makes you think that?" Nazario frowned. "Most of the men on her hit list have been East Coast. We should know. We've been driving up and down the coast from Maine to Miami. I mean, hell, Sammy's murder was in Boston."

"Jefferson Pearce, remember the guy?" Deputy Frost didn't wait for an answer. "He was abducted."

"He was *what?*" Nazario straightened up. "That former Marine? How in the hell was he abducted? When? Why...what does he have to do with any of this?"

"Oh yeah, almost forgot...um...he's Informant F," Frost conveyed nonchalantly, like he was talking about what he had for lunch. "He's got some talent for the computers. We've reason to believe he's got other aliases."

"He can't be Ace," Nazario said baffled. She didn't know what she was picturing, but she hadn't pictured the traumatized soldier they'd met. "The drunk soldier? He was playing us, wasn't he?"

"He was playing us until he got played. Been missing for twenty-four hours," explained Frost. "The same man who had Sammy killed took him and knows Dr. Wilder's the killer. Looks like they found out Jefferson was the hacker and our informant —playing us all against each other. One of our cyber guys dug up the email exchanges. Jefferson led Sammy to Boston. We think that's how the bastards got to Jefferson and knew where Sammy was."

"So, Jefferson was a part of some underground hacking club

on the dark web? He knew Von Schlange's identity this entire time—that *motherfucker*." Nazario speculated.

"Yep, some of my men at the bureau found the site and the email exchanges. Sammy was desperate to find her big sis, hadn't been in contact since Dr. Wilder left the hospital after the attack."

"So, who's got Jefferson?" Huxley injected.

Frost replied with that same even tone. "Jerry Bell."

"The brotherhood's leader? Not possible." Nazario laughed.

Huxley sat up and grabbed the phone from Nazario's palm. "His ass is in San Quentin. I should know. I helped put him there for money laundering, drug trafficking, and an illegal weapons charge."

"Released early," Frost corrected. "Should've kept him in much longer."

Nazario threw her hands in the air. "How in the hell did this happen, and when?"

"Guess which judge pulled strings for early release?" Frost said. It was a rhetorical question they all knew the answer to. "Been out about six weeks now. What's more interesting is that his release was kept mighty, mighty private. No one in the news media or law enforcement was notified. It's unbelievable. I've spoken with fellow peers in the FBI, had a chat with the CIA, and your peeps, Nazario, at LAPD. Put a lot of phone calls in sitting on my derriere and got nowhere. Hell, I even pulled out some of my old contacts, called my buddy at the *L.A. Times,* and tapped other media sources. No one had a clue. Bell's release should've been *big* news. It was *no* news. And that warden— tried talking to the guy—*real* a-hole, wouldn't answer any of my questions."

"The judge responsible is hanging from his Miami vacation home," Huxley said.

Nazario swore under her breath.

"Like by a literal rope?" Deputy Frost said.

"Affirmative," Huxley said. "We just got back from the scene...technically still here. Sitting in the driveway looking at him dangling out the front window. ME hasn't cut the body down just yet."

The cool January breeze swayed the judge's lifeless body, a grim reminder that he wouldn't be *hanging* around Miami anymore.

Frost whistled into the receiver.

"We got no clue where Bell is, do we?" Nazario punched the dashboard hard enough to leave knuckles sore and a bruise for later.

"Truth be told...haven't a trace of the guy," Frost admitted, "but we think he's somewhere here in Cali."

"Oh, c'mon, give us more than that to go by. Shit, California's a big-ass state, sir," Huxley seethed. "*Somewhere* means a hundred and sixty-three thousand, plus or minus, square miles. He could be in Sacramento or in fucking Barstow!"

"Yeah, I know. He can be somewhere in between." The deputy chuckled. Huxley and Nazario exchanged a deadpan expression, one that didn't share Deputy Frost's levity.

Nazario leaned into the phone. "That's it? Drop everything and head back?"

"Yep, orders are stat," Frost directed. "Oops...my new Apple Watch is telling me it's time for my walk. See y'all home."

"Hang on...Deputy, can you send us pictures of Bell? Any identifiable tattoos?"

"Sure, I'm right in front of his file. Sending it over now." Deputy Frost hung up, and the car continued to idle.

The windows moistened, thawing the mild Miami chill from the defroster's blast as quiet consumed the space between them. It dawned on Nazario that they hadn't even left the famed honorable José Estevan's Miami vacation home, and already they were ordered to return to L.A.

"What's our plan, Huxley?" Nazario finally said just as an email chimed.

"Find Bell and our killer doc before anyone else does," he said.

Nazario tapped on her email on the phone, and watched pictures populate of Jerry Bell.

On his right shoulder was that damn tattoo of the Confederate flag.

TWENTY-TWO

THE HUNT FOR VICTIM FIVE

SHE REMEMBERED *Jefferson knocking on her apartment about a year ago. Like all the other times, she'd given him grief. He wasn't supposed to cross her boundaries this way.*

"What're you doing here showing up like this?" Von had scolded him, attempting to slam the door. "I said no more."

"Double the offer." Jefferson had said sticking his black combat boot between the door. "Ten minutes of your time and you can pay me a grand instead of two."

Von huffed, raking a hand through her hair. "I said I have enough info. You coming down here like this—it's stupid Jefferson. It's fucking stupid. I've paid you enough. I told you they've been following us, and you can't just show up like this. I told you the rules from the get-go, man. I work alone."

"You need this one," Jefferson had insisted, "he ain't like the others, Von."

Von clutched the door, opening it just enough as Jefferson handed her a photo. "Is this some joke? He's at San Quentin."

"Not for long," Jefferson warned. "Dude's about to bounce. This is major intel on a silver platter, man. It's the main honcho. Bigger than all the rest."

"We're supposed to be hanging low. Our deal's done. I told you. You supplied what I needed. This is where you're supposed to not be coming up here, just begging to be caught. This isn't being careful?" Von bit out, frustrated.

"Quintientos dólares," Jefferson said in his native tongue.

"Five hundred dollars," Von sighed, "and for what? Thought you said a grand?"

"Deal of the day. Half off my original offer. Get the money and I'll hand you proof."

Von stalled for a beat, studying Jefferson. The young veteran soldier wasn't lying. She could tell by the determination in her eyes. She swore under her breath, disappeared briefly in her apartment and returned with an envelope with three thousand. Between her savings, proceeds from the sale of her clinic to her ex, the hospital's settlement for the botched surgery, and the home she sold in Casper, Von had seventy-two million in the bank after accrued interest. That wasn't counting stocks and several money market accounts she'd set up years before the worst night of her life. She had enough money to pay very close attention to a list of men on the FBI's list. She hadn't planned on Jerry Bell. He had been the orchestrator of the entire gang and had been in control even while on the inside, locked up.

Von handed Jefferson the envelope with the amount agreed upon and then Jefferson handed her a piece of paper. Von reluctantly scanned it. There were direct orders from Judge José Estevan granting Jerry Bell early release. Jefferson had easily hacked into the judge's emails and all of the exchanges were there. Pages upon pages of back-and-forth correspondence. Once again, she'd doubted Jefferson, but his hacking and research skills had come through.

"One more thing about this guy...he's got a Confederate flag with two hammers in the shape of an 'X' in front of it. This means *something to you, don't it?" Jefferson queried, and all Von could remember was being shocked.*

It sure did mean a lot to her. He'd definitely found the third and final man.

Von would have had no idea Jerry Bell would be released early if not for Jefferson.

"Damn good intel, Pearce. Damn good," she gave him a rare compliment, handing him an additional five hundred. "Let's make it a grand. I'll honor your original offer. Need to know where he'll be when he's released."

"Somewhere in California," Jefferson confirmed. "I'm like ninety-nine percent sure the dude'll remain in the state."

The truth: Von didn't have the last man's location on her list because he'd virtually been a ghost since his release. No one caught wind of Bell's release except for Jefferson and Von. Von didn't believe it for herself, not at first. After all, Jerry Bell had been in prison for multiple counts of rape and sex trafficking of minors.

As the former head of the Aryan Nation Brotherhood, Jerry Bell spoke German and had a surprising number of contacts: wealthy executives, businessmen, judges, doctors, and lawyers—people you wouldn't expect to be associated with such a man.

Von now understood that Jefferson had been pulling the strings, hiding behind anonymity.

She thought involving him had been her idea, but he was the one who had sought her out.

Jefferson got to know her as Ace, the anonymous hacker who helped her learn how to use spyware. That was the point in time when he must've planted himself in the library for her to "discover" him. While she thought she was daring him to hack the FBI's top-secret files, Jefferson had already hacked her computer and was the sole person to know of her plans. He had to have been cyber stalking her, knowing her moves. Jefferson knew she was in Florida and somewhere along the East Coast, but he never went to the cops.

Regardless, she still felt guilty and hoped the former Lance Corporal was still alive.

What she knew: Jerry Bell was released from San Quentin, and it was off the books. It was no easy task. In fact, to anyone with half a brain, the notion of a criminal getting early release from San Quentin would appear to be utterly ludicrous and virtually impossible. Several guards and the warden all got paid to keep it from ever reaching public ears. And before the judge scrubbed his emails and computer, leaving no digital trace of the transaction, Von had made copies. The email exchanges lived in Jerry Bell's folder and not in Estevan's because she didn't want to lead the detectives to him, not before she got to him first. She didn't have his location, but that didn't mean the detectives and FBI weren't aware.

Von thought about her parents calling out to her. For a moment, there was a heaviness in her heart that made her feel like she was drowning in despair. Then she thought of not just Sammy or the victims she rescued but of the countless underage young girls she didn't—victims of kidnapping, sex trafficking, rape—and the mental scars they'd forever carry. She thought of law enforcement not acting quick enough, causing more girls to be abused by the hands of evil men.

No, Von wasn't sorry for the true animals she'd taken out. They were subhuman.

In their hotel room, Von opened her folder on Jerry Bell, trying to see if she missed anything. But she knew she hadn't, and time was running out for her to find him. Von took out the box of four-milligram nicotine lozenges and plopped one of them in her mouth. If she was going to die, she'd much prefer a quick shot to the head rather than cigarette-induced cancer eating away at her body.

She turned on the television and switched to the news stations. The judge's death had hit all the major news outlet, making headlines everywhere. She flicked through the local Los Angeles network news channels. A satisfied grin spread across her lips. She unmuted the television.

"A local and prominent California judge, José Estevan, was found hanging from his two-story vacation home in Miami two days ago. Further investigation is underway, but authorities believe he first shot and killed a Miami police officer before taking his own life. Presiding in the infamous Aryan Nation sex trafficking ring case more than eight years prior, Estevan was accused of intimidation of witnesses, including a key witness found murdered in Boston within days of his suicide."

"What in the—" Von sat up on her bed. Another cover-up. The detectives working the case and the FBI had to have known that Montoya was dirty, based on his well-known, public record. Then there was the call Montoya made claiming Alisa Estevan had killed herself. There was no way in hell they thought José killed Montoya, then hung himself. She'd left Estevan's folder with the sex tapes. While part of the news report was true, the death was homicide. Murder.

Why were they covering up for her? Why were they feeding the media lies? What would be their motive? What would they stand to gain? Save their reputation for having sat too long on these cases? It still didn't make sense. What disturbed her most was that the Feds were falsifying facts to hide the truth. Concern and anxiety riddled her mind: What game was the FBI playing? If they could make up whatever story to cover up for these deaths and the killer's identity, what were their plans for her?

What did she expect? Personal convictions or no, her actions had consequences.

Then, out of nowhere, her burner phone, an unlisted and private number, rang for only the second time ever. The first time when Sammy was killed. Her heart slammed against her rib cage, causing a sharp pain. She breathed through it clutching her shirt. It was the closest to a heart attack that she'd ever experienced. Had Bell gotten to her parents? Killed them, too? Could it be Nazario or Huxley? Did they find a way to get a hold of her number?

By the third ring, she pushed the answer button and waited to speak.

"Yo," A familiar voice whispered into the receiver, "V?"

"T-Tommy?" Von pinched the bridge of her nose, and her shoulders sagged. A deep exhale escaped from Von's lungs as relief persuaded her body to slump into the rickety motel chair. She leaned her forehead against the window, cooled by the January chill.

"Ace sent me," he said. "Got the message at three this morning. One of them auto-triggers. Calls it the panic button. Made me promise if something ever happened, I'd make the delivery."

"Please tell me you know where Ace is?"

"I wish." Swallowing hard, Tommy, her tattooist, blew out a breath that caused the receiver to static on her cheap burner phone. "I don't know nothing. Just passing this on for Ace. You better write this down. JW," Tommy said.

"Is?"

"Jamal Wagner. Ex-con. Was in prison with Bell. Each was head of their own gang, and in a way, respected each other. They're both bosses. JW the black leader. Bell the white. You need to talk to JW, but it won't be easy."

"Got it. They didn't necessarily hang in the same circles on the inside. So why in the hell would this Jamal know where the head of a white supremacist gang is hiding?"

"People respect him. Scared shitless of him. Has his resources. The only one that Jerry Bell stayed far away from. They...have their own rules in there. He's the only one that knew that Bell was released, and I think he bargained a way to get himself out, too."

She swiveled around in the chair and snagged the pen and cheap note pad from the desk.

"Where can I find JW?" Von asked, and Tommy quickly spat out an address.

"This part is important. Ace put it in bold font in his auto-triggered encrypted message he sent me this morning. Said JW hates dogs and doesn't trust easily. Money won't be enough. You'll have to prove yourself to him," Tommy warned.

"Got it." Von stroked Zeus, words steady despite her hammering heart.

"And...at some point, Ace said you might need to contact some detective," Tommy paused as if trying to read a note. "A Detective Anaya Nazario."

Von shoved herself up from the chair. Frustration swelled as she paced, tongue slipping into German. *"Kontaktieren Sie den Detektiv, der meinen Arsch jagt?"*

"Whoa," Tommy whispered, "don't know what the hell you just said."

"Contact the detective that's hunting my ass?" Von repeated in English.

"Message here says you'll know when it's time to call the detective," Tommy said and then recited Nazario's cell number. Von quickly scribbled it down. "Ace insisted I give you the 411 on the detective."

"Don't care to know anything about—"

"She was Sammy's instructor."

"She what?"

"It says here, Detective Nazario was Sammy's Taekwondo instructor and that you'd get what that meant."

A rush of emotions strangled her throat, making it hard to breathe or talk.

"You there?" he asked after a five count.

She breathed heavy into the receiver. "Y-yeah."

Detective Nazario had been Sammy's fight instructor all these years? This detective, the same one chasing her down helped her little sister defend herself so creeps wouldn't take advantage of her again? Von was gobsmacked. This one small fact had suddenly changed everything.

"Look, Von, this whole thing's got me spooked. I'm only calling you as a favor to Ace. I don't even know what any of this means."

"O-okay," Von gulped, raking a hand through her hair. "Sorry you got involved in my shit, Tommy. Really, I am."

Tommy interrupted. "One last thing the message said. This part really makes no sense to me. It might to you. It says: *If you have nowhere to go, Doctor—*"

Von cleared her throat; she hadn't been referred to as doctor since before her surgery.

"What do you mean if I have nowhere to go? Tommy? Hey, Tommy?"

The line went dead.

———

Von dabbed Dermablend and spread it across the right side of her freshly shaved scalp. Next, she concealed her forearms, which required less cover-up. The makeup was adequate enough to assuage her concern about her tattoos showing.

Von cleaned her hands then eagerly ate her vegan burger,

washing it down with Diet Coke. After the quick lunch, she secured her hair under a nylon cap. The brunette wig made of human hair came next. Its librarian bangs and feathery, wispy strands framed her face. She put on the wig and adjusted it. To complete her look, she changed into a plain, fitted gray one-piece business dress that came to her knees. The outfit was complete with a black blazer and regrettable five-inch black stilettos.

Zeus made his whiny sound as he tilted his head curiously at her.

"*Es ist vorübergehend,*" she said. *It's temporary.*

When she arrived at the bank, she told Zeus she'd be back and left the dog in the car. It wouldn't be wise for her to be on camera with Zeus accompanying her.

Her high heels clacked boisterously against the waxed linoleum floors and through the too quiet privately-owned bank. She was swiftly greeted by the branch manager. Charles Rowland was over six-feet-six, a gangly man who seemed as if his limbs were exaggerated in an unnatural way. He took enormous strides, arms dangling back and forth at his sides. What was most peculiar was his long horse face and neck, which triggered the image of a giraffe. Rowland had been with the branch for more than twenty years and always personally managed her accounts.

"Dr. Agatha Jones, it's so very lovely to see you again."

Rowland only knew her by yet another alternate identity she'd created five years ago. From passports, driver's licenses, social security cards, and even birth certificates—not only was her legal name Von Schlange, but Dr. Agatha Jones, too. Now more than ever, she didn't regret picking her middle name as her third alias. It helped her hold on to a piece of her former self, reminding Von that she hadn't lost everything.

He was in front of her before she could reach his office door.

"It's been ages. Can I offer you a cup of coffee, tea, or perhaps a cold bottle of Perrier? It used to be your favorite?"

Charles Rowland had an impeccable memory—not just for numbers, but for details about his clients that made each one feel special. At least his charm had worked that way on her. His long bony fingers swallowed up her petite hand.

"Charles." Von shook his hand. "Kind of you to offer, but I just had lunch. Thank you anyway."

He ushered her into his private office and closed the door.

"It's been almost six years...five years, and ten months to be precise since you've come in," he said, typing into his computer and then turning to give his undivided attention. "What brings you in? Another deposit? I'm impressed that you haven't once touched your accounts."

"I've other means for regular daily expenses," she admitted. His elongated face twisted in disappointment. She sensed a bit of jealousy that she kept other money elsewhere.

Von cleared the air with a disarming laugh.

"Oh, don't look so sour; I can assure you it's a modest sum. The majority of my funds are under your management."

A modest half-million, originally in a separate checking account under Dr. Agatha Jones at a generic public bank, had been used primarily for living expenses over the past five years. She hadn't been focused on owning anything: no new wardrobe, expensive vehicle, or property. In fact, other than dog food and a vegan diet, she lived a very inexpensive, thrift-store life. While she couldn't explain her choices to her famous well-off parents or to anyone who knew her as Dr. Wilder, one person would've understood—Sammy.

Her throat constricted, and she willed the tears away.

Pull it together, Von—not right now.

Today, she had to play the part of her former identity.

"Withdrawal," she began, "twenty-one thousand ought to

do. Large bills, please, and in this suitcase. It's for a...business transaction."

She knew the Feds would eventually track her down, all her accounts were under Z *Dog Walking Services*. The owner's name, Dr. Agatha Jones, was strictly hidden from the public on all the accounts. But if uncovered, no one would connect Dr. Jones to Von Schlange.

"Twenty-one thousand in large bills," Charles repeated, and she hoped he didn't ask her any more questions. "Very well, you were at fifty-four million. It's been six years. Before the withdrawal, you were up to seventy-two plus with accrued interest. I'll have the receipt for you with your total balance minus the twenty-one."

Forty minutes later, Charles was counting the money and placing it in her suitcase.

"Thank you, Charles. I admire your years of loyalty at this branch." She shook his hand.

"It is your loyalty that I truly appreciate," he said with a broad smile and a formal bow of the head. "This...business venture...I do wish you the best of luck. Please do stay safe, Dr. Jones."

Something in his tone sounded suspicious. Nonetheless, Rowland was someone she trusted.

When she got to the car, Zeus waited for her with his head down as she instructed. She quickly walked him for a bathroom break and then, once at the hotel, topped off his food and water. At last, she yanked off the wig, itchy nylon cap, painful heels, and the awfully constricting business dress. Sammy, who always gave her a hard time, was right. How on Earth she used to dress this way boggled her mind. Von jumped in the shower, washing off the coverup makeup and any trace of her façade.

To meet JW, Von Schlange must show up, not Dr. Friedrich nor Dr. Jones.

TWENTY-THREE

THE DEAL

ASIDE FROM A LARGE black bouncer guarding the front door, no one else was around. There was no indication the remote warehouse just outside of Compton was home to one of LA's most exclusive underground clubs. The walls must be well insulated, Von mused, by some sort of soundproofing technology.

The bouncer looked at her and Zeus suspiciously. He folded his massive arms across his chest, bulging his pectorals and biceps. His large bald head sported a tribal design Von admired.

"This a private spot. It ain't open to the public. I don't know how you heard, but uh...people like you... don't belong up in here. Get what I mean? We definitely don't allow dogs."

In the presence of the intimidating bouncer, she found herself fumbling for words.

Von raised her brow. "What if I said a crazy hacker with a little PTSD and too much time on their hands told me about it."

Her delivery was spot on, and the bouncer took it as she intended—a cute little joke.

A wave of heat suddenly ignited her skin. *Fucking hot flashes.*

The bouncer rocked back, releasing laughter that boomed into the night.

"That's the only way your white ass could've heard about this spot," the bouncer chuckled in deep baritone. "Girl, you must be crazy comin' up in here. But I am diggin' the ink. That's some sick-ass detailed art. It must've taken while and hurt like hell, huh? Mine took two days."

Von saw her opening. "Five eight-hour days. The pain was much worse than taking a bullet out of my arm and stitching myself up without anesthesia or Patrón."

The bouncer smiled wide. "C'mon, you fuckin' with me? How *you* get shot? Forget to set the safety at the shootin' range?"

Von rolled up her sleeve, and the bouncer whistled as he inspected the stitches.

"You should've seen the other guy." Von smiled at him brightly, recalling Sean Martin and what became of him. She shrugged. "Who knows, I could very well be a serial killer."

"All five foot of you?" the bouncer hooted, a hearty laugh barreling out of him once again, causing his entire body to convulse and Zeus to shift in place. "Girl, you crackin' me up with the shit you sayin'. You really are crazy, but I'm kind of diggin' you. What you really here for?"

"Need to see JW," she said.

The bouncer stopped laughing, and his face turned to stone.

She looked him in the eyes and didn't flinch.

"You ain't jokin'."

She opened the briefcase, and his eyes bulged. Von removed ten Benjamin Franklins and closed the suitcase. Twenty-one thousand was precisely how much she needed. One thousand for the doorkeeper and the rest for the head honcho.

She extended the money to the man and incredulity spread across his face. "All you have to do is walk me to him. It has to be the dog and me. I don't go anywhere without him. I'd give you more. The rest is reserved. It'll be the easiest grand you make."

The bouncer hesitated and then took it. "You ain't packin'? You got nothin' to protect yourself with, do you?" he said, knowingly concerned. "Everyone up in here's packin'. Like I said, this ain't no place—"

"I don't like guns," she sighed, "and don't worry, I don't do cops. Feel me? We'll be fine. No gun, no threat."

"You don't like guns? Girl, you may not come out alive," he said, stuffing the money in his pocket.

"That's the chance I'm willing to take," Von said.

The bouncer blew out a loud breath. "You know the drill," he said.

Von assumed the position to be frisked and the bouncer patted her down. Satisfied, he opened the door. They made their way down a flight of stairs and along an underground cement tunnel. At the very end of the walkway was a massive metal door with a passcode keypad.

"Turn around," he ordered Von, and the bouncer typed in the code. The triple-thick metal door slid open. If she had to guess, it was bulletproof.

Clouds of smoke were dense, turning the room opaque and sooty. However, no one seemed to mind the lack of ventilation. Von inhaled a mixture of cigar, pot, and cigarette smoke, greedily filling her lungs with what her body had been craving. The low ambient lighting and old-school gangster rap offered the right atmospheric blend. It was not at all what she'd expected. It wasn't obnoxiously loud with rowdy crowds like most raves.

There were no young, college-aged drug dealers making the rounds with an assortment of pills as monotonous techno music played. Instead, there was a full bar and a scattering of expensive leather sofas and chairs. Tastefully designed modern tables where heated card games were taking place. Gorgeous women dressed to the nines accompanied by armed men. She scanned and noticed handguns of various sizes everywhere.

The classy, upscale atmosphere cloaked the danger lurking beneath.

"They all glockin'—every last one of them," the bouncer warned, and then she noticed the bulge under his own shirt in the front. She must either be really stupid or suicidal.

As she walked behind the bouncer with Zeus and her brief-case, a stillness came over the room. Bodies stiffened and paused, people stopped drinking, and their eyes trained on her. It was perfect room temperature, but her body felt like it had been set ablaze.

She pinched at her shirt trying to allow air to fan the perspi-ration beading on her chest.

Hot flashes from hell.

They wove through the card tables to the back, where a large leather sofa and coordinated leather chairs were arranged around it. Drinks and ashtrays were spread across the glass cock-tail table. Von inspected the scene quickly: Two mid-sized henchmen with tattoos sprawling across on their arms sat in leather chairs flanked on the right and left of the sofa. Both carried guns. Each man had a drink in one hand and a cigar in the other.

Her gaze finally shifted to the sofa. A massive, muscular man sat with his arms outstretched on either side, resting on the top of the sofa cushions like a king. Every inch of his upper torso from his fingers to his neck was covered with tattoos. She made out that some were verses; one was a cross that appeared to be covered in barbed wire and flowers. Letters were inscribed down each of his fingers, but in the low light she couldn't make out the message. The rest of his ink crashed into an unintelligible canvas of symbolism. A cigar dangled from his lips, and thunderous laughter roared out, juddering his entire body.

JW wasn't surrounded by an entourage, and she understood why he wouldn't want to be.

There was movement to the right and left of her periphery. The two henchmen started to their feet, both drawing their weapons. Number One pointed his automatic at her face, and Number Two, to her right, targeted Zeus.

"She's clean," the bouncer said, "ain't packin'."

"I wouldn't point your gun at my dog," Von warned, raising her hands in the air.

"And what's he fixin' to do?" Number One hollered, barrel aimed at her head.

Controlled, Von smiled. "Y'all are so brave with your big guns. How about you find out what my dog's made of."

"That's an unarmed woman. Stand yo ass down," JW ordered Number One in a cool tone.

Henchman number one did as he was told and sat in his seat, watching with sharp eyes.

Henchman number two on the right continued to stand with his gun pointed at Zeus. Her dog wasn't growling or moving but was in a ready position, and she was the only one that knew it.

"Let him," JW continued calmly, "bring his game on."

JW nodded at Von, communicating that he accepted the challenge.

It was a test Zeus couldn't get wrong.

Henchman two stepped closer to Zeus with the gun. The aim was undoubtedly precise and would kill her dog with certainty. Just as the man drew near, Zeus, acting on instinct and without command, launched in a run no one expected but her. The entire moment seemed to go in slow motion. Von knew better than to move. Like any lethal predator in the animal kingdom, they'd strike and kill her, code or no, if she tried to intervene. Time suddenly crawled, nearly stopping altogether. His finger began to squeeze the trigger, though he hesitated for a split second. Number Two looked startled that the one-hundred-pound canine was rushing toward him full speed, like a linebacker on four legs.

The last-second hesitation was all that was required. The henchman on her right let out a frightened scream as Zeus leapt through the air, teeth clamping down on the man's gun hand. The henchman and his gun clattered to the floor. His beefy frame slammed hard enough to shake the drinks on the nearby cocktail table. Zeus stood on the man's chest and then barked at JW. After a beat of silence, the boss broke out into roaring laughter. He began slapping his knee, laughing so hard he held his stomach.

The henchman's trembling hands went up in surrender.

"Alright...you got me," he said to Zeus. "Now would you get up off?"

Zeus stepped off his chest, padded over to the gun, and picked it up in his mouth.

All eyes followed the dog as he walked the gun over to JW, put it on the ground, and then with his nose, shoved it next to JW's feet. Von was relieved that two things didn't happen: a) the gun didn't go off and start a shootout, and b) Zeus didn't seriously injure the man.

Zeus must've had an intuitive sense that these men weren't like the ones on her list.

"Are you bleeding?" Von asked.

"It's all good," Number Two muttered, avoiding eye contact. He smoothed out his shirt and his jeans of unseen wrinkles and then awkwardly sat back down in his chair, weaponless.

"You good? For real? You sho screamed like you wasn't good," the bouncer said. He, JW, and Number One burst out laughing. But Von didn't find it funny. Number Two got really lucky.

"Bitch, don't you got a job to get back to?" Number Two sniped.

"Oooh-wee...I done seen it all." The bouncer shook Von's hand. "You one crazy white girl coming up in here. But that dog...I want me one of him."

The bouncer turned to JW.

"She got something in that suitcase you might be interested in, boss."

JW waited for the bouncer to leave before picking up the henchman's gun from the ground. He turned it around and pointed the handle at his embarrassed second-man.

"Ask the kitchen to cook up a steak. Cut it up for our new guest," JW ordered Number Two and then turned to her. "You hungry?"

"I don't eat meat," Von said, "but Zeus isn't a vegan."

Number Two took his gun from his boss, warily eyeing Zeus as he headed for the kitchen.

"Well, Zeus is one fine name for a bad-ass dog," JW exclaimed. "My man was right, you crazy as hell comin' up in here unarmed. I can see you got yo'self somethin' a whole lot better than a gun."

JW put his hand out for Zeus. Zeus stared for a beat before walking closer and letting JW pet him. That was not what she expected at all, but it made her relax a bit. If Zeus could trust him, so could she.

"Get her a chair," JW told Number One, and the man did as he was told. He returned quickly with a leather chair. Von thanked him and sat down. Number Two came back with a plate of chopped steak; it made her stomach turn at the sight and smell. He set it down along with a bowl of water. Zeus looked at her as if asking for permission.

"*Essen*," she said, directing Zeus in German to eat.

After both henchmen were seated, JW smashed out his cigar and pulled out a pack of Newports. While she used to be a Marlboro Reds girl, menthols didn't sound too bad right now.

She opted for her nicotine lozenges.

"What in the hell are those?" JW leaned in for a closer look. "Nah, you fixin' to have a real cigarette. None of this vape shit, lozenges, or that nasty-ass gum."

He gave her a cigarette, and she inclined forward for the light. She inhaled a long puff of menthol smoke into her lungs. Nothing could be better at this moment than this cigarette. JW took a drag and exhaled smoke out of his nose.

"Before we get to the suitcase...who are you and what's this about?"

"Von. Here for Jerry Bell," she said. "Need his location. Heard you can find him."

JW picked up his drink and took a sip. He paused contemplatively.

"I don't mess with that fool. I didn't on the inside and don't now."

Number One broke in. "He's a motha-fuckin' Aryan. A skinhead, man."

"Yeah, JW," Number Two agreed, "why can't we go—"

JW put his hand up and both men blew out angry breaths.

"I know what he is. I know all about Jerry Bell," their boss answered. "Here's the thing, San Quentin, it ain't no place any fool would like to revisit. Feel me? I got out early pullin' some strings—"

"Judge José Estevan?" Von asked. "He helped Bell get out, too. I know. I don't care what deal you had to strike with Jerry to keep peace on the inside or with that judge. By the way, Estevan won't be wheeling and dealing no more. Last I saw him, he had a noose around his neck and was dangling out the window of his vacation home in Miami while his dirty cop buddy took three to the chest, one to the head—with his own gun. That piece of shit was unplanned," Von admitted, taking a drag of her cigarette. "I don't like guns, but I had no choice."

"That was all over the news. You sayin' you killed Estevan and that cop in Miami? It was no suicide like they sayin'?" Number One cut in and threw his hands in the air. "You expect us to believe that shit?"

JW sat up and leaned into her. He looked her in the eyes, and she didn't look away.

He took a drag of his cigarette and then nodded. "You ain't lyin', are you?"

"Easy to assume just by looking at someone," Von said, "but no one knows what anyone is truly capable of." Lifting her shirt, she uncovered the hideous serpent keloid.

The men gasped.

She told them about the initial trial, Judge Estevan's involvement, the witnesses shutting down on the stand, and the inevitable non-conviction of sex trafficking.

"Well, that fool's dead now. Burned up in his home," Number Two said.

"Let her finish," JW said, glaring at both of his men. "Von, please continue."

"Five years ago, Fischer got out after serving time for the only charges he was convicted of—dogfighting. When he did, he had a plan. He wanted to send a message to my little sister, one of the witnesses...one of the victims," Von paused for a beat, reflecting on Sammy. "He...he came after me...and my fiancé at the time."

She detailed being left for dead and the physical ramifications on her body due to the attack. How, if not for Zeus covering his body over hers, she would've bled out and froze to death in the snow.

Von paced and took a drag of her cigarette and then pointed at the dog.

"For five years, we've been preparing. So, I know all about that house fire."

She paused, took a drag of her cigarette, and looked each of them in the eyes.

None of them looked away.

"I haven't told anyone. Why am I confessing to you and your men? Because you won't say shit to the cops or the Feds. Trust me, they're both looking for me."

She smoked the cigarette down to the filter, nearly burning her fingers before extinguishing it.

JW lit another cigarette for her and handed it to her. She took it without hesitation, drew another long drag, and continued.

Sharing her untold story was the ultimate release. For the first time in years, she felt a semblance of freedom. She had nothing to lose at this point. The FBI and the cops were looking for her and likely already knew her identity. Nothing she shared with JW and his crew would make matters worse than they already were, especially now that it had cost her Sammy.

She spent the next ten minutes telling them the rest of her story.

One of the henchman cursed under his breath, while the other slammed a fist down on the arm of his chair and yelled, "We need to take that mothafucka out, man!"

A few men playing cards glanced their way and then casually returned to what they were doing. No one in this private underground club flinched at talk of murder. The patrons all minded their own business like they were abiding by some unsaid rule.

JW handed her a drink. It was whiskey. She slammed it down.

"We got one rule: children, young girls, and women," JW said evenly, "are off-limits. We'll take care of him."

"No." She opened the suitcase. "Enjoy your freedom and keep your hands clean. Here's twenty thousand. All you have to do is tell me where Mr. Bell is hiding. No one touches him but me. That's the deal."

JW and both of his henchmen shared the same look of both contemplation and anger.

"Von, we misjudged you. We misjudged Zeus. I got mad respect. What you shared—goes to our graves. Feel me? You take out Bell, and we promise we'll help you find a way out," JW said, handing her a pen and paper. She wrote down the number to her burner phone and handed it to him. "We'll find that mothafucka in two days."

JW took the suitcase, and they shook on it.

TWENTY-FOUR
THE FIFTH VICTIM

SNOWFLAKES QUIETLY WHIRLED outside her window. For miles, there was nothing but virgin powder blanketing the pearly terrain. Although in California, Von found herself surrounded by snow once again. The smell of the old log cabin alloyed with freshly brewed coffee, warming her hands. She slowly sipped, savoring the moment as she gazed out at the frosty landscape. Everything about Big Bear brought back fresh nostalgia of when she'd lived in Casper, Wyoming, where this all started.

It had been five years since her surgically induced menopause. Despite the cold, she had at least three hot flashes this morning alone. For the most part, an all-natural, over-the-counter supplement helped her manage the symptoms. However, she noticed them returning. First, at the underground club, and now this morning, stress the likely culprit. At every turn, her body reminded her again and again how the parts that once made her a woman were shredded, making her thirty-five-year-old body behave like it was fifty-five.

Von never thought she'd come to resent buying menopause supplements, but she needed them and had little choice. She was almost out of them and needed to make a pharmacy run. The cashiers always eyed her with suspicion—a paradox of youth and age. The bigger dichotomy was sweating despite it being below zero outside and not having the heater on.

The frigid, scenic beauty had distracted her from that fiery, internal burning.

In the morning hours, the sun touched the snow at the perfect angle making the tiny ice crystals sparkle like a trillion diamond flecks. At night, the onyx sky turned the white mounds into glowing blue. Even Zeus, during his bathroom breaks outdoors, hopped through the snow like a puppy. It had been almost a week since she last spoke with JW. He called exactly two days after their meeting, as promised, to inform her that Jerry Bell had a remote cabin rental in Big Bear. She managed to rent the closest cabin thirty-five feet away. She was distant enough not to be seen by Bell, yet close enough to keep tabs on him.

Both odd and infuriating, the man hadn't left his home. In fact, it'd been three whole days without coming or going. The light inside turned on each evening around 5:30 p.m. and didn't turn off until around two in the early morning—Jerry Bell's bedtime. Von had tracked his sleep and wake patterns. Of course, since Bell had spent years in a six-by-eight cell, staying in a thousand-square-foot cabin for a few days was a luxury.

Using her audio app, she'd been able to track every move Bell made within the cabin. Other than listening to what was on TV, he'd been relatively quiet. There had been no sign of Jefferson. If the marine was there, she would've heard him. From day one, she had deduced that he must've been moved, alive or dead, especially after she'd peered through each window and seen nothing.

On that first night, she also found out that Bell was an extremely light sleeper. She'd been at the window testing to see if they were locked when, at the slightest creak, Bell sprang out of bed and was in the living room within seconds. He stormed outside, not even bothering with a jacket or shoes. Barefoot, he tramped through the snow with a shotgun, circling the cabin like a lunatic.

Von and Zeus were lucky they weren't caught. She'd gotten away with sneaking into the other homes but with Jerry Bell, not a chance. As desperate as she was to rescue Jefferson, it would do no good if she wound up killed before getting an opportunity to find the kid.

She had to be ultra-careful.

Von checked her watch: 1:34 a.m.

Bell would be asleep in thirty minutes.

Zeus lifted his head from the ground and looked at her.

"*Es ist Zeit.*" she told Zeus. *It's time.*

He got up knowingly, walked to the door, and stood obediently next to it.

She quickly slung the binoculars around her neck and donned the snow jacket she had brought with her. The bastard was in there—she knew it. JW and his boys wouldn't have gotten this one wrong. The audio spy app confirmed his movements, though up in the mountains, it could cut in and out. At some point, he'd have to leave.

Her silver, waterproof, all-weather boots rose just below her knee, making it easier for her to wade a path through the fresh snow ahead of Zeus so that he didn't have to hop through. They crunched swiftly through the snow, careful not to be seen, following the same course they'd taken all week. Behind her cabin and into the woods. Outside, Zeus took a much-needed piss on the first tree.

Von crept through the shadows, safely out of sight from the cabin door, hidden behind a cluster of majestic towering spruce trees. Zeus paced at her side, his ears perked and body tense.

Her heart was a pounding war drum as they approached Jerry Bell's parked white Ram Tradesman pickup. The crunch of snow beneath her boots felt like walking through a field of land-mines, each step a calculated risk.

If Jerry caught them, Zeus and Von would easily be dead within seconds.

The sound of windows sliding open cut through the quiet, snowy woods.

Her devoted canine froze in place, ears perking up as a low growl escaped.

"Shit," she whispered, dropping to her knees and sinking into the snow. They took cover behind a cluster of large trees. She watched Jerry Bell emerge from his home. Her watch read 1:38 a.m. Earlier, she'd finally seen him, and in person, he'd gained weight from his prison pictures. Bell was an average-looking man: stocky, possibly six feet tall, with a crew-cut and a soft middle, likely from a nightly six-pack diet.

Von reached the truck, her breath a whisper in the still air. From her pocket, she pulled out the Tracker XT-200, a small, black device no larger than a matchbox. The tracker was state-of-the-art, boasting a range of 2 miles, GPS precision within 5 feet, and a battery life of 72 hours. It was designed to sync seam-lessly with her iPhone via Bluetooth, allowing her to follow its signal in real-time.

Von slid underneath the truck, her pulse quickening. The world above seemed to fade, re-placed by the cold, metallic underside of the vehicle. She found a secure spot near the rear axle and pressed the tracker into place. The XT-200 clicked softly, its magnetic hold firm. The chill from the snow seeped through her gloves, numbing her fingers as she worked.

As she backed out, the soft creak of a door pierced the silence. Jerry Bell stepped out of his cabin for a second time—without his hostage. He glanced around, his suspicions sharpening, as if his life as a former prisoner had given him an instinct for sensing unseen eyes. Where the fuck was Lance Corporal Jefferson Pierce? The question spun in her mind, numb to the chill of the snow as she hid among the trees, watching.

Instincts screamed Jefferson wasn't inside, but this was her only chance to search the cabin, Bell's heavy footsteps a symphony of dread. Von froze, every muscle in her body screaming for action yet paralyzed by fear. She and Zeus ducked behind the truck, her heart now a wild, erratic beat.

She could hear Jerry's breath, a dragon's growl in the dark, as he moved closer. The scent of gasoline and rust filled her nostrils, mingling with the acrid taste of fear. Von's mind raced, every second stretching into an eternity. The night air was thick with tension, as palpable as the ground beneath her.

Zeus whimpered softly, sensing panic. Von pressed a hand to his head, willing him to be silent. Jerry's footsteps paused, mere inches from their hiding spot. Her heart hammered so loudly she was sure it would give them away. Each beat was a thunderclap in the quiet night.

Von's gloved fingers still felt the bite of the frosty winter as she fumbled with her phone, activating the Bluetooth. From their vantage point, she and Zeus were completely concealed from the dangerous ex-convict, leader of the sex trafficking ring, and head of the Aryan Brotherhood. She could taste the proximity to danger, feel the weight of being his next target, his next possible victim, a casualty of his sadistic thirst. The night air was thick with menace, each second stretched by the suffocating anticipation of being caught.

Her phone's screen lit up, showing the tracker's location. Relief washed over her, but she didn't dare move. She held her breath, listening as Jerry's footsteps resumed, walking to his truck.

When the door to the pickup slammed shut, Von allowed

herself to breathe again, glad that she'd have time to search the cabin now with Jerry gone, then follow his truck, thanks to the tracker hidden under the truck. The tracker's signal glowed on her phone like a beacon in the night. Once the white Ram was out of sight, Von quickly ran to his cabin. She checked the door, but she'd watched him lock it. Von recalled Bell opening one of the windows and noticed it was still slightly cracked open. A fusion of lingering pot and cigarette smoke hit her nose.

She slid the window wide enough to crawl in and then closed it behind her.

She ran through the home, screaming the soldier's name, but got nothing in return. Inside, Von unlocked the front door and wasn't surprised to see Zeus already waiting. An extra-large black plastic trash bag was full of empty beer cans—as expected. A blank notepad rested on the dining table. She saw the lines in the paper where Bell had pressed down hard while writing. She took the pen lying next to the notepad and sketched lightly over it.

What Bell had written down clearly popped up in white.

At the center of the notepad was a location: San Pedro Warehouse.

Von did another sweep of the cabin before running out the door.

Von felt a grim satisfaction. The hunt had begun, and she was ready.

———

It took her almost four hours to reach the cheap motel room in San Pedro. Skipping sleep, she gulped lukewarm instant coffee, clicked open a map on her laptop, and scanned the location. She reviewed a list of warehouses in San Pedro. There were several storage places, a grill cleaning service, small shops, wholesalers.

None of these places made any sense. Bell had been in the woods for a week without leaving his cabin.

"He wouldn't choose a crowded, public warehouse. Right, Zeus?" she asked.

Zeus eyed her without lifting his head from the floor.

Then she scrolled down on her list of searches, and something stood out.

She opened another browser window and located an abandoned warehouse. The only landmark close by was the San Pedro cliffs, where dozens of suicide victims had jumped to their death. One person, a depressed, suicidal sixteen-year-old angry with her mom, actually survived but no one else had.

She took out the paper with the detective's phone number. Before she was ready to make the call, she needed to scout the location first. It didn't take her long to find the deserted warehouse. She parked several blocks away and at a distance where her binoculars would be put to good use.

"Bingo," Von said, adjusting the focus on the white Ram pickup.

She and Zeus waited in the car for about forty-five minutes. Then, just past 6 a.m., Jerry Bell stepped outside. She followed him with her binoculars as he stepped back into his pickup truck, reversed for about a mile down the driveway, spun around kicking up snow, and headed down the street.

"Show off," Von bit out, checking the time on her watch.

They didn't have much time.

She put down the binoculars and eyed her aluminum baseball bat wedged between Zeus's massive frame and the passenger door. Suddenly, she felt exposed. The others on her list hadn't been prepared. Jerry Bell, however, had called her. He was expecting her and would be returning to this location soon. Then it hit her. Why didn't she think of it before? Her father had the most extensive gun collection of anyone she knew. The Republican, gun-owning, recreational hunter of innocent wildlife was the reason why she hated guns. He was now her only answer.

To prepare, she knew what she had to do.

Von dialed Dr. Anton Friedrich's cell and began heading in that direction.

It rang once. "Wil—*Von?*" Before she could answer, he responded knowingly. "What do you need? Whatever it is...you can trust me."

In their native tongue. *"Ich brauche eine Waffe. Etwas Gutes für die Arschlochjagd."*

I need a gun. Something good for hunting assholes.

The brain surgeon was silent for a ten count.

Anton responded to his eldest and only living child in German. *"Ich habe die perfekte Waffe, kehre in fünfzehn Minuten hierher zurück. Kannst du das tun?"*

I have the perfect weapon; return here in fifteen minutes. Can you do this?

"Ja," she agreed. *Yes.*

"We say nothing to your mother."

He hung up, leaving her unexpectedly astounded that her father would have any part in her mission. But perhaps the prudent surgeon understood when it came to avenging his youngest child.

They at least agreed on one thing.

Kill the bastard who had killed Sammy.

From San Pedro, she took 25th Street West to Palos Verdes Drive South and was back at her parent's Palos Verdes estates in under fifteen. She couldn't get used to how her childhood home remained looming and lonesome in its cloud of foreboding darkness. The front door, once again, was unlocked. In the dim, nebulous corridor, she followed a light past the kitchen. It was the back room that her father always kept locked. Anton stood before a shiny onyx gun case with a collection of various hunting rifles. In his hand was a stunning silver pistol unfamiliar to her.

"It is an Ed Brown Special Forces Carry 1911, 45mm ACP, fiber optic front sight with a stainless-steel light rail frame. Skeletonized hammer and trigger. The slide is stainless as well and very fluid." Anton's explanation was foreign language. He pulled back the slide atop the gun to demonstrate. It moved with a smooth, barely audible clink. "I'm sure you haven't a clue or care about the specs given your...*aversion* to guns."

He turned and stared for a long beat. Father and daughter exchanged a sobering moment before he handed her the gun and a box of bullets.

"I've loaded it for you," he continued, filling the silence. "It's light and powerful with an extremely tight tolerance. Your grandfather owned one of the first Ed Browns. I still have it, but this one is brand new. Custom designed but similar to the one I had you practice on when you were fifteen. I haven't even fired it yet."

"When it comes to guns...I," Von paused, before asserting, "trust your opinion."

"It's a sleek gun, truly extraordinary," the explanation came out soft and whimsical from her father's lips. "A precise machine with an extremely sensitive trigger. Sometimes...the most beautiful creations can be the most dangerous."

Her father's grey eyes met her own—they no were no longer talking about the gun.

"You recall how to use it?" her father asked, breaking the tender spell.

Von turned the lightweight gun in her hand. It really was a beauty.

"You made sure Sammy learned to shoot. It's one of the few things we used to do together, one of the few moments we spent together when you weren't working," Von responded to Anton's guilt-filled eyes. "How can I forget?"

"And you have always had excellent marksmanship and nearly perfect aim. It's what made you a great doctor," he said. The compliment startled her. "I'm sorry I wasn't...more there for you and your sister. I'll never forgive myself for putting my career...it doesn't matter now. I should've been focused on being a better father."

Von put the gun and the bullets in her duffle bag.

"I should be going," Von whispered.

Anton handed her a bulletproof vest as he closed the gap between them.

"*Sei bitte vorsichtig,*" he said and hugged her fiercely. *Please be safe.*

———

Upon closer inspection, the abandoned warehouse stood a mile from Point Fermin Cliffs. Battered by weather, the paint on the walls had eroded. She parked a few blocks away and sat in the dark. Zeus put his head down and waited for her lead. Von rubbed his ear, and he turned to lick her fingers. The bullet-proof vest felt weighty, yet it made her feel safer.

Waves of anxiety caused her heart to beat wildly.

To calm her nerves, she reminded herself: Jerry Bell was a monster.

His connection to Sammy and why he targeted her had remained unclear until this moment. It dawned on Von that Bell must have orchestrated not only the initial kidnapping eight years prior but also the attack that left her unable to conceive. Bell had discovered her true identity—that Von Schlange was actually Dr. Wilder Friedrich—and took the one thing that mattered most to her. The realization hit her hard: he knew how to inflict the kind of hurt she would never recover from. How did he know he was on her list? He had to have his own hacker tip-off on Jefferson's connection.

Von pulled out her phone, quickly navigating to the Tracker XT-200 GPS app. Her heart raced as the screen loaded, confirming Bell's signal—he was exactly where she had researched online, at the abandoned warehouse on Point Ferman Cliffs.

She stared at the paper she'd been clutching in her hand. Von dialed without bothering to block her number, as there was no point now and no going back.

The phone rang twice before the detective answered.

"Are you and Special Agent Huxley back in Los Angeles yet?" Von began.

A rustle on the phone. "Dr. Wilder?" The intonation in her voice shifted to disbelief.

"I changed my name."

"It's Von now, correct? I'm...I'm very sorry about Sammy. She was a student of mine. She was in my self-defense classes. Sammy was...she was very special to me."

"All the martial arts and training won't stop a bullet to the head, now will it?"

The detective sighed, and the silence that followed was suddenly as impenetrable as the night. Lighting exploded, reaching across the sky, then, rain veered from a light drizzle into a high-speed, reckless torrent. The downpour turned visibility from her window into an amorphous blur.

Von half-expected a barrage of questions, but none came. So, she led.

"Pregnant and still chasing me? The LAPD and Feds must be desperate. Now you're working with the FBI, flying everywhere to find me. You and your unborn child weren't meant to be dragged into this mess."

"I know...I know what happened to you—" The detective was losing the battle to retain her professionalism, and Von knew it.

Von checked her watch, she had to make this quick.

"Don't got time for sentimental chit-chat. You and Huxley and no one else. Involve anyone else and you don't get Jefferson."

"I'm not saying I know exactly what it feels like. I can't imagine the loss. But I do know trauma and almost dying; I've lived through it. Don't handle Jerry Bell alone—"

"I know this game; you're trying to keep me on the phone. Not gonna work."

"Please, he's dangerous. Turn yourself in, and we—"

"And you'll what? I've murdered five men, including that cop. Montoya was...incidental. It was him—or me and Alisa. You'll explain to the judge and jury that they all deserved it? According to the law, Detective, murder's murder no matter how much someone deserves to die. Will you explain the FBI's incompetence? The fact that these...*animals* were allowed to be free, to continue to prey on innocents, to victimize, to torture, and rape?" Anger filled her voice.

"Von...listen to me. I promise you; we'll figure something out. Together. I'm on your side. We're on your side. Let me help you."

Von noted the desperation in the detective's tone. The sincerity was evident. But there was no way in hell she was turning herself in or trusting law enforcement's help.

"There's an abandoned warehouse a mile from Point Fermin Cliffs. I'll secure Jefferson, and if he's alive, he'll be safe with me. But I promise you, on Sammy's life, I'd rather die trying than give Bell to you guys." Von threatened. "Consider this yours: Butch and Josh Schultz...those were Sammy's last words. Look into it. I don't have the time to do your job."

"The Schultz brothers," Nazario said, and Von could hear the FBI agent's baritone voice announce in the background that he was writing it down. "Are there any other requests? Anything you need from us?"

"Time's up, Detective. If you want Jefferson, you and Huxley come alone," Von warned.

"Hang on, please," the detective begged, "this is suicidal, and I can't accept that ending your life this way was your ultimate goal! Von, you don't know what—"

"He's mine," Von interrupted and hung up.

TWENTY-FIVE

THE FINAL KILL

NAZARIO HAD no time to recover from the shock of having Von, the serpent woman, ring her mobile. While Huxley quickly jumped on his laptop to start searching his FBI files and going through the list they'd been sent of the brotherhood, she called Deputy Frost.

He picked up on the second ring.

"Can you get someone to run a check on the Schultz brothers," Nazario cut to the chase.

"They were in Boston," Huxley spoke without looking up from his laptop.

"If they're in Boston, they had a hand in Sammy's murder," Nazario surmised. "Working for Jerry Bell. We need to know if they boarded a plane to Los Angeles. We need this *now*, sir."

Detective Frost urged, "My men are on it."

When they hung up, Huxley turned to her.

"We can't just go in there solo," Huxley said pointedly. "We're not prepared. Yes, we're armed, but we really don't know what we're getting ourselves into."

"Huxley, we got no time. She's going in there alone. Von

could be walking into an ambush. We could lose Jefferson in the process."

"Neither of us packed vests," Huxley said. "We need to stop by my house—"

"On the 405 in heavy, rush hour traffic? It'll take us two hours or more to go there to retrieve them, flip a bitch, and then head back to Long Beach. We can't do both. We'll *never* make it on time. We have to go now. Besides, mine won't even fit me no more."

Nazario pointed to her belly.

"Got an extra that's large enough for you," Huxley said, putting his hands on her shoulders. "Look, I'm not worried about me. We can't go renegade and go in on this alone. We need to let the team know."

"Frost was right; you truly are a Boy Scout, but remember what he said? Honesty isn't required to do our jobs, Huxley."

"We need to call the deputy. It's by the book on this one, Detective."

Nazario shook her head. "We promised her. We must keep our word on this. Come too damn far to let this one slip away."

"And I can't lose you or the baby," Huxley's voice rose. "This is dangerous, Anaya!"

"What about Arizona?" Nazario said, catching him off guard. "You don't think I know about that kid and the mother whose deaths you helped fake so they could disappear? You went rogue on that one, and it worked out just fine."

"How in the hell do you even know about that?" he hissed, as though someone else could hear. "You know what? Never mind how you found out. Arizona was different. My partner at the time and I had planned it out in advance. We weren't driving in there blind."

"You're the only agent, hell, the only individual I'd trust

with my life going into a hot building," Nazario said. "But if you're not coming, I'm going solo."

He swore, shut down his laptop, and began packing their things, scouring the hotel room for any last-minute items he missed. Nazario's phone rang. It was Deputy Frost.

"Whaddya got?"

"Your hunch was dead on. Butch and Josh Schultz boarded a plane from Boston to Los Angeles three days ago," Frost said. "Stayed at a hotel near the Boston Harbor for about a week. Checked out, then flew on red-eye the night Sammy was found."

"Thanks for the intel, sir."

"I need one thing from both of you," the deputy asked.

"Yeah?"

"Not a word to anyone. Clear?"

"Ah...shit," Nazario hissed. "And what's that mean?"

Tone clipped, Frost clarified, "Means confidentiality, Detective. The bureau has its reasons."

Nazario let out a loud gust of air into the receiver.

"You know we'll keep our mouths shut, sir," she answered, "but I'm not happy about it."

"Stay safe," Frost said, ignoring her feelings and hung up.

Nazario looked up to find that Huxley had got their bags ready. He stood in the front with the door wide open as if to say, "after you." She paused and met his eyes, detecting a mixture of concern, love, and fear.

Huxley's hand trembled slightly as he clasped hers. "We're putting everything on the line," he whispered, his voice cracking. "Our careers, our lives..."

She could see the weight of his words in his eyes, the fear that mirrored her own. "I know," she replied softly, squeezing his hand. "But we have to see this through."

His eyes darted around the room, then settled back on her. "What if it's all for nothing? What if we fail?"

Nazario took a deep breath. "Then we'll face it together. Like we've faced everything else."

His jaw clenched, the vulnerability in his expression making her heart ache. "I'm scared, Nazario. Scared of losing everything we've worked for. Scared of losing you."

She reached up and touched his cheek, feeling the warmth of his skin. "We have everything to live for, and that's exactly why we're doing this. Because it's worth it."

A tear slipped down Huxley's face, and she felt a pang in her chest. "And the baby..."

Nazario's hand instinctively moved to her stomach. "We're gonna be safe. We're gonna be fine," she promised, though the weight of uncertainty pressed down on her. "We gotta finish this, Blake. We can't stop now. We've come this far. We need to do this for—"

"For whom? For the victims or for this serpent woman, this Von Schlange?"

"Can't answer that. C'mon, this ain't so black and white and we both know it. We gotta take these assholes down." Nazario said, pulling Huxley into her. She rested her forehead on his. "This is our chance to catch Jerry Bell, the head of the brotherhood, and Von, she's leading us right to him. We have to save Informant F— Lance Corporal Jefferson Pierce."

"I'm still scared shitless," he said, eyes pooling with emotion.

"So am I...so am I."

As they walked through the door, the gravity of their situation settled heavily on both of them. Huxley followed silently behind her, his fear palpable. She thought about her father's rigid view of the law, the black-and-white world she had grown up in. But she knew better now; she understood the shades of gray that her father never acknowledged.

In different circumstances, she knew she could have been tempted by the same choices that Von had made. There was an inner kinship there, an understanding that scared her as much as it reassured her. She wasn't just doing this for the case or for justice; she was doing it because she understood why Von had done what she did. And that terrified her.

As they stepped into the uncertain future, Nazario held onto Huxley's hand a little tighter, silently vowing to protect him and their unborn child, no matter the cost.

———

By the time Von and Zeus had run in, they were soaked. Inside the dilapidated building, the walls, brittle and crumbling in ruins, echoed spirits of another life. The hammering rain danced to the stench of mildew.

Normally, Von wouldn't just storm into a place like this, but her binoculars had revealed something intriguing—the abandoned warehouse was unguarded. Jerry Bell didn't have any of his cronies guarding the building. She wondered if she was running into a trap, but she had to push her fears aside. Jefferson needed saving.

Most of the windows were broken and knocked out, forcing the cold, wet breeze to fling in the rain that had already pooled a few inches on the ground. Several feet apart, floor-to-ceiling, corroded rebar exposed by the broken concrete had been eaten away by the sea air over the years. The rain screamed against the old roof, hard enough to make it feel like it might cave. They sloshed through the eerily quiet warehouse, despite Mother Nature's lashing outside.

Von walked ahead of Zeus with gun in hand. It was the second time she'd ever used one, and she noticed Zeus eyeing it with caution. Piles of left-over wooden planks lay scattered about like broken bones torn from the building's body. Random graffiti tagged the metal beams and brick walls. The warehouse was three stories tall. The rain dripped through the fractured ceiling. A small pond formed on the staircase and in other random places.

"*Zimme...folge mir,*" Von pointed at a door in the far corner. *Room...follow me.*

They jogged their way across the warehouse, dodging trash, slabs of crumbled concrete and drywall. Following her instincts, they sprinted down a hallway and stopped at the first door on the right. When they got to the room, Von tried the door. Locked. It looked old enough not to need much effort to pry open. She kicked the door with her boots a couple of times before the wood splintered down the middle. One more final blow and the knob splashed into the runoff. The room reeked of musty rusting metal like the rest of the warehouse. The rain had come through the roof, wetting the moldy mattress on the floor that was as old as the building.

The Marine lay handcuffed to a metal pipe that ran horizontally above his head.

"Jefferson," Von yelled.

"Von...I knew you'd come for me," Jefferson said, voice heavy with desperation.

She inspected his face and assessed his body. He looked to have broken ribs, a broken nose, a black and blue face that had suffered repeated beatings.

"I didn't tell them jack-shit," he mumbled then coughed and winced at the pain.

Von quickly inspected the handcuffs and shook the metal pipe. It didn't budge.

"Fuck," Von hissed. "Keep your arms apart, and don't move."

Jefferson's eyes were partly shut as it was, his eyelids fluttered closed.

"Don't miss. Don't miss. Don't miss." The words scraped out of his throat.

She pointed the gun at the links at the center of the cuffs that held them together.

Bang!

Jefferson jumped and then opened his eyes exhaling loudly.

"You alright?" she asked. "We need to hurry. Your legs okay?"

Jefferson nodded as Von inspected them quickly.

"They're fine, Doc. He always shows up around this time every night," he explained, the words quivering out. "He almost killed me twice, but I managed to bribe him out of it."

"Never mind what you had to do." Von swiftly helped Jefferson up from the bed. "We've got no time for a kumbaya talk-it-out session. Anyone else inside the building?"

"They come and go," he said, voice hoarse from disuse.

Jefferson blinked weakly down at the broken cuffs still on his wrists, though with the links at the center blown off, he was no longer confined to the pipe and his range of arm motion was back.

Von hoisted an arm over her shoulder, and together, they carefully wove through piles of decomposing lumber. "Should've never talked to you at the library or involved you. Get your legs moving, Jefferson. C'mon, we're out of time."

"Trying," Jefferson said, taking larger breaths as he struggled to keep up. "Think my ribs are broken."

"They are," Von confirmed, "grit through it now and cry later, soldier."

Jefferson managed to catch his second wind, despite seeming to be in a lot of physical pain. They hurried through the warehouse and out into the pouring rain, pushing the injured veteran to his limit. Thunder and lightning erupted across the sky. They ran back to the car. She unlocked the doors, entered on the driver's side, and retrieved a chocolate bar from the center console.

"Hungry?" she asked, handing him the candy. "It's vegan dark chocolate and all I've got."

"Starving," he admitted as he tore open the candy bar.

"Don't you dare leave this car unless your life's in danger. Keep your head down."

"Gimme a gun," he coughed, wincing again in pain. He finished the candy bar in three large bites. "I can shoot them motherfuckers from this range."

"Only have one gun, and I'm not about to hand it over. I know what you're capable of, but this isn't your battle. It's mine." Von looked around, surveying her surroundings. When she saw nothing unusual, she continued with urgency. "You're too damn smart. Use that brain of yours for a good cause," she said, tapping Jefferson's temple. "Go ahead with that deal you told me about that the Feds want you to agree to. They're willing to grant immunity in exchange for what you can do for them. Do it, Jefferson. Work with them or wind up wasting your life in jail. Those are your only two choices. You're too fucking talented to keep doing this."

"Fine, I'll do it," he rasped, "but don't you dare think about turning yourself in."

Von handed him the car keys and spoke quickly. "The title is in the glove compartment with an envelope. The car's yours, and so is the check."

"You've already paid me," he said, adjusting on his back. He groaned in discomfort.

"Well, that check is intended to set you up for life," added Von, "get off disability and use what you got for good."

In the distance, lights from an old truck made their way toward them.

"Shit, it's him." Jefferson covered himself with a blanket in the back seat. "He threatened me, said I shouldn't try to escape because he wasn't going to be long and that he was bringing his friends."

"Friends?"

"Yeah, for backup, I suppose. Told me if it wasn't for the fact that I'd served my country, they would've already killed me. Guess serving your country really do have its perks—dodging a bullet from my own citizens instead of the Taliban."

Von and Zeus exited the car, and the retired Marine locked it.

They charged out in the rain, back into the dilapidated building, and climbed up the stairs to the second floor to hide.

———

The burst of rain was harder than anything Nazario had experienced in Los Angeles. The deluge obscured the road in front of them. High beams did very little to improve visibility. Huxley made his way closer to the abandoned warehouse. Then they spotted a lone black Jeep Renegade in the empty lot. It was brand new and still didn't have license plates.

Something was suspicious about the vehicle. Then a head popped up and quickly ducked.

"Over there!" Nazario pointed to a Jeep. "Did you see that? I think someone's hiding in that Jeep. Remember when Joey said Von ran him back to her vehicle? He said she had a black Jeep Wrangler, which had to have been a rental. Couldn't've driven across the country. No time to. Our girl most likely flew and bought this fresh off the lot. Von's got a thing for Jeeps."

"It has to be hers." Huxley pulled up behind the vehicle. "Let's hope that was Jefferson."

He shut off the lights and the ignition. They drew their weapons and flashlights cautiously, exiting into the rain. Nazario positioned along the right of the vehicle and Huxley on the left. They peeked into the Jeep, and sure enough, someone was lying in the back underneath a blanket.

Nazario tapped the glass with her Maglite. When the body remained rigid, she tapped again.

"Jefferson?" Nazario queried. "It's Detective Nazario and Supervising Agent Huxley."

The body hiding in the back of the Jeep barely moved. Fear rose through her, worried that they were too late. Jefferson unlocked the doors, and she opened the passenger side. Huxley walked around to join her.

"Damn...they did some number on you," Huxley said studying his face, which was badly beaten. Judging by his fists, it looked like he fought back hard. The ex-Marine was weak, but alive.

"They...they jumped my ass," the words came out muffled. "If I had my gun—"

"They'd be dead. We know. Don't talk, Jefferson," Nazario instructed, "lay back down and stay down. Keep the doors locked."

Nazario quickly got in the front seat, soaked to the bone. She took her phone, relieved it was protected with a waterproof casing from her inside coat pocket, and dialed Frost.

"I was just about to call you," Frost said, sounding like he was on speaker.

"We need to go, *stat*. So, we're doing this under radar is that it, sir? That means no backup, correct?" Nazario asked, trying to get final clarification.

"Wasn't that Von Schlange's request?" the deputy threw the question back at her.

Nazario exhaled loudly. "Yeah, those were our specific instructions."

"If it were up to you and my man Special Agent Huxley, what would serve the best interest of the situation?"

"You really asking me now, sir?"

"Yes, I am."

"We wouldn't want Dr. Wilder spooked," Nazario admitted honestly. "If we went by the book, we would get back up here, a bunch of squad cars, but..."

"But?"

"Well, I now get why you wanted confidentiality, sir. Von Schlange requested no back up and...well, I feel it in my gut. We have to honor her request."

"Someone'll be there to escort out Mr. Pearce in fifteen," Frost returned. "We can have the building under surveillance on the down-low if you need."

She thought about it. "That won't be necessary, sir. She'll detect surveillance of any kind and run. We can't risk it."

"Very well," Frost said.

"Jefferson's weak, but alive. Laying down in the back of the Jeep. He needs immediate medical attention. Have our guy knock twice on the window to let Jefferson know he's getting transported out safely," Huxley said. "We're out of time, sir."

"Y'all be safe. The bureau sees the good work the two of you have done and it hasn't gone unnoticed. Discretion is imperative. It's the best course; that's why, other than you, Nazario," Frost said, "the LAPD doesn't know and will not know you're doing this solo. If they did, they'd shit bricks and cause a huge problem."

"Understood." Huxley hung up the phone, his eyes lingering on Nazario's belly with weary concern.

Following instructions, Jefferson relocked the door and lay down, covering himself with a blanket.

BANG! BANG! BANG!

Live fire rang through the night.

Nazario and Huxley crouched low, as they hurried across the field toward the warehouse.

———

Bell was back. Von froze in her hiding place upstairs, Zeus beside her behind a stack of rusted steel and wood piles. The cast-off lumber formed a maze that made it both difficult to find her way through and an ideal hiding spot.

She'd know that voice anywhere.

She'd heard it when she'd surveilled the cabin, and from courtroom tapes of the leader of the brotherhood organization.

"The boy's across the way, down that hall, the first door to the right," Bell said. "Butch, take care of him."

"But...I thought he was bait?" Butch said.

"Kill that fucking jar head," Bell ordered. "Josh, ass your way over there. Make sure it's done."

"Yes, sir."

Footsteps splashed across the warehouse floor, now covered in a foot of water.

Von readied herself, gun positioned, as she poked her head from behind a pile of steel. Any minute now, they'd find out Jefferson was gone.

Within seconds footsteps slopped back across the room.

"He's not there," Butch hollered. "Marine's gone."

"She's here." Bell motioned to the men. "Josh, upstairs. Butch, spread out. Find her."

The rain came down heavier, causing a stack of nearby

wood to come loose and cascade into the water. Josh's footsteps sloshed closer to her.

From where she was hiding, she could see the back of his head as he approached the fallen planks. He aimlessly shot three times, randomly hitting scraps of abandoned building material in an attempt to track the source of the sound.

He inched even closer.

Von held Zeus by the collar, keeping him at bay. Otherwise, her highly intuitive dog was prone to act independently and leap out without her command. It'd happened before. She was but inches behind him now as she moved to close the small gap between them.

Zeus followed suit, both master and dog so quiet, neither could be heard.

"Little Sammy broke my nose and got Butch in the nuts," Josh began. "Fought us like hell. So, we took turns on the little bitch after we killed her. The Heineken bottle was our favorite."

Livid, Von's body tightened. Her heart sped, leaving her short of breath. Adrenaline hit her veins, and all she saw was red. Feeling her father's gun in her waistband gave her the sudden urge to use it in a fit of rage. She hadn't known how much pain her little sister had been in or if she was tortured. Von clenched her fist, her nails digging into her palm, grounding herself in the pain. Her breath came in slow, deliberate inhales and exhales, a thin thread keeping her from breaking. She could feel her heartbeat pounding in her chest, each beat a reminder of the rage she had to contain.

Her muscles were tense, a coiled spring ready to snap. The image of her sister's suffering replayed in her mind, each detail a stab to her heart, but she forced herself to stay focused. Von's jaw was locked so tightly that she could feel the strain in her temples, the tension radiating down her neck.

Her eyes narrowed, the cold fury in them tempered by the

necessity to stay in command. She needed to be methodical, precise. She couldn't afford to lose herself in the storm of emotions raging within her. Her hands itched to pull the trigger, to exact vengeance, but she knew she had to wait. She had to be patient.

She felt a bead of sweat trickle down her back, the physical manifestation of her internal battle. The killers were close, too close, and the last thing she could afford was to alert them to her presence.

She wished she hadn't known this added detail about Sammy. It took all her strength to keep control instead of pulling the trigger, giving away her location. She forced her mind to focus on the need for justice, not revenge. She couldn't fail her sister now.

She was outnumbered and had to be strategic.

Butch Schultz and Jerry Bell called out for her from below using the same cheap tactic, taunting her with disgusting words about Sammy. What it was like for them to first kill her and then defile her corpse. Wrath plowed through her body, enticing her to do the wrong thing, make an irrational move, get sucked into making a mistake, one that would force her to join Sammy and the others as another fatality, yet another victim. She pictured Sammy's sweet smile, and it calmed her like an elixir. Von's body went very still. Relaxed. In control.

She stepped even closer to Josh, so close she could reach out and touch him.

Von tightened her grip on the steel baseball bat she brought for good luck and swung, connecting with Josh's occipital bone. The heavy rain clanking on the roof swallowed the sound of Josh Schultz's body collapsing into the rainwater.

She'd have loved nothing more than to tie him up and torture him but had no time to indulge in fantasies. She squatted down low and snapped his neck. Josh's body jolted twice before it went completely still. His hands automatically seized into fists the way the body sometimes did during death, teeth clamped tight, as his eyes rolled to the back until the whites were showing.

She checked his pulse and, when there was none, dragged him back to her hiding place.

"FBI!" a male voice suddenly came from below, and she recognized it as coming from Supervising Special Agent Huxley.

"LAPD!" Nazario screamed.

Rounds of gunshots exploded and then stopped.

Footsteps thundered upstairs.

"Josh...Josh..." Butch whispered, running through, frantically looking through the maze of plywood. "No...no...no...."

Butch crouched next to his dead brother's body. Von and Zeus watched from the perfect hiding spot—behind him. Butch launched to his feet and then spotted her across the room. He was fuming and snarling with anger. He ran toward her.

Von tapped Zeus, who charged at full speed using his hind legs to propel him forward. Zeus's jaw clasped securely around Butch's neck.

They tumbled together to the ground.

Von quickly peered below and saw Nazario and Huxley cautiously make their way across the building with guns drawn. Her father's vest was heavy with rain, but the weight made her feel protected. Yet the pregnant detective and her partner were walking straight toward Bell's obscured position without one.

Von wouldn't be able to live with the knowledge that she had caused another murder at the hands of Jerry Bell. Sammy's death remained on her conscience, and now Detective Nazario's life and that of her unborn child were, too. The brotherhood had taken life from Von's womb, a child who'd be five years old now.

No one should endure such a loss, especially not an expectant mother.

It wouldn't happen as long as Von was alive.

She noticed a set of stairs running down and around the back of the building. If Bell was hiding at the north end, she could take the stairs and get to him before they did.

She crouched above Butch's head as he struggled desperately to buck off her German Shepherd, hoping she had time to get down there before they took Bell out first.

Grasping Butch's skull between her hands, she snapped his neck, then signaled to Zeus, who released his grip from the dead man's throat. Von and Zeus hurried down the back stairs leading to the north side of the warehouse. They proceeded down a long hallway with caution. She saw a flash of silver from behind rusted iron girders, Detective Nazario and Huxley looking in a different direction. Bell, totally concealed, trained the barrel of his pistol on Nazario.

"*Nach dem Mann,*" Von whispered to Zeus. *After the man.*

Zeus dashed in Bell's direction. But would he get there in time?

Simultaneously, Von ran toward Nazario.

Startled, the detective shot but hit a wall.

"Get down!" Von yelled. Nazario spun and locked eyes. The detective and the supervising agent finally saw Bell but were too late. And Zeus hadn't covered the space in time.

Von sprinted hard, her quads burning as she dove in front of Nazario.

BANG! BANG! BANG!

The bullets slammed into Von's Kevlar vest with bruising thuds, knocking the detective back onto the ground as water splashed in all directions. Huxley returned fire, attempting to target Jerry, but it was evident to Von that he was shooting blind, alarmed for the mother-to-be and their unborn child.

He'd hesitated, providing Von the perfect opportunity to catch her breath and honor her vow by finishing Jerry Bell herself.

With her weapon still drawn, time nearly froze. Von breathed evenly through her nose despite the cramping spasm to her ribs. From the corner of her eyes, she could see Huxley pulling Nazario behind a wall, the pair trying to collect themselves for the next attack. Von would never let them have Bell. She closed her left eye, aimed at Bell's heart, and shot: one, two, three, four, five, six. His body jerked as the bullets riddled the center of his chest.

One left.

As Bell's body swayed in death's grip, she aimed between his eyes and squeezed.

———

Pain shot through Nazario's hip as she hit the floor. Huxley knelt beside her, panic in his eyes. "You alright?" he begged. Gunshots echoed in the distance. Nazario could barely process the chaos around her. She heard Von's gunshots, and before Huxley could spin to fire, Jerry Bell was already falling.

One minute, Nazario was walking toward the north side of the building. The next, Von was sprinting at her full speed. Bell's hiding place had been invisible to her and Huxley, catching them both off guard.

Dazed, Nazario shook her head to clear the ringing in her ears. "I'm okay," she managed to say to Huxley, who looked relieved. As the world stopped spinning, they saw Jerry Bell's lifeless body on the ground. Nazario glanced up in time to see Von and Zeus sprinting out of the warehouse toward the south end of the building.

Huxley swore.

They took off after her and into the pouring rain, calling her name, expecting to be running towards some getaway vehicle.

Huxley and Nazario paused at a reasonable distance, each drawing their weapon. Nazario had the back of the serpent woman's head at bullseye. Knowing Huxley, he was also locked in. They could kill her right now. End a murder spree that had already claimed at least eight victims, including Josh and Butch Shultz, likely dead somewhere in the warehouse. Nazario's mind swirled with conflicting emotions. Von Schlange, the vigilante killer, was a paradox—a murderer who had taken lives yet saved many more. Faces flashed before Nazario's eyes: Kang Lee, Joey Worshom, Mia Hong, Alisa Estevan, Jefferson Pearce —each one saved through Von's twisted sense of justice.

But it wasn't just strangers Von had saved. Nazario's own life and the life of her unborn child were among the many. Von had thrown herself in front of the bullets meant for Nazario, the vest Von wore absorbing the impact, saving both Nazario and her baby.

Now, the serpent woman and her dog raced in an unexpected direction.

Other patrol cars had arrived on the scene despite Nazario's request that they hold back because they feared it would spook Von. Outside, other officers gave chase on foot, but Von and Zeus were already much further ahead.

"Oh no...Huxley, she's heading for the cliffs!" Nazario panicked. "They'll never make it."

They looked at each other and lowered their guns, opting instead to scream for Von to stop. Suddenly, Jefferson joined them from behind. They turned to see the soldier, who'd been standing next to a non-descript federal agent. Jefferson Pearce broke free from his transporter's grasp.

"RUN...VON SCHLANGE...RUN!!!"

Von and her German Shepherd did exactly that.

———

The inky abyss and sound of waves angrily crashing against the rocks below drew closer to Von with every burning stride.

"Von...no!" Nazario screamed. "Doctor Wilder, stop! Don't you fucking do it!"

"*Wir müssen springen!*" she commanded Zeus that they must jump.

The rain pelted their bodies, but they picked up speed, running faster.

Then she heard an unexpected voice call after her.

Jefferson?

Jefferson screamed, *"YOU NEED MORE MOMENTUM TO CLEAR THE ROCKS...RUN FASTER!"*

Had Jefferson calculated the speed needed to avoid hitting the jagged rocks a hundred feet below? Von picked up her pace, running faster than she's ever run in her life. Reaching land's end, Zeus sprang with his hind legs, catching incredible air as he stretched out, propelling into the night. Von opened her arms, arched her back, and inhaled deeply as the rush of ocean air hit her face, the night enveloped them. Jefferson's instructions, relayed by Tommy, echoed again in Von's mind. She finally pieced together what the soldier was trying to tell her before the line went dead.

"If you have nowhere to go, doctor—"

Jump.

But Point Fermin Cliffs was a jump no one was expected to survive.

TWENTY-SIX

THE DETECTIVE

DOZENS OF DIVERS scoured the Pacific Ocean, with an equal number of FBI agents combing up and down San Pedro's shores and along the coast.

There was no trace of the woman or her dog.

"No way in holy hell they made it," Huxley said to Nazario. "They don't call this place the Suicide Cliffs of San Pedro for nothing."

"Then, where are the bodies?" Nazario asked after a long beat.

"Do we need them?" Huxley raised a brow. "This isn't what we planned for, Detective, but it turned out to be for the best. We no longer have to repeat Arizona."

"No, it definitely won't be Arizona," Deputy Frost said, startling them. She didn't hear him walk up. Nazario noted the expression on Huxley's face. It seemed as though Huxley hadn't known that his boss, Deputy Frost, had been privy to the plot to help stage someone's death in order to help to start a new life and put a criminal behind bars. How much more was Frost not telling them? She didn't know and was too tired at this point to dig deeper. For once, Nazario had reached her limit. The case had drained her, and she was finally okay with the reality that she hadn't won this round.

She hadn't apprehended their perp, and for the first time, she felt at peace with it.

Deputy Frost pointed at Huxley's left hand. "Thought the two of you would at least invite me to the wedding?"

Huxley and Nazario burst out, talking in unison.

"I broke my necklace..." Nazario said.

"I'm just keeping it safe..." Huxley said.

Footsteps behind them prompted them to turn around to the source, breaking the brief moment of levity, which had become more and more rare in their profession. A couple of federal agents walked up, escorting an older couple Nazario hadn't met before.

Huxley whispered, "Dr. Wilder's famous parents. Guys, let's keep to our theory."

"Will do," Nazario returned.

"Yes," Deputy Frost agreed, rewording it so that it reduced appearance of any wrongdoing on the bureau's part. "All we're doing is sticking to what we know."

Deputy Frost introduced the two doctors, who each wore a somber look. While Katrine appeared to have been crying all morning, Anton was more stoic and unreadable. He didn't appear to be a grieving father who lost his only remaining daughter to suicide.

Nazario shared her sympathy with both and explained what they "officially" knew.

Her rendition of the events: She and Huxley arrived on scene after the Schultz brothers and Bell were killed. They'd chased Von out the warehouse, but the heavy rain made visibility difficult. Poor weather conditions combined, along with the fact that Nazario and Huxley had been too far away, meant they had no time to even draw their weapons, much less shoot or detain her. That was when Wilder and her dog jumped to their death. It was likely suicide, she had explained, theorizing that a strong current had possibly dragged their bodies into the depths of the Pacific Ocean. Huxley added that the search team hadn't recovered their bodies but that the FBI and the LAPD homicide team had deemed it a suicide.

Anton and Katrine's response wasn't what they expected.

Katrine began to laugh through her tears, covering her mouth with a hand.

Nazario stared, stunned, the rest of the FBI and LAPD personnel equally confused.

Anton walked toward the edge of the cliff and looked down. He remained silent for quite some time. His wife was still laughing and crying. Grief did strange things, but this was something Nazario hadn't seen in any parent who had lost a child. On homicide, she was used to heart-wrenching wails, but not this type of response.

"I believe we missed the joke," Nazario finally said.

Von's father turned around and faced them.

"Our daughter has been cliff jumping since she was a little girl," he said. "She's jumped some of the highest cliffs in the States. Zeus as well—since he was a puppy. She used to jump with Samantha. It was what they did for recreation."

Nazario and Huxley exchanged a wide-eyed look, all of them now even more perplexed.

The brain surgeon continued, "If there's anyone who could've survived Point Fermin Cliffs, it's Wilder. And if there were ever a canine that could've survived such a jump, it would be her German Shepherd."

Deputy Frost whistled.

"What're you getting at, Dr. Friedrich?" Huxley said.

"Are you implying that your daughter—" Nazario began.

Anton cut her off.

"There's no implication. Report what you wish to the media. Call it a suicide. The Wilder we knew died when she was attacked. You won't find their bodies." He walked to the edge of the cliff and glanced down. "I bet my life on this: That our daughter—Von and Zeus—are alive. Look all you want for them, but you won't find them. They're long gone." Dr. Friedrich looked at the officers surrounding him, then begged, voice raw with emotion. "We hope...we hope you'll leave our daughter and her dog in peace. Leave them *dead*."

A week later, a local fisherman reported an abandoned motorboat along the shore near the Long Beach Convention and Entertainment Center and in close proximity to the airport. While finding a floating boat along the coast wasn't unusual, what made it so was the six-seater Marex 375 was registered to a Jamal Wagner. Left behind in the boat, an Ed Brown Special Forces Carry 1911, 45mm handgun registered to Dr. Anton Jörg Friedrich. The same gun, according to the FBI and LAPD homicide, that was used to shoot Jerry Bell.

When questioned, JW claimed his boat had been stolen from the harbor, but he didn't file a police report. Regarding knowledge of Dr. Wilder Friedrich (A.K.A. Von Schlange), JW insisted, "I don't know that crazy white woman."

When asked about the gun, the prominent neurosurgeon had a sudden case of amnesia.

TWENTY-SEVEN
THE NEW DOCTOR

THE WOMAN LOOKED out the airplane window, noticing how the elevation had placed her above the cirrus clouds. Just below, alabaster wisps spread their fingers while the vast cobalt skies gradually prepared for the shift toward night.

Her dog panted as he adjusted, trying to get comfortable. She bent and massaged his body, starting with his shoulders and working down his back. Dr. Jones stroked his hip with care, in tune with the canine's whimpers. She dug into her handbag and took out the prepared injection.

"Cortisone?" asked the man sitting next to her in first class. "Is he hurt?"

She nodded. "When cortisone and steroid injections are taken regularly together, they're effective for temporary relief," she explained evenly, injecting her dog in the hip and then returning the used syringe to her black bag. He takes cortisone during the day, and then I give him the steroid at night. He took a leap. His hips are slightly bruised, though not broken, and thankfully, not hip dysplasia, which is very common in larger breeds."

She avoided the man's eyes.

"Don't I know you?" He tilted his head, scanning her face. "Haven't we met?"

"I don't believe so," she said to the handsome man. "Dr. Agatha Jones."

"I'm sorry," he apologized and then introduced himself. "Dr. Damião Sequeira, I treated a patient that...well...she looks a lot like you. She also had a German Shepherd like yours."

"And what happened to her?" Agatha asked, lifting her eyes to the handsome Brazilian doctor. She caught the subtle way his eyes raked across her face, studying her.

He looked down at his hands. "Her name was Wilder. She was viciously attacked. I saved her life, but the courts...they found merit that the surgery hadn't gone how it should've. She... she recently...well, I learned that she'd committed suicide. That's why I'm leaving the states, returning to my home country. I feel responsible. I never quite got over her. She was a patient that, I don't know, has stayed with me."

Agatha paused for a long beat. "Someone else's actions aren't your fault. We're only ever responsible for ourselves, for the way we react and not how someone else will."

The flight attendant stopped at their row. "Dr. Jones, I received the note that your service dog has special needs. Does he need water? Or would you care for a complimentary drink? Mixed cocktail? Beer? Red or white wine?"

"Not yet on the water. Maybe later? But I'll have a glass of red," she said.

"And for you, sir?"

He rose a brow, as if intrigued by her given name and the professional title they shared.

"I think I'll have the same," Damião said.

Once the attendant left, he asked Agatha, "Family medicine?"

"Veterinarian." She smiled in reply.

His eyes grew wide, brows furrowed, and mouth fell open.

They remained in discerning silence of a shared secret until she broke the moment.

"I'm opening up a clinic," added Dr. Jones. "It's in Rio de Janeiro. I love the Amazon rainforest, and how many of the remote areas require going on a boat to reach them. But most of all, I love that the Amazonia National Park is home for thousands of species of wildlife."

Dr. Sequeira looked stunned. A flush of red stained his cheeks.

"That's where I'm going. I have family there. That's where I grew up."

She put a hand on his and then squeezed. His hands were warm and soothing to the touch. He closed his fingers gently around hers and, with a trembling voice, continued. "Looks like we're both looking for a fresh start. Dr. Jones, allow for me to be your guide through Rio de Janeiro?"

"No need for the formality," she corrected, "just Agatha will do."

"Agatha?" he repeated, brows furrowed.

"Yes," she said, "why?"

"I...never forget a name," he said wistfully. For a brief moment, she thought she saw a hint of remembrance behind his dark brown eyes and wondered if the doctor was good at recalling middle names.

"It must make you a great doctor. Every patient wants to be treated like a human. Especially if they're in the hospital for months." She smiled softly, and his eyes moistened. "And...a tour around your home country sounds lovely. Perhaps dinner, too."

The flight attendant returned with their wine. They thanked her. Agatha rose her glass.

"To new beginnings?"

A smile widened across Damião's lips. He reached for her hand, and their fingers wove together. A static charge passed between them. "To new beginnings," he whispered.

They clinked their glass, sipped their wine, and gazed out the window, at the eternal blue heavens. From victim to vigilante—to free. The burden of her sins shed like snakeskin.

For the second time in her life, she was reborn.

ALSO BY S.Z. ESTAVILLO

The Serpent Series

The Serpent's Bridge

The Serpent Woman

Twilight of the Serpent

ABOUT THE AUTHOR

SZ Estavillo has been passionate about writing since childhood, with a defining moment in second grade when her teacher predicted, "You're going to be a writer someday." Her biracial heritage, being half-Korean and half-Puerto Rican, deeply influences her book themes. As a staunch advocate for diversity and inclusion, SZ works tirelessly to amplify the voices of underrepresented and marginalized communities within the publishing industry.

SZ is not only a feminist whose principles echo throughout her works, but also a true crime aficionado, having devoured every episode of true crime on networks like Discovery ID and Oxygen. Her interest in justice is deeply rooted in her family history. Her uncle, Nicolas Estavillo, retired as the highest-ranking Puerto Rican cop in New York's history, and her father, Jose Estavillo, has served in both the Air Force and U.S. Customs and Border Patrol. These familial connections to law enforcement enrich her storytelling and understanding of justice.

Balancing her roles as a devoted mother and an enthusiastic digital marketer, SZ brings her professional expertise into her personal passion, amassing over 85,000 followers on social media. She uses her platform to inspire and uplift the writing community with motivational and positive content. Along with her two children and two senior dogs, she enjoys the simple pleasures of family sushi outings in their Los Angeles home.

If you enjoyed this book, consider following her on social media or posting a review. Your support helps extend the reach of voices that matter. Thank you for reading and being part of this journey Stay tuned for her upcoming books, "The Serpent Woman" and "Twilight of the Serpent."

Please follow SZ Estavillo:

Goodreads: https://www.goodreads.com/author/show/
49349032.S_Z_Estavillo
X: @szestavillo
Instagram: @szestavillo.author
TikTok: @szestavillo.author
Facebook Page: https://www.facebook.com/sonyozofiaestavillo